MAFIA KING OF LIES

AN ARRANGED MARRIAGE DARK MAFIA ROMANCE

KINGS OF BLOOD AND VOWS
BOOK 1

KAYLA MASON

Copyright © 2025 by Kayla Mason

All rights reserved.

No part of this book may be reproduced in any form or by any electronic or mechanical means, including information storage and retrieval systems, without written permission from the author, except for the use of brief quotations in a book review.

❀ Created with Vellum

1

MARIA

There's a buzz of death in the air—clinging to my skin like static as the storm rages outside my bedroom window.

It's morbid as hell, but I can't shake the feeling that something is coming for us—something that wraps around my throat and won't let go.

I can't focus. I paint to quiet the noise in my head, but tonight, the storm outside is louder than usual—and so is the silence inside me. Something crawls beneath my skin, whispering that everything is about to change.

The wind gusts into my room—and then comes the thump. A sharp, clustered snap in my chest, like something breaking in my heart.

"Oh," I gasp, nearly spilling my wine on the easel. "Well... that was strange."

I inhale slowly, pushing the chill out of my chest. Fear doesn't get to live here. Not in this body. Not with the last name Faravelli.

I stare out at the dark clouds that loom ever closer to the

manor. I can smell the scent of rain in the air as it wafts through the open window. I close my eyes and allow the scent to calm me. It's not the storm I find peace in—it's the first breath of rain, the brief hush before everything breaks.

My family and I have been living in Florence ever since I was ten years old. This is the place that shaped me and created the ideas and dreams that lay in my chest. I was not born here, but it feels more like my home than New York.

I draw my glass back to my lips to take another sip. But just as the glass kisses my lips, a rippling scream shatters my eardrum, and I drop my glass onto the floor. Small little shards scatter everywhere, and another wail makes its way into my room.

What in the world is going on?

My heart pounds in my chest. I jump over the small shards and make my way to the door, running with bare feet and heart in hand.

The screams come from the foyer, echoing through the hallway like a prophecy already fulfilled. The dread cements itself onto my bones, growing heavier with each step toward the top of the stairs. I stop and stare down at the scene unfolding below.

Three people stand in the middle of the foyer.

My father's second, Elliot, stands drenched in blood and pale as a sheet. He stares at my papa with somber eyes. My mother rests at his feet, her body collapsed on the floor. Her face is red as she screams Bloody Mary, her cries echoing into the foundation of the home.

Death. Just as I had felt.

I swallow hard as I try to release the lump that has lodged itself in my throat.

Breathe, Maria. Breathe.

"Papá..." I don't even recognize my voice. It feels more like that of a stranger.

The two men turn their heads to where I stand at the top of the stairs. All the color has drained from my father's face. My mother continues to wail on the floor, and Elliot looks like a broken man.

I open my mouth to ask what has happened, but deep within my soul, I know. I felt the tether snap—I believe I knew before they all did.

"Antonio is dead, cara."

Four words. That's all it takes to shatter my world.

"He's gone, cara."

I hold onto the railing to steady myself, to keep from falling over. I press my hand over my heart and will myself to breathe.

He's... but... I just spoke to him this morning. There is no way that my twin is... No. No. No. This isn't real. Antonio was just here. Laughing. Breathing. Living.

The world tilts beneath me. My knees hit the cold marble floor, the impact barely registering over the crushing weight in my chest. My breath comes in short, jagged gasps, my ribs caving in as if the air has been punched from my lungs.

My lips part, and like my mother, I let out the most gut-wrenching wail—one that comes from the mist-broken and bitter parts of my soul.

My brother is dead.

∼

48 hours later

. . .

My brother is dead. I will never again hear his boisterous laugh moving through the empty hallways. I will never share a coffee with him in the morning after our runs. This world— all it does is take from us.

I try not to let the bitterness of it all consume me, but it's hard. I bat my eyes and try to push back the tears that threaten to spill. I've cried enough to fill Lake Como. It has been nothing but tears and heartache for the past forty-eight hours.

"Il mio bambino, Dio ha preso il mio bambino." My baby, God took my baby. My mother's cries can be heard throughout the cemetery. She clings to my father for dear life, his sunglasses on, his face stoic and unchanging.

The cries pierce right into the deepest chambers of my heart. I hear it crack, the soft flesh-like thing shattering like glass under the weight of a mountain. Tears streak down my face as I stand beside my wailing mother, a single white rose in hand.

The breeze blows, weaving through my hair and kissing my cheeks as if the heavens sent it to wipe my tears.

"And so from dust you were formed, and to dust you shall return." The pastor holds his hand in the air and makes a cross. The coffin begins to lower into the ground, and my mother's wails increase. "We lay you to rest, Antonio Marcelo Faravelli. May the Lord open His arms to you at the gates of heaven, and may you find everlasting peace."

The soft strumming of the violin begins to play. The gathered crowd watches in sorrow as my brother finds his new home in the dirt.

Fuck. I thought I could make it through this day. I thought that somehow I would manage, but now... I realize I'm holding on by a mere eyelash.

Pain. This can only be described as the most gut-wrenching pain I have ever experienced in my entire life. I want to be strong. I want to hold fast, but...

I lift my gaze—and freeze.

Across from me, a pair of dark brown eyes lock onto mine. Cold. Calculating. They're an electric storm, raging and roaring in silent dominance, promising destruction without a single word. My breath catches. My pulse stutters.

I'm staring into the face of a man I haven't seen since I was ten—a man from the past, now cloaked in flesh and power. A name that shifts the air in any room, stilling every breath.

Feared like a god. Obeyed like a king.

They call him the Warlord.

Matteo Davacalli.

And not without reason. Because he doesn't negotiate. He annihilates.

They say he once wiped out an entire rival family in a single night. No survivors. No mercy. Just blood and silence.

What is he doing here? I knew that back in the day, he and my father had been friends. But as the years passed and we relocated to Florence, the man had turned his back on us. As far as I remember, he looked down on my father for wanting to pull us out of New York before the turf wars that nearly took his son—Daniele.

So why is he here now? Maybe it's simply a courtesy, an obligation of sorts that he wants to fulfill to honor his old friend.

My parents step forward, and my mother's wails have now dropped a few volume levels. They throw their roses into the grave and step back.

His gaze lingers a second too long, like he's searching for

something beneath my grief. I rip my eyes from Matteo Davacalli and step forward. I stare down into the hole, the coffin now resting at the bottom. I never imagined this is how my year would unfold. Antonio just never seemed like the dying type. He is—was—invincible in my mind. My superhero brother who defeated all the bad things that went thump in the night.

And there he is, in a box, six feet deep in the ground.

"Mi hai lasciato il cuore spezzato, fratello." You left me brokenhearted, brother. The tears trail down my cheeks again. The wind blows once more, lifting the wisps of hair that hang against my face. "I love you for all eternity."

I step away from the grave and allow the others to throw their roses inside. My father has taken my mother off to the side, giving her the privacy and decency to break away from the proximity of the crowd.

I lift my head again, and like before, he is watching me. His eyes are like lasers—precise and deadly in their sharpness. His expression is blank. I can't get a good enough read on him to guess what he could possibly be thinking.

All I know is that this man's presence alone is enough to make me feel uneasy. If the Warlord is here, it means that death and chaos are not far behind.

I SPLASH my face with cold water, trying to wake myself up. The chardonnay has finally caught up to me, and my body is beginning to feel the downhill effects. I lift my head and stare at my now bare face in the mirror.

My eyes are bloodshot from all the tears I've cried. My neatly pinned bun has stayed in place all day. My cheeks are flushed from the icy water, but other than that, I don't seem too off-putting.

"Smudged mascara, red eyes—time to paint over the wreckage." I reach under my bathroom sink and pull out some concealer. If I didn't have to go back down and mingle with the rest of these people, I would be on my second bottle of chardonnay. It's what my brother would have wanted.

Antonio always used to say, "Every second is a good time for bubbly."

I choke out a laugh as I apply my concealer. Tears brim in my eyes, but I do my best to hold them back. The last thing I need right now is to ruin my makeup for the second time.

Go down. Talk to parents—mainly my father. Then drink my sorrows away in my bed.

That is my game plan, and a solid one at that. I'm sure the wine will be a better conversationalist than the people currently in my home.

I come out of my room after about twenty minutes. I walk to my parents' door and open it slightly. There, I find my mother lying on the bed, her chest rising and falling gently.

The pills worked.

I am not in favor of drugs helping her cope, but I popped a Xanax this morning to get through the day. If this is what helps her sleep and keeps her from being hysterical, then it's a win for all of us. I hate hearing her bloodcurdling scream. I hate not being able to soothe her pain.

"Fuck, Antonio," I curse my dead brother as I make my way down the stairs in search of my father. There are still people lingering around the house to 'console' us. But I know this world like the back of my hand. These people are just circling sharks who linger because they can smell blood.

The Faravelli heir is dead, and their family is weakened.

The anger pours into my system all over again. I have been robbed of my brother because of nothing but greed and a thirst for power. I have this undeniable bloodlust that fills my system. I am murderous. Whoever killed Antonio will rue the day they ever laid a hand on a Faravelli.

"Maria, a moment, please?" a woman I don't recognize calls out as she sees me walking down the hallway.

"I need to go and call my father," I say with an apologetic smile, though truly, I don't want any more of their fake condolences. "I'll be back."

Her shoulders sag in disappointment, but I could give two shits what makes her sad or not. I'm in mourning. Not her.

I round the corner and come to a halt when I see my father and Matteo Davacalli walk into his office. They've been having hushed conversations all day. At first, I thought they were simply catching up, but now my little spider senses are tingling—something isn't right.

"What are you up to, Papá?" I whisper under my breath. I wait for the door to close, then tiptoe toward it, wanting to hear what they're saying.

I stand outside my father's study. I can hear the muffled voices of the two men inside. There's something about Mr. Davacalli that stirs something in me. I don't know if it's fear or something else. I shake my head, trying to rid myself of anything that could otherwise be considered inappropriate.

I am at my brother's wake, for God's sake.

I step closer to the door and strain my ears to catch what's going on inside. I hear the words, urgent and necessary. As far as I know, my father has been staying clear of any heavily connected links within the mafia—particularly the Italian sector, which just so happens to be Matteo Davacalli. So why is he meeting with him? What could this man possibly have to say to my father?

"This will be for the betterment of your family, Marcelo." I hear Matteo Davacalli's deep voice seep through the door. Heavy footsteps follow, and I stiffen. I step away and quickly rush around the corner to hide.

Seconds later, the door opens—and out walks the mafia king himself. As before, his stature is domineering and demands attention. It's almost impossible to look away. My lips part as I gaze at him, but this time from behind the shield of the wall.

He easily towers over the majority of the men who attended today's funeral, including my father. His short black hair is slicked back, the style revealing the sharp features of his face—chiseled jawline and high cheekbones that look like they could cut diamonds. Not to mention the way his tailored suit hugs his body, leaving you wondering just how chiseled he really is.

A rush of heat moves throughout my system, and I catch my breath, embarrassed at how intensely I'm staring. There is no way in hell that I am... ogling my father's old friend. There is no way I can—*shit*.

Matteo rounds the corner and smacks right into me. His hand shoots out and helps to steady me so that I don't completely lose my balance. Little sparks of electricity move from the place where his palm touches my back.

He smells like expensive whiskey and something darker—something dangerous. His grip is firm, warm, steadying. I pull back, resisting the urge to shiver, and avert my gaze to the floor. His eyes scan me—slow, assessing.

"Careful, Miss Faravelli. You look like you've seen a ghost."

"I'm so sorry. I didn't see you there, Mr. Davacalli. I was on my way to see my father."

Why am I explaining myself? This is my house. I live here. If anything, he should be the one explaining why he was—

"That's all right," his deep voice filters into my ears, and I all but lose my shit. It's this silky, textured kind of symphony that kisses my eardrum.

Is it hot in here? My chest heaves up and down, trying to take in as much air as possible before I finally release my breath. A shiver travels up and down my spine until I steel my back and remember where I am.

"Um, thank you for... uh... coming to the funeral. I'm sure my papa appreciated your presence." I force a smile onto my lips and look into his eyes.

He stares into my pupils as if searching for something. His gaze is unnerving—it feels like he has me under a microscope. I clear my throat and break eye contact, unable to take the heaviness of his presence.

This man is intimidating. I've met many dangerous and ruthless men in this world, but there's a silent danger about Matteo that gnaws at my chest.

"Safe travels back to the States." I give him one last smile, then sidestep him toward my father's study. I'm almost at the door when he starts to speak again.

"Actually, I believe I will be staying a while. Some matters require my urgent attention here in Florence." He says to my back, "I will be seeing you, Miss Faravelli. Quite a bit, I imagine."

I don't know why, but his words slither down my spine

like a premonition. A promise. A threat. Whatever this man wants, it is more than just a courtesy visit.

I look over my shoulder at where he stands, but the man is no longer there. I stand in place for a few seconds and wait. The interaction with Matteo is not something I had been anticipating. I try to shake him from my mind and continue toward my father's study.

I stand at the door, raise my fist, and knock.

"Entra." Come in. I hear his muffled voice from inside.

I let out a shaky breath, preparing myself for whatever awaits me inside. Mamá is always the easier one to handle of the two.

I open the door. I find my papa by the small bar cart, pouring himself a whiskey neat on the rocks. From the drink choice alone, I know he's deep in his sorrow—Papá only ever reaches for the whiskey when something's broken inside him.

"Papá, stai bene?" Dad, are you okay? I walk in cautiously, as if I'm approaching a wild boar. My heels click against the hardwood floors, and the strong scent of oak and cigar smoke filters into my nose.

He grunts his reply and then takes a sip of his drink. He turns to look at me. His dark brown eyes smolder with despair —and something else I just can't place. He gestures for me to sit by the loveseat in the center of his study. I make my way over to the expensive leather seat and settle into the cold fabric.

The air is thick, and my heart hammers with anticipation of what lingers in it. I have a feeling that whatever he's going to say is likely to shift the entire trajectory of my life.

I try not to let my mind get ahead of itself, but I can't help it. There's something that isn't settling well within my soul.

"How is your mother?" Papá leans against the bar cart and stares at me. He's stalling. "Is she asleep? The doctor said he gave her one of those pills to calm her."

I nod my head once. "I just left her room before I came here. There are still some guests who have lingered behind, waiting to speak with you, I'm presuming."

Back straight. Chin up. Legs crossed.

This is the posture that has been drilled into me from the moment I could speak. I have been raised to be the perfect woman. In our world, the class and elegance of a woman is a father's pride. I am a reflection of the success of my father and my mother. I can never afford to walk out of step or speak out of tone when it matters most.

"And you? How are you keeping?"

"My twin brother is dead, Papá. I think it's safe to say I am between deep depression and suicide." There is no humor in my voice because I am deathly serious. The only reason I was even able to make it through today is because of chardonnay and Xanax. "I saw Mr. Davacalli walk out of here before I came in."

My father and I never speak of mafia business. That was something he always did with Antonio. But now, with my brother gone, maybe I could fill the hole that has been—

"I've been made an offer that I can't refuse." My father kicks off the bar cart and walks to the large floor-to-ceiling window that overlooks the grounds. The sun has just begun to set beyond the horizon, drawing a close to a day I hope to forget. "An offer that will, hopefully, soften the blow of losing my heir."

I gulp and wait for him to continue.

"You will marry within the coming days," my father utters as he sips on his expensive whiskey. "Matteo has proposed a deal that I can't refuse."

My heart stops dead in my chest.

"You can't be serious, Papá."

"It is done."

"No. No, you always said—I was free to choose who I marry—"

"That was before Antonio died."

"So I'm nothing more than a bargaining chip?"

Every cell in my body screams to fight this, to run, to burn it all down. And I stare at my father, waiting for him to take it back. Waiting for him to tell me this is all some sick, grief-stricken joke.

But he doesn't. His face is unreadable, cold and final. Like a tombstone sealing my fate. I am being traded like I am nothing. And worst of all… I have no way out.

I blink and watch my father by the window. His eyes are cast out toward the backyard of the manor. I have never seen my father so downcast before. He is always a man of few emotions and even fewer words. But within the last forty-eight hours, I have watched the big, strong man I grew up with barely hold onto his composure.

Truth be told, I want him to break. I want him to shatter and come undone like the rest of us.

We all lost Antonio. He is allowed to grieve—he doesn't have to be the big, strong capo.

"I don't understand, Papá." I grit the words from my lips. "Marry who?"

My father sips on his dark liquor again, wincing as the liquid travels down his throat. "Daniele. You will marry him within the next two weeks."

Daniele. I haven't seen him since I was ten, and he was the shadow in the corner, always two steps behind Antonio. And now he is to be my husband? What kind of man has he become? The thought sends ice trickling down my spine.

"This union will join the Faravelli and the Davacalli names as one. With my heir gone, I need to secure our power somehow and allow our legacy to live on. You will marry Daniele, and in exchange, Matteo will offer his resources and protection to help us rebuild and sustain what decades of our bloodline have built."

I ball my fists at my sides. I have to bite down on my tongue to keep from speaking. The last thing I want is to speak out of turn, but the situation begs me to do so. I am not some meek little woman without a backbone—I am not my mama. I do not take shit lying down, but I know that, in this moment, my father just needs to be allowed to speak. But only for a few moments.

"Your marriage will protect the legacy that is now left without an heir. You will marry Daniele, and you will produce an heir for me—a son. I will groom him, and he will carry the name Faravelli to continue our bloodline."

"This all sounds so archaic," I mutter under my breath—then my voice rises before I can stop it. "You want me to marry a man I don't even remember, to save a legacy I didn't ask to carry? What about what *I* want, Papá?"

When I catch my father's cool gaze, I clear my throat and look him dead in the eye. "Papá, you have an heir. You have me."

"You are a woman, cara. You cannot lead this family. We will be the joke of society. Don't act like you don't know our customs and our ways."

"All those people live in New York, Papá. We have our dealings here. We pulled out of the States a long time ago—why must we care what they think of us?"

"Maria, my word is final. You will marry Daniele within a fortnight. The arrangements are already in place." He downs the rest of his drink and walks to the cart again to pour another. "If you want to truly help me, then you will do this. You will marry this boy, and you will save our family."

"I didn't realize our family was under threat, Papá."

I hear him curse under his breath as he slams the glass down onto the cart. "Do you think these people are here to console a man who just lost his son?"

The silence that forms is deafening. I know the answer already—no. These people are here to deliver their final blows to my papa. A family without an heir is like a castle with no wall.

"They are here to see the easiest way to end me. Our family has been around for almost a century, Maria. Your ancestors built our name from the ground up, and I thought that by getting you out of New York—by pulling us out of the depths of that war—we could continue that legacy in peace. But I was wrong, and here we are. I... I need to protect what is left of my family. You and your mother are the most important things to me on this earth. You are what I live for. What I will always be willing to die for.

"We need Matteo. He is powerful and connected, and no one will dare to touch us under his watch. You will marry Daniele and move back to New York, where you will live with your husband and bear your children."

I gasp. "Papá, I can't leave you and Mamá. She just lost one child—you cannot ship her last one across the ocean."

"And if you remain here, you will die." My father doesn't mince his words. "And if you die, Marta will kill herself in all her agony, and I will be left alone—with no children, no wife, no legacy."

He turns back to face me. There is a resolve in his eyes that tells me there's no winning this. He has made up his mind, and trying to go against him will prove pointless.

And so, I bite down on my tongue to keep from speaking and swallow my fate whole.

"Congratulations, cara mia," my father lifts his glass in the air in a toast. "You are now engaged."

And just like that, the last piece of me is buried six feet under, too.

I had been right earlier today—wherever the Warlord is, death is not far behind.

Matteo Davacalli didn't come for condolences. He came to bury me, too—just slower, and in silk.

2

MATTEO

I've always known I'm a monster. But it wasn't until the end of the funeral that I felt it in my bones. I looked into her eyes and saw the man I killed. Mistake or not, his blood is on my hands—and nothing will bring him back.

I replay that day over and over again in my head. I think of ways it all could have ended differently. The information had been wrong, and Antonio had just been in the wrong place at the wrong time. How was I supposed to know he was Antonio Faravelli?

I groan and rub my eyes, trying to shake the weight of sleep. After the funeral, I made my way back to my estate in Milan with a heavy heart. The deal has been made, and now it's all but a matter of time.

The air in the study is stifling. Smoke from my cigar curls upward, a thin veil between me and the quiet judgment in the mirror across the room. I replay the conversation I had with Marcello. I gave him the deal of a lifetime. I know the offer is far too tempting to pass up. My name carries a lot of weight in this world.

Marcello Faravelli—the man I used to call a friend—trusted me. And now, his son is dead because of me.

I run a hand over my face, exhaling slowly, trying to summon the right words for a conversation I've been dreading since I woke this morning. The decision to do all this had been rash, but it soothes a part of my guilty conscience.

A knock comes at my door, and I pause. I lean back into my chair and roll my shoulders. It's Daniele.

"Entra." Enter.

The door creaks open behind me. Daniele's heavy footsteps follow, confident as ever. He doesn't know yet. I watch the smile slip from his lips the moment he sees the grave expression on my face. He walks over to the other end of my large desk and sits.

"Papá." He speaks sharply, as he always does when he enters my space uninvited. "You wanted to see me?"

He wasn't at the funeral, but I don't blame him. If I were in his place, after everything that happened, I wouldn't want to be in the presence of the family we destroyed, either. Hearing Marta's voice slice through the air was nothing short of gut-wrenching. I can't even begin to imagine the pain they must be feeling.

"I did." I set my cigar down in the ashtray. This is a conversation I never thought I'd have with my son. Beatrice and I had always been adamant that he wouldn't fall into the trap of an arranged marriage. We wanted him to choose.

"What's this about?" He crosses his arms over his chest. His warm caramel eyes stare at me anxiously. He's trying to assert dominance, but I don't have the energy to challenge him. Not today.

"We need to discuss your future."

His brow furrows. "What about my future?"

"You will be marrying Maria Faravelli within the next two weeks." The words hang heavy in the room.

He straightens, his posture stiffening. "Excuse me?"

"It means you'll marry Maria Faravelli within two weeks. After what happened with Antonio, I think this is a necessary arrangement."

In other words, a way to ease my guilt—marry her into our family so they can reap the benefits of the Davacalli name.

Silence. It stretches between us, thick and suffocating, until Daniele laughs. It's humorless, bitter, and cuts through the air like a blade. I know my son—and from the look in his eyes alone, I know I have a fight on my hands.

"You're joking."

"I'm not."

"Jesus Christ, Papá." He steps back, dragging a hand through his hair. "I told you I don't want to be tied down, and you agreed that I was free to make whatever choice I wanted—as long as it didn't infringe on my duties as heir to all of this."

He speaks the truth. But that was before everything changed. My mind flashes to the gun, the blood. So much fucking blood.

I slam my hand on the desk, silencing him. "You don't have a choice in this, Daniele."

He stares at me, anger simmering in his eyes. "Why? What could possibly make you think you have the right to throw me into a marriage I didn't agree to?"

I hold his gaze, letting the silence carry the weight of my guilt. When I speak, my voice is low, steady. "Because I owe Marcello Faravelli a debt. You know this better than anyone, my son. You were there when the gun went off and Antonio dropped to the ground. You saw it. I saw it. And now we owe a debt. It's our duty to help replace what was lost."

Daniele's jaw clenches. "So you want me to suffer for the sins you caused? Papá, please. Surely there's another way to appease your guilt?"

"Antonio's death is on my hands, and this"—I gesture to the room, to him, to everything we've built—"this marriage is the only way to make it right."

Daniele's laugh returns, harsher now. "You think marrying me off is going to fix this? Do you even hear yourself?"

"You think I don't hate this too?" My voice rises, and for a moment, I see him flinch. "I'm not doing this because I want to. I'm doing this because it's the only way to ensure the Davacalli name doesn't go up in flames—and to avoid a bloodbath. Do you have any idea what would happen if Marcello found out?"

He glares at me, defiant as ever. "And what about Maria? We'd be stripping away the freedom of a girl who doesn't deserve this."

"She doesn't have a choice either," I admit, my throat tightening at the memory of her standing in the hallway, her face pale, her eyes wide with grief—and something else. Something that made my chest tighten in a way I couldn't explain.

"She's innocent in all of this," Daniele mutters.

"I know." My voice softens, betraying the storm inside me. "But this marriage will be good for her. Our name carries weight, and she'll be far safer as a Davacalli than a Faravelli. The vultures have already begun to circle them."

Daniele shakes his head. "You're a coward."

I let the insult hang in the air, unchallenged. I know he's speaking from a place of emotion, acting on his anger.

Normally I'd never let that shit slide—but today, I'll allow it.

"Maybe," I say, "but this decision is final, and you can't change my mind. If you want to sit on the throne after me, then you'll marry this girl. End of story." My tone leaves no room for argument.

He balls his hands at his sides, the vein in his temple protruding, anger rolling off him in waves. He doesn't say another word. He just rises from his seat, gives me one last look, and storms out of the study.

I watch him go, and I know one thing for certain—I'll carry the weight of this guilt for the rest of my life.

And yet, despite everything, one thought lingers in the back of my mind. A thought I dare not entertain.

Maria Faravelli.

Her beauty. Her fire. The way her presence commands attention without even trying. The brush of her arm against mine shouldn't have burned. But it did. And I haven't stopped thinking about it since.

Damn it.

I stay in the study long after Daniele slams the door behind him. The silence is deafening—but somehow, the stillness is welcome. My glass is empty, but I don't pour another drink. The alcohol isn't doing its job. It's not enough to drown the memories I wish I could forget.

Maria Faravelli.

I've known her since she was a child. Her father and I used to sit on the Faravelli patio in New York while the kids played in the garden. Back then, she was just a little girl with scraped knees and a shy smile.

But the woman I saw at the funeral wasn't the same.

She stood tall despite her grief, a fire in her hazel eyes that didn't match the black veil she wore. Even as she mourned her brother, she commanded attention. The room shifted when she walked in, and for the first time in years, I felt something crack in the armor I've spent decades building.

It's wrong. Disgusting, even, to think of her this way. She's young enough to be my daughter—and soon enough, she'll be Daniele's wife. But none of that changes the way my pulse quickens when I picture her standing there, her lips trembling as she spoke to me at the funeral.

This has to stop.

I push myself out of the chair and head out of the study toward the damn pool. I need to cool off. I step onto the back porch, kick off my shoes, and dive in—fully clothed—as the moon hangs high above me.

I submerge myself in the water, desperate to drown the thoughts of the woman who has somehow stopped me dead in my tracks. The only other person who ever managed that was Beatrice. And now—now the first woman to stir something in me in decades just so happens to be the one I've arranged to marry my son.

This is fucking great.

3

MARIA

I look at myself in the mirror in my walk-in closet. I am the vision of the perfect bride-to-be. A white midi dress that hints at my femininity without showing too much. The strapless bodice cups my cleavage perfectly, giving my breasts the ideal roundness. My neck is adorned with one of my mother's sapphire necklaces. It's a small teardrop-shaped pendant that hangs on my chest—a gift she received from my brother.

Antonio. Oh, how I wish he could be here. Had he still been alive, none of this would be happening.

I touched up my makeup and kept my face a little natural to avoid looking too caked and overdone. I smack my lips together, mixing in the light lipstick I had applied.

I hear her footsteps before she comes into view in the mirror. Our eyes connect, and she smiles, looking me up and down. I press my sweaty palms onto the skirt of my dress, nervous.

"How do I look, Mamá?"

"You look beautiful, cara," my mother gushes from the

door of my closet. She is dressed in a black dress, a sign that she is still in mourning. "Ready?"

No.

"Yes," I push down whatever reservations I have. I straighten my back and roll my shoulders. "Are they here?"

She nods and holds her hand out to me. "They're in the tea room with your father. They've been here for some time, but I wanted to give you some space to yourself."

Her words ease me a little.

"Okay." I walk over to my mother and place my hand in hers. There is a sense of unity between us. We are both women forced to conform to the pressures of our society. My mother, of course, is more inclined to do it—whereas with me, it is more of a forced disposition.

"Mamá?" My voice is loud against the thickness of the silence.

She lifts her face; her caramel eyes meet mine through the glass. "Si, amore?"

"Do you think he will like me? Do you think we will find love like you and Papá?"

It seems silly that one would hope for love in an arrangement like this, but I can't help it. As a little girl, I dreamed of the grand kind of love I read about in novels and watched on the big screen.

"Of course he will like you, amore. You aren't marrying a stranger."

The softness in her tone does little to ease the tension that still riddles my heart.

We walk out of my room, hand in hand, as we head down the stairs.

With each step I take, I feel the world closing in on me. My chest heaves up and down, trying to pull in as much air as possible to stay calm. We make it into the front foyer, and I can already hear their voices echoing through the space.

This is it. I pat my free hand against the skirt of my dress and brace myself for what's to come. My mother and I walk hand in hand until finally, we come to a halt in the archway of the tea room. The scent of expensive cologne and alcohol wafts into my nostrils.

I clutch my mother's hand for dear life. She is the only thing grounding me. We stand in the archway, staring at the three men in the tea room.

"Mi amor," my mother calls out to my father. "We're here."

My father's hazel eyes meet mine, and I catch the slight glint of pride radiating from his gaze. My eyes shift to Matteo, who sits in the chair beside him. His striking steel eyes watch me with great intensity. That gaze of his—it will always pierce right through me. My breath hitches—only for a moment—before I steady myself.

"Benvenuto, Signor Davacalli." I even go so far as to drop my gaze to the floor as a show of respect to my elders. "It's good to see you again."

When I lift my eyes, there's a small hint of a smile on my father's lips. Of course, he's proud. I'm being the obedient little Italian girl he raised me to be—the perfect bride for a family like the Davacallis.

"Ciao, Maria." Matteo's thick voice fills the room. He turns his head toward his son. "Daniele, you know Maria, of course."

Finally, my eyes move to the man standing by the window of the tea room. He's dressed in form-fitting dress pants and a white button-down, the sleeves rolled up to his elbows, revealing a sleeve tattoo beneath.

Our eyes meet, and my heart thunders in the center of

my chest. I blink. My hazel eyes lock with his warm caramel ones. I haven't looked into those eyes in over a decade. The innocence that once shone so brightly within them is now gone. I can see the years have turned him into a man.

His brown hair is styled to perfection. His body stands a solid six feet off the ground, his head held high like he's already wearing his crown.

The mafia prince. In all his glory and wonder. The man many women in our world want to bed—and many men want to kill.

"Ciao, Maria. It's been a long time." His lips curl into a charming smile.

"Ciao, Daniele," I respond.

The time apart hasn't dulled him—it's refined him. My ten-year-old self would be screaming that her childhood crush turned out to be sex on legs. Okay—at least the attraction is there. Now, we just take the next steps, day by day.

"Please, sit." Daniele gestures to the empty loveseat and steps away from the window. He walks toward the seat and waits for me to come to his side.

My mother leans in and whispers gently in my ear, "You got this, cara. Amore, I have some calls I need to make. I'll be in the study."

I drop her hand and make my way to my awaiting fiancé. My heels click against the wooden floor until I reach his side. I offer him a small smile and take my seat, and he swiftly follows. The air in the room is thick with tension and nerves. Matteo and my father watch us expectantly, as if waiting for something to happen between Daniele and me.

I don't know what they want. I'm not going to jump the man's bones in front of them.

"Dad," Daniele cuts through the silence, "you both staring at her is making things a little awkward."

"Oh." Matteo clears his throat and glances at my father, who suddenly seems a little flustered. "Well, I think for now we can leave you two to get to know each other a little while we discuss what needs to happen in the coming days."

"You're dismissing us?" I try to keep the attitude out of my voice, but it's hard when I can feel irritation simmering just beneath the surface.

"Yes," my father quips. "We need to discuss other matters, but I think you two should get reacquainted after all these years. Show him to the gardens, Maria."

The edge in his voice tells me everything I need to know —I shouldn't push back. I nod and glance over at Daniele, who is already looking at me. There's a hint of a smile on his lips.

"Let's go."

Before I even have a chance to rise, Daniele is already on his feet, offering me his hand. I stare up at him, surprised by how chivalrous he's being, but I try not to let the expectation get the better of me. I place my hand in his and lead him out of the tea room, leaving our fathers to talk.

His large hand swallows mine, but his warmth radiates up my arm in small, electric tingles. It's a subtle sensation— but it wobbles the very foundation I stand on.

Everything's been set in motion. Now it's just a matter of time before I do what's expected of me—fulfill my duty to my family.

I only hope that through it all, I don't lose the parts of my soul that still make me... me.

4

MATTEO

We sit in silence for a moment. Neither of us dares to speak in the thick of the tension. I have a hard time looking at the man after all that has transpired. Every time I stare into his eyes—just like with his daughter—I see Antonio's eyes staring back at me.

Stay with me, Antonio. Don't die. I press my bloodied hand over his stomach.

The memories of that night haunt me. I cannot escape them, and I fear they'll stay with me for the rest of my life.

Marcello Faravelli sits across from me, his face hollowed by grief but his shoulders upright—a man holding himself together by sheer will. His hazel eyes, once sharp with command, are now dulled, haunted by the loss of his son.

I should look him in the eye. Instead, I stare at the whiskey in my glass, swirling the amber liquid in slow, deliberate circles. Anything to keep my thoughts from spiraling further.

"Daniele will take care of her," I say, breaking the silence. My voice is low, steady. "He may not like this arrangement, but he'll respect it—he'll honor her and their vows. Maria will be safe with him."

Marcello exhales, long and tired. "She doesn't have a choice but to accept this. The death of my son has left my family vulnerable."

His words echo in my head, only adding to the pressure of the guilt that surrounds me.

"I've always tried to shield her from this life," he continues, his voice heavy with regret. "She's not like Antonio. She's... softer. She doesn't have the stomach for what we do, Matteo. I moved us here so she could live a more normal life. But now..."

He trails off, his gaze dropping to the drink in his hands. He doesn't need to finish the sentence. I know what he means. Maria doesn't belong in this world—but the world has found her anyway.

"She's stronger than you think," I offer, my voice firmer than I feel. "She'll adapt."

Marcello's laugh is dry, humorless. "That's easy for you to say. It's not your daughter being married off to secure an alliance."

My grip tightens around my glass, and for a moment, I almost respond. Almost say something reckless—something that would unmask the guilt eating me alive. But I don't.

Instead, I set my drink down, the glass clinking against the table. "This isn't just for you, Marcello. It's for both of our families. You've lost Antonio, but you still have Maria. If this alliance can protect her—can protect both our legacies—then it's worth it."

His eyes narrow, suspicion flickering across his features. "You speak as if you're not the one benefiting from this. As if you're doing me a favor."

I meet his gaze, forcing my expression to remain unreadable. "I *am* doing you a favor."

The silence stretches between us, his eyes searching mine for something he won't find.

Marcello stares at me for a moment longer, and I brace myself for his next words. But then he sighs, leaning back in his chair, the fight draining from him.

"Let's hope this marriage brings us what we need," he mutters. "But if your son hurts her, I promise I will unleash hellfire on him."

"And I would expect nothing less from you, old friend."

Marcello rises abruptly, draining the last of his bourbon in one swift motion.

"We'll finalize the details tomorrow," he says, his voice clipped. "Make sure Daniele understands what's expected of him."

I nod, standing as well, though the stiffness in my limbs betrays the calm I'm trying to project.

"He does. And he'll do what's required."

Marcello looks at me for a moment longer, as if trying to read between the lines, to pick apart the words I won't say.

"If you'll excuse me, I need to go and find my wife. You and your son are my guests until the wedding is over. My home is yours," he says before turning and leaving me in the tea room, standing alone.

I let out a heavy sigh. The weight of all that is happening presses down on me.

I have killed many men. They used to call me the Warlord. But those were people who deserved to die.

Not Antonio.

I feel their pain, and every time I look into the eyes of the Faravelli family, I cannot help but remember the lifeless ones of Antonio.

Marta is the one who devastates me the most. Hearing her bloodcurdling scream sent shockwaves through my entire system. I have never heard so much agony in one voice.

I hear laughter outside the window, and suddenly, I'm moving toward it.

I step to the large, arched glass—its frame as old as the house itself. The view outside is serene, a stark contrast to the storm inside me.

And there they are.

Daniele and Maria sit by the pool, their legs dangling in the water as they talk. The faint sound of her laughter drifts through the open window—light and melodic. I see glimpses of the little girl who used to run around our yard with Daniele.

Maria leans forward slightly, her posture relaxed, her lips curved in a soft smile.

The setting sun catches the golden tones in her hair, and for a brief, foolish moment, I can't look away.

She's beautiful.

It's a simple thought—one I shouldn't have—but it slips through the cracks of my mind.

The realization twists something in my chest, a sharp pang that feels like betrayal. She's my son's fiancée.

My son's future wife and my future daughter-in-law.

I tear my gaze away, clenching my jaw so tightly it aches.

This has to stop.

I grip the edge of the window frame, forcing my breathing to steady. Whatever this is—this fleeting, unwelcome attraction—it's nothing. It has to be nothing, for the sake of peace within my own home. I've forced this union on my son; the least I can do is not lust after his woman.

Daniele says something, and Maria laughs again—the

sound light and unburdened, as though she hasn't just lost her twin brother. Selfishly, I am happy. She deserves peace. Happiness. A future untainted by the shadows of men like me.

I remind myself of that as I turn away from the window, retreating back to the tea room's suffocating stillness.

She's not mine to want.

And even if she were, I'd destroy her.

The proof of that is my very dead wife, ruined by the darkness in my life, and punished for the mistake of loving a man like me.

5

MARIA

We walk out into the garden area hand in hand, not a single word uttered between the two of us from the tea room to the porch outside. The air hits my face, and I breathe in the fresh Italian air. I close my eyes for a moment, relishing in the freshness.

When I open my eyes again, I'm met with a pair of warm caramel eyes that move over my face. His gaze is far less intense than that of his father's. I feel the heat rise to my cheeks, and I turn away.

"Why are you looking at me like that?" I drop his hand and walk down the stairs. I head over to one of the lounge chairs by the pool and glance back at him still standing on the porch. He has his hands in his pockets and watches me with a cocked brow. He still has that same mischievous glint in his eyes whenever he's up to no good in his head.

"Checking me out, Faravelli?" He chuckles and makes his way down the stairs. I haven't been called by my last name in years. He walks up to me with a smile on his face and drops down to one knee to help me out of my shoes.

"What are you doing?" I'm surprised by how easy it is to

feel so at ease with him. It's like fourteen years haven't passed since our last meeting. We're back to being those ten-year-old kids who laughed and joked with each other. Except now, we're engaged to be married.

"The weather's too nice not to feel the water. And last I remember, you love being in the water." He looks up at me through his lashes and smiles. He gently takes off my shoes and places them to the side. "Come on."

He takes my hand in his and leads me to the edge of the Olympic-sized pool. The movements between us feel so natural, like we've been doing them all our lives. It both scares me and gives me hope for what the future holds for the two of us.

I try not to let my heart get ahead of itself. When people are in mourning and faced with despair, any shred of light becomes dangerously addictive. I can't allow myself to latch onto it.

We settle onto the edge, our feet in the water and the calm of the Florence summer around us. The silence passes between us, but it's not awkward.

"You look well, Maria," he says. "When my father told me about our union, I'll admit I was shocked. Marriage was never a topic of discussion until recently. He always said I should marry whom I choose—the way he chose my mother. But I guess times have changed."

I guess we both have that in common.

"I'm sorry that you got stuck with me."

He clicks his tongue on the roof of his mouth. "Please. As far as I see it, I hit the jackpot of arranged marriages. We know each other at least, and you aren't some airhead bimbo who can't tell the difference between a fork and a spoon."

I choke out a laugh. "Who have you been dating over the years, Danny?"

His nickname slips from my lips easily.

"You don't even want to know my dating history. A lot of life lessons and character development there." He laughs under his breath, and the sound makes me feel all warm inside. "What about you? How has your love life been?"

Heat rises to my cheeks. "Oh, well… that has been non-existent for me. I was just so busy with school and then my art, so…"

The truth is that my brother and father had me under a watchful eye. Every time a boy wanted to take me out on a date, they had to pass the Antonio test. Spoiler: very few made it ten minutes.

As a sister, I should have been annoyed, but I didn't mind. I knew he was looking out for me, and at the time, I had no interest in men. To be honest, I still don't—but with the turn of events, I'm glad I can at least speak with my fiancé, and he isn't some weird old man.

"Maria Isabella Faravelli, are you telling me that you are a virgin?"

My blush deepens. "I mean… I've kissed a man before, if that's what you mean?"

I am quite underdeveloped compared to the average twenty-something-year-old. While many are experimenting and clubbing, I lock myself away in my home and paint and draw to my heart's content. I find comfort in the silence of creating. Bringing all of my thoughts and imaginations to life is something that I love to do.

"So you are a virgin."

I duck my head and turn to the side to hide my heated face from him.

"Maria."

I keep my gaze averted, not daring to look his way. Why do I feel so mortified?

His hand comes up to cup the side of my face. He gently draws me toward him so I can meet his gaze. There's a gentleness in his eyes that eases the slight chaos inside me.

"In the world we live in, your virtue is gold, Maria. Own that." He strokes his thumb against my cheek. "There's nothing to be embarrassed or shy about at all. And to be honest, I think it's quite admirable that you've kept your innocence for so long. Most women are... loose these days, and willing to let anyone between their legs."

"But aren't you used to more experienced women? What if... I don't satisfy you the way you need me to? I know sex is a very big part of marriage, and I need to make sure that you enjoy it with me."

His eyes smolder with a gentle warmth. "And we can take things as slow as you want. We don't need to dive in headfirst." He drops his hand from my face, and I lean away from him, feeling a little awkward.

"Take it slow?"

He nods. "We're going to be together for the rest of our lives. We can take things in stride. I'm not in a rush for anything—are you?"

I shake my head. The weight that's been pressing on my chest since my brother's wake lifts a little, and some of the anxiety I've been carrying subsides. This is all going far better than I hoped it would.

"Good. So don't stress or feel embarrassed. And as far as wives go, I don't think you're all that bad of a pick, do you?" He kicks his feet in the water. He turns his head to the side and shoots me a smirk that leaves my insides fluttering. "Easy on the eyes, knows how to hold a fucking conversation, and doesn't like pineapple on her pizza."

A laugh rumbles from my lips. "Thank God I don't like pineapple."

"Anyone who likes it is inhumane, in my opinion. And we're Italian—isn't it heresy to like it on our sacred dish?" He chuckles and dips his hand into the water. He swirls his fingers about before lifting them and flicking me with water.

I let out a little shriek that didn't sound like it came from me at all. Who am I right now? I'm not this gushy, girly kind of person. But I guess Daniele has a way of bringing out the little girl in me.

Our laughter fades, and we settle into a comfortable silence. We sit and listen to the birds chirping in the trees and the gentle breeze that whistles through the leaves around us. I love our backyard—it's one of the places I like to spend most of my time.

"I'm sorry about your brother, M." Daniele nudges his shoulder against mine. "I know how close you were with him."

I knead my fingers together in my lap and stare at the water.

"Thank you." I bite down on my lower lip, not wanting to dwell too much on the negative emotions. "I know this should've come sooner, but I'm sorry about your mother. I don't think I ever reached out when she died."

His eyes soften. "It's okay. We had lost touch at that point, and I had my dad, so... it's okay. I think she would be over the moon if she knew we were getting married. I remember how she used to tease us about getting married—and how you'd be the perfect bride for me."

Beatrice had wanted us to get married. She didn't have any other children besides him, so she viewed me as her daughter. She always gushed to my mother about what the wedding would look like. Only now, hearing him say this, does my mind take me back.

That's where my crush began.

We talk by the pool for what seems like minutes, but it turns out to be two hours. We joke, laugh, and tease each other like we've known each other all our lives. I learn more about the man he's become, and he asks me questions about the woman I am—and hope to be.

For the most part, we steer clear of any wedding or marriage talk, which I'm grateful for. But at the end of our conversation, he walks me back to my room—bare feet against the cool marble floor. We come to a halt by my door. He hands me my shoes, and we just stand there, staring at each other with the goofiest grins.

"Thank you for today. I had a great time getting to know you all over again," I say, smiling up at him.

He steps closer, the space between us almost non-existent. For a moment, I think he's going to kiss me. My eyes flutter shut as I feel him inch closer—but his lips never meet mine. Instead, I feel the soft brush of a kiss against my cheek before he pulls back and stands to his full height.

"You thought I was going to kiss you, Faravelli?" His warm caramel eyes lock onto mine, dancing beneath the hallway lights. "On the first day? I'm a gentleman. I'll wait until tomorrow."

With a wink and a kiss on the back of my hand, he saunters down the hallway toward the stairs—leaving me floating on cloud nine.

I want to believe this is truly going to work out. That this arrangement might actually become something good.

But if life has taught me anything, it's that everything can change in the blink of an eye.

Thunder rumbles through the walls of my bedroom, and I jolt upright in a cold sweat. My chest rises and falls rapidly as I struggle to calm my panic. I run a hand through my messy hair and lean against the headboard.

"Jesus," I groan, tilting my head back toward the ceiling.

Nightmares. They've been relentless lately. So vivid, so terrifying—I don't think I've slept properly in days.

A flash of lightning spills into the room. I rub a tired hand over my face and sigh.

A storm.

I usually love the rain, but I've never been able to sleep through Mediterranean storms. It has a lot to do with the accident that happened when I was a little girl—one of the reasons Papá decided to fly us across the ocean.

I throw the blanket off my legs and head for the kitchen. When I wake during a storm, there's only one thing that eases my nerves: hot milk. I don't know what it is, but the warmth calms me. Grounds me. Makes me feel safe.

My bare feet touch the cool marble as I move quietly through the dark halls and down the stairs. But as I round the corner into the kitchen, I come to a sudden halt at the sight of a shirtless man leaning against the counter, a cup in his hand.

"Shit," I hiss, turning to make a run for it. The milk will have to wait. The last thing I need right now is to be alone with a half-naked Matteo Davacalli.

"Maria," he calls after me. "You don't need to leave. I only came for some water."

I curse under my breath, briefly closing my eyes before turning back to face him, a smile plastered on my face. I walk over to the counter, nerves skittering through my body.

"Sorry, I didn't think anyone would be up at this time." I shift on my feet uncomfortably. I try to keep my eyes on his face, but his chest is on full display—and it's hard to focus when you have a masterpiece in front of you.

Oh my God. No. I cannot be thinking about him like that. He's my father-in-law. Well, soon to be.

"No need to apologize. This is your home, Maria. I'm merely a guest here." He gestures toward the fridge behind him. "Did you want some milk?"

My eyes go wide, feeling a little too exposed. "How did you know that I…"

"You used to sleep over at my home quite frequently, once upon a time. I'm not a man who forgets details about people." He holds my gaze with great intensity. "Warm milk calms you during storms. Allow me."

Before I can stop him, he goes to the fridge, pulls out a carton of milk, and pours it into a cup. He microwaves it while I stand on the other side of the counter, silently watching him.

I am well aware that I'm standing in the middle of the kitchen, in the middle of the night, with my future father-in-law—who just so happens to be shirtless. I don't miss the way his muscles flex as he reaches up to retrieve the cup from the microwave. When he turns to face me, I quickly avert my gaze from his body.

Why did it suddenly get hot in here?

"Here you go." He slides the cup toward me.

I accept it with a small smile. "Thank you. I should head back to bed."

I don't want to stay and make small talk with this man. Ever since my brief encounter with him at the wake, I've wanted to avoid him as much as possible. Something happens to me internally whenever I'm near him, and I don't understand it. That's why I don't like it.

"See you in the morning, Mr. Davacalli." I turn and begin to walk away from the counter.

"Maria," he calls just as I'm about to turn into the foyer.

I pause and glance over my shoulder. There's something in his eyes—something raw, threaded with deep emotion.

"He's a good boy, my son. He'll take care of you well."

I swallow hard, trying to find my voice. "I'm sure he will. Goodnight, Mr. Davacalli."

"Goodnight, Maria."

And with that, I turn—hot milk in hand—and scurry toward the stairs, feeling this strange fluttering sensation in my chest. It's unlike anything I've ever experienced. I have no idea if it's fear, intrigue, or a mixture of both.

All I know is that Matteo Davacalli is not a man I should be alone with. And I should avoid him at all costs.

But how is that even possible, when I'm literally marrying into his family within the coming week?

6

MATTEO

I loathe people. But what I hate more? A party full of them. If I had it my way, Maria and Daniele would have eloped by now. But I have to honor Marcello and his daughter by granting her a wedding for the ages.

The violin strums in the background, setting the mood for a classy and elegant aesthetic. A ballroom filled with drug lords, murderers, and prostitutes—all dressed to the nines to hide the ugly red stains we pretend we don't carry.

"Fucking boring." I brood in the corner of the room, away from the hustle and bustle of the mafia elite.

I watch Maria and my son work the room like pros. She smiles and hangs on to him with a light in her eyes that is not only captivating but makes you stop and stare. Something in the way she carries herself draws your eyes to her.

She is beauty personified.

I shake my head and try to rid my mind of these thoughts. This is wrong. I shouldn't be having these thoughts—not when she's wearing my son's ring. She's meant to be a Davacalli. My daughter-in-law. I take a sip of whiskey and grimace. Surely Marcello could have sprung for the good liquor. I'm paying a hefty fee for this wedding to begin with.

"Enjoying the party, Mr. Davacalli?" Marta Faravelli, Marcello's wife, comes to stand beside me. She offers me a small smile and a raise of her glass. "I must say, the ring chosen for my daughter is stunning. And her birthstone, no less."

I know little of the madame of the house, but from what I do know, she has Marcello's ear and is one of the main reasons he's been so successful—after the clusterfuck of a head his father was before him. She made the man who now stands in the corner of the room, smiling with the rest of the wolves.

"I must say, you've outdone yourself, Marta. The hall looks impeccable on such short notice." I offer her my appreciation. She's had less than a week to make this all work, and she's done well.

"Mhmm." She hums her agreement. She holds the stem of her wine glass and pats her palm on the skirt of her midnight-blue, floor-length gown.

"Thank you. And I'm sorry for being such a bother, but matters like these require the highest urgency."

"I'm aware. The murder of my son has left my family... in need of some power. And you just so happen to be willing to lend a helping hand."

There is accusation in her tone, but I don't indulge her. I've already taken from her. I can take whatever thoughts or grievances she may have. She's a grieving woman—and her son's body is still warm.

The crack of the gun and the whizz of the bullet ring in my mind. I have to force myself to remain composed as the memories try to trickle their way back in.

"You know this world we live in, Marta." I sip the shitty

whiskey to keep my mouth preoccupied. "This world is all about power plays and moves. Your husband was once invaluable to me, and now he can be again. My son needs a bride, and I need a trusted ally. We all win here."

She manages a grimace of a smile. "Yes, everyone wins. My son is dead, and you can't wait to make a power move. But what am I to expect from the Warlord himself?"

This time, I give her my full focus. It strikes me just how much of her was in her son—the same son who lies dead in a hole thanks to me. Her eyes are locked on our children on the other side of the room, but I know her words are meant for me.

"I'm truly sorry for your loss, Marta," I say gently. "Losing a child... I can't imagine that kind of pain."

She stiffens. Her eyes stay on our children standing nearby, but I see her grip tighten around the glass in her hand. She's barely holding it together. Planning this wedding has been her distraction—her way of avoiding the grief. But in moments like this, when Antonio's name lingers in the air, I can see her break a little. The pain hits, and so does the reality—he's never coming back.

She wipes at her eye and then turns to look at me.

There's hurt in her eyes, yes—but also something sharper. Anger.

"This world already took one of my children," she says, her voice low and steady. "And now you and your son want to take the last one I have left. You're dragging her back into the middle of all this—excuse me—bullshit. Right into the line of fire."

She steps closer. She's small—barely over five feet—but right now, she feels ten feet tall. Her rage fills the space around us.

"You may be feared. You may be powerful. But if a single

tear falls from her eyes—if one hair on her head is harmed—I swear to God, I will burn your world to the ground. No amount of power, money, or reputation will protect you from me. She is my last child. I carried her for nine months. I labored for eighteen hours to bring her into this world. You better honor that—and keep her safe."

She doesn't blink. Doesn't waver. Every word hits like a strike to the chest.

And for the first time in a long time, I have nothing to say back.

"You have my word that I will keep her safe."

"I will hold you to that promise." She gives me a lasting nod before making her way to the other side of the ballroom, where her husband stands with a few of our *colleagues*. It's comical, really.

Outside of this event, we're plotting and planning to kill each other. And yet here we are—congratulating and smiling like I didn't have a gun to their informant's head a week ago.

I raise my glass in the direction of Gallagher, the head of the Irish mafia. He's a man I despise deeply, but I'd rather have him as a friend than a foe. He lifts his glass to me, then turns back to the group he's speaking with.

My eyes shift to the corner of the room where I see the bride and groom looking rather tense. My son says something in her ear that makes her visibly stiffen. Then, he proceeds to step away and walk out of the ballroom, leaving his bride standing there at a loss.

"Dammit, Danny," I mutter, downing the rest of the liquor before walking out after him.

I follow him into the hallway and turn left when he does. The Faravelli estate is built more like a castle. It's a maze of rooms and corridors that make getting lost easy. I keep an eye on my son until he finally breaks out onto a balcony and grips the ledge. I pause for a moment, assessing his body language.

Low shoulders, tense back, and from the looks of it, his fists are clenched tight. A telltale sign that he's battling something. He's always done this—even as a boy. I know him like the back of my hand.

I step onto the balcony. The cool breeze hits my face, and the moonlight kisses my features. "Daniele."

"Leave me alone," he mutters, not turning to look at me. "I want to be alone right now."

"This is your engagement party. You can't be out here while your fiancée is left alone inside. Whatever's on your mind, we'll talk about it later. Come." I allow my authority to seep into the words.

He stays in place. His grip tightens on the ledge, nails digging into the concrete. I can feel the fury rolling off him in waves. Whatever's bothering him, it's shaking him to the core.

"Daniele, don't make me repeat myself." I walk up to where he stands. "Go back into the room. Now."

His neck snaps toward me, and the fury in his eyes takes me aback for a second. But I keep my face neutral, unphased by whatever tantrum he's about to unleash.

"How could you?" There's a crack in his voice—a telltale sign of emotion lodged deep in his throat. "You knew. All these years, from the very beginning—you knew."

My heart falters for a beat.

He knows.

That look in his eyes... it can only mean one thing. For decades, I feared this moment. That he would find out the one truth Beatrice and I swore we'd take to the grave.

The betrayal and anguish in his stare make me look away, even if only for a second.

"Look at me," he seethes. "How long did you think you could keep this from me?"

"Daniele, I—"

"I don't want to hear it." He shakes his head in disbelief. "All this time, you played me for nothing but a fool. And now you have me here, cleaning up your mess."

I glance around to make sure there's no one within earshot.

"Watch your tongue, Daniele."

He scoffs. "Oh, forgive me, Father. I know you don't want anyone finding out that you killed the only heir to the Faravelli fortune."

"Daniele, that is enough," I seethe, my voice laced with a bitter kind of fury. "Now is not the time or place to speak about this. You're getting married in two days, and the last thing you need to be doing is causing a scene."

"Married? Fuck that. I want no part of this." He steps away, the anguish in his eyes clear for all to see—and I feel like the biggest dick in the world. It was never supposed to come out this way. "I'm done, Matteo. I won't be part of this anymore."

"What do you mean you won't be part of this? We have a debt to pay, my son. Need I remind you that—"

"I don't owe shit, Matteo." His eyes lock onto mine. "You hid this from me."

I open my mouth to speak, but no words come out. I'm at a loss. I try to reach for him, but he pulls away from my grasp, and my heart clenches. My son is twenty-four-years old. I've watched him grow from the womb to the man he is now, and never in all those years has he looked at me the way he is looking at me now.

"Danny boy," I try to reach him again, but he's already shaking his head.

"I need to get out of here." He sidesteps me and walks off the balcony, leaving me alone in the warm night air of Florence.

I stand there, completely lost for words. I have no idea what the fuck just happened—or how the hell he found out. This was meant to stay under lock and key, and the only people who knew the truth were me and…

I shake my head.

Surely not. Surely he wasn't stupid enough to go to my son.

The rage simmers just beneath my skin, threatening to break through. I ball my fists at my sides and breathe deeply, trying to calm the urge to kill that laps at my senses.

I want his head on a platter for what he's done. He's trying to undo my life, and I refuse to let that little cockroach win. I should've put a bullet in his head when I had the chance, and now I'm stuck dealing with the aftermath of a pest that refuses to die.

The blood rushes to my head, the pressure increasing with each passing second. I groan as I try to rub away the tension that's settled in my face. I close my eyes and lean against the ledge, trying to center myself.

I have a room full of guests who will expect to see the groom, and he is—

"Mr. Davacalli?"

A sweet, angelic voice snaps me out of my reverie.

My eyes rip open. "Maria."

She stands by the door in her white cocktail dress, her hair flowing in the breeze. The light behind her hits her features perfectly, casting a gentle glow on her face. She shifts from side to side, unsure whether to come closer or stay where she is.

Stay where you are, little dove.

I'm a monster who can't be trusted.

My unspoken words must reach her, because she remains at the threshold.

"I'm looking for Daniele." I watch the small ball in the middle of her throat bob up and down. "He left the ballroom suddenly, and the party is about to end."

"He had some business to attend to. As you know, our world waits for no one." The lie falls from my lips easily. "He'll be out shortly, I'm sure. I'll go and find him."

She doesn't seem convinced. "Is… is everything okay?"

"Yes. Why wouldn't it be?"

Her hazel eyes take on a much bluer tone under the moonlight. They reflect the hue of the moon in them.

"It's just… you're a little tense. If everything is okay, then I'll just head inside and wait for him to come back."

I don't like the way her eyes carry that sad gaze.

What alarms me more is how much I… care for this girl.

I don't know if it's because she reminds me of a lamb in a world full of wolves, just waiting to devour her.

You better keep her safe.

Marta Faravelli's words echo in my mind, and I snap out of it.

"Go back inside. Don't worry yourself with Daniele. He'll be in shortly."

She still seems unsure, but she nods and makes her way inside.

I watch her body retreat down the hallway without so much as a glance back my way. Her scent drifts onto the balcony behind her, and I have to physically stop myself from inhaling it like a starving man.

She is not mine to have. She never was.

It becomes a chant of sorts as I force my gaze away.

I have much bigger issues to deal with—the last thing I need is a brown-haired, hazel-eyed distraction plaguing my mind.

I need this wedding to go off without a hitch.

The future of the mafia world depends on this union going through. And come hell or high water, Maria will become a Davacalli.

Even if I have to drag my son down that aisle myself.

7

MARIA

I stare at myself in the mirror. This is the dress of my dreams. I never gave much thought to my wedding day, and to be quite honest, I don't care much for it now. But after speaking with Daniele, I feel hopeful that we could build a good life together.

But I still haven't seen the groom in over twenty-four hours. The last time I spoke to him, he stormed out of the ballroom with his father in tow. I didn't see him all of yesterday, and now I stand by the mirror, dressed in my gown, ready to marry this man.

"Oh, you look stunning, cara." My mother comes into view in the corner of the mirror. She's dressed in a lavender gown that compliments her skin perfectly. Her brown hair is swept up into an elegant updo, and her face is dusted with the softest makeup to accentuate her features. "I've seen the dress already, but seeing you now, all dressed up... a true princess."

I give her a small smile in the mirror, letting go of a shaky breath as I look over my body. A beautiful floor-length gown with a tight sweetheart bodice holds my breasts perfectly. The skirt cascades down to the floor with a slight side slit that allows me the freedom to move. My hair flows down my back in loose curls, and I wear a tiara—a family heirloom my mother dusted off for this day.

I hear the door to the bridal room creak open, and in walks my father, dressed in his tuxedo. I expect him to at least look somewhat pleased that this deal is finally going through, but instead, I see only the tension locked into his features.

I turn around, my heart already slipping to the floor. "Papá, stai bene?" Dad, are you okay?

His eyes find mine, and from that stare alone, I know something is wrong. A cold weight sinks in my stomach, rooting me to the spot. My mother moves to stand beside him, her face drawn with concern.

"Marcello?" She places a hand on his shoulder. "What's wrong?"

My father runs a hand through his graying hair. His shoulders are tight, his jaw clenched.

"Daniele is gone."

I blink. "What do you mean he's gone? Gone where?"

"Matteo tells me he left in the night. Headed back to the States," he explains, and I catch the slight bitterness in his tone. "You won't be marrying Daniele..."

There's a flicker of disappointment, but it's followed—almost instantly—by a rush of relief. I'm free. I had come to accept that marrying Daniele wouldn't be so bad. But now that he's gone—likely running from the very thing I feared—it feels like a weight has finally lifted from my chest.

"So... that's it? No wedding?" I ask, hope fluttering like a dying bird in my chest. I try to keep my voice steady, but it trembles despite me. As much as I hated the idea of marrying Daniele, my father had been counting on it. I had been preparing for it.

"No," my father says, voice tight. "There will be a wedding."

I blink. "I... I'm sorry—what?"

"You heard me."

"I'm pretty sure a bride needs a groom to have a wedding," I say, my heart picking up speed.

His eyes find mine. Cold. Unblinking. "You have a groom."

Something in my body freezes. A sudden, unnatural stillness, like the air before an earthquake.

He breathes out the words like they don't carry the weight of a thousand knives.

"Matteo."

My entire world splits in two.

Silence. Deafening. My breath catches, and I swear the room tilts.

"No," I whisper, shaking my head as if that might erase what I just heard. "No, Papá, you're not—"

"I am," he says. "It's done."

"Matteo Davacalli. No." I take a step back, like the space between us will undo what I've heard. "No, this isn't happening. You can't do this. This wasn't the plan. I was supposed to marry his son, the boy I once knew, not... not the devil wrapped in silk and power!"

My knees almost give out. My hands shoot out to the vanity for support, my knuckles going white. My chest tightens, and I forget how to breathe.

He doesn't flinch. "The deal stands. The name stands. The groom changes."

I stare at him—this man who raised me, protected me,

once swore he'd never hand me over to monsters. And now here he is, offering me up to the biggest one of them all.

The silence stretches. Suffocating.

And then, softly— "You're feeding me to the Warlord."

"Marcello, what are you talking about?" my mother asks —voicing exactly what I'm thinking. "She's marrying Matteo now? As in... the father of Daniele?"

"That's what I said, isn't it?" My father sighs heavily, placing a hand on his hip. "The wedding will still take place. You will still get married, and this deal will still go through."

I can't believe this.

Only a week ago, we buried my brother in a cemetery just twenty minutes from this very cathedral. That same day, I was betrothed to my childhood friend. And now, a week later, I'm set to marry his father.

I shake my head. "No. Papá, I won't marry him. I'll find Daniele—I'll talk to him. Just two days ago, we were steady, aligned... we were ready to face this together. He can't just be gone..."

There's no way he would abandon me. He gave me his word. He promised me.

"There is no other choice, Maria."

"He's a widower. His wife passed away not long ago. How do you expect me to be the bride of a man who already had a wife?"

My father pinches the bridge of his nose, trying to maintain his composure. I know he hates when I push back—but I refuse to let him dictate this.

"You won't be the first woman to marry a widower, and you definitely won't be the last."

I throw my bouquet onto the armchair and step toward him, rage and desperation mixing in my blood. The hairs on the back of my neck stand as I close the space between us—

the man never meant to be challenged. But right now, I don't give two shits. This is my life he's playing with, and I refuse to marry the Warlord.

"You can't do this to me. I don't agree to this." I seethe, my anger rising higher than it's ever dared with him. "If fucking Daniele isn't here, then there is no wedding."

"Watch your tongue, Maria." The fury in his eyes makes me falter, but the fire inside me pushes through. "I am still your father, and you remain under my care."

"I am twenty-four, Papá. I'm an adult. I can walk out of here right now, and you can't stop me."

I see the muscle in his jaw twitch.

"Not with my name, you don't. If you walk out of those doors, you'll be stripped of it all—my fortune, my mercy, my name." My father storms over and grabs my wrist. "If you leave this cathedral, you will never again be allowed near this family."

My lips part. A gasp slips free.

"Marcello," my mother says, her voice sharp and low. "She's our daughter—my daughter. You won't speak to her like that. She is the last of our children. Your heir. You'll disown her over my dead body."

My father's eyes dart to hers, and I see the regret hit him immediately. He does love me—I know he does. But he's running on grief and desperation. We all are.

He blinks, then turns his gaze back to me. Guilt and remorse flicker in his eyes.

"You will marry this man, or our family will pay a price we cannot afford." His grip on my wrist tightens. "Do you want your brother's blood to be for nothing?"

"Marcello," my mother gasps again.

"You know it's true, Marta," my father snaps, turning to where my mother stands. "Do you think I want to give her away? To force her into a life she didn't choose? I don't have a choice. Without Matteo, we will drown in the pool of blood Antonio left behind."

My heart clenches at the mention of my brother. I don't want to accept that he's gone, but every time we speak of his death, I'm plunged back into the nightmare I'm trying so desperately to escape.

The room falls silent. The only sound is the gentle strumming of a violin as guests begin filtering into the cathedral. I can hear the faint, distant rhythm of my heart breaking with every beat.

"I'm sorry, my daughter," my mother says, her voice breaking the heavy silence.

Tears brim in my eyes, threatening to spill, but I hold them back. I push down the despair clawing at my chest and dig deep for the strength I need.

"Maria, listen to me. This isn't just about you—it never was. It's about our family's survival. Since your brother's death, we've been exposed. Vulnerable. They hover at the edges, drawn to the scent of weakness. If we're humiliated now, in front of all these families, we lose everything. Respect. Power. Support. No one will stand with us."

I swallow hard. "So, this marriage... it's just politics to you?"

"It always has been." His voice didn't waver. "Matteo needs this alliance as much as we do. He wants control in Italy, and we're the perfect bridge. That's why he'll never walk away from this union—because it strengthens both our names. This marriage is our insurance."

My hands curl into fists at my sides. "This isn't fair..."

"No. It isn't." His tone didn't soften. "But fairness has no place in our world. Think about your mother. Think about what happens if we fall from power. She becomes the easiest target. They'll go after her first. Do you really want that?"

The knot in my throat tightens. "I... I don't want that..."

"Then you need to understand something, and you need to understand it now." He stepped closer. "If you walk away from this, you're not just walking away from a marriage. You're turning your back on your family. On everything we've built. On the people who love you."

He paused, eyes locked on mine. "Is that a risk you're willing to take?"

"I will marry him," I say, my voice steadier than I feel.

I hold my father's stare, refusing to let my eyes waver, refusing to give him the satisfaction of seeing me break. But inside, something splinters—quietly, irrevocably.

"I'll wear the dress. Smile for the cameras. Play the part of the dutiful bride," I continue, each word tasting like ash. "But don't mistake my silence for submission."

I finally look away, not out of defeat—but because I've made peace with the war I've just agreed to enter.

"If this is what it takes to protect what's left of this family..." I pause, my voice hardening, "then so be it. I'll give them a wedding. But don't ask me to give him my heart."

"You have ten minutes, and then we need to begin. Come, Marta—you need to take your seat."

My father holds out his hand to my mother, which she takes, though with a slight hesitation. Her caramel eyes are clouded with resignation and regret, but she says nothing.

The perfect wife of a Mafia boss.

My father's word is law, and she never challenges it—no matter how deeply it conflicts with what she wants.

Is this what my future is doomed to be?

They leave the bridal room, and I'm left alone to sit in the wreckage of what today has become.

I fucking knew it. It had all gone too smoothly.

I knew something would go wrong, but never—not even in my worst nightmares—did I imagine it would end with me marrying the Warlord.

I leave my room exactly ten minutes later. I find my father waiting by the closed cathedral doors, a cigarette perched between his lips—unlit.

"Mamá will kill you if you light that," I say, stepping up beside him. "You told her you quit."

He chuckles, but there's no humor in it. He rips the cigarette from his mouth and tucks it into his pocket.

"It's only for the scent. I never light it. Your mother made it very clear she doesn't want me smoking—and her word is law."

If that were true, you wouldn't be giving me away to a man almost your age.

I think it, but I don't say it. What's the point now? It's over. I'm seconds away from walking down that aisle, and nothing I say will change it.

"You look beautiful, Maria."

The doors open, and dread lodges deep in my stomach.

The violin strums the gentle classical piece I picked out just days ago. A piece that once sounded like hope... now sounds like surrender.

I knew it. Things were going too well. I should've braced for the collapse.

"Rendimi orgoglioso, Maria." Make me proud, Maria.

My father's voice is steady and cold.

There's no turning back.

The guests see us step into the aisle, and all rise to their feet.

I'm going to be sick. My stomach churns violently, and if it weren't for Papá's firm grip on my arm, I would've run—

bolted down the aisle and never looked back. My heart aches with every step toward the life I didn't choose.

This. This is exactly what I wanted to avoid.

I don't want to marry a man twice my age.

I keep my gaze fixed just a few feet ahead as we walk. The sweet, angelic music that fills the cathedral feels all wrong now. It will forever be etched in my memory as the soundtrack to my walk toward the slaughter.

Because that's what this feels like.

I am the lamb, and waiting for me at the altar... is the wolf.

I steal a glance at Papá. His expression is set, stern, eyes locked forward.

But I—I can't bring myself to look at Matteo. Mr. Davacalli. My fiancé.

We come to a stop at the altar. I keep my eyes on the floor, trying to steady my breath as the blood rushes through my veins like a storm.

The priest begins to speak, but his voice is distant—muffled beneath the roar in my ears.

"I do," my father says, his voice cutting through the haze. "I give my daughter to this man."

Fuck. Here it is.

Papá gently removes my hand from his arm—but I resist. Just for a second. I don't want to let go. I don't want to do this. This cannot be my fate.

But he doesn't give me a choice.

With practiced calm, so as not to draw attention, he pries my hand off his arm and places it in a much larger, waiting palm.

I can't bring myself to look up. Not yet. Not at the man I'm about to marry.

But I feel the heat of his touch, the command in the way he holds me.

"Ti do la mia cosa più preziosa." I give you my most precious thing. My father murmurs, just loud enough for those at the altar to hear.

"Take care of her."

I force my eyes up.

The heaviness in my chest is unbearable—like wet cement pouring in, layer by layer, pressing against my ribs, refusing to set, building until I'm on the brink of suffocation.

"Ti amo, amore," he says softly as he kisses my cheek. I love you, my love.

When he pulls away, I catch it—the sadness in his eyes. But he buries it quickly behind a hollow smile.

Then he steps back, releasing my hand fully into Matteo's grasp.

The moment our skin touches, a flutter stirs in my chest—soft, disorienting—followed by the sickening churn deep in my stomach. My gaze traces the path from our joined hands, up the length of his arm cloaked in smooth black fabric, until it finally collides with his eyes.

My breath catches. "Mr. Davacalli."

My voice comes out no more than a whisper. But against the thick silence of the cathedral, I may as well have screamed to the heavens and beyond.

Fuck.

"Maria." His voice is thick, laden with emotion. His eyes pierce through mine, stripping me bare—leaving me with nothing to shield myself.

"You're breathtaking, Maria."

His compliment catches me off guard, so much so that the priest has to clear his throat to get my attention, urging me to step forward with my fiancé. Matteo helps me up, his hand still wrapped securely around mine.

"Please face each other," the priest says, his white cloak draped elegantly around him, a serene smile on his face.

"Join your hands, please."

I hand off my bouquet to one of the women seated in the front row—someone I've only seen once or twice before. Then, I place my hand into Matteo's. The warmth that travels up and down my arm is not only distracting but unnerving.

I don't know why my body decides to short-circuit whenever he's near me—let alone touching me.

"We are gathered here today..." the priest begins the ceremony, but it all just blurs into the background. My mind circles back to one unshakable truth—I'm about to marry a man I don't want to marry.

I woke up hopeful this morning, believing I was stepping into a future filled with light. But instead, here I am—being cast to the lion.

Had this been the plan all along? Were they all in on it?

I resist the urge to glance back at my parents.

The ceremony moves on, my thoughts stealing most of my attention. Before I know it, we're exchanging rings, and the priest finally moves to the part I've been dreading.

"Do you, Matteo Angelo Davacalli, take Maria Antoinette Faravelli to be your lawfully wedded wife—to honor, cherish, and protect her, for as long as you both shall live?"

The words echoed off the stained glass windows.

"I do."

Matteo holds my gaze without a hint of shame. His hands squeeze mine ever so slightly at his declaration. He then reaches down to the ring bearer and takes my ring from the velvet pillow. With careful precision, he slides it onto my finger—a perfect fit.

It's stunning. A sleek platinum wedding band. It's the kind of ring I would've chosen for myself—had I been given a choice.

"Do you, Maria Antoinette Faravelli, take Matteo Angelo Davacalli to be your lawfully wedded husband? To honor, cherish, and love him as long as you both shall live?"

Love.

Such a heavy word—especially when paired with the Warlord.

How does one love the darkness?

Is that even possible?

"I do," I say, forcing the words past the lump in my throat.

I'm handed Matteo's platinum band, and I slide it onto his finger. The expensive metal shines against the sun rays that stream in through the window of the church.

A sigh echoes softly, likely from my father in the front pew.

He was probably holding his breath, worried I'd make a scene.

But I've committed to this.

And now, I have to see it through.

"You may now kiss your bride."

The words fall like a gavel in my mind, locking my spine into place.

No.

We remain facing each other, our eyes locked in a silent war.

Neither of us moves.

I freeze, uncertain how to navigate this moment.

I had braced myself for the younger Davacalli—the boy I once made mud pies with in the backyard.

But the man standing before me now is no boy.

He's the deliverer of death. Warlord.

The Warlord.

How do I kiss darkness and walk away unscathed? How do you kiss death—and survive it?

I must hesitate too long, because Matteo lifts his large hands to cradle my face. He leans in, and the air between us crackles with electricity.

Sparks kiss the surface of my skin and bounce back into the atmosphere.

His thumb strokes my cheek gently. The pad of his thumb heats the skin he touches, branding me. The cathedral, filled with people, fades away. My eyes flutter shut. I wait, caught between fear and anticipation for what's to come. This man has assaulted my senses from the moment I saw him across my brother's grave.

And now...

Inches vanish.

Our breaths tangle together in a cloud of tension—

And then...

He presses his lips to mine.

Fireworks. No—detonations. Explosions of heat and electricity ripple through me, setting my nerves ablaze and short-circuiting every carefully constructed defense I've built. My body, traitorous and unthinking, leans into him— into the storm—melting into the impossible warmth of the man who shouldn't feel like home.

The kiss lasts mere seconds—five, maybe—but it fractures something deep within me. When he pulls away, his eyes are no longer cool and distant; they're the raging sea. For a heartbeat, I see it all—passion, hunger, danger. A man on the edge of ruin, and I am the tether he both fears and craves. It calls to me, beckons me closer like prey to its predator.

And then he blinks—shutters it all—and the veil falls back into place.

The crowd erupts into cheers, and just like that—the trance is broken.

"May I introduce to you Mr. and Mrs. Davacalli. May their union be blessed, and may they be protected by the Almighty," the priest announces to the congregation.

They all rise, clapping and cheering.

I tear my gaze away from my husband, the ring on my finger suddenly feeling as heavy as a two-ton truck.

Matteo clutches my hand in his and turns to face the crowd with me, presenting us for the first time as husband and wife.

My lips still tingle from the kiss, and I can't help but think back to it. My eyes catch my mother, who has tears streaming down her face at the front. My father, standing beside her, remains stoic—his expression unchanged—but I catch the glint of unshed tears in his eyes. Still, I know he won't let a single one fall. The predators are watching.

Matteo leans down, his mouth brushing against my ear, tickling my senses. "Welcome to the family, Maria."

He pulls away—no smile, no warmth, no joy. Just the gaze of a man carved from stone, one who carries only a void within his soul, filled with every drop of blood spilled by his hand.

And just like that...

I am officially Maria Davacalli.

The bride of death.

8

MATTEO

I stare at the ring that lies heavy on my finger. It's a snug fit—my son has much thinner fingers than mine. I'll need to get it resized. The reception is loud and filled with laughter, drunkenness, and regret. The last one comes from me, but it lingers in the air like cheap perfume.

I am married.

The words still don't feel real, even on my lips. I vowed that after Beatrice, I would never marry again—but my son has forced my hand.

I hear a sniff beside me at the high table where we sit. I turn my head to the side and find my wife staring at her lap, looking miserable. She isn't happy about this union, either. I get it. But I'm trying to make the best of it. We have a show to put on—for her parents, my colleagues, and the rest of the world. She carries a heavy name now.

"You could at least try to look like you're not having the most miserable time of your life." I lean toward her and utter the words into her ear. Her body shudders—the kind of reaction that would make one think she fears me. "You just got married, Maria. Smile a little."

She sucks the air between her teeth sharply. "I didn't know people smile when they're going through torture."

She turns her head, our breaths mingling in a plume of heat. I'm taken back to the church where I kissed her. It was brief, a short kiss—but it did things to my internal system that I didn't expect.

"Where is your son, Mr. Davacalli?"

I clear my throat, trying to remove the lump that has formed in it.

"I'm sorry things didn't turn out as you had hoped, Maria. But this... marriage between you and me is for the best."

She bites down on her lip, trying to keep the words from escaping. She wants to speak—she's seconds from an explosion—but the poise and composure she's been groomed for since birth holds her tongue.

"This is by no means a real marriage." From the jut of her chin alone, I know she's trying to be defiant. It's amusing, watching her try to go toe to toe with me. "I may hold the title of wife, but I will not perform the duties that come with it."

I hold the corner of my mouth down to keep from smirking. I stare into her eyes—the fire in them intrigues me. Most people can't even meet my gaze. This past week, she hasn't dared to look me in the eyes for more than a fleeting moment—yet here she is, challenging me with my ring on her finger.

"Are you talking about fucking me, Maria?" I watch with great amusement as her cheeks heat with embarrassment. "Don't be shy now."

She grabs her wine and sips it, tearing her gaze from mine. She looks out at the happy crowd celebrating our union on the dance floor.

"That's not what I meant. Look, Mr. Davacalli, I—"

"Matteo," I correct her. "You'll need to start calling me Matteo to keep people from getting suspicious."

She blinks. "No. We just need to get through this night and head to our rooms."

I notice she says rooms. I'm not objecting to having separate spaces, but from what Marcello said, he wants an heir within the year. I don't want to start trying soon either, but we need to keep up appearances.

"Of course." I lean back in my chair and reach for my glass. "But you do know that, in time, you'll need to learn to just accept what happened. We're married. That's not going to change.

No divorce will free you—unless, of course, you put a bullet in the middle of my head. But if you do that, then your family goes right back to square one."

I hear the grinding of her teeth, but she says nothing. Music fills the silence between us, and we sit watching the wedding unfold from the table we've been placed at—to be adored by all the guests.

I'm not foolish enough to think these people are happy about this union. Her marrying my son was going to be a seismic shift in mafia society. But now that she's my wife, I'm sure the whispers have already made it to the East Coast. Which means this game is only going to get bloodier.

"Excuse me." My bride gets up from her seat beside me and heads—likely—to her mother. She doesn't look back, and I'm fairly certain that'll be the last I see of her until we're forced to leave for the manor.

Two hours later, and after many forced, fake goodbyes, we finally make it back to the Faravelli manor. Marcello and Marta left an hour earlier, leaving us to mingle with all their cokehead relatives.

The walk into the manor is silent—as expected. The woman hates me. She loathes everything I represent in her life. And who can blame her? She was meant to wear the Davacalli name beside my son—not wrapped around the man who forged it in blood and power.

Her heels click against the marble floors, the train of her dress trailing behind her like a cape. I want to offer to help, but she'd likely chew my head off. And I'm in no mood to deal with my ever-pleasant wife tonight.

She leads the way to her room. I follow closely behind her. I have no intention of sleeping. The last woman I fucked was my wife, and ever since then, I've had only my own hands for company—and it's been enough. I haven't needed to bury my cock anywhere—for now.

"You don't need to follow me, Mr. Davacalli." Her back is still turned to me as she leads us up the stairs.

"Are you forgetting it's our wedding night, Mrs. Davacalli?" The words sound foreign on my lips. She is my wife—the realization hits me like a two-ton truck. I don't want to accept it. "Besides, I need to walk you to your room."

Her steps falter at the top of the stairs, but she doesn't turn back. She continues with determined strides and makes her way to her room. She opens the door, and I follow her inside. I close the door behind us and stride in with a confidence that probably shouldn't be allowed.

I place myself on the edge of her bed and take it all in. In the corner of the room sits an easel with a few strokes painted onto a white canvas. A painter—I never would've pegged her as the type. I imagined her room being far more... vibrant. But this... It's rather dull and beige.

"So this is your room? It's less colorful than I would've thought. Beige is rather dull for a woman like you." I make the most obvious observation. Just by looking at her, she screams polished perfection. Rich, spoiled, a Mafia princess with access to more resources than the average girl. "You're not what I imagined you to be, I must say."

My bride stands in the middle of the room with her arms crossed over her chest, looking uneasy.

"It's been a long day, Mr. Davacalli, and I—"

"Matteo," I correct her. "We're married now. There's no need to be formal. You're my wife, and it would be strange if people ever heard you call me 'Mr. Davacalli.'"

"Right." She shifts her weight from foot to foot. "Like I was saying, it's been a long day and I just want my bed, so it would be great if you could leave my room. I want to shower and wash this whole day off."

I stifle a laugh. "Odd thing to say about one's wedding day."

"Go, please." She shudders and hugs herself, trying to find some comfort. "I understand that I'll have to give you a baby one day—but tonight is not that night. Leave. Please."

I hold up my arms to show her I'm not a threat. "I won't ever force myself on you, Maria. When the time comes for a child, there are plenty of ways to get there without me having to find myself between your legs."

In the corner of the room, I see three suitcases lined up against the edge. I guess she's all ready for tomorrow.

"Do you have to be so crass?"

"It's the truth. Never in my life have I had to force a woman to fuck me—and you won't be the first. If and when you want to fuck me, all you need to do is ask." I watch the heat tint her cheeks, even through the layer of makeup she wears.

She scrunches her nose in disgust, but it doesn't make my words any less true. I never wanted another wife. I'm a widower. My love died the day I lost Beatrice. I have nothing left inside me to give.

"You can leave now, since we've cleared that up," she bites out. "There are plenty of guest rooms—take your pick. I'll be staying here for my last night."

I lift myself from the edge of the bed and stand to my full height. I want to cross the distance between us and offer some solace, some comfort—but nothing I say will ease any of this. I'm struggling with her. I have no idea where my son is, and now I'm left with a wife I never intended to have. I am as pleased as a pig in a slaughterhouse.

"Goodnight, Maria. We take off tomorrow morning. We should be in New York by 9 a.m. I have a lot of business to attend to."

Mainly finding my son and making sure he doesn't make a mockery of himself—or our name.

My wife says nothing. She just hugs her body tightly. Her eyes stay locked on the front wall, and she looks like she's seconds from falling apart. In this moment, I'll give her the freedom to break in peace.

I walk out of the room without another word. I don't even turn back to make sure she's okay. We have no relationship beyond what the papers say.

I close the door and let out a breath I hadn't realized I was holding. For the first time since this fucking day began, I can breathe. The entire day has been nothing short of a shitshow, from the runaway groom to now having a wife.

I glare down at the ring on my finger. The thing feels more like a shackle than a symbol of love or loyalty.

"Fucking hell."

My voice echoes through the empty halls of the Faravelli estate. Everyone is likely asleep—or hiding in their rooms, much like I want to be.

But first... I need to take the edge off.

I make my way down the stairs and into the kitchen, where I find Marcello's less-than-stellar liquor collection. It'll have to do for now. I pour myself a glass and head out through the sliding doors that lead to the back porch.

This is the only peace today will afford me.

Tomorrow, when the sun rises, there will be a long list of fires to put out. I'll need to account for my son and his disappearance. I'll need to make sure all loose ends are tied up before we leave.

And most importantly, I'll need to keep my new bride alive.

I saw the reactions at the wedding.

The vultures may not be circling just yet—but they're close.

They can smell the tension in the air.

"Are you not meant to be in bed with my daughter, Matteo?"

His voice catches me off guard. I glance to the side and find him by the sliding door of the kitchen. He's still in his dress pants and shirt, but he looks far more disheveled than he did at the ceremony.

I don't bother sitting up in my chair.

"I see you found my liquor supply."

I raise the glass in the air. "It tastes like shit. When you left New York, did you also lose your taste for the finer things in life? You've had better whiskey in my basement, Faravelli."

I glance back at my old friend, and he manages to let out a low smirk—against his will, I'm sure.

We've known each other a long time, and never in a million years did he expect me to marry his daughter .

He simply walks onto the porch and takes the chair beside mine that looks out to the yard.

The moon kisses the surface of the pool, casting a gentle blue hue over the area. You can hear the whistle of the crickets and the soft hum of the summer breeze weaving through the trees.

"You are married to my daughter."

Those are the first words that come from my father-in-law.

"Yup." I sip on the bitter liquid. "I know you pictured me joining your family a little differently. But we are family now, Faravelli—and my word still holds. From this day forward, you are under the protection of the Davacalli name. Your daughter will want for nothing. She will be the most protected woman on the East Coast—if not the entire country."

Marcello remains quiet. He looks out over the water, his face pulled tight in a deep frown.

"You can't even keep your son in check. How can I trust you to keep your word when it comes to my daughter?"

I pause, my glass halfway to my mouth. "I was caught off guard. But make no mistake—my son will answer for what he's done."

He scoffs. "You're meant to be the most feared man in the world, and yet you can't keep a leash on your own boy? I am not happy, Matteo."

"And neither am I." I glance back at him. "What happened is unfortunate, but you still got what you wanted. The Davacalli name. Our resources. They're yours now. The picture may not look exactly how you imagined, but you know me, Marcello. I'm not a man who would ever dishonor your daughter or shame her. She's in good hands. Trust is a rarity in our world, but I'm asking you for it—just this once."

I turn my head fully to look at him—and he meets my gaze.

As a father, I understand him.

And as a mafia boss, he understands me.

My intention with this union is to ease the guilt weighing down my chest for taking his son.

And his is to protect the last of his blood.

We may not like each other, but we need each other to reach our goals.

"I will never fully trust you, Matteo," he says slowly. "But I trust my daughter. And I trust that if she ever needs to, she'll make the call—and I will get her out of this marriage. To hell with what may come after. She is the last of my blood, and I will not allow her to suffer because of this world."

His words carry conviction—unshakable, clear.

"You make a single tear fall from her eyes, or you harm a single hair on her head... I will personally hold the gun that puts a bullet in the middle of your eyes."

I hold his stare. "I will honor her as I did my last."

I try to keep the image of a smiling Beatrice out of my head. I haven't thought of her in a while—work usually keeps me busy enough that my mind is never idle. It's only in the thick of the night, when the silence presses in, that I feel the void in the shape of her.

We sit in the weight of silence. Neither of us dares to speak first.

We both know.

No matter what is promised in a moment like this, it's the heavens that decide what happens next.

I will honor Maria.

She is my wife. I made a vow.

My word is my bond—and I'll uphold that part of the bargain.

She'll never have to worry about a wandering eye. She'll never need to fear a scandal or a divorce. She will have my loyalty, and she will have my protection.

But one thing she will never be able to claim is my heart.

That has been locked away... for all eternity.

9

MARIA

I see the sun's rays peeking out just beyond the horizon. Just like that, my wedding came and went, but the outcome was nothing like I had imagined.

The large diamond on my finger feels like a shackle—heavy and suffocating. I fight the urge to rip it off. My gown lies abandoned on the floor, exactly where I left it last night after kicking my husband out of my room.

I barely spoke to him, yet I felt his presence like a shadow lingering in the air.

Matteo Davacalli. My husband.

A man I know nothing about, yet one I am now bound to for life.

I didn't even see his reaction when I locked the door on him last night—did he care? Or was I just another transaction to him?

I wish it were all a bad dream. But no matter how many times I close my eyes and take a deep breath, when I open them... I'm still here.

"Fuck." I roll into my pillow, stifling the scream building in my chest. "Why?"

The questions torment me, playing on an endless loop.

Why did my brother have to die? Why did I have to get married? Why did Daniele leave?

Why did I have to leave behind everything I knew?

But it's not just that. I can't stop wondering—what kind of man have I married? A ruthless killer? A cold strategist? Or something even worse?

I flip onto my back and stare at the ceiling.

I could run.

If I packed a bag now and left at dawn, I could be in Milan by eight, on a plane to some remote island by ten.

No one would find me.

I glance at my closet. The thought of grabbing a bag, stuffing it with essentials, and slipping out before dawn is tempting.

But no matter how far I ran, the weight of my last name would catch up to me.

Matteo would catch up to me.

And something tells me he isn't the type of man to let his wife simply disappear.

Then, I remember my parents. They never forced me into this world. They never asked for anything from me—until now.

With Antonio buried six feet under, there's no one left to shoulder the burden of the Faravelli name.

Except me.

I throw the sheets off my body and head into the bathroom. The house is still, the world outside still asleep. The hot water burns against my skin, but I let it, hoping it will wash away the weight pressing down on me. It doesn't. In just a few hours, I'll be on a plane to a place I haven't seen in almost a decade.

By the time I'm dressed and step out of my closet, my

mother is sitting on my bed, clad in black. She is still in mourning.

She lifts her head at the sound of my footsteps, her eyes red-rimmed, tears glistening in the soft morning light.

"Mamá." I sit beside her. "It's early. Why are you up? You did so much yesterday at the wedding."

She shakes her head. "I only have a few more hours with you, amore. I need to spend as much time with you as possible. How are you feeling?"

I hesitate. "I'm fine. Tired, but fine. You packed my bags for me."

She follows my gaze to the neatly lined suitcases. A faint smile tugs at her lips. "I didn't want you to have to worry about anything." She turns back to me. "I packed a few of my jewelry pieces—things you may want for galas and events. You'll need them as Matteo's wife."

My stomach tightens. "Mamá, you didn't have to—"

"I wanted to." She takes my hand. "Promise me you won't lock yourself away in your room and draw all day. Go out. See the city. Experience life."

I scoff. "Do you really think the overbearing mafia Warlord is going to let me go clubbing in Manhattan?"

She cups my cheek, a small, wistful smile on her lips. "Not clubbing, cara. There is more to life than drowning yourself in alcohol. I want you to breathe. To live. To love."

Her words are hopeful, but hope is a foreign concept to me now. My fate is sealed. I can try to find the light amid the darkness, but one thing is certain—the light won't be found in a city I barely know or in a man I will never love.

She sighs. "You are so brave, my girl. I wish you didn't have to go, but I feel in my heart that, as unfair as this is, it will be good for you."

I lean into her touch. "I wish I didn't have to go either, Mamá."

Tears well in her eyes. "We have been joined at the hip since you were born." Her voice wavers. "But now, you are a wife. And soon, you will be a mother."

A heavy silence falls between us. She doesn't need to say what we're both thinking. Antonio should have been here. We should be celebrating love, not mourning loss.

A knock at the door breaks the moment.

"Come in."

My father steps inside, his face unreadable. The dark circles under his eyes speak louder than any words.

"We need to get to the tarmac," he says. "Matteo has a tight schedule."

I nod. "Of course."

Without another word, he leaves. My mother exhales shakily.

"Papá and I..." She trails off, her lips pressing together. "This whole ordeal has been hard. We have never been at odds before."

Guilt twists in my gut. "I'm sorry, Mamá. He's trying to do what's best for the family. For you."

"It's going to take me some time to come to terms with the fact that I'll only see you during the holidays now—not whenever my heart aches for you."

I nod, her words settling between us like a quiet weight. "We should go."

The longer I stay, the harder it becomes. I need to walk away before the ache has a chance to take hold.

"Okay."

THE DRIVE to the airport is steeped in silence. Tension thickens the air, a heavy weight pressing on my chest.

Matteo sits beside me in the back, his attention fixed on his phone, fingers moving swiftly over the screen. Every now and then, he flips through a file, his expression unreadable. He hasn't looked at me once. Not in the car. Not since this morning.

What is he thinking?

I sneak a glance at him from the corner of my eye, searching for something—anything—that might reveal what goes on behind that face. His jaw is sharp, clenched, as if he's grinding his teeth in concentration.

Is he already regretting this marriage?

Does he resent me as much as I resent him?

I barely know him, yet I am bound to him. Matteo Davacalli—the man whispered about in the mafia underworld, a figure as feared as he is respected. But what is he like beyond the reputation? As a man? As a husband?

I know nothing about him.

A part of me wonders what he was like with his first wife. Did he love her? Did he look at her with warmth, with care? Or was she just another obligation, just as I am?

The thought unsettles me, though I don't know why.

The jet looms ahead, and reality crashes down with full force.

I'm leaving.

"Say your goodbyes."

Matteo's voice is calm, detached. The first words he's spoken to me all morning. Then, without another glance, he strides toward the jet, his presence commanding even in silence.

I watch him for a moment—his calculated movements,

the way he barely acknowledges me. A stranger. A ghost of a man I am meant to call my husband.

He doesn't care.

I shouldn't care either.

"Come, Maria."

My father steps out of the car first, followed by my mother. I force myself to follow, my body stiff, resisting every step. The staff come to the car and begin to offload the car with all our bags, and I just stand there next to my parents.

My mother pulls me into a tight embrace, her tears soaking into my shoulder. "Call me as soon as you land. FaceTime every week. Reply to my messages so I know you're safe."

I nod, swallowing the lump in my throat.

"If you need me, I'll be on the first jet out—"

"We don't have the jet anymore, amore," my father interjects gently.

She whips around, glaring. "Then you will buy one, Marcello. You are still in the doghouse."

A flicker of amusement crosses my father's face—just for a moment.

That alone tells me they will be fine.

She turns back, pressing kisses to my cheeks and forehead. "Ciao, cara mia."

I cling to her warmth, memorizing it. "Ciao, Mamá."

When I step away, my father meets my gaze. "You have made me proud, Maria. I have asked much of you, and you understood your duty. If you ever need me—no matter how big or small—I am a phone call away."

The sincerity in his words is rare, but I hold onto it.

I walk into his arms, breathing in the familiar scent of him. For a moment, I am a little girl again, safe in his steady embrace.

"Ciao, Papá."

I turn and walk toward the jet, my steps measured.

Matteo is waiting.

His hands in his pockets, his expression impossible to read.

I study him—his posture is relaxed, but there's an underlying tension in his shoulders. Controlled. Measured. As if nothing in the world could rattle him.

Does he feel nothing?

Or is he simply that good at hiding it?

I step past him. He barely acknowledges me, shifting slightly to let me go first—just enough space to force me to brush against him. The briefest contact.

I glance back one last time. My mother is openly crying now, my father holding her close.

I press a hand to my chest. "Ti amo."

They mouth the words back.

The entire ride from the manor to the airport, he has kept a distance from me, as if allowing me to have these last moments with my parents undisturbed.

I guess the Warlord is capable of compassion and empathy.

Then I turn away, stepping into the jet.

"Good morning, Mr. and Mrs. Davacalli. My name is Stephanie, and I'll be taking care of you today."

She barely looks at me. Her attention remains fixed on Matteo, her gaze lingering far longer than necessary.

Blonde. Skinny. Blue-eyed. Starving for attention. How typical.

I shake off the irritation and move past her. She doesn't offer to take my bag, but when Matteo steps in behind me, she practically stumbles over herself to relieve him of his laptop case.

Pathetic.

The flight attendant deposits his bag beside him, her hand 'accidentally' brushing against his rolled-up sleeve.

I resist the urge to roll my eyes.

I do not care. I do not care.

I move to my seat, and Matteo drops into the one directly across from me.

I steal a glance at him. Our eyes meet for a fraction of a second.

There's something in his gaze—it's not cold or cruel.

I don't know what it is.

But it terrifies me.

Then, he looks away and flips open his file.

What's going on inside that head of yours, Matteo?

Stephanie leans in unnecessarily close. "Is there anything else you need, Mr. Davacalli?" Her voice is syrupy sweet. "Water, wine..."

I nearly choke. Is she serious?

My eyes snap to Matteo, waiting for him to shut this down. But he simply nods, flipping through his file as if she doesn't exist. "Thank you, Stephanie."

She preens under the minimal acknowledgment. "Of course. I'm at your beck and call."

My fingers curl against my thigh.

I do not care. I do not care.

But I do.

I unbuckle my seatbelt and rise. Fifteen minutes before takeoff. More than enough time.

Stephanie startles when I step into the galley.

"Yes?" she asks, her tone clipped.

I smile, resting my hand on the counter—making sure my wedding ring catches the light.

"Stephanie," I say smoothly, "I get it. My husband is

attractive. Most women seem to think so. And while I usually find it amusing, what I don't tolerate is blatant disrespect. Especially not in front of me."

Her lips part, but I lift a finger, silencing her.

"The only acceptable response here is 'Yes, Mrs. Davacalli.'"

A pause.

"Yes, Mrs. Davacalli," she murmurs.

I offer a sweet, pointed smile. "Good. Now, bring my husband a bottle of water. Mine should be sparkling—room temperature."

I clap once and turn away, feeling victorious.

I pause when I see Matteo holding my notebook. My breath catches.

I storm over and rip it from his hands. "Excuse you."

Shutting the book, I press it to my chest. "Has anyone ever told you it's rude to dig through people's things?"

"You're actually really good." He ignores my irritation, his eyes piercing through my soul. "Quite good, I might add."

Heat rushes to my cheeks, and my fingers tighten around the notebook. "Stop touching my stuff, Matteo. It's not yours to snoop through."

I drop into my seat and buckle my belt, refusing to meet his gaze. I can only hope he didn't flip through it. No one has ever seen my sketches—I never allowed anyone to. They were deeply personal.

Matteo leans back, watching me. "It fell to the floor, and I accidentally saw the drawing. I was just curious—I didn't mean to."

He tries to engage me again, but I keep my mouth shut and my eyes locked on the window.

What do you see, Matteo? What are you thinking?

But I don't ask. I don't want to know.

My parents are no longer on the tarmac, and the jet begins to roll out.

This is going to be a long flight.

And an even longer life with this man.

10

MATTEO

"Can you not stare?"

After almost seven hours of flying, those are the first words my wife says to me as we begin our descent to JFK. Her tone is sharp, laced with irritation. "It's weird and creepy."

"I've been called worse." I close my files and fasten my seatbelt, giving her a slow, amused smile. "Try a little harder, kitten."

Her scowl deepens. "Don't call me that."

My brow lifts. "What? Not a fan of your new name? Funny, I didn't think you had it in you to put a woman in her place like that."

"I didn't take you for the kind of man who lets women disrespect his wife," she shoots back. "There should have never been a need for me to do that in the first place. If you hadn't indulged her, she wouldn't have stepped out of line."

"Indulged her?" I let out a short laugh. "How, exactly?"

"You didn't tell her to back off," she huffs, frustration burning in her voice. "She was flirting with you, and instead of shutting it down, you answered her."

I blink. "Maria, indulging her would've been bending her over this table between us. Did I fuck her? No. I simply responded."

Her jaw drops slightly before she snaps her mouth shut. "Must you be so... so crass?"

I smirk, enjoying her discomfort. "I'm telling you the truth. But if it bothers you, I'll take note of it and make sure it doesn't happen again."

She eyes me suspiciously. "Is that meant to be an apology?"

I shake my head. "No, because I'm not sorry. But I will make an effort to ensure women know their place around me."

She clicks her tongue but doesn't reply. The rest of the landing is spent in thick silence. She refuses to look at me, and I don't press her. In time, she'll learn to open up to me, to speak her mind in ways that don't always involve biting remarks. Until then, I'll keep gnawing at her, wearing her down until she bends.

When the jet comes to a halt, I waste no time getting up. As we disembark, I notice Stephanie, the flight attendant, watching me from the back of the jet. I don't miss the glare Maria sends her way, and something about it makes my cold, thorn-pierced heart thrum with satisfaction.

She was jealous.

The cool summer air of New York greets me, the distant hum of sirens and city life filling my ears. I'm home.

Maria trudges behind me, her tension so palpable I can almost feel it pressing against my back. She's out of her depth here, but she'll learn. She has no choice.

Two large SUVs wait for us on the tarmac.

"Welcome back, Mr. Davacalli." Emily, my housekeeper,

smiles warmly. "You've been missed." She turns her gaze to Maria. "Welcome to New York, Mrs. Davacalli."

Maria steps out from behind me, hesitant but intrigued. "You're the first person to greet me with a smile," she says, extending her hand. "Maria. It's nice to meet you."

For the first time since we left Florence, I see the ghost of a smile on her lips. Her posture eases slightly in Emily's presence, and I feel my own body loosen in response. I knew she'd take to Emily, but I'd been prepared for resistance.

"I have business to attend to," I tell Maria. "Emily will take you to the penthouse and show you around. If you want to explore Manhattan, you may, but you'll take Tony and Curtis with you." I nod toward the two bull-like men by the SUVs. "They're your security detail from now on."

Maria's gaze sweeps over them with thinly veiled disdain. "I don't need them."

There's that defiance again. It makes her a pain in the ass at times, but I can't deny how much I enjoy watching her fight against me.

"Yes, you do."

She folds her arms. "You just want them to spy on me."

She's right, but I'm not about to admit that.

I resist the urge to sigh. "This isn't up for negotiation, Maria."

"I think Emily will do just fine."

"Emily is not trained to protect you. No offense," I add, glancing at Emily, who merely nods. "Her job is to manage the household, not keep you alive." My voice is low, controlled. "Let me make this simple—you are no longer a Faravelli. You're a Davacalli now, and with that name comes enemies."

Maria's jaw tightens, but she doesn't argue. She knows I won't bend.

I turn to Tony. "Take them to the penthouse. If she goes anywhere, you go with her. I want tracking updates." My gaze shifts back to Maria. "I already put my number in your phone. It's under 'Matteo.' If it's urgent, call. Otherwise, a simple text will do."

Her brows knit together. "How did you get my number?"

I lean in, brushing a whisper against her ear. "I have my ways. Behave while I'm away, kitten."

She stiffens as I press a fleeting kiss to her cheek before stepping back. I acknowledge my staff once more and slide into the waiting SUV.

As we pull away, I pull out my phone and dial my son's number.

Straight to voicemail. Again.

"Hi, you've reached Daniele Davacalli. Leave a message."

I exhale sharply. "Danny, I'm getting worried. Call me back."

I pocket my phone and stare out at the city as we weave through the streets of Manhattan. Daniele is my heir, the only one meant to inherit my throne, but he's slipping further away. He could be on a beach somewhere, drink in hand, or he could be plotting his next reckless move against me.

Either way, I need to find him before someone else does.

The SUV pulls up to my business headquarters. Among all the illegal dealings, I run a few legitimate fronts to clean my money. This place is one of them.

As I step inside, the atmosphere shifts. People tense, bodies pressing against walls to clear a path for me. Their fear is almost tangible, and I welcome it.

Gretchen, my receptionist, rises from her desk, her face flushed. "Mr. Davacalli, I didn't know you'd be in today—"

"Spare me the flattery. Bring me the files on the west

harbor's layout. And a double espresso from Brooklyn, piping hot."

Before she can reply, I step into the elevator and hit the top floor.

The doors open, and I am met with people milling about. When they see me—just like at the reception—they all press their backs against the walls, making way for me to walk. The wedding band on my finger feels like a large billboard, drawing everyone's attention.

My assistant, Marcus, rises from his chair, ready to greet me. "Welcome back, Mr. Davacalli. I trust you had a good trip?"

"Hello, Marcus. You gained some weight while I was away—lose it," I grunt under my breath. "Before you start allowing people to bombard me, I need a few minutes alone. Hold my calls and keep my door shut."

"Of course, sir," Marcus says before I disappear into my office.

I walk in, and the scent of mahogany and cigars hits me. The familiar aroma settles deep in my senses, wrapping around me like a comforting embrace. For weeks, I have been bombarded and forced out of my areas of comfort. It feels good to be somewhere that still feels like mine.

"Welcome back to the kingdom." I stare out of the large floor-to-ceiling windows that make up the majority of my office. "Long may the king reign."

I never once thought of myself as a king. I never wanted to rule. I just wanted power, and that goal has never changed. I want my name to be the most powerful and most feared there ever was.

Flashes of my son assault my mind, reminding me again of how strained our relationship has become. He is my heir, and his name rests on my throne. But he won't even return my calls. How can I convince him to wear this crown?

I am only in my chair for a few seconds when the door opens without permission. Valerio struts into my office with the arrogance of a fool, his hands in his pockets, a toothpick clenched between his teeth. I wait for him to take a seat on the other side of my desk before I reach for my landline.

"I'm sorry, sir. Mr. Delchini pointed a gun at my head and told me he would drop me dead if I didn't let him in." Marcus's shaky voice filters through the receiver.

I sigh in disappointment. "I should fire you. But I won't —for now. If you allow anyone else in, Marcus, I will personally put a bullet in your head."

I don't wait for him to respond. I hang up and turn my attention to my second-in-command. Raven-black hair, deep Mediterranean skin, and eyes that could drop the panties off a nun. Valerio Delchini.

"A gun to his head, really, Valerio? The kid is only twenty-one."

Valerio rolls the toothpick between his teeth. "He'll need to learn about the world soon enough. The kid nearly pissed his pants when he saw the barrel. You should fire him for being so much of a pussy, if you ask me."

"What do you want, Valerio?" I lean back into the thick leather of my chair. "I'm currently trying to enjoy a moment's peace, and you are disrupting all of that with your... presence."

"You wound me." He feigns hurt feelings.

"Out with it or leave, Valerio." I rub the side of my head, trying to ease the headache forming behind my eyes.

"You're married." The words tumble from his lips all at once. "To a woman half your age."

"She is not half my age. Almost, but not exactly." The technicality doesn't make it any better.

"Give or take five years." The sarcasm drips from his voice. "You married Marcello Faravelli's daughter after killing his son? Do you have any idea how unhinged that is —even for you?"

The words are a slap to my face. "That was an accident and something we will not discuss. It's done, and my penance is paid."

"It still doesn't negate the fact that it was your finger that pulled the trigger, Matteo. Do you have any idea the kind of shit this could bring? It was bad enough you wanted Daniele to marry her, but now you? What happens if he ever learns the truth?"

"He won't find out." I will make sure of it.

"There's no guarantee of that. Daniele knows the truth, and as we both know, your son can be quite volatile. What if, to spite you, he decides to inform Maria or Marcello?"

"He won't do that. I know my son, and right now, he's a little... taken aback. But he will come to his senses soon enough."

Valerio scowls. "Matteo, I have been with you since the days of your father. I have walked this road with you and stood by you. So you know I will always tell you the truth."

I run a tired hand over my face. "Go ahead. Give me the advice I never asked for."

"Marrying her was a mistake, Matteo. But what's done is done. We will deal with making sure the story is dead and buried. For now, we have even bigger issues regarding Giacomo."

My blood turns to ice. "What about him?"

"He's been moving a new drug. They call it Hushies. It's

like molly but stronger, and most of it is laced with fentanyl. He has the cops all over our operations now with these overdoses. I managed to speak with the chief to cool things off, but we need to take care of this."

I dig my nails into the leather of my chair. Giacomo Feriamo has been a thorn in my side since we were young boys. We grew up together, and for a time, we had been friends. But life got hard, and he got greedy.

"And what about our new shipment of weapons from the Russians? Is the transaction set for Friday with the Mexicans?" I try to keep my mind from straying to Giacomo, but it's hard. The man is a hydra—no matter how many times you cut off his head, two more grow in its place.

"We have them all stored in the warehouse. We will do a stick count before Friday. Diego is set to fly in at 1:00 p.m., but we need to be quick. He's on Interpol's radar."

"Fucking fantastic." One thing I hate about dealing with these lower-level leaders is that they are never clean about their reputations. "We need to make sure this is a clean, in-and-out job. I don't want the cops coming in and giving us an even bigger issue to contain."

"Yes, boss. But we also have the Charlotte Gala to attend. You are a major donor, and the prospective governor will be there. It would be good to make friends."

My stomach churns at the thought of schmoozing politicians, but I need them to ensure my business runs smoothly. "Fine. I'll be there."

"With your new wife."

"What? Why would I take Maria with me?"

"You just got married. The rest of the mafia world needs to see your wife. The rumors are flying, and the longer you keep her hidden, the weaker she appears. And the last thing we need is for people to make her a target."

Before I can answer, my phone buzzes. When I pull it from my pocket, I see a name on the screen I wasn't expecting.

Maria.

It's a text that reads: *Will you be home for dinner?*

My heart does an odd skip before thudding in my chest. I must be getting sick.

For a moment, I stare at the message, unsure why she even cares. It's not like this is a real marriage.

But something about the simple question—for the first time in years, someone expects me to come home.

Matteo: No, we have a gala to attend. I'll have a dress sent over, and a car will bring you to the venue.

I expect her to reply with some snide remark. But she doesn't.

That, for some reason, irritates me more than it should.

Even after I send the message, I find myself staring at the screen, waiting... For what? I shake my head and put my phone away.

I look up the moment I hear, Valerio hiss under his breath.

"What?

"The warehouse. The one with Diego's shipment..."

I sit up in my chair. "What about it?"

"It just got hit. The warehouse caught fire. Everything is gone. Almost three million dollars' worth of arms—burned to a crisp."

A sharp pulse beats against my temple. My vision narrows. Three million dollars—gone in smoke. My fingers dig into the leather of my chair, the fine grain creaking under my grip.

"We need to go."

We are out of our chairs before we can even blink.

Whoever did this wants war.
Fine.
I will turn them to ash.

11

MARIA

I watch as the SUV makes its way off the tarmac, leaving me with Emily. The wind picks up and blows my hair into my face. I take a deep breath and exhale slowly, trying to calm the storm raging inside me.

"Shall we go, Mrs. Davacalli?" the little sweet voice pierces my eardrums. I turn my head to the side and catch a pair of wide blue eyes. Her blonde hair whips around her face as the wind picks up. "All your bags have been placed in the car. Would you like to stop anywhere before we make it home?"

Home.

"Umm, no. We can go." I look up and see the two burly men staring at me. Irritation immediately riddles my mind. "I get that he made you his lapdogs, but can you at least try not to breathe down my neck?"

The black-haired one, Tony, looks to his counterpart, then turns back to me. "We are instructed whatever is necessary for your safety. We will keep at least ten paces behind and ensure there are no active threats that can get close to you."

His answer is so mechanical and rehearsed. But what gets to me is the lack of emotion that touches his features. He is stoic and... blank.

"I see. Well then," I clutch my notepad to my chest. "Shall we?"

I get into the backseat of the SUV with Emily on the other end. I remain quiet, my body glued to the door. I watch the tall buildings move past as we drive down the pathways of the concrete jungle.

New York is a jungle of steel and glass, a sharp contrast to Florence's sun-kissed vineyards and cobblestone streets. The scent of fresh basil and olive groves feels like a distant memory against the city's constant hum of honking taxis and burnt coffee.

"I hear that you used to live in New York when you were younger." Emily breaks the thick silence.

I turn to face her, and she has this megawatt smile on her face. I will be honest and say that it is a little unnerving how one person can be so... bright.

"Yes. But not in the city; we were just on the outskirts. I was closer to New Jersey than central Manhattan."

"Did you ever miss it?"

"No." My answer comes almost immediately. "I left this place when I was far too young, so I hold no real attachment to it. Italy is my home—the rolling hills, the blue water lakes, and the peace. There was no evident violence, and this world—the guns, the blood, the death—is far removed from it."

The smile on Emily's face falters a little. "Oh, I see. But I'm sure that now you are a married woman, you will enjoy it more than you did as a child."

"I doubt it." I turn back to the window and continue to stare as the world passes us by. I don't want to be a bitch to

Emily but I also can't lie. "But maybe it will grow on me in time."

Even as the words slip out, they feel empty, like echoes in a hollow space. But what choice do I have? If I don't believe them, who will?

After about a thirty-minute drive, we finally make it to Matteo's building. Along with his other nefarious deals, he also owns a construction company responsible for several skyscrapers. You would think that since he does honest work, he would drop the mafia overlord persona, but it's engraved into his DNA. You can never separate the two.

When we make it to the top floor of the building, I can't say I'm surprised at what I walk into—a full glass wall overlooking the city, an open floor plan, and an ultra-modern interior.

"Welcome home, Mrs. Davacalli," Emily announces as I make my way into the penthouse.

The color scheme is no better than mine back home. White, black, and gray—monotone, one-dimensional, and dark. Much like the character of Matteo.

Tony walks in with my luggage and walks past me, heading to the stairs. Emily stands at the center of what must be the foyer. She holds back a shit-eating grin as she observes my reaction to the penthouse.

"It's nice." Those are the only words I offer. Her smile slips, and she blinks.

"Would you like a tour?"

My eyes continue to move from the living room to the dining area and then to the large grand piano that sits off the corner.

"No thank you," I say absently. "I think I need some sleep right now. We can do all the grand tours later."

"Of course, please follow me to your room." There was a

subtle emphasis to the word 'your' but I don't think on it too much. "Mr. Davacalli made sure that it was ready upon your arrival."

We walk up the spiral stairs that take us to the second floor. I notice as we walk that there is little to no personalization in this place.

"Has Matteo lived here alone long?" I ask as I look at the empty walls. No family. No friends. Just a cold and void mansion with no real life.

Emily looks over her shoulder at me. "Mr. Davacalli used to live on the outskirts of the city. The Davacalli manor. But after his wife died, he decided to come back into the city. The reasoning was he wanted to be closer to work, but I think it's because he misses his late wife—Beatrice."

Her name sends shock waves through my system. Until recently, she had been married to him. She had been the one at his side, and now I had come in as her replacement.

"He loved her?" The questions slip past my lips.

We pause at one of the doors at the end of the hallway. Emily turns to me fully with a distant glint in her eyes.

"She humanized him. She brought out the softer side to his darkness that the rest of the world never got to see." It's the softness that she speaks of her. I can tell that Beatrice made lasting impacts on everyone. "Here is your room, Mrs. Davacalli."

She opens the door and I am immediately stunned.

"This..." I walk into the oak-floored room as my eyes dart from corner to corner. Apart from the wall of windows that displays the New York skyline, this is a dead ringer for my room back home. The beige and white color scheme litters the room, from the bedding to the white oak furniture that decorates the area.

"Mr. Davacalli gave me inspiration from your old room.

He wanted you to feel right at home. He requested that the same fine bed linens be imported from Italy." Emily still stands at the door. "I will leave you to rest. I will be back with lunch a little later. Or would you like something to eat now?"

"Uh, no, I ate on the jet. Thank you, Emily." I tear my eyes from the paintings that hang from the wall. "You've been lovely, truly."

Her eyes light with joy and she nods before she closes the door, leaving me in my room.

I close my eyes and breathe in the fresh scent of wood and fabric softener that wafts into my senses. I walk over to the bed, my heart lurching in the center of my chest.

He did all of this...

The sight of my room—a near-perfect replica of the one I left behind—catches me off guard. I shouldn't feel grateful. But the warmth creeping into my chest tells me otherwise.

"I guess you aren't as much of a brute as I thought." I plop myself onto the bed and take out my phone from my back pocket. I scroll through my contacts until I reach one particular name that I never imagined I would ever dial, but here I am.

"Don't be a wuss, Maria." I try to give myself my version of a pep talk. "He's just a human who bleeds red and breathes air like the rest of us."

I click on the name, a lump finding its way into the center of my throat. I bite down on my tongue, my fingers hovering over the keypad before I finally decided to type the first word.

Will you be home for dinner?

I toss my phone onto the mattress, my chest rising and falling in frantic waves. I can't believe that I am panicking over sending a text to my husband.

My phone vibrates. I reach for it, not sure what to expect as his response.

No, we have a gala to attend to. I will have a dress sent over to you and the car will bring you to the venue.

"A gala?" I spit. "Already? Day one?"

I know there will be many galas that I will need to attend, but I at least thought he would give me a little heads up. I just got off a plane no more than two hours ago, and now he wants me to be ready for a party even though I am battling jet lag? Criminal.

I throw myself back onto my pillows and sigh heavily to the ceiling. The morning rays stream in through the large windows. The sight from this high up is beautiful. But the anxiety of what is to come keeps me from fully appreciating its beauty.

"Fucking hell." I turn back into my pillow and scream. Fatigue finds me, and suddenly, I'm plunged into a sleep my body so desperately needs.

The next time I open my eyes, the sun is setting behind the skyscrapers. Before I can answer the door, it opens, and in walks Emily with a rack of gowns and that same smile on her face.

I wonder if she has any expressions other than that one.

"Mr. Davacalli says that you have a gala to attend. We have just under three hours to get you ready." She claps her hands together. "You can get the shower going, and I will unload your luggage. But Mr. Davacalli did take the liberty to stalk the closet for you."

I rub my eyes and sit up in my bed. "What?"

Emily chuckles and walks over to where I sleep. "You need to get up and get ready. You can leave the rest to me, okay?"

"Okay." My mind is still foggy with sleep.

"Let's make you look fabulous." She grabs my hands and pulls me to my feet.

A shower, some scrubbing, and a few curling iron mishaps later, I stand in the middle of my walk-in closet with a full dome mirror in front of me.

"Your car is here, Mrs. Davacalli." I hear Emily's voice call from the room.

I don't say anything. I am too lost in my thoughts for me to even articulate what I want to say properly. I pat my hands on the skirt of my gown and fidget with the embroidery on the bodice.

Finally, after a long pause, I answer, "I will be right out."

I give myself the once-over in the mirror. The floor-length gown I wear hugs me at the bodice, the boning sucking me in and giving my chest that added lift. The white cloth dances against the overhead light of the walk-in closet; I'm not too thrilled about the color, but Emily says that I should take advantage of it as a newlywed.

"You look stunning," Emily comes up from behind me with a brush in her hands. She loosens my curls and smiles at all her handiwork. "I knew this dress would look good on you. The image of a perfect bride."

"Perfect bride," I mutter under my breath as I look myself up and down. "I don't feel like the perfect bride. If I'm being honest, I feel really out of my depth here. I am the wife to the mafia warlord."

"And he also happens to be the best of them, Maria." She offers me a thoughtful smile. "As much as he is tainted in many ways, the man cares for his own, and you are a part of his tribe now. He will honor you and protect you."

Her words do nothing to ease all the anxiety in my body. "I want to believe that, but after all the rumors and things I read about him, I…"

The words trail off into the atmosphere. I cast my gaze down to the floor. I catch the glint of my ring against the light. It's a large billboard and serves as the symbol of my imprisonment.

"You've worked with this family for some time, right?"

Emily nods. "Almost eleven years. Mrs. Davacalli—uh, I mean—Mrs. Beatrice Davacalli, Mr. Davacalli's first wife, picked me herself."

The first wife.

"What was she like?"

"She was beautiful, warm, and incredibly kind. Much like you, she didn't seem to fit the world of the mafia darkness." She walks off to the center drawers that contain the jewelry. She pulls out the most gorgeous sapphire necklace that sparkles against the light. "This will go well with your dress. May I?"

"Are you sure? My mother gave me some of her jewels to wear and I think that they will—"

"You are a Davacalli now, and you need to be wearing the jewels. This is the first time you will be presented to this world and I think it's only appropriate that you are decked out in the finest the name has to carry."

I hadn't realized how deeply politics ruled this world. There are so many rules and regulations I am not used to. Since my father took us out of New York, I didn't need to know all these 'protocols,' so to speak. I need to get accustomed to it if I want to acclimate quickly.

"The women in this world don't get to say much, but they can speak volumes through what they wear. This necklace is a statement piece. It has been in the family for generations and worn by almost all the Davacalli women."

She walks up behind me and places the necklace around my neck. When the cool jewels hit my skin, I can't help but feel like I have been adorned like a queen. They are heavy but they make me feel... powerful for some reason.

I hold my head high and watch myself in the mirror. I hardly recognize the woman I am right now. All in the space of a month, I lost my brother, got married to the mafia king, and am now thrust into the thick of the world my parents tried to run from.

"Let's get this night over with, then." I turn away from the mirror and leave the closet with Emily in tow. I walk out of my bedroom and find Tony on the other side of the hallway. His eyes look to me and he says... nothing. "Tony, do you ever crack a smile? Or is that against your contract?"

He blinks. "My job is to protect you and not—"

"—make childish conversation. I know, you told me." I look back at Emily, who hands me a clutch and my phone. "Oh, thank you. You always seem to know what I want before I do."

Her lips tilt up into a smile. "That is my job. To make your life easier."

It is a little unnerving but I don't let those words pass my lips. "Shall we go? I'm sure Matteo is waiting for me."

Tony grunts in response and leads the way down the narrow hallway. I follow, clutching my bag for dear life. My palms are slick with sweat, and my heart hammers against my ribs. This isn't just a party—it's a battlefield dressed in silk and diamonds.

The idea of standing beside my husband in a room full of power-hungry sharks sends a chill down my spine. But if this is my fate, I have two options—sink or swim. And I refuse to drown.

12

MATTEO

I hate these formal events, but what I hate even more is having to play nice when the taste of blood is still fresh on my tongue. I pull at my collar trying to loosen the bowtie. "Fucking hell."

"You need to be calm," Valerio mutters beside me. "You can't look like you're on the verge of killing someone."

"I do want to kill someone." I am still heated from the warehouse. "Two of my men were strung up on a lamppost like trophies."

Valerio clears his throat as Mayor Collins walks past us with a smile on his lips. "We will get to the bottom of it, but for now can you please be calm. Where is your wife? Tell me, brother, is she allowed to drink yet?"

I elbow the man in the ribs and he doubles over, but instead of whining, he laughs. "Careful, Matteo. Your feelings are starting to show. And it looks like someone can't take a joke."

"I can take a joke—just not yours." I give him an incredulous stare. "You are not funny, not back in high school or now. Now, where is my wife?"

I look down at my watch and see that she is late. I gave her strict instructions to be here on time. I'll need to teach her about her tardiness.

I dig my phone out of my pocket and search for her number. But just as I am about to dial it, I hear the hushed whispers fall over the entire hall. I lift my head and look to the entrance where I see a woman dressed in all white, looking like an angel.

Wait, is that... Maria? The bartender places a whiskey in front of me, but I push off the hardwood and make my way to my wife.

My eyes move over her body while she is distracted by all that goes on around her.

My God. She is breathtaking in every sense of the word. The dress fits her body so well, like it was made for her. White is truly her color. But she could also wear Barbie pink and still look incredible.

Her makeup is striking, making the green in her eyes even more vibrant. A waiter passes me and I grab two flutes from off the tray, my heart doing little weird pitter-patters in my chest. I don't miss the wandering eyes trailing over her body. An ugly green jealousy rears its head in the center of my chest. Then my eyes move from her face and down to her neck, and I still.

Why is she wearing that?

That necklace... It's Beatrice's. Something turns in my stomach as the flashes of brown eyes move within my mind. I push the feelings down, trying to regain my composure. I cannot afford to be so destabilized amidst so many enemies.

I roll my shoulders and make my way toward her.

Her eyes finally find mine and her lips part. I catch her eyes moving up and down my body appreciatively.

"Well, if it isn't my wife," I speak as soon as I get into

earshot. I hand her a flute and she takes it with a small smile. I can tell from the way her eyes move from place to place that she is out of her depths.

"You didn't wear the dress I sent for you." My eyes remain locked on her neck.

She sips on the champagne and then looks at me. "Emily thought this one would suit me more, seeing as I am still a newlywed and all."

"And the necklace?" I finger the pendant and a rush of memories fill my head. I remember placing that necklace on Beatrice's neck and the way she had beamed at—no, I will not think of her tonight, her ghost already plagues me enough.

"It's beautiful, isn't it?" She looks down at the pendant. "I think it matches my dress perfectly."

A muscle ticks in my jaw. The necklace. I shouldn't care but I do. It looks good on Maria, but it belongs to a ghost. A ghost that still lingers in my mind, in my bed, in my goddamn heart. The memories claw at me—Beatrice's laugh, the way she tilted her head when she wore this very pendant.

I shove the thought away, but it sticks—like blood that won't wash off.

I ball my fist at my side to hold myself together. That necklace should not be on her neck, but I can't make a fuss about it now. We are too exposed here for me to blow a gasket.

"It is beautiful but next time, I would suggest not wearing it."

She tilts her head to the side, confused. "Why?"

"This one you just can't wear, Maria. I don't need to explain my reasonings to you. When we get back home, leave it in my study to be kept in my safe."

"You can have it after you tell me why I can't wear it, Matteo." She grips her glass tightly and holds my gaze. Why must this woman be so stubborn?

"Your job is to obey, Maria. I don't have to explain myself."

She scoffs, eyes flashing with rebellion. "I am your wife, not a servant. You cannot tell me what to do."

"Yes, I can," I bite out. I see that she also has a knack for getting under my skin. After the day I have had, the last thing I want is to fight her. "We are not about to start a fight in the middle of a gala. We will speak about this later."

"No, thank you." She turns from me and sips her drink, disregarding everything I have said.

"Well, if it isn't the newlyweds!" Dario De Luca comes into view with his wife, Ginny, hanging on his arm. Her eyes move between me and Maria as she analyzes us. They come to a halt right in front of us.

"Dario," I sigh heavily and look to my wife, who looks at the couple in front of us with great intrigue. "It's good to see you up and about. I heard the Russians did quite the number on you."

That makes the smile on his face falter a little. "What can I say? I'm a survivor. Much like you, I hear."

"Yes, you always manage to survive like the cockroach you are," I throw it right back at him. The man easily gets on my nerves. He is a fairly young leader, thirty-five and at the height of his career. He is known to be as ruthless and cutthroat as me, but since being with his wife, he has softened. We have this love-hate relationship that we have established. "Ginny, I see you haven't come to your senses yet and divorced this fool."

Ginny cracks a smile and lets out a low laugh. She leans into her husband as she speaks. "It's good to see you Matteo, it's been a while. I didn't expect that the next time I saw you, it would be as a newlywed."

"Yes, well, I do like to keep you all guessing."

"I heard you stole her from your boy."

The grip on my glass tightens. "Watch yourself, Dario."

The smirk on his face intensifies. "Just the rumors flying around. I'm offended, Matteo. I had the courtesy to extend a wedding invite to you, but you could not do the same for me?" He adds an extra effect by clicking his tongue on the roof of his mouth.

"The amount of testosterone wafting in the air is enough to make me nauseous. Maria, shall we grab another drink?" Ginny gestures to my wife's now empty flute.

When had she downed that?

"Yes, please." Maria doesn't even look at me as she walks away with Ginny. I watch her make her way with Ginny, arm in arm like they have been friends for ages. I should feel somewhat relieved that she is being friendly to others, but part of me is a little jealous that she isn't so... warm with me.

But do I want her to be warm with me? I am as closed-off as they come. What is the use of her opening up to me when I won't do the same? It's only cruel to try and get close to her when I won't do the same for her.

"I never thought I would see the day you put a ring back on your finger. A wife. We all believed that Beatrice was it for you." Dario broke the thick silence between the two of us. "What changed?"

He is prying. Dario has no real concern for me. "You know how marriage is. It's nothing but a business agreement between two families. That's what yours was meant to be, if I'm not mistaken. You just happened to fall in love with your woman. My arrangement is nothing more than that."

"So you took your son's woman and beat him to the

altar." I can see the amusement floating in his eyes. Dario has always had a knack for getting under my skin.

"The union is better and stronger with me in it. Now mind your business, Dario. We have more pressing matters than my marriage."

He holds his hands up in surrender. "Only curious, old friend. And what pressing matters are these?"

"Giacomo."

As soon as I say the name, the amusement on his face dissolves and his hard gaze returns.

"So you know what he's doing?" I give him my full undivided attention. "How sure are you of your intel, Dario?"

"We've heard the whispers. We know what we could potentially be up against." Dario smirks. "If he knows what is good for him, he will stay far away from me and my business. Otherwise, I will put a bullet in the middle of his head."

"Do you really think Giacomo is not a madman? The fact that he is pushing a new product should concern us all." It seems I am the only one concerned. I know this man better than most. He has been silent up until a few months ago. He is up to something, and my gut tells me that a war is coming.

Dario's eyebrow tips upward. "Don't tell me that the great Matteo Davacalli is scared?"

I let out a low rumbling growl that escapes my mouth. "I fear no one. I am doing you a favor, Dario, by warning you ahead of time. Don't get ahead of yourself thinking that you are some invincible man. You are still human, and not even you can account for what Giacomo will do next. The man is a deranged psychopath who will stop at nothing to get what he wants."

Dario pats my shoulder. He is young and ambitious and

has too much power at his disposal. "I appreciate the heads up, and I will look into what's moving in my corners."

"Okay," I say under my breath.

In the thick of the conversation, a bellowing laugh makes it to my ears. It's a sound I have memorized and engraved into my psyche. I whip my head to the side, and sure enough, I see the mop of black raven hair on the other side of the room.

As if he senses my eyes on him, he turns his head, dragging his attention away from the group he is with.

"Daniele..."

I have been looking for my son for almost a week. He just left Italy without so much as a word, and now here he is reappearing like a risen spirit. I can see the hurt flashing in his eyes before he blinks and looks away.

My heart clenches. I hurt him. I knew the truth and hid it from him upon his mother's request. I move to take a step in his direction, but then I pause when I notice a flash of brown waves moving across the hall.

"No, Maria," I mutter the words under my breath. "Don't..."

There is a look of sheer determination and resolution in her eyes. If she starts something in the middle of this event, not only will it shake her down, but she will cause a scene and everyone will see.

I need to separate them—fast. I know how my son gets when he's upset. And from what I've seen, Maria is just as explosive.

Maria comes to stand at the group Daniele is with. I see her say something that makes the woman hanging off of his arm laugh. Maria bites down on her lip, and even from here, I can see the glossiness in her eyes.

I don't know if she is on the brink of tears or about to raise hellfire.

She and my son go back and forth before she grabs his arm and pulls him away from the group—out of the hall, away from prying eyes—my eyes.

Shit. I move, fast. Maria is about to start a war she doesn't understand, and my son is too angry to care.

I weave through the crowd, my pulse hammering in my ears, but I'm too far.

Too late.

Maria and Daniele disappear behind the heavy doors.

13

MARIA

"This corset is so tight, I don't even know how I'm breathing right now... I think..." Ginny's words fade into the background. My eyes are focused on a man who has not been answering my calls or my texts.

Daniele throws his head back in laughter, and I freeze. He looks so... normal. My life for the past seventy-two hours has been completely upended and ruined, and he stands there like he is having the time of his life.

The annoyance pours into my system faster than I can gather my restraint. My legs are already moving long before my brain has a chance to analyze the situation. Ginny calls after me but I only have one thing on my mind.

Daniele Davacalli.

My strides are long and rushed, afraid that, like the day of my wedding, he will vanish before I can get to him. My blood sizzles with every inch I devour between us.

Be calm. My brain keeps repeating it like a mantra. I need to keep my cool—I am a Davacalli bride, and with that comes an image I must uphold.

When I'm just a few feet away, he looks up, and our eyes lock. The joy slips from his face.

"Daniele." I come to a halt. "What the hell?"

I have a million and one questions I want to ask but that one slips forward first.

"Maria Faravelli—my mistake—Davacalli. I hear congratulations are in order, step-mommy."

The crowd he is with snickers, and the blood rushes to my cheeks.

"We need to talk," I press him. "Preferably somewhere private."

"How about no?" He winks at me. "Go find your husband, I'm sure he is missing his shiny little trophy."

I hate how he speaks to me.

"No." I stand my ground. "We need to talk, you at least owe me that, since you ran from the altar like a coward."

"I think it's best that you leave, Maria," he says in a bored tone. The woman who hangs off his arm smothers a laugh and my cheeks heat.

Enough of this.

I grab his wrist and the blonde gasps, but I ignore her. "Come."

Surprisingly, the man allows me to pull him away from his group. The man must have a conscious, after all.

I drag him all the way out of the ballroom with every eye on us. I'm sure this little action of mine will cause a plethora of rumors, but to hell with them. I need closure, and he is the only one who can give me that.

We walk until we come to a secluded corner away from the eyes and ears of the masses. I let go of his wrist and turn to give him my full attention.

"What can I help you with?" He places his hands into his pockets nonchalantly, like he didn't even do anything.

"You're kidding, right?" I scoff.

He shrugs, his body language completely relaxed and unbothered.

"Do you have any idea what you did to me? One day everything is great and fine, and the next you leave me at the fucking altar, Daniele. You hurt me." I stare into his eyes.

All my walls are down and I bare my feelings and vulnerability to him. But I don't get the same back. The man is nothing more than a blank slate, emotionless.

"I don't understand what you want here, Maria. An apology? You will never get one out of me. I did what was best for me and my future. The last thing I needed was to be tied to someone like you." His words pierce me like a knife. "I chose me, and I would have thought you would have the balls to choose yourself. But I should have known you were weak and pathetic."

"You have some nerve coming at me like that after everything you've done," I grit out through my teeth "I didn't want to marry you either, but at least I didn't run with my tail tucked in between my legs like a coward."

Daniele's eyes flick to the necklace at my throat before locking on to mine, dark and vengeful in a way I've never seen before.

"You shouldn't even be wearing that necklace. It was my mother's and my grandmother's. They were women of true power and formidability. You are nothing more than a meek little waste of space who would be dead within seconds in this world were it not for the Davacalli name."

The words are a double-edged sword that pierce between my soul and flesh. But it's not his words that get to me. It's the hatred in his eyes. But now it also made sense as to why Matteo was being weird about the necklace.

It belonged to his mother first... and then Beatrice. His

first wife. His love. The woman whose presence lingers in the walls of his house, whose ghost still curls up in his bed at night. The woman he still protects, even in death. A woman I can never compete with. My stomach twists. I shouldn't care. But the sharp sting of bitterness digs its claws into me, unrelenting. Why does it bother me?

Right now, I should be bothered more by how we got to this point and why Daniele left me. Only a few short days ago, there had been light in those irises of his. The caramel brown in his eyes had been molten and warm. I don't recognize the man who stands before me.

"Why are you being like this?"

He hooks his finger on the diamond-encrusted chain around my neck. "You should take this off. You aren't even worthy to wear it around your neck."

I grab his wrist and rip his hold from mine. "I am a Davacalli wife. This necklace belongs to me as much as it did your mother." The words slip from my lips without intention. But it's too late to take it all back.

His features contort into a scowl that makes him look all the more dangerous.

"Daniele, I—"

"You know that you will be nothing more than a whore to him, right?" He steps toward me, the distance between us virtually gone. "He will fuck you and put a baby in you to seal the deal. You are nothing more than an incubator and a means to an end."

The truth of what he says lodges itself in my throat and refuses to come up.

"It's a pity your family had to sell you like cattle all because your brother couldn't dodge a bullet."

I hear the slap before my palm feels the impact of connecting with his cheek. I stare at him stunned, my eyes moving between my hand and his face in pure and utter shock.

Daniele huffs, but there is no humor in his tone. He turns his head ever so slowly in my direction. I can practically see the steam coming out of his ears. The man's face is bright red, and his body trembles with rage.

Shit.

"Daniele..." I look around but we are alone in this hallway. I should never have asked to talk with him here. "I think we both need to calm down."

"So, you're a tough girl. Funny, I didn't peg you for much of a fighter." He leers toward me, his chest rises and falls dramatically as he breathes in heavily. "Let's see how much of a fight you put up."

He goes to reach for me, but the roar of a loud voice breaks us apart. I snap my neck to the side and see Matteo storming down the hallway toward us. His face is cool but his steps are deliberate and strong.

He is a man on a mission.

"Oh goody, if it isn't my daddy dearest come to the rescue of my step-mommy." The ridicule in his tone is obvious.

"Enough of this, Daniele." He comes to a halt and drags me behind him, a shield between father and son. "I taught you better than this. Your mother taught you better than to raise a hand to a woman."

Daniele's nostrils flare. "Don't speak about my mother. You went and married *her*."

"Only because you ran from your commitment, Daniele. Do you have any idea what you did that day?" Matteo is surprisingly soft with his son. He is never this... gentle when he speaks to other people. "You almost screwed everything up."

Daniele steps toward his father, and they are now toe to toe. The tension in the air is thick and laden with electrical charge. It feels like one wrong move could set this entire thing on fire.

"I didn't want to clean up the mess that you made, Papá." There is an edge to his voice. "I think things worked out exactly how they were supposed to, don't you think?"

The silence that follows is deafening. The two Davacalli men stand in front of each other. The king and his heir in a faceoff. And all I can do is stand off to the side, praying that this does not come to blows.

Matteo huffs. "Learn your place, Daniele. Or I will teach it to you—I am still your father."

Daniele clicks his tongue. "How could I forget, Daddy Dearest? Forgive me."

He steps away from his father and then whips his gaze to meet mine. "Careful, Maria. You're in bed with the devil."

"Daniele." Matteo hisses but it's too late. His son turns on his heel and makes his way toward the ballroom, leaving me with his father.

The air is laden with tension and anxiety. I have no idea what I just witnessed, but the Daniele who stood in front of me is not the same boy I grew up with back in New York. He isn't the same man who sat with me for hours on the edge of the pool and talked.

I clear my throat. "I think we should head back. People will be missing us."

I start to walk in the direction of the ballroom but Matteo's hand whips out and stops me dead in my tracks. I look over my shoulder at him, confused.

"What?" I pull my hand out of his hold and, surprisingly, he allows me to. "I am getting very tired of men just grabbing me when they feel like it."

"That necklace—who allowed you to wear that?" The force in his voice throws me. He stares at the necklace like he has seen a ghost. "Who?"

I flinch at the anger in his tone. "Emily. She–she said that it belongs to every Davacalli bride. It's an heirloom."

"It was my mother's," he quipped. "You have no right to be wearing it."

It was his previous wife's necklace.

"That necklace holds a lot of sentimental meaning. You can't wear it."

His comment ignites something inside of me. I raise my left hand and thrust it in his face showing off the ring that he put on my finger. "I am sorry about your wife, Matteo. But you can't treat me like I am beneath you. I don't know if you get this but we are married. *Married*. I am sick and tired of both you and your son discounting what I am and who I am in all of this. I signed that marriage certificate just like you did. We both said yes to this. And I am your wife; as much as it might pain you to see me with this on, it deserves to be on my neck."

He is silent. He doesn't answer me back; he simply watches me, taking in my little outburst.

"I need some air." I walk away from him, leaving him standing in the hallway alone. There is a part of me that wants him to chase after me. A part of me wants him to stop me and apologize for what he said and what Daniele said. But it never happens.

I quicken my pace, nearly breaking into a run as I round the corner. I can feel the emotion raging through my veins and I need to feel the air on my face. I run down the hallway and make my way to the balcony door. When I breathe through into the cool air, I let go of the breath I have been holding.

Fuck him. The tears prick my eyes. I try to hold them back but they betray me and tumble one after the other from my eyes.

A low broken sob escapes my lips and my heart cracks only by a few inches, but it is enough to have me latching on to the stone ledge and gasping for air. I don't want to cry; men like Daniele do not deserve my tears, but his words play over and over again in my mind.

I blink to the night sky, searching for some kind of sign, an answer of sorts. I am surrounded by luxury, power, and wealth, yet I feel like a captured bird, unable to fly. What is it to gain the world but to lose your freedom?

"A pretty woman should never have tears in her eyes."

I jump at the voice that comes from the shadows on the other side of the balcony. I swipe at my tears, looking for the speaker.

"Who's there?" I tried to make my voice sound decisive and firm but it came out meekly.

A man dressed in an all-black suit and a scar that travels down the side of his jaw walks into the light. The smile that splits his lips can only be described as eerie. There is a dead look in his eyes, like there is no soul behind the glass.

"Forgive me." He steps toward me, and I take a step back on instinct, feeling the growing threat.

Shit. That is a mistake. The smile on his lips deepens. I have no idea who this man is, but I know his kind well. They feed off fear. They indulge in making people feel uncomfortable, and often seek out the weak in order to exploit them.

"No need to be afraid, I'm not going to hurt you, little dove." He steps closer, but this time I hold my nerve. "Good, was that so hard?"

"Who are you?" I jut my chin up to feign confidence. "It's creepy that you were just waiting in the shadows."

I observe him for a moment and take him in. Raven black hair and icy blue eyes that penetrate right through your flesh. He carries an air about him that unsettles me.

"I was here first," he shoots back. "If anything, you disturbed my private moment with your tears."

"I was not crying." I look away from his gaze. "I just needed a breather."

"No need to defend yourself from me, Maria. We all need our moments."

My head whips to him so fast, I fear I may get whiplash. "How do you know my name?"

The smile returns to his face. "I make it my business to know all the important people. And you, my dear, happen to be the most important piece in the board."

A shiver runs down my spine but I try to not to let it show.

"You are far better-looking than the last, I must say." His eyes move over my face, drinking in every single feature on display. "I guess he got lucky by grabbing a young one. Oh, forgive me, where are my manners?"

Without warning, the guy grabs my wrist and pulls me toward him. He lowers his head and presses a kiss on my skin, and I recoil.

"My name is Giacomo Feriama. It's a pleasure to meet you." He lifts his gaze from the back of my hand and looks up at me. "You are far more beautiful in person, I must say."

I try to pull my wrist from his hold but his grip just tightens. He straightens to his full height and pulls me toward him.

"Don't be rude, little dove. Why don't you accept my advances?"

"Let go of me," I hiss through my teeth. "You are making a huge mistake. My husband—"

"Matteo Davacalli." He smiles but this one has far more malice behind it. "I know him well. In fact, we happened to fuck the same girl once upon a time. Maybe we could do that again?"

Giacomo leans into me. I try to shy away from his face but the wall behind me provides no room to maneuver. I pull at the arm locked tightly in his grip and inch away from him, but no matter how hard I try, he won't budge.

"I see why he is taken by you, such a beauty you are." His tongue darts out of his mouth and kisses his bottom lip. "If only I can have a little taste. To sample what belongs to the great Matteo Davacalli. After all, he sampled mine..."

"Let go of me!" I squirm on his hold. I can feel his hot breath fan my face, and every cell in my body is repulsed by his closeness. "I will scream."

"No one will hear—"

Before my scream can ripple through the air, Giacomo's grip falls away, and I fall backward. But before I hit the ground, an arm wraps itself around my waist and pulls me into a hard body.

I gasp and my eyes blink up to Matteo. His eyes move over my face in a panic, as if he is searching for injuries. When he is satisfied, he steadies me, and then he turns to Giacomo, who laughs from the ground.

"I was wondering why you left your bride unattended. Not a very smart thing to do, all things considered." He spits blood and ambles to his feet.

I can't see my husband's face, but from the tension locked in his shoulders, I can tell that he is murderous. He wants blood.

I should be scared. I should be on edge. But instead, heat

pools low in my stomach, slow and dangerous. A spark, a flicker, a wildfire waiting for ignition. Matteo's body hums with raw power, his breath still ragged from the fight. His grip on my wrist is firm—possessive. A silent declaration. My pulse jumps at the way his fingers flex, like he's restraining himself. Like he wants to do more. He's still furious. Still on edge. And somehow, despite everything... I want him to be.

"You touch my wife again and I will end you, Feriama." The venom in his voice is so potent that I even feel it sear my tongue. "You have no business with her."

"Oh, Matteo, after all these years, you are still the ray of sunshine you have always been." He smiles, showing his bloodstained teeth. "Tell me, how well does she ride your cock?"

Matteo snaps at his words. He lunges for Giacomo and grabs him by the collar before dragging him to the ledge. I let out a shocked scream as I witness the Matteo of rumors come to life.

The wind howls through the night, electricity crackling in the air as tension coils tighter with each passing second.

"Careful, Matteo," Giacomo chokes as the grip on Matteo's hands tightens. "You don't want to scare away your new wife, do you?"

Matteo's head snaps toward me. The rage blazing in his eyes roots me to the spot. He is not human in that moment. I see something far more ferocious and feral. But then he blinks, the humanity returning to his body, and then he looks at me, torn.

"But then again, she needs to see the real you," Giacomo hisses. "The true you. The uncaged, unhinged version of yourself that you are at your core."

Matteo whips his head back to Giacomo. He leans down

and whispers something in his ear that I don't catch. He then releases him and takes a few steps back, but his eyes are still trained on Giacomo.

"You got lucky this time, asshole. But make no mistake, come near her again and that's a bullet to your chest. Maria, come." He holds out his hand to me, keeping his gaze trained on his enemy. I take it without hesitation. "I'm watching you, Feriama."

Matteo turns, leading me away. His grip is firm, unyielding. Possessive. A silent warning that I belong to him.

I shouldn't, but I steal one last glance over my shoulder —straight into Giacomo's eyes.

His smirk deepens, slow and deliberate, like he knows something I don't.

"Until next time, beautiful Maria." He blows me a kiss, and a shiver rolls down my spine. I rip my eyes away from him.

Why does it feel like this is only just the beginning? Like a game has started, and I don't know the rules...

14

MATTEO

I storm back into the ballroom with my wife in tow. She hisses at me to let her go, but I hold on to her wrist even tighter. I can feel the eyes on us, but I don't give a shit. They can think what they want.

This is not the debut I would have wanted but the night did not go according to plan. We need to leave before things get ugly and floors are stained with blood.

"Matteo, please stop." She tries again to pull me to a halt. "People are looking at us."

"Let them." We are on our way out anyway. And besides, these low-level thugs need me more than I will ever need them. They all know this; it's why they play nice in front of me. "We are leaving."

"Matteo?" Valerio comes to my side, leaving a woman he was chatting up by the bar. He looks between me and my wife and then trains his gaze on me. "What happened?"

"Giacomo is what happened. He's here, and so is my son—Daniele. Keep an eye on them both; do not engage, and report back to me what you see. I'm taking Maria home. Tell the governor I am sorry, and we will have to reschedule our meeting."

We break out into the open air, my second still at my side and my wife now silently trailing next to me. We come to a grinding halt, waiting for the valet to bring my car around.

"I will, boss. But before you go…" He steps around me to stand in front of my wife. "I wish we had met under more pleasant circumstances, but I'm Valerio—the man tasked with keeping your husband's head out of his ass."

I shoot him a glare, but Maria manages a small smile, quelling some of the tension coursing through my body.

Maria takes his hand in hers. "It's nice to meet you, Valerio. Hopefully we can sit down and have a nice chat some time?"

The little shit goes the extra mile and takes the back of her hand and kisses it. I clear my throat, uncomfortable with this little exchange. But from the smile on Valerio's face, I know he is only doing it to get under my skin.

"It would be my pleasure. Maybe we can exchange numbers and—"

"Oh, would you look at that? The car's here." Right on cue, it pulls up, and I nudge Maria forward. "You want her number? Sure. I'll give it to you… never."

My second lets out a low chuckle after succeeding at getting under my skin. He rolls his eyes and heads back inside.

The valet opens Maria's door, and I help her inside. The smile has dropped from her lips and she looks pensive. Her eyes move over my face for a few seconds before she opens her mouth to speak, but I cut her off.

"Whatever you have to say, can you save it? I need to put as much space between me and this place as possible." I manage the words, but thinking of what just happened makes my blood sizzle a little.

"Okay."

I shut the door and round the car so I can take us home. Giacomo is like a rat; he only lives in the shadows and in the deep underground sewer. If he has resurfaced, it means he is up to something, and I need to find out what it is.

The drive back to the penthouse is silent. We ascend the elevator, not a single word uttered between the two of us. I am still fighting off the last shrivels of anger still lingering in my system.

I am holding it in for her, but had I been on my own, I would have made my way to my range and blown off some steam.

We walk through the door, and I loosen my bow tie and breathe a sigh of relief. Today has been nothing short of a clusterfuck of events.

The heels of our shoes hit against the marble floors, sending the sound to the walls and then back again.

"Who was that man?" She finally fills the silence of the house. "Why does he seem to hate you?"

I ignore her and walk over to the bar, where I find my favorite bottle of whiskey. I pour myself a glass and throw the harsh liquor back. I wince but I appreciate the burn as it sears my throat.

"I have many people who hate me, Maria. That is the name of the game." I watch her, standing in the middle of the open area looking like a vision in white. So pure. So innocent. "Are you okay? After everything that happened tonight."

She looks at me with furrowed brows.

"Daniele?" I prompt.

She sighs heavily. "Truthfully?"

"Yes, always."

"No." She shakes her head. "Only two months ago, I was thinking about where I wanted to exhibit my next pieces, and now... well, now I am the wife to one of the most dangerous men on the east coast, and the only person I could call friend hates me for some unknown reason."

He doesn't hate her. He hates me and for good reason, but I can't tell her. This is a secret I have carried since the day he was born and one I do not intend to divulge.

The pain in her voice stirs something in me. I push the unknown feeling down, not ready to address such things.

"In the span of a month, I lost my twin brother and married a man who seems all but soulless toward me. Do you know that you haven't even asked how I am doing through all of this? I had to let go of the only life I knew and could find comfort in. I'm in a strange new world and I... I'm barely treading water. I feel like I'm either seconds away from crying and melting down or breaking something. There is no in-between, and it's driving me to insanity."

Her words hang in the air. The weight of them press down onto my chest.

Antonio Faravelli.

There has been blood on my hands for decades, but his blood mars my hands, and I don't think I will ever be able to come to terms with what happened. This is why she should have married Daniele. My debt would be paid and I wouldn't have to see her every day in my home.

"I sometimes forget that you are still grieving the loss of your brother. You handle the grief so well that I... I forget." My words are sincere that they even throw me for a loop. "I know I have said it once before, but I am sorry for your loss."

Her eyes linger on me. A flicker of something unreadable

flashes through them—so fleeting, I almost miss it. She takes a few tentative steps toward me, and I pause. She looks like she is on a mission but there is a hesitance in her actions.

That's when I see it. The shift in her eyes—raw, unfiltered desire. A silent plea wrapped in fire, a challenge and surrender all at once.

"Maria..."

She swallows hard, her breath uneven, but still, she moves toward me.

"We may never love each other," she murmurs, her voice thick with something darker than want. "But I can't stop needing you." Her lashes lower, her breath uneven. "It's maddening—the way I burn when you think of her. When I see the ghost of her in your eyes, in your silence, in the way you hold yourself back from me."

She exhales shakily, fingers curling at her sides. "And it's unbearable—the way I ache when you touch me." Her voice drops lower, almost a whisper. "I don't know what this is, but I don't want to fight it anymore. I don't want to be in a battle I've already lost to someone who isn't even here. I want you to want me the same way."

Her words seal my fate.

Something snaps inside me. A dam breaking, a beast unchained.

She's standing before me—bare, vulnerable, but not fragile. No, Maria has never been fragile. She is fire and steel, reckless and beautiful, daring me to take what she's offering. Daring me to make her mine.

She steps closer—so close I can smell the lingering traces of her perfume, the soft mix of vanilla and danger. Her eyes, wide and doe-like, lock onto mine, searching, waiting.

She reaches behind her, fingers trembling slightly, and then—one by one—she lets the straps of her dress slip from her shoulders. The silk glides over her skin, pooling at her feet in a whisper of fabric.

My breath catches.

No lace. No undergarments. Nothing.

She stands before me, bare, utterly unashamed, the flickering light casting golden shadows over every curve of her body. A vision of temptation—pure sin wrapped in delicate, unmarked flesh. I clench my fists at my sides, every ounce of my self-control hanging by a fragile thread.

Her chest rises and falls in uneven breaths, but she doesn't waver. She doesn't shy away from my gaze. She wants me to look. She wants me to burn for her.

And God help me, I do.

"Make me yours, Matteo."

Her voice is quiet, but the steel in it is undeniable. She takes a step forward, her bare skin brushing against my suit, her warmth searing through the fabric. My jaw clenches. My pulse roars.

She has no idea what she's just unleashed.

"Don't make me beg for something that is mine by law," she continues, her nails grazing slightly over the fabric. Her lips part, her breath mingling with mine. "I can see you want to."

Christ. Can she?

I lift a hand, trailing my fingers over her collarbone, feeling the way her pulse thrums beneath my touch—fast, unsteady. For me. She gasps softly, her breath hitching, and fuck, it's the sweetest sound I've ever heard.

"You want me to want you the same way?" My voice is low, rough. Possessive.

I tilt her chin up, forcing her to look at me. Her pupils are blown wide, her lips parted, waiting, wanting.

"You have no idea how much I already do."

Then I crash my mouth to hers, swallowing her gasp, tasting the fire she's kept buried for far too long. And in this moment, in the way she melts against me, in the way her nails sink into my skin, I know—

She's mine.

Tonight, tomorrow, forever.

I rip my lips from hers and lean my forehead against hers. I see her dilated pupils and the way the green in her eyes slowly begins to dissolve.

"This body of yours is mine tonight. I am claiming you—as mine," I pant against her breaths. "Let me work your body into oblivion."

She smiles and steps back before she takes my hand in hers and leads the way.

We make our way up the stairs as she leads us to her room. My cock strains against my trousers and it takes everything in me not to slam her against the wall and have my way with her.

We arrive at her door just in time. The hunger in me is getting to a point where I can't hold back much longer. I shouldn't have this visceral reaction to her being this close, but I do. She is like a siren calling me into her waters, and I am helpless to resist her.

We walk into the room and, without wasting time, I capture her lips in mine and shut the door.

Maria's lips are plump and swollen from my kiss, a sight so intoxicating I nearly lose myself all over again.

"My God, you are breathtaking," I murmur, my voice thick with hunger. My thumb brushes along her jaw, the soft skin warm beneath my touch. "Everything about you is... magnificent."

She holds my gaze, her dark eyes glistening under the dim light, an unspoken challenge flickering in their depths. A slow smile spreads across her face as she reaches up, her fingers barely grazing my cheek, her touch featherlight but searing.

"You always say the right things," she whispers, her voice husky.

I capture her wandering hand in mine and press my lips to her palm, lingering there, savoring her scent, her softness. A foreign sensation claws at my chest—gentleness, tenderness, restraint. I don't recognize this version of myself, but the thought of not touching her, not taking her, is unbearable.

"I only speak the truth," I murmur.

Maria is living artwork—every inch of her designed to undo me.

Her breath catches, and her chest rises, pushing against me, teasing me with the promise of more. I shouldn't lean into this, shouldn't lean into her, but I do. I always do.

"I'm going to claim you, Maria," I tell her, cupping the side of her face, my thumb brushing her lower lip. "I will try to be gentle, but that is not the man I am. I want to ruin every man who came before me. I want to be the only one you think about."

Her eyes widen slightly, but there's no fear—only desire, dark and deep, burning as fiercely as my own. She tilts her head, her lips brushing the pulse at my wrist before she whispers, "Then don't be gentle."

My control snaps.

A growl rumbles from my chest as I grab her, lifting her effortlessly. Her legs wrap around my waist, her back hitting the wall hard enough to rattle the frame beside us, but she only gasps, her fingers tightening in my hair. She wants this. She needs this.

"Matteo," she breathes my name, a sound so sweet, so full of hunger, that I nearly lose myself then and there.

I take her mouth in a searing kiss, my hands mapping the curves of her body, tracing the swell of her breasts, the smoothness of her thighs.

Needing more, needing all of her, I lift her into my arms and carry her to the bed, dropping her onto the mattress with a controlled roughness. She bounces slightly, her dark hair splayed across the pillow like a masterpiece.

I kneel between her legs, my hands gliding down her inner thighs. "You knew exactly what you were doing to me tonight, didn't you?" I murmur, my lips tracing the path my hands made.

She shivers, her fingers grasping the sheets. "I hoped."

"Clever girl." My mouth finds her breast, sucking, biting, leaving my mark as my hand slides between her thighs. When my fingers finally touch her, she gasps, arching against me. She's soaked, ready, desperate.

I smirk against her skin. "You're already so wet for me."

"Matteo, please..." she whimpers, grinding against my palm.

I press a single finger inside her, slow, teasing, savoring the way her body clenches around me. Her head falls back, a moan escaping her lips. I add another finger, curling them just so, watching her fall apart in my hands.

"You like that?" I whisper into her ear, my fingers working in slow, deliberate strokes.

"Y-yes," she gasps, her body trembling beneath me. "More."

I slide down, spreading her thighs wider as I replace my

fingers with my mouth. The moment my tongue flicks against her, she cries out, her hands tangling in my hair, pulling me closer. Her body bucks, but I grip her hips, holding her in place as I feast on her.

"Matteo—" Her voice is a breathless plea. "I can't—"

"You will," I murmur against her. "You're mine, Maria. Come for me."

A scream tears from her throat as she shatters, her body convulsing, her nails digging into my scalp. I don't let up, drawing every last tremor from her until she's panting, spent.

When I rise above her, she's a vision—flushed, glowing, her lips parted in breathless exhaustion. I palm my belt, unbuckling it with one hand, my gaze never leaving hers.

She watches, transfixed, as I free myself. Her eyes widen slightly, her tongue darting out to wet her lips. "My God..."

I smirk, gripping my cock, stroking it slowly. "Too much for you, cara?"

She grins, sitting up on her elbows, mischief in her eyes. "I didn't say that."

Her hand wraps around me, soft and warm, moving with an innocent curiosity that nearly undoes me. I groan, my grip tightening in her hair as she strokes me, learning what makes me weak.

"Enough," I growl, pushing her back down onto the bed. "I need to be inside you."

Her legs spread wider in invitation. I hover over her, teasing her entrance with the tip of my cock. But then I pause, my forehead resting against hers. "Tell me you want this, Maria. Tell me you need me."

Her fingers slide up my arms, her nails raking lightly down my back. "I've never wanted anything more in my life, Matteo. Now, take me."

With a single thrust, I bury myself inside her, groaning at the way her body clenches around me, so tight, so perfect. Her breath hitches, her nails digging deeper. "Oh, Matteo—"

I grit my teeth, fighting for control, letting her adjust. "Tell me when."

Her hips roll against mine. "Now."

I move, slow at first, deep and deliberate, savoring every inch of her. But it's not enough. Not for either of us. When her nails rake down my back, my restraint snaps. I grip her hips and thrust harder, driving into her with the force of every unspoken desire.

"Harder," she begs. "Don't hold back."

I obey, pounding into her until the bed shakes beneath us, the sound of our bodies colliding filling the room. Her moans grow frantic, her thighs tightening around me. She's close—so am I.

"Come for me, Maria," I growl, my fingers finding her clit. "Let go."

She shatters with a scream, her body writhing, her walls clenching around me so tightly I follow, groaning her name as I spill deep inside her.

I collapse beside her, pulling her into my chest, her body still trembling.

"Are you all right?" I ask, brushing a strand of hair from her face with unexpected tenderness.

She smiles. "I'm perfect."

"I wasn't too rough?" The question feels foreign on my tongue. Since when do I care about such things? Since when do I ask instead of take?

She laughs softly, the sound vibrating against my chest. "You were exactly what I needed." Her fingers tracing lazy patterns on my skin, leaving goosebumps in their wake.

"Besides, I believe I was the one who told you not to be gentle."

I capture her wandering hand, bringing it to my lips. "So you did."

The moonlight casts shadows across her face, highlighting the curve of her cheek, the fullness of her lips. I find myself memorizing these details, storing them away like precious artifacts. This isn't like me. I don't linger. I don't savor. I take what I want and move on.

"Sleep." I bury my nose into her hair. "Tomorrow is another day."

She doesn't reply. Her eyes are already closed and her chest rises and falls slowly. I try to close my eyes but sleep never finds me. Instead I stay awake with my stare focused ahead and my wife in my arms.

It's the calm after the storm. Maria lays on my chest, her hair sprawled out on my skin and her leg and arm draped over me. Her naked body molds into mine perfectly, like she is made for me.

I don't even want to entertain the thought of her being my perfect fit. I need to keep everything as surface-level as possible.

I look down at my wife. Her face is at ease and she sleeps peacefully in my arms. I dare to brush the stray strands that kiss her cheeks and tuck them behind her ear. She only stirs a little and my heart lurches in my chest when she snuggles into me.

I don't like the way my heart melts like ice when I am near her. It's bad enough I need to mask it all, but here, in the thick of the silence with only my thoughts as company, I fear that the truth is too hard for me to face.

This is just sex. It can only be just sex. But it doesn't go beyond that. It can't.

I cannot allow myself to get to close, not again. She is an obligation that I have to fulfil and one that I cannot afford to fumble. This is nothing more than a part of the business agreement.

I don't know if I am trying to convince myself into believing it.

I will do well to remember my place in all of this. And most of all, I will remember—Maria will never be mine. Not truly. No matter how much I fucking wish she was.

15

MARIA

The sun streams in from the outside and kisses my naked back. I moan into the sheets and feel the silk wrap around my body. The ache between my legs is evidence of what happened last night.

My eyes blink open and I catch the sunrise trickling into my room. I look to my left and see the bed is empty. I had expected that, but the one thing I did not expect is the hard rock of disappointment.

I told myself I wouldn't care if he wasn't here. But the cold sheets beside me still feel like a rejection I wasn't prepared for.

I sit up in my bed and lean against the headboard. I look out the window at the rising New York skyline. The yellows and the oranges bleed into each other, casting gentle shadows behind the large skyscrapers.

I much prefer the lakes of Italy to the concrete structures of New York. But there is a certain beauty to the concrete jungle.

I turn my head to the empty pillow beside me. I reach

my fingertips out to the sheets but I quickly retract them when I realize what I'm doing.

I rub a tired hand over my face and look around the room. The floor is free of any of the clothes we stripped away last night, and even the necklace that graced my neck last night is gone.

He must have taken it.

"This body of yours is mine tonight." His words fill my skull and cause all the blood in my body to rush down to the lower region.

I can't believe I'm no longer a virgin. I gave it to the man whose name once stirred nothing but fear in me. It's so crazy to think this is where I ended up.

I pull the blanket off my body and walk to my closet to put on a pair of boyfriend shorts and a large T-shirt. Before I leave, I catch myself in the mirror, and I have to pause.

I walk over to my reflection and drink in my unruly sight. My hair resembles a bird's nest; my lips are plump and look freshly kissed. My neck has a small purple bruise on the side.

My breath catches. A hickey. A visible, undeniable claim. Heat rushes to my core as flashes of last night hit me like a drug—his mouth, his hands, the way he owned me. I should be angry. But instead, all I can think is: *He wanted to mark me.*

I shake my head and step away from the mirror. I rush out of the closet and make my way out of the room. The last thing I should be doing is picturing last night, even if it was one of the most memorable things I have ever experienced in my life.

I walk down the marble steps and go into the kitchen, where I find Emily behind the stove frying up some bacon. When she hears me, she lifts her head and smiles.

"Good morning, Mrs. Davacalli. I was going to bring breakfast to you but I was running a little late, I had to pop the laundry into the washing machine."

I look at the spread of food on the counter. It looks like she is preparing to feed an entire city.

"Morning, Emily. That's all right, I needed to get out of bed anyway. And please, call me Maria, no need for the formalities." I tangle my fingers with each other and shift my weight from foot to foot. "Is... is Matteo here?"

She shakes her head. "No, he left before dawn. He is usually out before dawn most days when it's a work day. Especially after the disaster at the warehouse."

"What?" I walk over to the high chair at the edge of the counter. "What do you mean, disaster at the warehouse?"

"He didn't tell you?" Emily places the crispy bacon on a plate before turning to the coffee machine. "What would you like? You look like a latte kind of woman."

"Cappuccino, please. Sorry, can you explain to me— what warehouse tragedy?"

"One of the organizations, warehouses, was burned down to a crisp. Almost everyone is talking about it. Mr. Davacalli views this as an attack—and no one is stupid enough to attack Mr. Davacalli without knowing there will be hell to pay after."

I try to hide my annoyance that she knows more about my husband than I do. I am still new here, and as far as the ins and outs of the mafia are concerned, I am as clueless as a newborn. I will need to become more invested and engaged in this world.

"I see. Did anyone die?" Saying the word at the end made my stomach churn.

"Two men, they were just boys. But I'm sure Mr. Davacalli will get to the bottom of who did it. He protects his own jealously and makes sure that no one under his protection is left out in the cold."

She spoke of him with such admiration. I guess that comes with working with the family for over a decade.

"Okay, how many sugars would you like?" She finishes pouring the milk into the mug.

"Two, please."

"You two had sex." She slides me a cup of coffee with a knowing look in her eyes. "And from the look of it, it was some really good sex."

"H-how do you know that?" My cheeks are on fire, I'm sure the entirety of my face is beet red. "I... I mean we..."

Emily throws her head back and laughs. "You are so adorable. The hair is a dead giveaway and the fact you didn't bother to cover your hickey. Now, unless you are two-timing your husband, you had sex with him."

I grab the warm cup in both hands and sip on the caffeinated goodness. I watch her over the rim of my eyes. Her gaze is locked on mine, her eyes bright and her smile wide as the sea.

"So, how do you feel?"

I set the cup down and move in the chair a little. "Can I tell you something?"

"Of course."

I bite down on my lip and stare at the coffee. I have never really had girlfriends, so all of this is new for me. My brother was my only friend growing up. But Emily seems like a safe enough place to start making friends, even if she is technically the help.

"It was my first time, and it kind of hurt." I flicked my gaze up to meet hers. "But then it got really good after the pain. Like... really, really good."

Emily blinks, taking in what I just said. "Wait, you're—well, *were*—a virgin? How?!"

I choke out a laugh. "What do you mean how? I just never had sex. I didn't leave my house often enough to make a connection with anyone. And I was homeschooled all my life. I didn't even go to university; there was no point when I knew all I wanted to do was paint."

"I just... you're gorgeous, and I was certain that men were lining up for miles to have a shot with you."

I shrug. "Well, there were people who approached my father wanting to date or marry me, but he always refused. He said that the decision to marry who I want was up to me and no one else."

But that all changed when my brother died.

Emily leans her elbows on the granite counter. "So... you gave your virginity to Mr. Davacalli?"

I nod. "Yeah. He is the only man who will ever experience me in that way."

I squirm in my seat and drink the coffee before it gets cold. Emily looks over my face like she is trying to get a solid read on me.

"Do you regret it?" The question catches me off guard. "You don't have to answer that if it's too personal for you."

I shake my head. "No, it's fine. I wouldn't say that I regret it, but I do wish our relationship was a little different. We aren't the typical married couple—we were arranged, and not only that, but we don't know each other."

She ponders over my words for a moment. "You can get to know him."

I want to, but I feel as though he wants to keep me at arm's length. I know that life after his first wife died is hard for him. From what I know of her, she was his sunshine. He existed to revolve around her.

"But how do I compete with a ghost?"

"A ghost?"

Shit. I didn't realize I said those words out loud.

"I mean with Mrs. Davacalli—Beatrice. She still lives in his heart, I can tell. That is where most of his reservations come from. I don't think he will ever let her go. Not that I want him to forget her and focus on only me. But I can't help but to feel like I am fighting a losing battle."

"But what if there is room for the both of you in his heart?" she says. "Look, I understand where you are coming from. But that should not stop you from trying to get to know your husband. You don't have to be exchanging dark secrets and childhood traumas today. You can start off small—maybe over dinner?"

I muse over her suggestion. "I'm not opposed to that. Why don't I cook him something? What does he like to eat?"

My mother always says that food is a love language everyone understands. Maybe the same is true about my husband.

"That's an amazing idea!" Emily claps her hands. "He loves a good carbonara, and we have all the ingredients here to make it. But I think you should message him to make sure that he gets home on time for dinner."

"Right." I get up from the counter and make my way to the living room where I left my phone. I sit down on the couch, my heart in my stomach as I open our chat.

I'm making dinner for us tonight, what time will you be home?

It feels so odd to now call this place my home.

I wait for the message to come through. It feels like hours but really it is less than a minute before he responds.

I'll be there by 7. Don't poison me.

It takes me a minute to take in that he said yes. Well, he

didn't say the word, but this is a good sign. Maybe he really wants to try this out for real.

Two hours in the kitchen and a few burns and scrapes later, dinner is ready and I am dressed and ready to meet my husband.

"You look gorgeous, Maria. I doubt he will be able to keep his hands off you." Emily winks from the sink. "Red is your color."

I pat down the skirt of my dress on the chair. I kept it simple, with a cute cocktail dress that shows off my figure in the most tasteful way possible, and a fairly natural face.

"Thank you." I turn my head to the clock that hangs on the wall. "Any minute now, he will walk through those doors."

And so I wait. The time ticks on and the minutes bleed into the hours with still no sign of my husband.

"He will be here, Maria." Emily sets another tea down in front of me. She looks at the clock: 9:53. The man is about to be three hours late. "Drink some of this, it will calm you. I can see that you're a little tense."

I look at the floating tea bag in the water and thank her. I sip on the green concoction. "He said he would be here. Is he normally late?"

Emily opens and closes her mouth, unsure of what to say next. "He tends to be very punctual but I guess work kept him held up."

"I guess so." I sigh heavily. "Maybe this was all a mistake, and I jumped the gun."

"No, of course not. This is you starting to have a relationship with your husband. He will be here, just give him a little more time. I need to dash home."

"It's all right, you can go ahead. Thank you. For helping me." She rounds the corner and pulls me into a hug. It's oddly comforting coming from a woman I barely know. When she pulls away, I force a smile. "Drive safe."

She gives me another squeeze. "It was my pleasure, Maria. He will come, I'm sure of it."

She leaves the kitchen and heads out for the night. The silence that follows after is deafening and overwhelming.

"I'm not." I kick off my seat and head out of the kitchen. The carbonara will need to be reheated and the salad that sits in the fridge will likely go soggy if it stays out overnight.

I make my way over to the couch in sunken living room area. I grab the remote and flip through some channels until I finally land on a weird nature documentary. I look at the clock for what seems to be the hundredth time: 10:15.

I tip my head back and sip on my tea as I wait for my husband to return home, hours later than we had agreed upon. I don't know how long I sit on the couch for, but the next time I wake up, the nature show is gone.

I hear the door open and the sleep melts away. I sit up on the couch and look back to see my husband trudging in.

When he catches my gaze, he falters for a second. This is the first time I am seeing him since we had sex. I had thought that it would be awkward but surprisingly, my body feels charged, my pussy already filling with eagerness and anticipation.

I need help.

"You were meant to be home almost four hours ago," I tell him. My eyes take in his crisp and put-together self. "Clearly, you weren't in an accident. So what made you so late after you said that you would be here on time?"

He sighs dramatically and walks in deeper into the penthouse. "Not now, Maria. I've had a long day and I would much rather not argue with you." He pulls at his tie, trying to loosen the thing from his collar.

I stand from the couch but it seems a little too quickly. Without any support, I lose my footing and almost fall flat on my face.

"Whoa."

Within seconds, my husband is at my side, helping me to my feet. I allow him to do so for the first five seconds before my brain reminds me that I'm mad at him. I pull my arm from his hold and give him a hard stare.

"Are you okay?"

I shake my head and move away from him. "I'm fine, just a little lightheaded. Where were you?"

The softness on his eyes dissolves and he is back to his pensive self. "I do work, you know that, right?"

"I told you that we had dinner." I shift on my feet. The pressure in my head increases as I try to blink away the pain in my eyes. "And you told me that you would be here. If you got busy, you should have called so I wouldn't waste my time making you food."

He turns his head and looks to the set table. Something flashes in his eyes but as quickly as it came, it flees from his black pupils. He turns his head to me with a straight face. "You expect too much, Maria. I never asked for a wife—I needed a contract. If you thought this would be anything more, that's on you."

I ball my fist at my side to keep myself from punching this man square in the nose. The last thing I want to do right now is fight with this man. "We said that we were going to try this for real. This is going to be a real marriage, and real married couples sit and have dinner together."

He rubs his knuckles against the stubble that has begun to form on his jaw. "You are delusional, after all. You are young, so I cannot fault you for having these fantasies of what this union actually is. This thing," he gestures between the two of us, "is not a real marriage, nor will it ever be. Beyond us fucking, we have no relationship."

I want to protest and fight him, but the room spins and I feel lightheaded. I close my eyes, trying to swallow down the nausea that threatens to make its way up my throat. When I open my eyes again, Matteo is in front of me, looking rather concerned.

"You look sick." He reaches for my forehead to feel my temperature, but I move away from his touch. "Let me call the doctor."

"Don't bother." I swat his hand away again when he tries to reach for me. "I just need to lie down. I've had a long day."

"Come, let me take you to your room." Matteo holds his hand out to me.

I look between his hand and his face and then back again. "This isn't a real marriage, remember? No need to play the doting husband. I can make it up the stairs just fine on my own."

I turn on my heels and make my way to the stairs. I spare a glance at the table I had prepared. All that effort and those wishful thoughts I had of what this could all potentially be.

I don't look back as I ascend the stairs, but I feel his heavy stare on me the entire time.

"Asshole," I whisper.

16

MATTEO

A couple of hours earlier

I never should have said yes. This dinner is a mistake. Sleeping with Maria was an even bigger one. I should have never touched her. But I did. And now, I can't stop thinking about it.

I left her alone in the bed this morning, and all I have been able to think about is the fact that I was balls deep in her last night.

I've had my share of women. I've done everything there is to do in bed. So why did last night feel like my first time?

I lean my head against the cool glass of the elevator. This day has been an absolute clusterfuck. From dealing with the aftermath of my son going rogue and then me and Maria… it's a little much for me.

"If I didn't know any better, I would think you're depressed with all that sighing." Valerio quips beside me. He keeps his eyes trained on his phone as he reads through a file. "Do you want to talk about it? Shall we sit around a fire and express our feelings?"

"Fuck you." I open my eyes to look at him. He fires a wink my way. "Have I ever told you how annoying you are?"

"Three times this morning, once at lunch, and five times in the car ride back to the office."

"Smartass."

"Handsome smartass," he bounces right back at me. "Don't leave that part out, it's crucial."

Instead of indulging his childishness, I sigh and glance at my watch. 5:56 p.m. That dinner is fast approaching and I am going to have to face my wife sooner or later.

As much as I don't want to admit it, the sex with Maria scared me.

"You keep looking at your watch," Valerio utters from beside me. "Do you have somewhere you need to be?"

I turn my head and look to my second. "How about mind your business?"

"Damn, someone's on edge. You need to get laid, boss. Your chakra is all fucked up."

"And what the hell do you know about chakra?"

"Edith, she's this sexy little yoga instructor who came by the club the other day. She's teaching me all about finding my inner peace and shit."

I blink. The things that come out of his mouth surprise me every single time.

"Shut up." The elevator opens just before I have the chance to punch my second in his face. "Don't you have other things to keep you busy? I don't know, maybe you can go make me some damn money?"

"I already do that. In fact, I just made a few million this morning. The new shipment of arms came in from Moscow. The deal with the Turks is on the table now." He sounds like a gleeful schoolchild. "Meeting is set up for tomorrow."

"Good, you are useful for something after all."

Valerio places a hand over his heart and feigns hurt. "Um, hello? Did I or did I not get employee of the month ten months running?"

"No, that was Ingrid in accounting." I give him a flat look. The smile drops from his face, and he shoves me. "Work as hard as Ingrid and you may get it next month."

He pulls his finger at me and walks off to his office. As much as Valerio and I get on each other's nerves, I trust the man with my life. I would die for him and he would do the same for me.

At 6:30, the majority of the office is gone. I walk into my office and close the door so I can get to work. In the back of my mind, I have this dinner I need to attend.

I should have told her no.

I am only in my chair for five minutes when I hear my door open. I turn my head, thinking it is Valerio, but my body seizes when I take in his burly structure.

"What the fuck are you doing here?"

Giacomo spreads his arms out wide. "Not happy to see me, Matty? You wound me. The last time we came face to face, you were a little rude."

My nostrils flare. "Get out before I—"

He plops himself onto the chair on the other side of the desk. He makes himself comfortable and leans into the expensive leather. The smile on his face makes me want to punch out all of his teeth.

"How did you get in here?"

He shakes his head. "Let's not focus on the how but the why. Why do you think I'm here?"

Silence blankets the room, thickening the air between us.

"I must say, you and your wife did look like quite the pair. You did well."

"Don't speak on my wife." I bite the words and make sure to douse them in poison.

"Your wife, such a tasty little thing. I find it hard to believe that you were just going to hand her over to your son." Giacomo kicks his legs onto my desk, and my eye twitches. "She's quite the looker—dare I say, even more beautiful than Beatrice."

"Don't say her name." I launch out of my chair, sending it backward. "Go before I put a bullet in the middle of your head."

He waves me off, his body language completely relaxed. "Same old threats, Matteo. 'I'll put a bullet in your head, Gia.' 'I'll make you regret being born.' Blah, blah, blah. It's getting boring. Maybe try something new?"

I storm around my desk, and as I do, he rises to his full height. A slow smile spreads across his lips, like he's daring me to strike. I pause, as soon as I am in front of him.

He's baiting me. He wants to throw me off my cool and get me distracted.

"You have ten seconds to leave." I don't want to let him go but there is strength in exercising caution in this instant. "You forget that you're on my turf, my rules."

"Of course," he chuckles lowly, "how can I forget, the great Davacalli kingdom. But tell me, Matteo, where is your heir? I heard you two got into a little bit of a tiff at the gala. Trouble in the family unit?"

I shove him—hard. He stumbles a few steps but catches himself and takes a swing at me, but I easily dodge it. I grab his collar and throw him onto the desk. I hold him there, tempted to choke him out. I am moving on pure rage and vengeance.

"Oh, frisky, is this how you get it on with the missus?"

"Enough!" I growl. "Don't speak of her."

"Someone is a little touchy," he says in a singsong voice. "Fine, if you don't want to talk about your marriage, then maybe we can discuss how your warehouse burned to a crisp—sorry about that, by the way. My arson guy got a little carried away."

My nostrils flare. "You!"

He smiles up at me, his eyes gleaming with victory, "You were taking too long to figure it out, and I was getting bored. I wanted to speed things up a little bit."

"Bastard." I lift him up slightly and then slam him back onto the desk. "You killed my men!"

"They were just in the way." He cackles, the sound unhinged and grating.

Without warning, he shoves me hard, so I stumble a few steps backward, but I catch myself before I fall. "I only told you because I want you to know that I am coming for you, Davacalli. I am coming back for everything you took from me. Starting with that little darling wife of yours. Tell me, does she fuck as well as Beatrice?"

I want to grab my gun and shoot him where he stands. I want to put him down like the mutt he is but I hold myself. In moments like this, it is best to be silent.

"Leave, Giacomo," I bite out. "Before I get my security to throw you in a ditch somewhere."

"Promises, promises, Matteo. But fine, I will leave you." He makes a dramatic bow. "Until next time, old friend."

And with those parting words, he leaves me standing in the middle of my office, vibrating with the kind of anger that draws a man to kill.

I walk over to my desk and plunge my fist onto the hardwood. How the fuck did he even get up here? Someone is getting fired for this, maybe even in solitary confinement. I don't give two shits.

I close my eyes and try to quell the rage that moves through my body. "I'm teetering on the edge."

Whenever there is the mention of Beatrice, something inside of me snaps. All I can feel is rage.

I am still reeling with anger. My fist twitches against the hardwood of the desk. I have a thirst for blood—his blood.

Maria.

Her face flickers in my mind—soft, innocent, untouched by this world of monsters.

"He will never touch her." The words hang in the empty room, a promise etched in steel. As long as there's breath in my lungs, Maria is mine to protect. And he will never get near her.

My heart finally calms, and the anger subsides. I stand up straight and look at my watch: 6:58. I am late for dinner, but I can still make it in time.

I go to grab my keys when my door bursts open again, and this time, Valerio runs in, looking like a man who's just been hit in the balls.

My blood runs cold. "What is it?"

"Vortex, the club—it's been hit."

"What do you mean hit?" I am already walking to the door.

"Someone came in and shot up the place. We have the police on site and Sergeant Morrison already called in," he explains as we make our way to the elevator. "We think it's the same people who did the warehouse. We are working on finding out who—"

"Don't bother, it's Giacomo." My blood boils. "He confessed when he came into my office."

"Your office? When the hell was he in your office and why didn't you call me?"

"I had it handled. I should have put a bullet in his head."

The decisions we regret are the ones that pain us the most. "How many are dead?"

"A bartender and three of the bottle girls. The rest sustained minimal injuries. But Morrison wants to speak with us. We need him to cover a few details; the news will catch word of those, and we don't want people snooping around like last time."

The elevator doors slide open, and we step inside. My mind is moving a million miles a minute thinking of how I can murder Giacomo without turning everything into a complete bloodbath.

"The club is one of several of our hotspots for the molly and jungle gums." Those are our best-selling products. If the cops find our underground, we're screwed. "How many boots do we have on the ground?"

"Ten. I've already sent them to do some moving around. Don't worry."

This is why I chose Valerio as my second. He is thorough and does things before I even need to think of them.

The doors close on us and we head down to the parking lot. If Giacomo wants war, then I will bring the battle ground right to his doorstep.

Dinner would have to wait. Maria will have to understand.

Giacomo just signed his death warrant. And I'll be the one to collect.

17

MARIA

I thought that by the time I woke up, I would feel fine. Sadly, I am still upset about him missing our dinner date. I know he is a busy man, but for him to walk in like he had absolutely no care in the world gnaws at my insides.

I roll over in bed, feeling dejected. I want to waste the day in bed, but I know that's not an option. I can't let this man have so much effect on me.

I drag myself out of bed, feeling sluggish and drained despite having slept for over ten hours. As I make my way to the bathroom, I catch a glimpse of myself in the mirror and wince. My eyes are puffy and bloodshot from crying last night, my hair a tangled mess. I look as wrecked as I feel.

Shaking off the thought, I step into the shower, letting the hot spray wash away the dried tears and lingering disappointment. But no matter how much I scrub, I can't wash away the emotions twisting inside me—anger, hurt, loneliness.

Part of me wants to confront Matteo and demand answers, to make him see how his actions affect me. But another part of me is terrified of being vulnerable, of giving him even more power to hurt me.

As I step out of the shower and wrap myself in a fluffy towel, I smell the bacon coming from under my door. Emily is here.

After I change, I make my way downstairs and into the kitchen. I find her busy behind the stove, making an assortment of things for me to choose from. Normally, I would be salivating at the thought of food, but for some reason, my stomach knots and a wave of nausea hits me.

Emily spots me and gives a sympathetic smile. "Good morning, Maria. How are you feeling today?"

I force a tight smile in return. "I'm fine, thank you." The lie falls easily from my lips.

She eyes me skeptically but doesn't push. "I've made some breakfast if you're hungry."

The smell of bacon and eggs turns my stomach. "Thank you, Emily, but I'm not very hungry this morning."

Emily frowns, concern etching her features. "Are you feeling all right? You look a bit pale."

I wave off her concern. "I'm fine, just tired. I think I'll just have some tea, please."

As Emily makes tea, I sink onto a stool at the kitchen island. My head is foggy, my body aching—like I'm coming down with something. Is this situation really taking such a toll on my body like this?

"Here you go," Emily says, placing a steaming mug in front of me. "Some ginger tea to settle your stomach."

I wrap my hands around the warm mug, inhaling the spicy aroma. "Thank you."

Emily leans against the counter, studying me. "Mr. Davacalli called earlier. He said he won't be home until late tonight."

I nod, unsurprised. Of course he wouldn't be home. Why would I expect anything different at this point?

"Did he say why?" I ask, trying to keep my voice neutral.

Emily hesitates. "There was some kind of incident at one of the clubs last night. He's dealing with the fallout."

My brow furrows. "Incident? What happened?"

"I'm not entirely sure of the details," Emily says carefully. "But from what I gathered, there was a shooting. Some people were hurt."

My stomach drops. A shooting? No wonder he didn't come home. Still, a small selfish part of me wishes he had at least called to let me know. And none of that negates the fact that he said this isn't a real marriage.

"I see," I say quietly, sipping my tea. The ginger does help settle my queasy stomach a bit.

Emily watches me with sympathy. "The dinner didn't go as planned, did it?"

I shake my head. The tears prick my eyes and I hate myself for being so emotional. "I just don't understand him. I understand that we are arranged and there is no reason for us to form a connection. We are bonded for life, until death, that is what we vowed. And to make matters worse, he was my first."

Emily's eyes widen slightly at my admission. She pulls out the chair next to me and sits down, reaching out to gently squeeze my hand.

"Oh, Maria, I'm so sorry. That must make this situation even more difficult." Her voice is soft, filled with compassion.

I nod, blinking back tears. "I just... I don't know what I expected. But I thought maybe after we..." I trail off, unable to say the words. "I thought things might change between us. That he might see me differently."

Emily exhales. "Matteo is... complicated. He's been through a lot, and he doesn't let people in easily. But that doesn't excuse his behavior."

I catch how she calls him by his first name but I think nothing of it.

"I know he loved his first wife deeply," I say quietly. "I'm not trying to replace her. I just want..." I struggle to find the words. "I just want to matter. To be seen as desirable in his eyes."

It's stupid, but I can't help wanting him. When he touches me, it's electric. Like a storm brewing beneath my skin, waiting to strike. An out-of-this-world kind of feeling.

Emily leans back, tapping her nails against the countertop like she's thinking. Then, a slow smile spreads across her face.

"Okay," she says. "Do you trust me?"

I frown. "Yes? Why?"

She grins. "We're going shopping."

I barely get a word out before she's already pulling me to my feet.

"We'll get you some sexy lingerie, and then I'm teaching you Seduction 101. If you want something, you take it."

I blink. "And by 'something,' you mean Matteo?"

She winks. "Exactly."

This is a bad idea. A really, really bad idea.

But at this point, what do I have to lose?

I can't believe I let Emily talk me into this.

I stare at my reflection in the mirror, my breath catching at the sight. The red lingerie clings to my body, leaving little to the imagination. Never in my wildest dreams did I think

I'd do this, but here I am—ready to seduce my own husband into wanting me.

I shake my head. Matteo is the only man who has ever touched me like that, the only one to kiss me with such force that it feels more like a branding. I crave him in a way that defies reason, making me reckless.

"He's going to lose his mind when he sees you," Emily says, stepping into view behind me with a knowing smile.

Heat creeps up my neck. "You think so? I just feel…"

"It doesn't matter what you feel right now," she interrupts. "You want your man? Then go and get him. Sometimes, a woman has to play the game to win."

I nod, but the doubt lingers. "But what if he rejects me? Like he did at dinner?"

Emily scoffs, disappearing into my closet. "If that man turns you down looking like this, then he's blind. Just be bold, Maria. Tell him what you want. You don't have to fall in love tonight, but you can at least get an orgasm or two along the way."

I let out a breathy laugh, but my nerves refuse to settle.

Emily returns, tea in hand. She sets it down on the vanity, stirring it absentmindedly before meeting my gaze in the mirror.

"You have the kind of beauty that could launch a thousand ships," she murmurs. "The kind of woman men go to war for. Own your power. You wear his ring. You carry his name. If you want his heart, fight for it."

Something shifts inside me. A slow-burning confidence I didn't know I had.

"Okay," I say, straightening my shoulders. "I can do this."

Emily grins. "That's the spirit." She lifts the tea. "This will calm your nerves. Or I can make you a dirty martini."

I arch a brow. "Both?"

We laugh together.

I didn't have many friends growing up, but Emily feels like the first real one. And for that, I'm grateful.

The evening slips into the night as I sit on the couch in the sunken lounge. I watch the hours tick by until the clock finally strikes 11:00. It only turns to 11:05 when I hear him come in. His heavy footsteps hit against the marble floor, and I look back and see him.

My breath catches in my throat. He is walking sex on legs, and it's criminal that one man should look this good. The room immediately becomes supercharged.

We haven't had a conversation since last night. The last thing I told him was that this was not a real marriage. And I walked up the stairs. Now here I am in a silk robe with red lingerie underneath.

Christ.

"You're up." His husky voice fills the room. "I thought you would be asleep by now."

I gulp and stand from my seat. I place the empty martini glass down and turn slowly so I'm facing him. My robe is closed, concealing the red underneath.

My heart pounds heavy in my chest.

"I was waiting for you." My voice comes out rough. Laced with passion and lust all over it.

Matteo's eyes roam over my body, lingering on the silk robe that barely covers my thighs. His gaze darkens as it travels back up to meet mine.

"You were waiting for me?" he asks, his voice low and gravelly. There is something dark and enticing in his tone.

He takes a step closer, his presence filling the room. "And why is that, Maria?"

I swallow hard, gathering my courage. "I wanted to see you. I don't like how we left things last night. It was... rough. I wasn't aware what happened to your men."

He blinks but says nothing.

I take a deep breath and shake whatever fears I have. "I forget that this is the world I live in now. Every time you walk out that door, there is a chance you may not come back. This life you live is filled with blood and gore. You see darkness every day. You have become accustomed to it. The closest I have gotten to it was seeing my dead brother in a casket."

I play with the strands of my silk robe. "I am sorry for not being considerate last night. But I do feel like we need to talk, so I stayed up to see you for this specific purpose."

Another step closer. He's only a few feet away now, close enough that I can smell his cologne.

"See me for what purpose?" His eyes are intense, burning into mine.

My heart is racing. It's now or never. With trembling fingers, I reach for the tie of my robe.

"For this," I breathe, letting the silk fall open to reveal the red lace underneath.

Matteo stills, his gaze dragging over my exposed body. The air between us crackles with electricity. For a long moment, he says nothing—just drinks me in with a heated gaze that makes my skin tingle.

But the tension in his jaw gives him away. And then, just like that, the heat in his gaze turns to something else. He looks at me like I've done something unforgivable—like my existence alone is an offense.

His voice, when it comes, is a low, controlled snarl. "Maria... what the hell are you doing?"

I gather my courage and step closer to him. "I... I can't stop thinking about the other night." My voice is softer now, my breath shaky. Heat floods my cheeks, betraying me.

His eyes drag over the red lingerie I chose—for him— and I don't miss the flicker of something there. Heat. Want. Quick as a struck match. But just as fast, it's gone, swallowed whole by something colder.

"Why the fuck are you wearing this? These cheap little slut clothes?"

The words slam into me, each one a deliberate wound, meant to cut, to humiliate.

He steps forward, his body rigid with control, his hands flexing at his sides like he wants to grab me just as much as he wants to push me away. His next words drip with disdain, with barely leashed frustration.

"If I wanted a whore, I could get one."

The air between us is a live wire, buzzing with everything he refuses to say. Because I see it—I see it. The way his chest rises a little too fast. The way his fingers twitch, like he's dying to touch me.

And yet, he doesn't.

He won't.

Because Matteo is a man of control. Of duty. Of chains he locked around himself a long time ago. And I—no matter how much I try—will never be the one he gives in to.

I force myself to gather what little courage I have left. Because if I don't say this now, I never will.

"You know what? Fine." My breath is sharp, like I'm holding back more than just words. "I thought maybe—just once—you'd remember what you have. What's right in front of you. But no."

I take a step closer, daring him to look away. "If all you see is a slut, then that's your problem—not mine. I wore this for you. I wanted you to want me. I wanted to remind you that I'm still the woman who can set you on fire with a single look. And maybe—just maybe—you'd see me as something more than duty. More than some contract you're bound to."

My voice falters for half a second, but I catch it, turning it into a bitter smile. "But you'd rather spit insults than touch me, wouldn't you? Because if you touched me, if you gave in for even a second, you'd have to admit you still want me."

I take a step back, but the air between us hums like a live wire, stretched tight with everything we won't say. "Congratulations," I say softly, my voice like a slap wrapped in silk. "Message received. I won't make that mistake again."

"You think dressing like this gives you power over me?" His voice is low, almost a growl, but even he can hear the rough edge beneath it—desire fighting to break free. "You think I don't know what you're doing? Trying to seduce me like that fixes anything? You could strip naked right now, and it wouldn't change what we are."

He steps toward me, so close that my scent hits him like a punch. He leans in, his lips brushing against the shell of my ear, his breath hot and deliberate. His voice drops to a whisper, slow and taunting—a sinful mix of heat and venom.

"You want me to fuck you against this wall, is that it?" His words are a ghost against my skin, each syllable sinking into me, dangerous and intoxicating. "To prove you still matter?"

A shiver runs through me, my breath catching in my throat, but before I can react, he pulls back.

His face lingers inches from mine, his breath fanning against my lips, his presence swallowing up every inch of space between us. His eyes are locked on to mine, dark and burning, filled with the kind of hunger that could ruin us both.

He can see my breath catch, my pupils blow wide, and it's so fucking tempting—but instead, he steps further back. Because if he touches me, even once, he's done for.

His jaw clenches, his hands curling into fists at his sides—like he's physically restraining himself. His voice is lower now, rougher, almost strained. "You don't know what you're playing with, Maria."

I swallow hard, refusing to break eye contact. "Oh, I know exactly what I'm playing with." My voice comes out softer than I intend, a breathy challenge, but the way his eyes flash tells me he heard every ounce of meaning behind it.

The air between us is stifling, charged, suffocating in the best and worst ways. I can feel the heat of his body, the tension rolling off him in waves, the way his gaze drops—just for a second—to my lips before snapping back up.

He's struggling. Fighting himself.

And I want him to lose.

I tilt my chin up, just slightly, daring him to close the distance. "You want me, Matteo." I don't whisper it. I state it. Like a fact. Like the undeniable truth we both know. "So stop pretending you don't."

His exhale is sharp, his nostrils flaring as his control wavers for a split second. His fingers twitch—like he might grab me, might give in—but then he moves away.

His eyes are like steel now, his walls snapping back into place, forcing himself into that cold, emotionless mask I hate.

"Too bad," he mutters, "I'm not that easy."

The wave of disappointment nearly rocks me.

"Go to bed, Maria." His voice is hoarse, rough, but there's no mistaking the finality in it. "Before I forget myself."

Matteo's jaw tightens, his fists clenching like he's holding onto something just out of reach. His eyes—those dark, reckless eyes—burn into mine, but he keeps himself locked behind the bars he's spent years building.

And then, like a blade sliding between my ribs, his voice cuts through the silence.

"One woman already claimed my heart. There's nothing left for you."

18

MATTEO

"You want me, Matteo. So stop pretending you don't."

For a heartbeat, I say nothing. I just stand there, jaw tight, breathing hard like she's physically shoved me against a wall.

Because—fuck. She's right.

She's always been right, and that's the problem.

My fists clench at my sides because if I don't hold on to something, I'm going to grab her—fist my hands in her hair, drag her close, and kiss her until neither of us can speak. But I won't. I fucking can't.

Because wanting her is dangerous. Wanting her makes me weak. And if I give her that much power, if I let her see just how badly I still crave her—she could destroy me.

But God help me, she's standing there in those fucking clothes, all fury and heartbreak and heat, and I want her more than my next breath.

And yet, none of it matters.

I force the words out, voice low, cold, deliberate. A

sentence meant to cut her throat with a whisper. A dagger aimed at her heart.

"One woman already claimed my heart. There's nothing left for you."

The silence that follows is deafening. It's not shock—not really. Maria has known this truth for longer than she cares to admit. It's the reason she tries so damn hard, the reason she puts on dresses I might like, cooks meals I never asked for, touches me like she still has the right.

She knew. Of course she knew. But hearing it from my mouth—as a weapon—still slams into her like a fist to the ribs.

She stiffens, her throat working as if swallowing down a sob. Her nails bite into her palms, a desperate attempt to hold herself together when everything inside her is coming undone.

But inside? Inside, something cracks wide open.

Because no matter how hard she tries, no matter what she wears, what she says, how much of herself she's willing to offer—she knows she will never be her.

And I? I will never let her forget that.

But it's not just that.

If she knew the truth—what I've done, what my hands are stained with—she wouldn't just hate me. She'd run.

The thought slams into me like a wrecking ball, twisting in my gut, making it harder to breathe. My hands clench into fists at my sides, my nails biting into my palms as I fight the urge to reach for her—to take what I can never have.

Because the truth isn't just ugly. It's damning.

I didn't just betray her by loving another woman.

I destroyed her family.

Maybe not with my own hands, maybe not in the way that would leave blood on my skin—but the stain is still there. Permanent. Unforgivable. And if she ever finds out—*when* she finds out—this fire between us will turn to ash.

She will hate me.

She will leave.

And for that reason alone, I force myself to do what I do best.

I push her away.

The air between us hums, so thick with unsaid words it's suffocating. For one wild second, maybe she thinks I'll take it back. That I'll reach for her, pull her close, kiss her like it's the only language we still understand.

But I don't.

I cover the want with anger, drown the ache in cruelty.

I just stand there.

A man holding back a hurricane. A man fighting a storm, I know will win.

And Maria?

Maria has no choice but to become the storm.

The low rumble of thunder pulls me from my sleep, the remnants of my nightmare clinging to my skin like a second layer. My jaw clenches as I sit up, pressing my palms against my face. The room is too quiet, too still, and for a moment, I feel the weight of the past pressing down on me.

I exhale sharply, running a hand through my hair before pushing the sheets aside. Sleep won't be coming back anytime soon. I can feel the heaviness in my chest settling in. I need something to take the edge off.

Pulling on a pair of sweats, I make my way downstairs to the kitchen, my bare feet soundless against the cold marble. The storm outside is intensifying, flashes of lightning illuminating the dimly lit hallway. It's fitting, really—my mind is just as chaotic as the weather outside.

Reaching for a glass from the cupboard, I fill it with water, taking slow sips as I lean against the counter. My thoughts are a jumbled mess. The scent of her lingers in my sheets, taunting me, reminding me of the night we spent together. Of how she felt beneath me, how she looked up at me with something dangerously close to trust in her eyes.

I close my eyes and inhale deeply.

I never should've touched her.

A soft sound breaks the silence.

Footsteps. I hear them move across the marble floor, just barely audible beneath the crack of thunder.

I turn my head just as Maria appears at the entrance, dressed in one of those silk nightgowns that shouldn't be allowed around a man like me. Flashes of her in the red lingerie invade my mind, and I have to push them back forcefully so I can focus.

Her chameleon eyes widen slightly when she notices me, but she doesn't turn away. Instead, she walks to the fridge without a single word, pulling out a bottle of water. The tension between us is thick and tangible, and for a moment, I consider letting her leave without a word.

There is no need to try and bring her to a stop. All that needed to be said was said last night. My words have pricked and scarred her little heart. I should let her go.

But I don't.

"Maria."

She stills. I see her back visibly tense, and my heart clambers to a pause in the middle of my chest. I deserve her coldness. I had been too harsh with her last night. She was only trying to take steps toward something real. The only problem? I didn't want anything real. I can't allow this to happen.

"Look at me, please." The words are meant to come out as order but instead they are much softer.

Slowly, she turns, gripping the bottle in her hands as if it's her only anchor. "What do you want?"

I hesitate, the words forming before I can stop them. "About last night..."

Her lips part slightly, a flicker of something unreadable passing over her face. I brace myself for her anger, for her disappointment. I deserve all of them.

"I thought maybe—just once—you'd remember what you have. What's right in front of you. And maybe—just maybe— you'd see me as something more than duty. More than some contract you're bound to." I was a monster. She told me something so heart-wrenching and I brushed it off like it meant nothing. She never deserved that from me.

She steps closer, hesitating only slightly before lifting her chin. "The next words that should come from your lips are either 'I am sorry' or 'Forgive me'. If those aren't the words you have for me, then I would rather just go back to bed. I have faced enough humiliation for one day."

On cue, thunder cracks outside the window and shakes the kitchen window. I can see the silhouette of the city just beyond the horizon. Even in the darkness, New York has a certain beauty.

I set my glass down with more force than necessary, my fingers tightening around the edge of the counter. The words are foreign, almost unnatural on my tongue—but when I meet her eyes, I know they need to be said.

"I'm sorry, Maria."

At first, she looks a little stunned. As if she cannot believe that I just apologized to her. My heart clenches in my chest. I have been an asshole to her all this time, and last night simply proved that to me.

She stood there, vulnerable in her lingerie, practically begging me to take her, to want her. And I had looked her in the eyes with nothing but cold brazenness and told her I didn't want her.

I had lied. I want her, I want her so badly that it physically pains me how hard I have to hold myself back.

"What I did last night, it was wrong. I shouldn't have turned you away the way that I did. You didn't deserve my harshness. I should have been more kind and understanding with you."

She casts those doe eyes to the floor and she shifts her weight from foot to foot. "Okay... I just wish things were different."

She wants this to be real, but I am not in the space or the capacity to give her that, and I don't think I ever will.

I want to tell her these words, but for some reason, they lodge themselves in my throat.

"Look, Matteo." She steps toward the center island and sets her bottle down. "I get it, okay? I was never meant to be yours. This whole marriage thing threw you for a loop the day Daniele decided to run away."

She exhales sharply, running a hand through her hair as if trying to steady herself. "And I know you've been trying to make the best of it, just like I have. But let's be honest—neither of us chose this. We've just been playing our parts, pretending like any of this makes sense."

Her voice wavers, but she doesn't back down. "I was the foolish one to think that maybe this—us—could be something real.

Her words hang in the air above us. They move through

the kitchen with a thick tension that hits me in the middle of my chest.

Her eyes hold mine, never once leaving my gaze.

I lick my lips, preparing to speak. I am a man who has stared down the barrel of a gun and never once did I flinch. But here I am looking at my wife, and my knees feel like they are buckling.

"I had a wife before you." The words slip past my lips before I can speak. "I loved her deeply and I lost her unexpectedly. The things that you want from me, I cannot give you. I won't apologize for that. But what I can say is this, I should have been more gentle with you. You deserved better."

The silence passes between us. She muses over my words again, digesting them one by one.

"I didn't want you to be kind or understanding. I simply wanted you to fuck me. Last night, I was under no impression that you would give me love or anything like that. I simply wanted you to have sex with me the way you did the night of the gala. You did things to my body that I never felt in my entire life. I... I want that again."

She speaks with such confidence in her tone, but the blush that tints her cheeks betrays her. She is still innocent, so uncorrupted.

"At some point, I forgot that you were a mafia boss. There is nothing kind or soft about you. You have jagged edges, and I cannot expect you to somehow find softness overnight."

"For you, I would have." The words slip past my lips on their own accord. But it doesn't make them any less true. For her, I would find the gentleness within myself.

"I never wanted it gentle. I wanted you to give me everything you had—and you did."

No, I didn't.

I hadn't even scratched the surface of what I was capable of with her. If I am to give her all of me, she would likely break apart. She isn't ready—not yet. But part of me thinks she never will be.

The silence is thick, pulsing with something dark and electric. A slow-burning current that hums between us, drawing me in, making it impossible to pull away.

She feels it too.

Her pupils blow wide, her breathing turns shallow, and her lips part just slightly—like she's already bracing for what she knows is coming.

Then, her voice cuts through the air—soft, but firm enough to own me.

"Kiss me, Matteo."

Not a plea.

A command.

I exhale slowly, but it does nothing to calm the raging storm inside me.

"If you want to show me you're sorry—kiss me."

My jaw clenches, every muscle in my body locking into place, fighting the inevitability of this. Of her.

This is a trap. A trap I should avoid. She wanted me to claim her last night, but unlike then, my resolve is weaker now—shattered. Guilt gnaws at me, but something stronger, darker, hungrier pushes me forward. Unlike last night—I can't walk away.

I move around the island, each step slower than the last, each one feels like surrender, spelling my own downfall.

By the time I stop in front of her, she's already breathless, her hands gripping the white marble edge like she needs something to anchor her.

She tilts her chin up, eyes burning into mine, daring me to make the first move.

She blinks up at me through her lashes, those perfect pink lips parting, her chest rising and falling in quick, shallow breaths.

I snap.

In one swift motion, I grab her hips and yank her against me—hard enough that a gasp rips from her lips. Her hands press flat against my chest, warmth bleeding through my shirt, sinking straight into my skin, my blood, my soul.

"Maria Davacalli." The name rolls off my tongue like it was always meant to be there. The way she shivers at the sound of it sends something wild, uncontrollable, fucking primal through me.

"You think this is a game?" My voice is rough, thick with something dangerous.

Her breath is unsteady when she speaks. "No, Matteo. I think this is fate."

I curse under my breath, my hand trailing up her spine, fisting into the silk of her nightgown.

Her eyes dart from mine to my lips and then back up again. Her actions send a wave of pleasure up and down my spine.

She leans in, her lips barely brushing mine. "Take what's already yours."

Fuck.

And then I do.

My fingers flex against her waist, my restraint snapping thread by thread.

And then her lips crash into mine.

Fire. Destruction. Something unstoppable.

The moment we collide, it's a detonation. A desperate,

all-consuming clash of mouths, of bodies, of everything we've been holding back for far too long.

She melts into me on instinct, like she was made for this, made for me, her body curving into mine, fitting against me like there was a space carved just for her.

I growl against her mouth, feeling the way her body molds into mine. My grip tightening on her waist, my fingers fisting the silk of her nightgown, pulling her even closer, deeper, like I could swallow her whole.

She gasps, but I devour the sound, tilting her head back, kissing her harder, deeper, bruising. Her nails dig into my chest, and instead of stopping, it fuels me.

She shivers, but she doesn't pull away.

No.

If anything—she presses closer.

Her arms wind around my neck, her body arches into mine, desperate, pleading, demanding more. Her tongue flicks against mine, teasing, and I growl, taking control, taking everything, losing myself in her the way I swore I never would again.

Because this is war.

And neither of us are surrendering.

I curse under my breath, my hand sliding up her spine, feeling every delicate dip, every subtle tremble beneath my touch. She's intoxicating—so damn intoxicating that I don't think I'll ever get enough.

Maria fists my shirt, her nails scraping lightly against my skin through the fabric, and it ignites something primal inside of me. I spin us around, pressing her back against the edge of the counter, caging her in.

She looks up at me through heavy lashes, lips swollen from my kiss, breath coming in short, uneven pants. "Matteo..."

My name on her lips sends a dangerous thrill through my chest. The way this woman affects me is unreal. She unhinges my normal restraint.

She's mine.

And God help me, I want to remind her of that in every way possible.

I lower my head, letting my lips graze the side of her throat. She tilts her head instinctively, granting me more access, and I take it—pressing a slow, open-mouthed kiss just below her ear. Her hands thread through my hair and they pull at the soft strands.

I feel all the blood rush down my cock. It strains against my pants, begging to be let loose into her. The need for her is raw, untamed, and out of control.

I nip at the sensitive spot beneath her jaw. "Tell me to stop."

Silence.

"I don't want you to."

I groan, dragging my teeth over the pulse in her neck before kissing the spot as if in apology. My hands travel lower, gripping the backs of her thighs. In one swift motion, I lift her onto the counter, stepping between her legs.

Maria gasps, her hands flying to my shoulders to steady herself. "You're insufferable," she mutters, but her fingers slide up, threading into my hair.

I smirk against her skin. "And yet, here you are, letting me touch you."

She huffs, but there's no real bite to it. Instead, she tugs on my hair—hard. I growl, capturing her lips again, kissing her deeper, slower, drawing out every ounce of tension that has been simmering between us since the moment we met. And it *has* been there, even though I did my best to deny it.

There has always been something about her that drew

me in. Like a siren call that draws sailors into her treacherous waters.

Her hands slip beneath my shirt, dragging across my bare skin. I feel the hesitation in her touch, the way her fingers linger like she's memorizing me. And damn it, I let her. Because as much as I don't want to admit it, I'm memorizing her too.

Every soft sigh, every small shudder. Every single piece of her. I want to know every inch of her.

I pull back slightly, ripping my lips from hers. My lips are bruised and tingling from her touch. My chest rises and falls rapidly as I try to catch my breath.

"We should stop."

Her brows furrow, her expression shifting from lust to frustration. "You're kidding, right? Don't do this to me again, Matteo. Not when you kissed me like you want to fuck me. I don't want to go through this back-and-forth with you again. Either you take me here and now or we move past this for good."

The anger that glazes over her tone is warranted. But it still catches me off guard slightly.

I shake my head, dragging a hand through my hair. "I can't—I won't let you get attached to me, Maria. I don't want you to confuse what this is."

She levels me with her stare. "Unless *you* are a little confused, I will tell you. This, what is going to happen between the two of us, is a normal action that occurs between husband and wife. If I'm stuck in this marriage with you, Matteo, then you're either going to fuck me—or let me find someone who will."

Her words flare something dark and dangerous within me. I grab her thigh with one hand, grip her chin, and tilt her face up to meet my gaze. "You would let another man have you?"

She sucks in a breath, but her voice doesn't waver. "The man I want won't take me."

My grip on her tightens. Fucking hell.

She tilts her head back, her lips inches from mine, her breath warm and unsteady. "So tell me, Matteo—should I give myself to someone else?"

The words ignite something dark inside me. My restraint—already threadbare at best—tears apart completely.

I grab her chin, forcing her to look at me again. My voice is low, guttural. "You think I'd fucking let that happen?"

Her lips part, and I don't miss the way her pulse flutters at her throat, the way her body trembles against mine—not with fear, but with anticipation.

"Then do something about it," she whispers, her voice barely above a breath.

Her words slam into me, knocking the breath from my chest, slicing through me like a blade.

The image of another man touching her—his hands where mine should be, his mouth claiming what's already mine—it's a sickness, a madness I can't control.

I shouldn't care. I shouldn't need her this much.

The thought of her belonging to someone else?

It makes me homicidal.

Maria isn't a possession. She isn't mine to keep. But fuck if I'll let another man have her.

And that's when I snap.

My restraint shatters, splintering like glass, torn apart by something dark and primal. A slow exhale escapes me—a warning, a surrender, a fucking admission of defeat.

I crash my lips onto hers, hard, punishing, possessive—devouring her like a man starved, like I need to erase the very idea of anyone else touching her.

Because tonight, she's not just my wife.

She's mine.

19

MARIA

The moment his lips crash against mine, I meet him with equal hunger, daring him to take more. He swallows my moan greedily, pulling me in. His body is fire, his heat seeping into my skin, branding me, making me crave more. He coaxes my lips to move and I follow without complaint.

He kisses exactly as I expected—lethal, all-consuming, overpowering. Just like the man himself. Passion and excitement surge through me in monstrous waves. His tongue tangles with mine, and I melt into him, starved for his touch.

We moan in unison, our hunger igniting, stripping away every last shred of restraint. My hands tangle in his hair, gripping the silky strands as heat pools deep in my core.

This is a feeling I have never experienced in my entire life. It's... cosmic. It consumes me and takes over all logic, and I move on pure, raw instinct. He rips his lips from mine, causing a whimper to escape my mouth.

"Maria," he breathes, his lips trailing wet hot kisses up and down my neck. I arch my neck to the side giving him more access to the sensitive parts of my skin. "Do you have any idea what you do to me?"

I open my mouth, but only pleasure-filled sighs escape. I pull at the hairs on the back of his head. My legs wind around his waist, pulling him even closer. I crave more—aching for him in ways that feel almost sinful.

A deep sound erupts from my throat, surprising even me. My back arches into him, his teeth grazing my soft skin.

"Matteo," I breathe his name like a silent hoping for—needing for—more. "Please."

I know exactly what I'm asking for, and I refuse to beg. He won't deny me what my body craves.

He pulls back, his eyes laden with lust, and his lips plump from their assault on my own. His chest heaves up and down, his hands squeezing my thighs hard.

"Say it." His commanding voice is laced with sex and need. "Say it, amore."

"Fuck me, Matteo." I lick my lips, trying to swallow down whatever timidness still resides within me. "Fuck me."

His eyes flash and he growls before smashing his lips back down onto mine. He lifts from the counter with ease and carries me toward what I presume to be my room. I am too lost in the taste of him to know exactly where we are.

I hear the kicking of a door and then, a few seconds later, the closing. My tongue tangles with his, my senses completely overtaken by his presence. His large hands squeeze my ass and I squeal into his mouth in shock. He chuckles, deep and low, into our kiss, and the sound alone drives me crazy.

He sets me down on my feet, our lips never once leaving each other. He grabs my face in both his large hands and forces our lips apart. My lips are bruised from his assault. His darkened gaze moves over my face, taking me in with a new kind of hunger I've never seen in them before.

"Are you sure about this?" I can see he is fighting his restraint.

I don't have the capacity to speak, so I simply nod my agreement.

As if possible, his stare darkens. "Strip."

I blink, my mind barely catching onto what he said. "What?"

"Take off your clothes, amore."

I bite down on my lip. This man has already seen me naked, but for some reason, I still feel so shy. Nonetheless, I push past it and peel off the fabric from my body. He is the only man I have ever been with. The only man I will ever have, and he sets my body alight in ways I can't quite put into words.

The fabric pools at my feet, leaving me exposed and bare to his gaze. My nipples are taut, begging to be kissed by his lips. My wetness slicks my inner thigh, my body ready for him.

"Perfection." His eyes move over my body drinking me in. "You are my Achilles heel, Maria."

I swallow hard, trying to keep my cool, but I want nothing more than to pounce on him and have him claim me.

"We will do this my way, amore." He grabs my hips and pulls me toward him. "It won't be kind, it won't be gentle, but I promise that I will adorn your body. What you give me is a gift and I will cherish it."

I don't speak. I simply press my hands on his chest.

"Get on the bed," he commands. "Spread those gorgeous legs for me."

I go onto the bed and move until my head is on the

pillow and my legs are spread wide for him. I wait in anticipation for his kiss. And without hesitation, he comes in between my legs and dips his head low.

His tongue flicks against my skin, stealing the slickness from my thigh, and I nearly lose control. His large hand trails up my torso and comes to rest on my breast. He squeezes my nipples between his fingers and a wave of pleasure moves down my spine and pools at my center. The bundle of nerves in my clit is on fire.

"Matteo," I moan into the dim lighting of my room. "Fuck."

His mouth comes over my clit, and he sucks me hard. My legs buck, and I almost close my thighs in on him, but I have to resist. His tongue moves up and down the sensitive skin, teasing every inch of me.

"Heaven," he mutters against my lips. "You taste divine."

I don't respond. I am too lost in the passion, drowning in the sweet abyss. I feel him in every fiber of my being. His touch overtakes my system.

Then without warning, he plunges two fingers into me and my back shoots off the mattress from the violent intrusion. His other hand presses me back down and he uses his hand and tongue to push me further and further to the edge of my passion.

"Matteo, please." I am barely holding on as he continues to work my body in the most sinful ways. "More."

I look down between my legs and I meet his amused gaze. He shoots me a devastatingly sexy smirk.

"Matteo!" I can feel my climax coming but I try to hold it off. I don't want this to end. I want to enjoy him more. "Oh, yes!"

"Come for me," he mutters against me, his fingers

pumping with a faster rhythm that forces me to come completely undone.

My muscles tighten around his finger, and the orgasm crashes over me, raw and consuming. My hand pushes his head into my pussy as I ride out the pleasure-filled wave with his tongue lapping me up.

Stars cover my vision, and my mind turns to complete and utter mush. I don't think, I can only feel. I blink rapidly, trying to bring myself back to the room, but I'm floating. The orgasm has me drifting on cloud nine, and I never want to come down.

Matteo lifts his head, his tongue sweeping over his lips as he savors every last drop of me. He stares down at me with a dark gaze. When my eyes drift down a little lower, I can see the tent that has formed in his pants.

My lips part. I can feel the ghost of his touch from the last time he entered me.

"Ready for me, baby?" he asks, breaking through the thick fog of sex and passion.

"Yes." I am surprised I even have the capacity to speak after something like that.

Matteo moves off the bed and strips down until he stands bare. My eyes are focused on his hard cock; he strokes it gently as he eyes my body. We take a moment to watch each other, neither one of us daring to break the silent moment.

Instinct takes over, and I move without thinking. I sit up on the bed and turn with all fours on the mattress. My heart thumps quickly in my chest as I turn to look over his shoulder.

"Naughty girl." He smiles wickedly. "Move closer to the edge of the bed. Come."

I move back and position myself so I'm right in front of

him. I watch as he moves the tip of his dick over my slickness. I push backward, wanting him inside but he pulls back and slaps my ass.

"Behave, amore mio. I am in charge." He slaps my ass again for good measure.

A deep sound erupts from my throat, surprising even me. He laughs lowly under his breath, and then, without warning, he plunges into me. I am so wet, there is little resistance.

"Oh, yes."

"Fuck, you feel amazing."

I squeeze my eyes shut and allow the initial pain to settle. For a moment, we're both still; the only sound that can be heard is our heavy breathing and the blood rushing past my ears.

The fullness is overwhelming, almost too much, yet I crave more.

Matteo kisses my shoulder from behind and grabs my hips. His dick only moves slightly but that is enough to cause a moan to erupt from my lips. When I feel my walls move to accommodate him fully, I relax against him. I press backward and take the very last inches of him.

Matteo groans, his grip tightening on my hips. "You were made for me, amore."

"Move." I give him the green light and he doesn't need to be told twice. The man pulls out of me and then moves back in with more force.

He hits every wall and we both groan. He continues these movements slowly, coming to a steady and perfect rhythm. The sound of skin firing against skin fills the room.

"Oh yes." My breasts bob up and down as he picks up the pace. "Matteo, you feel... ah!"

A hand comes down on my ass again and he slaps the soft skin.

"Again," I demand. "Everything. I want everything."

He does as I ask, and his pace picks up even more. He pounds into me relentlessly. The power of his strokes sent my brain into a completely different dimension. I've never felt so much… energy surging through me. Adrenaline rushes as we push our bodies to the brink. Desire obliterates all thought, leaving nothing but unrestrained pleasure.

I push my ass back onto him, his cock driving into me—desperate to take him as deep as I can.

Matteo presses me down until my head meets the mattress. He reaches around my waist, fingers finding my clit. He squeezes the bundle of nerves hard, and that is my single undoing.

"Matteo!" I scream his name, and I'm free falling over the edge.

"Fuck, Maria." He finds his own release and joins me.

The orgasm rips through us, consuming every inch of our bodies. We ride them out together until we are left in the thick of the fog that we have created.

Matteo pulls out of me, and my body slumps down onto the mattress completely and utterly spent. I can still feel the remnants of our sex in the tingles in my legs.

I turn and stare at the ceiling. Matteo stands overhead, watching me intently. His cheeks are flushed and little beads of sweat shine on his forehead.

"That was…" I try to look for the right word.

"…perfect," he finishes for me. He takes me into his arms and moves me up the bed and places the sheets over my body. For a second, I think he's about to leave, but he gets in with me.

The little lust bubble that we have enclosed ourselves in

begins to dwindle, and the outside world threatens to penetrate in.

I know I am meant to pretend that this doesn't mean more to me than just simple sex, but it does, and that is what scares the shit out of me. I try not to let those thoughts be the one thing that permeates through my mind, but I can't help it.

"Come here." Matteo opens his arms out to me, and without pause, I move into his embrace and rest my head against his hard chest. "Rest."

He presses his lips to the top of my head and pulls me in closer. The action alone makes my heart lurch, and I find myself blurring the lines of the physical and the emotional.

"Goodnight, Maria," he mutters over the roar of the thunder outside.

"Goodnight, Matteo." I listen to the gentle beating of his heart—a stark contrast to my own.

I close my eyes and let sleep come. Ironically, it comes easily to me in his arms. For the first time in weeks, I don't see the haunting eyes of my brother or the coffin that we lowered into the ground months ago.

Instead, I find myself dreaming of warm chocolate eyes that give me hope for a future that I know reality may not offer.

I think... I know. I'm falling in love with my husband.

20

MATTEO

When morning breaks, I don't want to leave her. She looks so peaceful, and for just a moment, I want to get lost in her softness. Her softness is a contrast to everything I am. My hands don't deserve her. And yet, if I ever tried to let her go, I think I'd rip myself apart. I fought these feelings from the very first day I saw her. She had me, but she didn't belong to me—until now.

She is my wife.

But the guilt of what I did never leaves me. It lingers in the back of my mind, somehow always reminding me of the penance I still owe. After a few minutes of watching my sleeping wife, I find the strength to leave the bed. But unlike last time, I make sure to leave her a little note.

Left for work. Make sure you eat and stay safe. —M

I still cannot promise her my heart, but I can at least meet her in the middle. She deserves that much from me, at the very least.

By the time I am leaving, Emily is coming in for the day.

"Good morning, Mr. Davacalli," Emily greets me with her usual warmth, her smile never faltering despite the early hour. "Is there anything you need before you head out?"

I shake my head, my mind still lingering on Maria upstairs. "No, thank you, Emily. Just... keep an eye on her today, will you? I've noticed she has been looking a little pale. Is she sick?"

Emily shakes her head. "Not that I know of, but I'll make sure she's well taken care of."

I leave the penthouse without another word. I force myself to leave her warmth behind. There's no room for softness where I'm going. Giacomo's growing bolder, and if I don't act now, he'll think he can get away with it. The war is coming, we can all feel it in the air. With Daniele now a free radical, I need to get a lid on things—fast.

By the time I get to my office, several of my men are already gathered around the conference table, Valerio at my right side. They all know what we are up against and want to avenge the soldiers we lost just as much as I do.

"War is coming." I settle into my seat and look at everyone's face individually. "We are under siege."

The realization settles over the room like a thick fog, suffocating and inescapable. The air is heavy with the scent of cigars and espresso, the usual vices of men who know their days are numbered.

Valerio leans forward, arms braced on the table, his sharp gaze scanning the faces of our gathered soldiers. "Giacomo's making his move," he says, his voice steady but edged with warning. "The ambush on our warehouse wasn't just an attack—it was a statement. He's testing us, waiting to see if we'll strike back or sit on our hands like the other families."

I exhale slowly, fingers drumming against the table's polished surface. Giacomo is growing bolder, but he's still underestimating me. A mistake he won't live long enough to make twice. But when I am to strike, I need to make sure that the hit is hard and it goes for the kill.

"The other families?" I ask, my tone even, though my patience is running thin.

Valerio's jaw tightens. "They're hesitant. Some are waiting to see which way the wind blows before they pledge their loyalty. As you know, boss, many of our allies are simply that because they fear retaliation from you."

Cowards. Just like when we attended that gala. They were all nothing but a bunch of serpents and sheep. They have no real backbone of their own.

I lean back in my chair, my gaze sweeping the room. These men have killed for me, bled for me, sworn their allegiance in the kind of oath that can only be broken by death. And yet, even among my own, I see flickers of unease.

"Send a message," I say finally, my voice quiet but firm. "One he won't ignore. I am not the kind of man who does not return a punch when it's launched at his face. Blood for blood—that is our way."

Valerio nods, but before he can press further, Dario, one of my captains, clears his throat. "There's another issue, boss. The Chinese want to discuss an arms deal out on the West Coast. It could secure a steady supply line for us, but they want to meet face-to-face."

I rub my temples, weighing my options. The Chinese syndicates don't trust easily. If they're extending a hand, it's because they think there's an opportunity to be had. And in the midst of a war, I need every advantage I can get.

"Set it up," I say. "We leave tonight."

Valerio nods, but I can see the unspoken question in his eyes. He doesn't need to say it—I already know what he's thinking: Are you sure you should be leaving now?

The man knows me too well and it annoys the fuck out of me.

I should be focused on war, on strategy, on the crumbling balance of power in my world. But instead, my mind keeps drifting—to her.

Maria.

Something shifted between us. There is a softness in my chest now when I think of her. Before, all I saw was my obligation. But now, I see her differently. And for the first time, she didn't look at me with this mixture of intrigue and fear. Instead, she looked at me with… warmth. The same kind of warmth I have seen her exude so easily to others but rarely to me.

I can't afford to want her. I still need to tread lightly when it comes to her. Besides, if she ever finds out the truth of why this marriage even happened in the first place, she will likely never forgive me.

I push back from the table abruptly, my chair scraping against the floor. "I'll be back before the week is out," I say, already moving toward the door. "With Giacomo's next move unknown, I need to gather as many friends as possible. Bolster security and make sure every major area is watched with hawk like precision. We do not give him another chance to hit us again. Dismissed." I stand to my feet. "Valerio, get the jet ready for me. I need to be out within the hour. I just need to go home first."

By the time I get home, the weight of the meeting still presses heavily on my shoulders. The war brewing with Giacomo, the uncertainty among the families, the deal waiting for me on the West Coast—it should all be my focus.

But as I step inside the house, my thoughts drift elsewhere.

To her.

The house is quiet, save for the faint murmur of a voice coming from down the hall. I don't need to listen closely to recognize it: Maria. I follow the sound, my steps slow and deliberate. The door to her room is slightly ajar, and I pause just outside, unseen.

She's on the phone, speaking in low, measured tones. There's a softness in her voice I don't often hear. A longing of sorts.

"I miss home," she murmurs, barely above a whisper. "I miss everything about it. The warmth, the familiarity... the way things used to be. America—New York, specifically—is a huge adjustment for me. The food, the people, the culture."

I lean against the wall, my eyes closed, listening to the longing in Maria's voice. It's a side of her I rarely see, this vulnerability that she keeps hidden behind a mask of quiet dignity. The pang in my chest deepens, mingling with an unfamiliar sense of guilt.

"No, Mamá, I'm fine. Really," she says, her voice wavering slightly. "Matteo is... he's been kind. In his own way."

I flinch at the hesitation in her words. Kind. Is that what she sees when she looks at me? A man who's merely kind? Or is she simply trying to reassure her mother, to paint a picture of a life less complicated than the reality she faces every day?

"The gala went well," she continues, a forced brightness in her tone. "Everyone was very welcoming."

More lies.

"My role here, it's... complex."

Complex. What a delicate way to describe the web of violence, power, and deceit she's found herself entangled in.

I want to push open the door, to tell her she doesn't have to pretend. But I remain still, listening.

She's homesick. I hear it in the way her voice falters, the way she softens just at the mention of home. It should've been obvious, but I was too absorbed in my own world to see it. Now, the realization sits heavy in my chest, like a stone I can't swallow. I've taken her away from everything she's ever known, dropped her into my world of blood and shadows, and expected her to adapt.

I should have known. Should have seen it sooner. She packed her bags in a matter of weeks and moved halfway across the world to a place she didn't even remember calling home. She's been isolated from the outside world, and she has no real contact with people aside from Tony and Emily.

"But I make do with what I have. I've seen a few restaurants I want to try soon." She lightens her previous words.

I shouldn't be listening. I should turn away and leave her to her call, but I don't. Instead, I remain in the shadows, unmoving, listening to a conversation that isn't meant for me.

Then, her voice changes—bright, forced, like a mask slipping into place. "Yes, Mamá. Matteo is good to me. The marriage is good."

Her voice is steady, her lie effortless. *The marriage is good.* But the words sink into me like a blade, slow and twisting. How many times has she told this lie? How many times has she forced herself to believe it? The truth? Our marriage is nothing but a cage made of gold, and she's still learning how to survive in it. I wonder how much of our life together Maria has sanitized for her family's sake. How much of the truth she's hidden behind reassurances and half-truths?

"I should go," Maria says softly. "I love you, Mamá. Give Papá my love."

There's a moment of silence, and I know the call has ended. I should leave, retreat to my study, and prepare for my trip before she discovers me eavesdropping. But my feet remain rooted to the spot, my hand hovering near the door.

I hear a soft sniffle from inside the room, and something in my chest constricts. Before I can stop myself, I'm pushing the door open, stepping into Maria's sanctuary.

She's curled up on the chaise lounge, her phone clutched to her chest, eyes glistening with unshed tears. For a moment, she doesn't notice me, lost in her own world of homesickness and longing. Then her gaze snaps to mine, and I watch as she straightens, composing herself with practiced ease.

"Matteo," she says, her voice steady despite the moisture in her eyes. "I didn't hear you come in."

I stand there, feeling like an intruder in this intimate moment. The silence stretches between us, heavy with all the things we never say.

"How much did you hear?" she finally asks a hint of resignation in her tone.

I consider lying, but something in her vulnerable posture makes me pause. "Enough," I admit, my voice low.

"I see." She nods in understanding.

"Come with me," I say, my voice rougher than I intended.

Her brows furrow. "Where?"

I don't answer. I just turn and start walking, knowing she'll follow.

Maria follows me in silence as I lead her down the hall, through the grand corridors of our home. I don't say a word as I push open a set of heavy double doors and step inside. This is something I had commissioned when we first made our way back to the States.

She hesitates on the threshold, her eyes flickering with curiosity before she finally steps in.

Her breath catches—sharp and audible, like she's been struck. The room is bathed in golden light, and for the first time, I see something in her eyes I rarely do: wonder. Her fingers graze the art supplies with the kind of reverence that belongs to something sacred. She turns to me, her lips parting slightly as if trying to find the words. But she doesn't need to. I see it in her eyes.

Canvases lean against the walls, some blank, some filled with soft brushstrokes of unfinished work. A massive easel stands in the center of the room, flanked by shelves of art supplies—paints, brushes, charcoals—all untouched, waiting for her.

Her fingers trail over the edge of the wooden table, tracing the outlines of the tools before turning to me, eyes wide with something I can't quite name.

"Wha—what is this?" She gestures to the room.

"This is your new studio. I figured, since I have a study, you would want your own creative space here."

"You... you did this?" she asks, voice barely above a whisper.

I shift my weight, suddenly feeling out of place. "You're always drawing and your father mentioned your love for arts."

She blinks as if trying to process my words. Then, cautiously, she steps further into the room, walking slowly as if afraid she'll wake from a dream.

I watch her, something unfamiliar twisting in my chest.

"I thought maybe if you had something of your own here," I say, watching her fingers brush against the smooth wood of the easel, "it wouldn't feel so much like a prison."

Maria's eyes widen at my words, her hand stilling on the

easel. She turns to face me, her expression a mix of surprise and something else I can't quite decipher. For a moment, we stand in silence, the weight of my admission hanging between us.

"Matteo," she begins, her voice soft and uncertain. "I... I don't know what to say."

I shift uncomfortably, unused to this vulnerability. "You don't have to say anything," I mutter, averting my gaze. "I just thought..."

But before I can finish, Maria closes the distance between us. Her hand reaches out, hesitating for a moment before gently touching my arm. The contact sends a jolt through me, and I find myself looking into her eyes.

"Thank you," she whispers, her voice thick with emotion. "This is... it's more than I ever expected."

I stand there, frozen by her touch and the raw gratitude in her eyes. This isn't how things usually go between us. Our interactions are typically stilted, and formal—a carefully choreographed dance of polite distance. But now, with her hand on my arm and her eyes shimmering with unshed tears, I feel something shift.

"You're welcome," I manage, my voice gruffer than I intend. I clear my throat, trying to regain my composure. "I know it's not Italy, but—"

"It's perfect," Maria interrupts, her voice soft but firm. She looks around the room again, wonder etched on her delicate features. "I can't believe you remembered my art."

I shrug, uncomfortable with her praise. "Your father mentioned it. I thought it might help you feel more... at home."

Maria's eyes soften at my words, a small smile tugging at her lips. "It does," she says quietly. "More than you know."

We stand there for a moment, the air between us

charged with a familiar tension. I'm acutely aware of her hand still resting on my arm, the warmth of her touch seeping through my suit jacket.

Not wanting to think too much of it, I grab her hips and pull her toward me. I lean in, slowly, giving her the chance to move away. She doesn't. Instead, her breath hitches, her lips parting just slightly.

I close the distance between us, brushing my mouth against hers, soft at first—testing. But the moment she exhales, surrendering, I'm lost.

I kiss her deeply, my hand sliding up to cup the side of her neck, my thumb grazing her jaw. She melts into me, her fingers gripping the front of my shirt as if she doesn't want me to pull away.

When I finally break the kiss, her eyes are dazed, her breathing unsteady.

"I have to leave for business tonight," I tell her, my voice low. "But when I come back... we can talk."

Maria nods slowly, her fingers still curled into my shirt.

I step back, letting my hand drop. But before I turn to leave, I notice something—her face is paler than usual, and there's a slight fatigue in her eyes.

I pause, studying Maria's face more closely. The color of her skin and the faint shadows under her eyes concern me. It's subtle, but noticeable to someone who has been observing her as intently as I have these past weeks.

"Are you feeling all right?" I ask, my tone softer than I intended.

Maria blinks, seemingly surprised by my question. She forces a smile, but it doesn't quite reach her eyes. "I'm fine," she says quickly. "Just a bit tired, that's all."

"Get some rest," I murmur, brushing my knuckles

against her cheek. I press my lips to her forehead and leave her with one lasting kiss.

This is the first time I'm tender with her without thinking too much of it. The actions are like second nature.

"I will text you when I land." And with those words, I leave her and head to my room to pack.

She watches me go, and something stirs in my chest—a flicker of something I thought was long dead. I wait for the panic to set in. It never does. And that terrifies me.

21

MARIA

Sleep clings to me like a heavy fog, my body weak from the past few days. Matteo has been gone for days, but true to his word, he texted me. The messages were light—teasing, almost. He's still keeping me at arm's length, but for the first time, I think he's trying.

My stomach twists violently, another wave of nausea forcing me still. The bathroom has become my second home, the cold porcelain of the toilet bowl an unwelcome comfort. Something is wrong with me—but what?

The door slams open, a sharp burst of sound shattering my half-asleep haze. "Maria!" Ginny's voice cuts through the fog, dragging me back to reality.

Crap, I forgot she said she was coming over today.

"Ginny." I sit up in the bed and look at her. "How did you get in?"

"You told the concierge I was coming. And besides, I saw your maid leaving and she told me you were sleeping the day away." She looks over my weakened body. "You look terrible."

I try to smirk, but it comes out more like a grimace. "God, you're always obnoxiously beautiful."

She crosses the room quickly, her heels clicking against the hardwood floor. As she reaches the bed, her hand presses against my forehead. "You're burning up. How long have you been like this?"

"A day, maybe two?" I mumble, closing my eyes against a fresh wave of nausea. "Emily has been taking care of me. She brings me tea and soup and makes sure I take some medicine."

She is a literal godsend.

Ginny's lips press into a thin line. "Has Matteo been here? Does he know you're sick?"

The mention of my husband's name sends an unexpected flutter through my chest. "He's... away on business. I didn't want to bother him."

I barely have time to react before she plops onto the edge of my bed, her signature smirk in place. "I think you need out of this bed and some fresh air. What do you say?"

I let out a groggy sigh, rubbing at my temple. "The thought of leaving my bed does not sound the slightest bit appealing."

She waves a dismissive hand. "You need some fresh air, some girl time—something other than being cooped up in this sky castle."

I hesitate, shifting against the pillows. The thought of stepping outside doesn't tempt me, but Ginny has been nothing but kind. Ever since the gala, she has checked in every now and then.

I do need to get out.

I sigh, finally pushing myself up. "Fine. But if I pass out in the middle of lunch, it's on you."

Ginny grins. "Deal. Now, get dressed."

By the time we're seated at a cozy café in the city, I realize just how much I did need this. The sound of people chatting around us, the clinking of silverware, the scent of freshly baked bread—it's a stark contrast to the suffocating quiet of the house.

Still, as I stir my drink absentmindedly, I can't shake the unease resting at the back of my mind. Ginny, ever perceptive, tilts her head. "You've been fidgeting since we sat down. Spill."

I let out a slow breath, tapping my fingers against the rim of my glass. "It's Matteo."

Ginny raises an eyebrow. "Shocker."

I feel a flush creep up my neck, averting my eyes from Ginny's knowing gaze. "It's just... things have been different lately. Not bad different, just... I don't know."

Ginny leans forward, her voice lowering. "Different how?"

I bite my lip, considering how much to reveal. "He's been... softer, I guess? We've been texting while he's away. Nothing serious, but it's more than we have done previously."

"Hmm," Ginny hums, a thoughtful expression crossing her face. "And how do you feel about that?"

How do I feel? Relief, certainly. A tentative hope. But there's something else, something I'm almost afraid to name.

"I'm... confused," I admit finally. "Part of me wants to believe this means something, that maybe he's starting to see me as more than just an obligation. But another part of me is terrified of getting my hopes up."

Ginny nods slowly, her eyes softening with understanding. "That's natural, Maria. You've been through a lot with him. If I could tell you the shit my husband put me through." She lets out a low laugh. "These men are hardened, shaped by a world that's never been kind to them. It takes them time to show affection. I saw the way Matteo looked at you at the gala. He may not admit it to himself yet, but he is in love with you."

"In love?"

My heart skips a beat at Ginny's words. In love? The idea seems so far-fetched, yet a small part of me clings to it desperately.

"I wouldn't go that far," I murmur, tracing patterns on the tablecloth. "He's just... trying, I think. It's more than I expected."

Ginny leans back, a knowing smile playing on her lips. "Oh, honey. You've got it bad too, don't you?"

I open my mouth to protest—but the words never come. My pulse stumbles every time his name lights up my phone. His touch lingers like a ghost long after he's gone. Maybe I don't need to say it. Maybe I've known all along.

"I... I don't know," I admit quietly. "Everything's so complicated. Sometimes I think I'm starting to understand him, and then he pulls away again."

I take a sip of my drink, letting the warmth spread through my chest. "It's not just that. I'm scared of... of wanting more. Of letting myself feel something for him."

"Because of who he is?" Ginny prompts gently.

I nod, my voice barely above a whisper. "Because of who he is, what he does. Because I know that in his world, attachments are dangerous. And not to mention Beatrice..."

Ginny's eyes soften with understanding. "Ah, Beatrice. The ghost that still haunts the Davacalli home." She reaches across the table, squeezing my hand. "Maria, you can't live in her shadow forever. You're not her replacement—you're your own person."

I nod, blinking back the sudden sting of tears. "I know that, logically. But sometimes... sometimes I feel like I'm competing with a memory. And how can I possibly measure up to that?"

Ginny leans in, her voice low and intense. "By being yourself. Beatrice was Beatrice, and you are you. Matteo married you, not her ghost."

I let out a shaky breath, mulling over her words. "I suppose you're right. It's just... hard sometimes."

"Of course it is," Ginny says, leaning back in her chair with a sympathetic smile. "But you're stronger than you give yourself credit for, Maria. I've seen it."

I offer a weak smile in return, grateful for her unwavering support. "Thank you, Ginny. I don't know what I'd do without you."

As we finish our lunch, the nausea that had momentarily subsided returns with a vengeance. I press a hand to my stomach, trying to will it away.

Ginny notices immediately, her brow creasing with concern. "Maria, you're pale again. Are you sure you're okay?"

I nod, though the motion makes my head spin. "Just feeling a bit queasy. It'll pass."

But as we stand to leave, a wave of dizziness washes over me. I stumble, grabbing the edge of the table for support. Ginny's arm is around me in an instant, steadying me.

"Crap," she says, her voice laced with worry. "Maybe we should get you home."

I nod weakly, letting her guide me out of the café. The fresh air helps a little, but my stomach is still churning uncomfortably. We walk toward the car, with Tony waiting nearby. He looks bored—until he sees Ginny helping me. Then, he jumps into action.

"What happened?" He crosses the remaining distance and relieves Ginny of her crutch duties. "Mrs. Davacalli, are you all right?"

I nod. "I just need to lay down. Take me back home, please. Ginny, I'm so sorry about this, I…"

My words die as a shadow falls over me. When I lift my gaze, my breath catches. Daniele. His eyes pin me in place, sharp and unreadable. He moves toward me, slow and deliberate, like a predator closing in.

Tony tenses beside me. "We should get you into the car."

I shake my head and pull out of his hold. The nausea still persists but I am able to push it back as much as I can in order to focus my attention on my stepson as he comes to a halt in front of me.

"Well, well. Step-mommy. Out and about without your leash. Does Daddy know?" Daniel sneers my way. "Ginny, I didn't take you for the type to be around harlots. You are meant to be the upper crust of the mafia world. Oh, how the mighty have fallen."

"Watch yourself, Daniele," Ginny snaps. "What are you doing here? Last I heard, Daddy gave you an ass-whooping for straying."

Daniele's nostrils flare. "Funny, I heard that you are running from your husband because you caught him red-handed with the maid—what a sad cliché."

"Watch yourself, Daniele." I try to sound intimidating but my voice has drained of all its power.

Daniele steps toward me. "You look like you're already halfway to the grave, step-mommy. Should I give you a push? Trust me—it'd be a mercy, considering what you're about to learn."

His joke is sick and twisted, and I want to slap him, but Tony pushes my wrist down.

"You may be the boss's son, but say one more threat, and I will personally hand your ass to you, Daniele." Tony plays the role of bodyguard to perfection.

"I only come bearing some words for my step-mommy, Tony, no need to get your panties in a twist." Daniele cuts his gaze to me. "The name you wear now, Maria? It's heavy, drenched in blood—maybe even your own. Watch your back. The wolves? They're starving."

I open my mouth to demand answers, but Daniele is already walking away. My throat locks up—no sound escapes. The world tilts violently. My skin turns clammy, my pulse erratic, pounding too fast, too loud. One step. Then another. My vision tunnels, black dots swallowing my sight. A gasp—Ginny's voice warps into a distant echo. My knees buckle. The last thing I feel is weightless free fall. Then—nothing.

Fear doesn't reach me. Pain doesn't touch me. Only regret. I never told Matteo how much he means to me. And as the darkness swallows me whole, I wonder—did I wait too long?

22

MATTEO

This has to be a nightmare. Maria. Unconscious. Hospital. The words hammer into my skull, looping over and over like a curse I can't escape.

Fresh off the plane, I had planned to surprise her. A nice dinner, just the two of us, where we could sit and talk—just be us.

She swore she'd rest, and take care of herself. So why the fuck is she behind those doors, fighting for her life?

"Matteo, you need to sit down." Valerio has been trying to calm me for the past hour. "They are doing all that they can for her."

"Don't tell me to fucking calm down, my wife collapsed in the middle of the damn street and I don't know why." My eyes dart to a crying Ginny, who sits in her seat somberly. "Why did you even take her from the penthouse? What were you thinking?"

Ginny's head snaps up, her eyes burning with fury, a storm raging behind them. "There is no way you are putting the blame on me for this one, Matteo. How about you take some damn accountability and ask yourself why your wife was even that sick in the first place? You didn't even care to check on her or take her to the doctor."

My fists clench at my sides, rage boiling through my veins. How dare she speak to me that way? I take a menacing step toward Ginny, but Valerio's hand on my shoulder stops me.

"Boss," he murmurs, "now's not the time."

I shake him off, my eyes never leaving Ginny's defiant face. "You have no right to insinuate that I do not care about my wife," I snarl. "You have no idea what I do or don't do for her."

Ginny stands, matching my aggressive stance. "I know enough. I know she's been miserable, lonely, and apparently sick enough to collapse. Where were you, Matteo? Where have you been all this time?"

The words hit me like a physical blow.

I don't respond. She is correct to some extent; there is a certain level of self-blame that I need to apply. I saw how pale Maria looked. Up until this point, I had been unkind to her. I acted like she didn't exist in my life.

"I was only trying to get her some fresh air. You, as her husband, should have seen that she was unwell. And your idiot son didn't make it any better, either."

Valerio and I snap our heads in her direction.

"What did you say? Daniele was with you guys?"

She nods. "He came out of nowhere and basically told her a bunch of bullshit that didn't even make sense. She was going to give him the middle finger when she fainted. It was weird and I think if he hadn't said that shit, she may not have collapsed."

My blood runs cold at the mention of Daniele. What the hell was he doing there? And what could he have possibly said to Maria to provoke such a reaction?

Would he have? No—he couldn't have. Because if he did, then Ginny wouldn't even be looking at me. She's loyal to a fault, and I know she would take my wife's side.

"Tell me exactly what happened," I demand, my voice low and dangerous. "Every detail."

"There isn't much to it. He came to us after we left the cafe and then he started talking about how she looks near death and how her new name carries a lot of blood—even the blood of her family."

That idiot. Daniele has taken it a step too far. My jaw clenches, rage coursing through me. Daniele has always been reckless, but this... this is obscene.

I turn to Valerio, my voice clinging to every ounce of rage I have. "Find him. Now."

Valerio nods, already pulling out his phone as he steps away. I run a hand through my hair, my mind racing. This is exactly what I want to avoid. He could ignite a war and all for what?

I open my mouth to ask more questions when the door bursts open and out walks a doctor in scrubs. My heart lurches as the doctor approaches, his face unreadable. I step forward, my voice hoarse as I demand, "How is she?"

The doctor's eyes flick between me and Ginny before settling on me. "Mr. Davacalli, your wife is stable now. We've managed to stop the internal bleeding and address the immediate concerns."

Relief floods through me, but it's short-lived as the doctor continues, his tone grave. "However, there are... complications we need to discuss. Perhaps in private?"

I nod curtly, following him to a secluded corner of the waiting room. Ginny tries to follow, but Valerio holds her back with a gentle but firm hand.

"What complications?" I ask, my voice low and tense.

The doctor hesitates, then speaks softly. "Mr. Davacalli... your wife wasn't just sick. Someone has been poisoning her —for a long time."

My blood turns to ice. "Poisoning?" I repeat, my voice barely above a whisper.

He nods gravely. "Yes. It appears to be a slow-acting toxin, administered over time. It's caused significant damage to her liver and kidneys. We're doing everything we can, but..." He pauses, his eyes meeting mine. "Mr. Davacalli, I have to be honest with you. Your wife's prognosis is not good. The next forty-eight hours will be critical."

I feel the world tilting beneath my feet. Poisoning. Someone has been poisoning my Maria. Four years ago, I watched Beatrice waste away from the exact same thing. And now, it's happening again. History isn't just repeating itself—it's hunting me.

I feel the walls cave over me. My vision blurs as memories of Beatrice's final days flood my mind. The same haunted look in her eyes, the gradual weakening, the helplessness I felt as I watched her slip away. And now, history seems determined to repeat itself with Maria.

I grip the edge of a nearby chair, my knuckles turning white. "Someone is going to pay for this."

The anger completely takes me over but I push it all down.

"Can I see her?"

The doctor nods. "She is in and out of consciousness. Follow me."

As I follow the doctor down the sterile hospital corridor, my mind races. The rhythmic beeping of machines and the hushed voices of medical staff fade into the background as I struggle to process what's happening. *Maria, my Maria, poisoned. Just like Beatrice.*

The doctor pauses outside a room, his hand on the door handle. "Mr. Davacalli," he says softly, "I must warn you. Your wife is in a fragile state. Don't be alarmed by all the machines and the tubes, they are there to keep her alive."

I nod, steeling myself for what I'm about to see. As the door swings open, my breath catches in my throat. Maria lies there, pale and small against the stark white sheets. Tubes and wires connect her to various machines, their steady hum a grim reminder of how close I came to losing her.

I approach the bed slowly, my eyes never leaving her face. Even in this state, she's beautiful. Her perfect hair fans out on the pillow, framing her delicate features. Her chest rises and falls with shallow breaths, each one a small victory and a sign that she is still alive.

I sink into the chair beside her bed, gently taking her hand in mine. It's cool to the touch, so fragile I'm almost afraid I'll break it. "Maria," I whisper, my voice rough with emotion. "I'm here, amore mio. I'm right here."

Her eyelids flutter at the sound of my voice, and slowly, painfully, she opens her eyes. Those emerald orbs, usually so bright and full of life, are now clouded with pain and confusion.

"Matteo?" she murmurs, her voice barely audible.

"Yes, it's me," I say, squeezing her hand.

Maria's eyes struggle to focus on me, her brow furrowing with effort. "What... happened?" she whispers, each word a clear struggle.

I swallow hard, fighting to keep my voice steady. "You collapsed, amore. But you're safe now. I'm here, and I'm not going anywhere."

A ghost of a smile flickers across her pale lips. "You came back early," she murmurs.

"Of course I did," I say, brushing a strand of hair from her forehead. "I couldn't stay away from you."

My heart clenches as the thickness in the air steals the breath from my lungs.

"Maria," I whisper, voice trembling with a mixture of fear and remorse, "I'm so sorry. I—I've been a terrible husband."

Maria's eyes flutter, struggling to stay open. "Matteo," she breathes, her voice barely audible. "Don't... don't blame yourself."

I lean in closer, desperate to hear her words. My thumb strokes the back of her hand, careful not to disturb the IV line. "How can I not? I should have seen the signs, should have protected you better."

A weak cough wracks her frame, and I reach for the water glass, gently lifting her head to help her drink. After a few sips, she settles back against the pillows, her gaze more focused now.

"Matteo," Maria whispers, her voice gaining a hint of strength. "You couldn't have known. I didn't even know myself."

I shake my head, unable to accept her forgiveness I don't deserve it. "I should have been there. I've been so distant, so caught up in..." I trail off, unwilling to burden her. She doesn't even know that she has been poisoned. I will save that for later. For now, she should rest and heal.

Her fingers twitch in mine, a feeble attempt at a reassuring squeeze. "I don't feel like you need it but I forgive you, Matteo. I'm not angry with you."

The selflessness in her words cuts me to the core. Even now, lying in a hospital bed, poisoned and fighting for her life, she's trying to comfort me. The realization of how much I've taken her for granted crashes over me like a tidal wave.

"No," I say firmly, bringing her hand to my lips. "No more excuses. I want to do this with you, Maria. I want to be all in with you."

Her eyes widen slightly. "Are you saying…?"

"Yes," I say, my voice thick with emotion. "I'm saying I want us to be real. No more pretending, no more distance."

Maria's eyes fill with tears, a mix of hope and disbelief shimmering. "Matteo, I… are you sure? This isn't just because I'm in the hospital?"

I shake my head. "No, amore. I've been thinking about this for a while now. Seeing you like this… it's made me realize how much I could lose. How much I've already been losing by keeping you at arm's length."

A small, tentative smile curves her lips. "I want that, too," she whispers. "So much."

I lean in, pressing a gentle kiss to her forehead. "Then we'll make it happen. Together."

She nods weakly, her eyelids fluttering as exhaustion begins to overtake her. "Matteo," she murmurs, her voice fading, "I'm so tired…"

"Rest, amore," I whisper, gently stroking her cheek. "I'll be right here when you wake up."

As Maria drifts off to sleep, I lean back in the chair, my mind racing. Someone has been poisoning her, and I have a sinking feeling I know who's behind it. Giacomo. But how? How would he have access to her?

Either I have a mole or an enemy from within. Regardless, whoever dared to touch my wife has already sealed their fate. And when I find them… they'll beg for death before I'm done.

23

MARIA

Nine days. That's how long I stay in the hospital. They monitor me closely, and my husband hovers like a helicopter. At first, it was endearing to have him so close, but then at some point, I got annoyed.

"I'm not going to break, Matteo." I scowl at him as I get off the side of the bed. "The doctor has cleared me to go home and you are going to have to stop being so... so... this." I gesture to his tall stature.

He gives me an incredulous look to which I just bat my eyelashes. It's crazy how easily we slipped into this new dynamic. And all it took was me being on the brink of death for him to finally give me—us—a chance.

"I just want you to be careful," he says, offering me his arm, which I take. "I need you to keep on this upward trend of getting better. You were being poisoned and I... I can't trust anyone near you right now."

My stomach twists at his words, and I shake my head, frustration bubbling to the surface. "Matteo, you can't just go around suspecting everyone. Not everyone is out to hurt me."

We walk out the door and are greeted by Tony. "Boss, ma'am."

"Tony, please get my wife's bag inside. I will take her down to the car and wait for you. I need to head to the eastern side of town."

My head snaps in his direction. "Well, this is a shock. You haven't left my side for nine days, and now the moment I'm going home, you're jumping at the first chance to leave? Unbelievable."

"Shut up." He kisses the side of my head and playfully nips at my ear. "I need to attend to the work I have been putting off. I will be home within three hours, not a second later. If I didn't need to go, you know I would be at your side."

My heart warms at his words. We walk to the elevator meant to take us down to the parking garage. "Thank you for being here with me."

We walk inside, arm in arm into the empty elevator. As the doors close, he pulls me into his chest and he holds me there. The silence that surrounds us is thick and filled with emotion. All I can think and feel is him. He surrounds me and consumes me the way a tsunami would a beach.

"You never have to thank me for doing my job, cara mia. I am meant to protect and honor you." He mutters the words into my hair. A shiver of pleasure runs up and down my spine. Matteo pulls away to look at me. "What's with the look on your face?"

"Nothing." I lean into his side and take in his warmth. "Nothing at all."

Matteo helps me into the car. Once I'm settled, he reaches over to fasten my seatbelt, his movements careful—almost reverent. But then he stills, his face just inches from mine, his breath warm against my skin. His eyes burn through me, cutting straight to the core of my being.

He leans in, his lips capturing mine in a deep, consuming kiss that sends me spiraling into weightlessness. My heart soars, pounding wildly—like a hammer striking metal, relentless and unyielding.

I will never get enough of him. Of this.

He pulls away, his eyes shining with a warmth I'm addicted to now. I want to be able to spark that light in his eyes every single chance I get. For a moment, the world falls away, and all that exists is me and him.

I once read that some people in this world feel like sunshine. That's what Matteo feels like to me. He is the light in my pit of darkness. It's ironic, seeing as he has a lot of darkness that surrounds him.

"Get some rest, I instructed Emily to make something light for you." He smiles and then presses his lips on mine once again. "I will see you at home for dinner in three hours."

"No more than that," I repeat his words from earlier. I dare to reach up and cup his cheek. "I will see you later."

He seems reluctant to leave but he pulls away just as Tony settles into the car after having put my bags in the back. Matteo's eyes cut to my guard and then back to me.

"Ciao, my love." He shuts the door before I can say anything, and I watch him leave.

My heart does these little flip-flop motions in my chest, and I have to forcefully push those feelings down. This will take some getting used to.

The ride home is quiet, thankfully. I am in no mood to speak. I reply to a few messages from my mama and Ginny, who have been on my case about communicating. I heard the incident between Ginny and my husband. I know she knows that what happened to me was not her fault, but I can tell from our interactions that a small fraction of her feels guilty.

"Here we are, Mrs. Davacalli." Tony opens the front door for me. I walk into the foyer and I wait to feel the warmth of being home, but it never comes. "Home sweet home."

Yeah. Home sweet home.

Emily is already waiting for me in the foyer, her usual polite smile in place. "Welcome home, Mrs. Davacalli," she says warmly, stepping forward to take my bag from Tony. "I've got it."

"No, no, I've got it." Tony moves his hand from her grasp. "Mrs. Davacalli is your main concern. The boss said we need to keep her off her feet and make sure she eats so she can take her meds."

Emily stills for half a second, something flickering across her face—surprise, maybe even frustration—but she masks it well. I almost don't notice it. Almost.

Tony heads upstairs without another word, and I am left with Emily.

"Mrs. Davacalli, please come to the couch. I will make you some tea or soup to help ease." Emily takes me by the arm and leads me toward the sunken living room. "It's good to see that you are alive and well."

"Yeah, thank you. I don't know what happened. They said I was being poisoned." I shake my head. "I don't know where the damn poison could have come from, but thank God I got to the hospital in time."

Emily helps me to settle on the couch. "Yes, we thank the heavens. I was praying for you. For a moment, I feared you would leave us—just like the first Mrs. Davacalli."

I didn't miss the way that she said the word, the first. There was a subtle emphasis to it.

Emily places a blanket on top of my body and my body relaxes into the expensive material. I want to pretend that my body is back to its regular form, but after all the hospital poking and prodding, I am still worn down.

"Thank you, Emily."

She smiles. "Of course. Shall I bring you your calming tea?"

I shake my head, my mouth already opening to yawn. "No, thank you. I just want to sleep right now. Maybe when I wake up."

She inclines her head, a gesture she hasn't done for a while. "Okay, please rest. Mr. Davacalli wants you healed in record time."

Her voice already fades into a distant echo as the fatigue draws me deeper into her darkness. The last nine days have been nothing short of a blur. The hours bled into each other, but one thing remained constant—my husband.

He's so attentive and present now. But there is also another thing that still lingers in the back of my mind—Daniele. His words still echo like a resounding gong in the back of my mind. He came out of nowhere with a warning I didn't understand.

I should let it go. But I am yet to bring it up with my husband. And there is a part of me that doesn't want to bring it up, for fear of what those answers will reveal. But I know that, eventually, I will need to address what is going on.

I wake up to the flickering glow of the television and the comforting weight of the blanket draped over me. The scent of something warm and rich lingers in the air; it's spicy and smells just like curry. My stomach immediately responds to the scents.

Food.

I stretch my arms and look out the window to find that the day has melted into the night, and the sun is gone.

"Jesus, how long did I sleep?"

I reach for my phone, which I remember placing on the coffee table, but instead, I find a small white sheet of paper. I pick it up, read the messy writing, and smile.

Join me for dinner?

I stare at the words for a moment, my chest tightening unexpectedly. Matteo. True to his word, he made it home after three hours and not a moment more. When did he get here?

I push the blanket aside and rise to my feet, moving toward the soft light spilling from the dining room. What I find there makes me stop in my tracks. The table is set for two, candles flickering between two plates of steaming curry and what looks to be jasmine rice—my favorite, but how did he know that?

The sight of it—of him—leaves me momentarily speechless. His eyes find mine, and the small smile that comes to his lips makes my heart pound in my chest. The candlelight contours his face, defining his already sharp jaw that much more.

Matteo stands near the table, his hands in his pockets, his posture a little too stiff, like he's uncertain about how I'll react. For a man who commands rooms full of killers without hesitation, it's almost endearing to watch him be nervous.

I step forward slowly, my voice softer than I intended. "What's all of this?"

His lips twitch slightly as if he wants to smirk but isn't sure if he should. "If we are going to do this for real, then I want to do it right. I think a first date is long overdue, don't you?"

"A first date? A little backward, aren't we?" I chuckle, feeling the blush rise to my cheeks.

"Yes, it kind of is. But I did agree to try." He rubs the back of his neck with his hand, and I have never seen him look so boyish. "Please join me."

I hesitate for a moment, taking in the sight before me. The warm glow of the candlelight flickers between us. Slowly, I step closer to the table until I come up to the chair. I reach to pull it out myself but he stops me.

"Allow me," he whispers right by my ear, sending a shiver down my spine. All the fatigue has left me now.

He helps me into his chair and his hand grazes my neck and I shudder. It's maddening how easily he unravels me—his touch, his scent, the mere sight of him.

Matteo settles into his own seat and looks at me waiting. "It's chicken curry and jasmine rice."

I nod. "I can see that. But how did you know to make this for me? You look like a steak kind of man."

That nervous laugh of his returns. His eyes shine like a thousand shooting stars as he stares at me. "I am but I wanted you to have some comfort food. Your mother tells me that you love a good chicken curry."

"You spoke to my mother?"

He nods. "After she scolded me, of course. She made sure to remember her promise to me on the day of our wedding. I told her it would stick with me for life."

I tilt my head to the side and observe him for a moment. "What promise?"

"She said she would find eighteen different ways to kill me if I didn't take care of you." He blinks at me. "She was deathly serious too. I believe her."

I sputter out a laugh and think of my sweet mother. "Of course she would."

"Try it—I tried to make it the way that your mother does back home." He waits for me to try the curry and I have to fight back a smile. This man is just too cute right now.

I pick up my fork and take a bite, and the moment the flavors hit my tongue, I let out a small, surprised hum. "This is actually good. It tastes like home."

Matteo exhales through his nose, the closest thing to a laugh I've ever heard from him. "I'm sure your mother would kill me if it wasn't. It's her recipe that I would have botched."

The tension between us shifts slightly—still present, still heavy, but no longer suffocating. For the first time since our wedding, aren't caught in a constant push and pull of resistance and surrender.

We're simply existing together.

The silence stretches between us, but it's not uncomfortable. If anything, it feels... oddly peaceful. Then, without thinking, I ask the one question I know I shouldn't.

"This is real, right?"

Matteo pauses, his fork hovering just above his bowl. He doesn't answer right away. Instead, he sets his fork down, leaning back slightly in his chair.

His gaze locks onto mine, something unreadable swimming in the depths of his eyes. "It is more real than it has ever been, Maria."

I should be relieved by his words. I should let them settle in my chest like a soothing balm, should let them wash away the uncertainty clinging to me like a ghost. But instead, doubt curls around my ribs like a serpent, whispering the cruelest question of all—what if this isn't real?

What if I'm just another duty he's committed to out of guilt?

What if, one day, the warmth in his eyes cools, and I'm left alone in the shadows again?

What if this isn't real? What if I'm just another fleeting moment to him—just a duty he's committed to out of guilt?

My fingers tighten around the fork, and I lower my gaze to my plate, suddenly unable to meet his eyes. I want to believe him—I need to believe him. But my heart has already learned the cost of trusting too easily.

And yet... he came back for me. He stayed with me.

"I want to believe you," I murmur, almost too quietly.

Matteo exhales. His voice, when he finally speaks, is quieter—but no less intense.

"I know why you hesitate, Maria. I know I've given you every reason to doubt this—to doubt me." His jaw tightens for a brief moment before he releases a slow breath, his shoulders softening. "But I need you to know this."

He leans forward, the flickering candlelight casting shadows over the sharp angles of his face. His gaze—steady, unwavering—locks onto mine, and for the first time, I see something in them that wasn't there before.

"I am here. I am yours. And I am not going anywhere."

The raw sincerity in his voice sends a shiver down my spine.

"I don't expect you to trust me overnight. I don't expect you to believe every word I say just because I'm saying it. But I need you to see that I'm standing right in front of you, choosing you. Every damn time, I will choose you." He pauses, his throat bobbing as he swallows hard. "I don't want to make this work out of duty, or guilt, or obligation—I want to make this work because I need you. Because you, Maria, are the only thing that makes this world feel real to me."

His words press against something deep inside me,

cracking the carefully constructed walls I've spent months building.

My breath catches. I swallow hard, feeling the sudden weight of his words settle between us. "I don't want you to hurt me, Matteo."

He lifts his eyes to meet mine and the world stills. I forget how to breathe. I can hear the blood gushing past my ears.

"I was unfair to you, and I cannot apologize enough for what I have done to you and your heart."

I open my mouth to speak but he holds his hand up to allow him to finish.

"I have not loved a woman since Beatrice. When I lost my wife, something inside me snapped. I thought I locked my heart away, convinced myself no one would ever reach it again. But you—"

His breath hitches, his fingers tapping against the table once before stilling.

"You were already inside before I even realized it. And that scared me."

I hold my breath, my chest tightening as he continues.

"I pushed you away because I thought it was the only way to keep myself from losing again. Because love—real love—makes you weak. It gives someone the power to ruin you." His voice drops lower, almost hesitant. "And I swore I would never be that vulnerable again."

He shakes his head, jaw tightening. "But when I saw you lying there in the hospital bed, Maria—when I saw you pale and unconscious, barely breathing—everything I thought I knew shattered. I wasn't protecting myself. I was punishing myself. I was punishing you for something you never even did. And I was so fucking wrong."

. . .

His voice is raw, thick with a kind of desperation I never thought I'd hear from him. His fingers tighten around his fork for a brief moment before he exhales, his jaw tightening.

"Do you know what it feels like, Maria?" His voice drops lower, barely above a whisper. "To think you're untouchable—only to realize too late that someone has already burrowed so deep inside of you, you can't breathe without them?"

He looks at me then, and for the first time, I see it. Not just the love, but the fear.

"That's what you are to me."

He finally looks at me, his piercing gaze locking onto mine. "You are the sun I revolve around, Maria. I will never let my fear push you away again."

I open my mouth, but nothing comes out. Because for the first time, I don't think Matteo is just saying something to manipulate, to control, to assert power. For the first time, I think he means it. I don't just hear the words—I feel them.

His words linger between us, thick with something I can't quite name.

"I don't care how many times you need reassurance I will be right in front of you telling you, that I am here and this is real. I will tell you every morning, noon, and night if I have to." His words are coated in conviction and truth. "You are my world, Maria. And there is no me without you, not now or ever. Okay?"

My mind is a frenzy of emotion and chaos. I don't have the right words to say so I simply nod.

"Good." His body eases and the tension releases from his body.

The rest of dinner passes in a quiet, unexpected calm.

Matteo doesn't push for conversation, and for once, I don't feel the need to fill the silence.

When I finally set my fork down, I realized just how much I needed this. Not just the food, but this moment. The warmth of a meal shared, the steady presence of this man.

Matteo watches me carefully as if trying to read my thoughts. "You should rest," he says, voice softer than usual.

I nod, but something in his gaze keeps me locked in place. The candlelight casts sharp shadows across his face. There is a tinge in his pupils, a flicker of heat that simmers just below the surface.

My fingers tighten slightly around the edge of the table. The electricity in the air crackles to life, and that subtle hum that passes between us whenever we collide smashes into us.

I don't know what comes over me then, whether it's exhaustion, the warmth of the evening, or the sudden pull between us, but before I can think better of it, I stand from my seat and walk toward him.

Matteo watches me carefully, his expression unreadable, his body as still as stone. The heat in his eyes begins to boil, and the gentle charge in the air intensifies.

"What are you doing, cara?" He looks up at me as I come to a halt by his chair. I stare down at him, trying to make sense of my own intentions.

"Fuck it." I don't give myself a chance to second-guess—I just move.

I lean down, brushing my lips against his in a kiss that starts soft but deepens quickly. Matteo doesn't hesitate. He responds instantly, his hand coming up to cradle the back of my neck, pulling down toward him. He pushes back to give me the room to settle in his seat.

The kiss is slow, sensual—an unspoken promise, a

confession in the language of touch. I taste the heat of him, the hunger, the depth of everything he feels but doesn't say. Fuck, it's good. Our tongues move together in an intricate dance that only they understand. It's this gentle push and pull of the tides that leaves my heart pounding ferociously in my chest.

When we finally break apart, my pulse is racing, my breath uneven.

"Take me to bed, Matteo," I whisper.

24

MATTEO

I take her into my arms, her body molding against mine like she is made for me. Her lips trail along my neck, slow and warm, then nip at my pulse point. A full-body shiver ripples through me.

Fuck. She's sin and salvation wrapped in skin. My kryptonite.

I carry her up the stairs, her mouth still working the sensitive spot where my neck meets my shoulder. When she sucks harder, a harsh exhale leaves my lips. Blood surges straight to my cock, and it's already throbbing behind my zipper.

"Maria," I warn, voice rough with restraint. "You're playing with fire, amore."

"Shh." Her breath ghosts over my throat. "Then let me burn."

She bites down, and I stumble slightly. Jesus. I tighten my grip on her thighs, then pick up speed, slamming the bedroom door behind us.

"My turn," I growl, tossing her onto the bed. She lands with a squeal, and before she can blink, I'm over her. I crash my lips into hers, devouring her mouth like I've been starving.

She moans into me, and I drink every sound like it's my last breath.

We kiss like we've done it a thousand times in dreams—tongues tangling, teeth scraping, a dance of hunger and heat. Her hips roll against mine, rubbing her soft core over my hard length. The friction damn near ends me.

I break the kiss, panting, my forehead pressed to hers, staring into her hunger-ridden eyes. The air between us is thick with sex. Her fingers thread through my hair, tugging gently at the small strands at the nape of my neck.

"You're perfect, Maria," I pant. "Utter perfection and no woman on this earth compares. Fuck, I need you."

"I need you too." Her hand glides down my chest before resting over my heart. There's a warmth in her gaze that both scares and thrills me. Like she sees past the want—into all the broken, buried parts I never let anyone touch.

Her eyes flicker with something deeper—hunger, maybe. Or something that terrifies me even more: trust.

"But first... I want to taste you."

She pushes me onto my back and straddles me. Her hands go straight for my zipper, and within seconds, my cock is free—rock hard and aching.

"Maria—"

She silences me with a kiss that brands my soul. It's not sweet. It's conquest. She kisses me like I already belong to her.

When she pulls back, her fingers grip my jaw.

"I'm doing this," she says, voice husky. "So shut up and let me."

Her hand wraps around my cock, and her tongue flicks the head. My hips buck. I groan—loud.

She takes me in, slow at first, then deeper. Her tongue swirls around the shaft, teasing every nerve. Inch by inch, she devours me until she gags, pulls back, then does it again.

She strokes my balls with one hand while working my cock like it's her goddamn mission.

"Fuck, Maria," I hiss, grabbing the back of her head. "You're gonna make me lose it."

I thrust gently into her mouth, her gag making my abs clench. My hand guides her rhythm as she takes me, owns me.

She works my cock like it's the only thing she wants in her mouth, and I'm close—too close. I yank her up before I come down her throat.

She lets out a frustrated sound, but I flip her fast, pinning her beneath me. Her protest is swallowed by my kiss.

She fights for dominance, but I'm not giving her an inch. Not now.

I tear her clothes off while our mouths stay locked—kissing like it hurts to stop. She fumbles with my pants until I finally sit up and rip my shirt off.

We're both bare, panting, high on each other. I can't remember ever needing someone like this.

Never again, I think. *I won't lose her. I won't let her go. Not ever.*

Her hand cups my face. "What is it?"

I kiss her palm, voice a whisper. "You're exquisite, Maria Davacalli."

And maybe that's what scares me most—how easy it is to fall for her. How impossible it is not to.

She lies beneath me, vulnerable but powerful. Something primal roars in my chest.

I'm in love with her. Maybe I always was.

"Fuck me, Matteo," she whispers. "Hard."

I don't need to be told twice. I line up with her entrance and drive in slow. Her eyes roll back, her back arches, and she lets out a guttural moan.

"Matteo... oh, fuck."

She's tight. So tight I forget how to breathe. I bury myself to the hilt, balls flush against her ass. I hold still, let her adjust. She stares up at me with wild eyes, and the last of my control slips.

"Move," she commands.

"Gladly." I pull out, then slam back in, dropping my face to her neck as I thrust.

"Ah!" she cries.

"You okay?" I ask, teeth grazing her shoulder, voice tight with restraint.

Instead of answering, she wraps her legs around me and pulls me in deeper. "Don't stop."

Her nails dig into my back, and I obey—pounding into her, searching for that rhythm only our bodies know. "That's it, baby," I growl into her ear. "Take it. Take every inch of me." Her cries rise with every thrust, raw and breathless.

I kiss her hard, swallowing every moan.

She's still so innocent in some ways, but it's intoxicating watching her unravel, learning her own hunger.

Our skin slaps together, sweat glistening under the dim light.

"Matteo," she gasps. "I didn't know it could feel like this."

I fuck her harder, chasing the edge. Her face twists in pleasure, hair fanned out like a halo while I wreck her body beneath me.

"You like being filled like this, don't you?" I growl, watching her fall apart. "Say it."

"Yes... Matteo!" she screams, and that name—my name—on her lips undoes me.

"Say you want more."

"Yes," she whimpers, hips rolling up to meet me. "More. Fuck me harder, please. Use me, Matteo. Make me yours."

I'm right there, held on the brink by her pulsing walls.

I don't just want to come inside her—I want to pour every broken part of me into her, like she could make me whole again.

"Let go for me, Maria," I growl, my thumb circling her clit. "I want to watch you fall apart."

Her breath catches—and then she shatters.

She convulses beneath me, thighs trembling, pussy clenching my cock so tight it rips the orgasm from me too. I groan as I spill inside her, buried deep, riding the high with her.

She looks like freedom. Like peace. Like everything I never believed I deserved—until now.

We stay tangled for a long moment, our breathing ragged and heavy in the silence.

I brush a few strands of hair from her damp forehead, my eyes drinking in the soft flush of her face as I marvel at her beauty. Her eyes flutter open, heavy-lidded and warm, filled with a slow-burning mix of satisfaction and longing.

"That was..." she whispers, seemingly at a loss for words.

"Incredible," I say, pressing a gentle kiss to her forehead.

She smiles. "I didn't know it could be like that between us. I hoped it would be. But this... this is more."

She traces lazy circles on my chest. I pull her closer, her body melting into mine like she was made to fit the pieces I thought would stay broken forever.

There's a world waiting for us—messy, dangerous,

uncertain. But for now? For this breath, this night, this warmth between us?

Nothing else matters.

I close my eyes, her heartbeat steady against my chest, and for the first time in years... I find peace. Not just in her arms—but in the way she sees me. And still stays.

I JOLT AWAKE BEFORE DAWN, reaching for Maria instinctively. My hand finds nothing but cold cotton sheets. My stomach plummets.

"Maria?"

I'm already moving before my brain catches up. The bed feels too empty, the silence too loud. Panic grips my chest like a vice, the ghost of that night—the hospital, the monitors, the poison—seizing me without warning.

I call her name, but there's no answer. I throw back the sheets, my heart already pounding. The panic that I felt that day returns and it takes every mental ounce of strength I have not to lose my shit.

I get my boxers on and head straight out of the room. I walk down the stairs and make my way to the kitchen, but I find it empty. I look to the living room, but no one is there. My mind goes to the worst possible place until I see the light that comes from her new studio room.

I make my way to the room, and my heart instantly eases when I see my wife—her messy bun and my white button-down—as she stands by her easel.

I step forward, but I pause and just observe her for a moment. Instead, I lean against the doorframe, mesmerized.

Her fingers move with practiced ease, coaxing color into life, breathing existence onto the canvas. She is completely lost in her art, unaware of the way she commands the space around her. The tip of her tongue peeks out in concentration, a habit I find both adorable and devastating.

How can she create beauty with hands that should be shaking? How can she love me with a heart I helped break?

I lean against the wooden doorframe and drink her in. Those legs had been wrapped around my waist not too long ago. Her mouth has screamed the most ungodly things in my ear and she—

"I can feel you staring, Matteo." She doesn't turn back. Her eyes never leave the canvas. "Instead of being a creep by watching me, you should come to greet your wife good morning."

The humor in her tone is apparent; I can even hear the smile in it.

"I like stalking you, don't you know?" I push off the doorframe and make my way into the studio. I feel proud every time I see this room. It is the first good thing that I did for my wife. "What are we drawing?"

I come up behind her, wind my arms around her waist, and kiss the side of her face, pulling her into me. I bury my nose in her thick locks and breathe a sigh of contentment.

I don't know how I ever survived without her. She eases all the aches and pains. She makes life make sense again.

Maria exhales a small breath, a wistful smile tugging at her lips. She melts her back into me and pauses for a moment to turn to the side and kiss me. Her kiss is brief but it is enough to shake the very foundation that I stand on.

She pulls away far too quickly for my liking and then turns back to her work. I move my eyes to the canvas and get a better look at what she is doing.

"A lake?"

"It's the one by our farmhouse in Tuscany. My brother

and I used to love going there every time we went down south for the summer." The sadness in her voice is hard to miss. "I just woke up thinking of him. I had a dream that we were back there, and I... I just wanted to paint it, in honor of him."

The guilt moves like a thick sludge in the middle of my chest. Antonio. A name I will never forget and I will never be able to pay enough penance for.

"He loved it there. He said the world made sense when he was near the water and me. I didn't get what he meant back then but now, since being deprived of the water, I get it." She moves her brush over the canvas. "There is a calmness that comes with the push and pull of the waves. It's like nature's melody."

I say nothing, allowing her this moment to speak of her brother. She carries her grief so well that I often forget she is still in mourning. I need to be more mindful of that. Especially the fact that I am the cause of that pain.

She dips her brush into a deep shade of blue, dragging it softly along the surface of the water she's creating. "Sometimes, I feel like I'm losing pieces of him," she murmurs. "But when I paint, I remember as the memories come flooding back to me. I can almost hear his voice again."

The truth is a curse I carry alone—a wound that festers, never healing, never fading. If I rip it open for her, it will only poison her too.

I should tell her. I should have told her the second she spoke his name. But how do you confess to the woman you love that you were the one who took away the person she loved most?

Her brother's blood is still on my hands, no matter how many times I've washed them. And if she ever finds out, she will never look at me the same way again.

I would rather live with this sin buried in my chest than watch the light in her eyes dim when she realizes who I really am.

So I lodge the truth deep into my psyche and lock it away.

I can't tell her...

"You won't forget him," I say, my voice lower than before. "He will forever be a part of you. And that will never change no matter how much time passes. He lives on in you, Maria."

She looks up at me then, her warm eyes searching mine. I wonder if she can see it: the weight I'm carrying, the sins I haven't confessed. But if she does, she doesn't say anything.

She presses her lips to mine and turns back to her painting. "I wish you could have met him. I think he would have liked you."

I did meet him, amore. And I was the one to lodge a bullet into his heart.

25

MARIA

For seven days, the world outside doesn't exist. Matteo and I vanish into the quiet luxury of the penthouse, wrapped in stolen mornings, hungry touches, and the illusion that time might bend for us.

But illusions never last. And I know, deep down, he'll have to go back to the world that waits for him.

"Stop that." I bump my shoulder against his arm. "How can you call yourself a New Yorker when you haven't even tried Starbucks?"

I laugh at his contorted face. He stares at the vanilla latte I ordered for him in disgust. The chill of the air tints his cheeks pink, and he looks like he is seconds from having a coronary.

He shakes his head. "Whatever this is, it's a crime against real coffee."

"It is delicious," I laugh and smile. "You have no taste for the finer things in life."

"Of course I have a taste for the finer things, Maria." He tosses the coffee in the trash without hesitation. "Tailored suits. Italian engines. A woman who can out-stare a storm. But *that*"—he nods to the cup—"that's an insult to caffeine."

The wind blows moving through my hair and momentarily covering my face. I pause and try to get the hair out of my face while trying to balance the coffee in my hands.

"Here, let me." He moves the hair from my eyes. He cups my face and then presses his lips to mine, and I taste the vanilla on his lips. My body melts into his instinctively and I feel my feet rise above the clouds. He pulls away far too quickly from my lips and I whimper.

"Careful," he whispers against my lips. You'll get addicted."

I bite down on my lip and look up at him through my lashes. "I could spend a thousand lifetimes with you and still not get enough. I thought you would know this by now."

His gaze darkens with emotion. "Then one lifetime will never be enough—for either of us. I wish I didn't have to leave you today."

"And why must you burst my bubble?" I pout my lips and continue down the pavement. "I was happy, and now you remind me of the disappointment that waits for me when we get back home."

Home. The penthouse still didn't feel like home on its own. He needs to be in it for me to feel like it is. He is my home—my haven.

"Come now, amore. You know I need to work, and besides, there is still your perpetrator on the loose, and I need to figure out who it is." He grabs my hand and interlaces our fingers. "I need to make this city safe for you again."

I breathe a heavy sigh, and my breath mists in the fall

air. "I know. But I got used to you being around. You were a nice distraction from everything."

And by everything, I mean all the questions I have about what Daniele said to me. I still haven't forgotten, and I am scared to bring it up with Matteo. I don't want it to turn into an argument, but I know that eventually, I will have to.

But today is not that day.

"Why did you choose to live in the city? I know you have the Davacalli estate out north, and you loved it there from what I remember." It is a question that I have been curious about for quite some time now.

Something flickers behind his eyes—just for a second. A shadow. A memory. He doesn't answer right away, and for a moment, I think I've overstepped. But then he breathes out slowly, gaze fixed on something far away.

"When Beatrice died..." he starts, his voice quieter than before, almost hesitant. "The estate didn't feel like home anymore. It became... a mausoleum. Every hallway echoed her laughter. Every corner whispered her absence. I'd sit on the porch and expect her to walk out, barefoot, smiling— and when she didn't... it felt like the walls closed in."

He swallows, and I catch the flicker of pain in his eyes, raw and unguarded.

"Grief... It's a strange thing. It doesn't scream. It seeps. It took everything I loved about that house and made it feel like a punishment. I couldn't breathe there. I was a ghost among memories, and it was killing me slowly."

I rest my forehead against his shoulder, keeping our hands connected, but he's still staring ahead, like he's looking back in time.

"Daniele was grown, off doing his own thing. I told myself it was practical, leaving. That the house was too big, too empty. But the truth?" He pauses, turning to me, eyes full of something so painfully human. "I ran. I ran from the silence. I ran from the guilt of surviving her. And I didn't stop running... until you."

I squeeze his hand, letting him know that I am here for him. The man has more demons plaguing him than I care to admit. He has seen many dark things and survived the worst of what the world has to offer. I know it's not easy for him to let me in like this. I don't take it for granted.

"You don't have to talk about it if it's too much," I say gently. Sometimes I forget—he's still carrying that grief, a wound that never truly healed, just learned to stay quiet.

He shakes his head. "You deserve to know."

"You know I'm not trying to replace her, right?"

He looks over at me, a soft smile touching his lips. "I know. And no one ever could. I'd never compare you to her —never pit you against her. You're two very different women... but somehow, you share the same kind of fire."

I tilt my head. "What do you mean?"

His smile deepens, laced with memory. "It's in your warmth. That quiet strength that doesn't need to shout to be felt. You both love with your whole hearts, but when you're angry—when you're pushed—you burn with a fury that can level anything in your path. It's beautiful... and terrifying."

A soft laugh escapes me. "And how are we different?"

He pauses, the smile fading into something quieter. "With you, it's... different. There's this pull—like a thread that's always been there. I felt it the moment I saw you at Antonio's funeral. I shouldn't have looked at you the way I did, but I couldn't help it. It was like... gravity."

My heart stutters. "Like we were meant to collide."

He nods. "Beatrice opened my heart. She changed the way I saw the world. She gave me my son. But you—" he takes my hand, gaze burning into mine, "—you feel like everything was leading to this. To you. With you, it feels like... destiny came full circle."

I blink, breath caught in my throat. "So what you're telling me is... I'm your destiny?"

His lips lift. "The inevitable kind."

I mean to say it as a joke, but my husband suddenly pulls us to a stop and turns to face me. His eyes—molten autumn and full of fire—hold a gravity that roots me in place. There's something in his gaze I can't quite decipher, something that makes the air between us feel too heavy, too still.

My stomach lurches. The teasing tone vanishes from my throat.

The intensity of his stare has my heart pounding like war drums in my chest. Every instinct tells me to brace myself—for what, I don't know.

Then his voice drops, low and certain.

"Sei l'inizio della mia fine, amore mio. E quando questo mondo finirà, farò in modo di trovarti nel prossimo."

You are the beginning of my end, my love. And when this world ends, I will make sure to find you in the next.

"Matteo..." I can't find the words to say it. So, instead, I lift onto my toes and press my lips to his. I pour all that I have into that kiss and hope that he feels it within him.

He is the beginning of my end and all the things in between. I am falling in love with him, and I am helpless to catch myself. I don't know what the future holds for us with all this chaos that surrounds us, but I know that as long as his hand stays in mine, we will make it out alive.

After a short walk around the park, his meeting time arrives, and we head back to the penthouse.

"Come, my love." He opens the door for me. "You will be fine while I'm gone."

I walk in, but before I can respond, a familiar voice calls out—

"Surprise."

Ginny steps forward with a wide smile, her arms already open. There's a sparkle in her eyes, but she's more graceful than frantic.

"I've missed you," she says as she pulls me into a warm hug. "You have no idea how good it is to see you in one piece."

I hug her back, my chest tightening with affection.

"I talked to you on the phone last night. What are you doing here? I thought you and Dario would be in Washington."

She pulls away and smiles. "That was all a lie. We were coming here to New York to see you. Dario has business with your husband, and I thought, why not drop by? Hello, Matteo."

"Ginny, lovely to see you." Matteo gives her a polite greeting. "Amore, I am leaving. Stay in the house, please, and if you must leave, make sure you go with Tony and text me."

Before I can answer, he smacks a hot kiss on my lips and then pulls away. He pecks me one last time before saying goodbye.

"Take care of my wife for me, Ginny," he says. "Emily should be back now, amore mio. Should you want anything, she will help you. And remember..."

"...stay alive." I roll my eyes at his overprotective stance, but truthfully, I find it all endearing. I love the fact that he watches over me with so much precaution. "Have a good day at work."

Matteo walks out the door, leaving me with my friend. I watch the door for a moment like a little lovesick puppy.

Ginny steps up beside me, her eyes dancing with amusement. "You've got that look."

I glance at her, wary. "What look?"

"The one that says, 'I've been thoroughly ruined by my husband.'" She smirks. "Was it everything you imagined... and then some?"

"Ginny," I gasp, heat rushing to my cheeks.

A pause settles between us. She raises her brows expectantly.

I bite back a smile, unable to help the flush that spreads across my face. "Yes. It was..." I exhale, dreamy. "It was incredible."

Her grin widens. "That's my girl."

Emily comes out from the kitchen with a tray in hand. She offers me a small smile when she sees me. There's something hollow in Emily's eyes lately. Like she's smiling with her mouth, but her soul hasn't caught up. It's subtle—so subtle I almost convince myself I imagined it.

Still, I can't shake the odd flicker in her gaze as she sets the tray down.

There is something that just doesn't feel right with her anymore. The light that used to shine in her eyes is no longer there. She isn't the same Emily that I knew.

"I brought you some tea and sandwiches, Mrs. Davacalli." She sets the tray down and gives Ginny and me one last look. "I will be in the kitchen if you need me."

"Thank you, Emily." I offer her a warm smile, but she doesn't return it. She inclines her head and walks back to the kitchen. I watch her until she disappears around the corner.

"What has gotten into her ass?" Ginny comments. "She used to be so… chipper and smiley."

I shrug. "Ever since I came back from the hospital, she has been off with me."

Ginny brushes off my comment and pulls me to the couch, where the tray has been laid out for us.

"Now, spill, how good was it?" She wags her eyebrows at me.

I blush, and my cheeks go up in flames.

"Oh, you have it bad, girl." She picks up her cup of tea and gushes. "I think we may need something a little stronger than what we have here. Emily!"

"Oh my God, Ginny…" I roll my eyes at her antics, but I can't help but smile.

Emily appears again, but this time, she looks like she is on the brink of irritation. But when she notices me watching her face, she blinks and schools her features.

"Yes?"

"Please get the bubbly out. We have some celebrating to do. My girl got laid!" Ginny smiles, and I laugh at her brazen nature. "Bring two bottles. My husband will come and pick me up."

Emily bites down on her lower lip, and a flash of emotion crosses her eyes. I don't catch it quite fast enough before she schools her features.

"Emily? Are you okay?" I pick up my teacup and hold it in my hand. "You seem rather… not yourself."

She shakes her head and then plasters on her polite smile—a fake one. "No, I'm fine. I think I'm just tired. I will get your champagne."

She leaves without another word, and I am left feeling

uneasy. Something is going on with her, and I don't know what it is. But I will need to get to the bottom of it. Her entire demeanor has me on edge.

I am about to get out of my seat to chase after Emily when Ginny steals my attention.

"So tell me, how do you feel?" She brings the cup to her lips, pauses, then looks down at the liquid, her brow furrowing before she continues. "And be honest."

I shrug. "I mean, I feel good considering that now he doesn't leave the bed or look at me like I killed his cat every time we get intimate. I think we are making strides in our relationship now."

"Are you happy?"

Matteo's face flashes in my mind, and my heart turns to mush almost instantly. "Yeah, I am."

Ginny tilts her head to the side. "But? It sounds like there is a but at the end of that sentence."

I sigh. "I mean, I can't stop thinking about what Daniele said when we left the café that day. It's been replaying in my mind over and over again."

"Have you spoken to Matteo about this?" She takes a sip of the tea and pauses. "What the fuck?"

The widening of her eyes has me on edge. My heart thumps heavily in my chest. "What is it?"

She sniffs the tea, places it on the table, and then takes my cup from me. She looks to the kitchen and then back at me. "I need you to call Matteo right now."

"What? Why?"

Ginny reaches for her bag and pulls out her phone. "I am going to call Dario. We need to get out of here now."

Ginny stares into my teacup again, her face draining of color.

"Okay. Don't panic," she says, though her voice shakes ever so slightly.

She sets the cup down with exaggerated care, like it's a ticking bomb. "This tea is poisoned, Maria. I'm serious."

For a second, I see something rare flicker in her eyes—fear.

Not her usual dramatics. Real, bone-deep fear.

"Poisoned?"

She clamps her hand over my mouth and hushes me. "It's a super rare plant, you won't be able to tell it's in there unless you are familiar with it. I don't have much time to explain, but I need you to text Matteo and tell him to get over here now. If this tea is poisoned, then it means Emily is the one who has been poisoning you."

My stomach churns violently. I feel like I've swallowed glass. The tea was halfway to my lips. My hands start to shake. Oh God—how long has this been going on?

No, there is no way that Emily of all people would do this to me...

She made me breakfast and asked about my dreams. She brought me soup. She made me that calming tea every time I was anxious. A breath hitches in my throat.

God—she was poisoning me with care.

I hear the first crack in my chest. The betrayal spreads through my blood like a thick sludge settling over every muscle.

I open my mouth to speak, but nothing comes out. I am too shocked, too stunned, and... scared. All this time, it was her. I think back to all the times she offered me that tea to 'calm me.'

"Oh my God." I pull out my phone and quickly type a message to my husband before reaching for Ginny's hand. "We need to get out, Tony should be outside."

I turn so we can leave, but then I pause. The hairs on the back of my neck stand, and a cold chill runs down my spine as I come face to face with eyes that could only resemble those of a cold-blooded reptile.

"Emily..." I stare at her, completely at a loss. A woman I thought was a friend holds a knife out to us. Instinctively, I place Ginny behind me, not wanting to put her in the direct line of fire. "Put the knife down, please."

My voice cracks before I can stop it.

"You tucked me into bed when I was sick, Emily. You held my hand when I cried over my brother, Antonio. You were there. You were my friend. How—how could you do this to me?"

"You took his love from me," she hisses, her voice trembling with rage. "He was supposed to choose me. I was the one who stood by him—who knew what he needed. But then you came along, with your pretty little voice and your innocent eyes, and suddenly I was invisible. You ruined everything!"

I see her left eye twitch. Her hand shakes while holding the knife. The temperature drops in the room, and I gulp.

"You were supposed to die." Her eyes are wide, like she is high or possessed. "Why didn't you die like you were supposed to, Maria? Now... now I have to kill you myself."

Emily's eyes gleam, unfocused. "Beatrice was supposed to make him strong, but she made him soft. She ruined him."

Her voice drops to a whisper. "I had to do what was necessary. And then you... you were worse."

She lifts the knife higher. "But I won't fail this time."

My breath catches in my throat.

This isn't just madness.

This is personal.

She took Beatrice from him—and now she wants to take me, too.

The betrayal stings so deeply, I almost forget to move.

But I can't freeze.

I won't.

I have to survive this.

For Matteo. For us. For everything we haven't had yet.

I will not let her take that from me.

26

MATTEO

Dario sits across from me in silence, arms folded, eyes distant. Beyond the curt greeting he offered when he arrived, he hasn't said a word.

My mood's been lighter lately—lighter than it has any right to be. Maria is healing. We're becoming something real. For once, the storm inside me has quieted. But storms never stay silent for long.

"Smile, Dario. Keep scowling like that, and people might think you're plotting a coup." I flash a grin. "Still surprises me how Ginny puts up with someone so intense."

He lifts an eyebrow. "Coming from the king of intensity himself? Matteo, please."

"I'm telling you, I definitely brood less," I say, the corner of my mouth twitching. The contentment that's been bleeding into my bones lately—Maria—still clings to me like sunlight.

Dario exhales, slow and flat. "Good for you. Some of us still have wolves to kill." He leans back, steepling his fingers. "But we didn't come here to swap emotional growth stories. Giacomo isn't going to choke himself out."

My mood cools. Every time I hear his name, a chill settles over me. I hate how even in his absence, he can still get under my skin.

"We are trying to get an exact shipment date on his next shipment." I crack my knuckles. "We need to cut him off completely from his big money. Then after that, we will go after the people he is working with."

A silence falls over us. Then Dario opens his mouth. "That list of people includes your son, Matteo."

"Except my son," I say too quickly. "He's just... lost."

But even as I say the words, something in me clenches. The truth is, I don't know if he'll come back to me—or if I've already lost him for good.

"How sure are you?" He leans his elbows on the desk.

The truth is, I am not so sure. I have no idea if he will come to his senses and finally believe me. I don't entertain his question with my answer—because I don't know it.

"I understand he is your boy, but there may come a time where you have to make a decision. We need to kill the entire hive, and if he is a part of it, then he will need to go down too."

I don't want to hear it. I don't even want to entertain the possibility of that thought coming to life. I will walk away from this with my wife and my son.

Just as Dario opens his mouth again, both our phones buzz.

I glance down. Maria. Her name lights up my screen, and for a split second, the chaos of the world fades. A smile tugs at my lips—instinctive, helpless.

How quickly she's become the still point in my spinning world. The calm in my storm.

I tap her name—and joy vanishes in an instant.

My stomach drops. Four words: *You were right. Hurry.*

I shoot up from my chair. Dario's already on his feet, eyes narrowed.

"What?"

"Something's wrong. Ginny sent me a message—'Get to Matteo's house. Fast.'" He scowls. "I thought you said that place was locked down tight."

I'm already on my feet, storming toward the door. "I do."

I made sure that not a single person could make it within a fifty-foot vicinity of her without me knowing. That place is an air-tight fortress—or so I thought.

"I need to get to her."

Dario's right behind me, his phone already to his ear. "Call your wife. I'm getting Gin."

He glances at me, voice low and dangerous. "If they lay a hand on either of them, Matteo... I won't wait for permission."

My hand is already dialing Maria. But it rings, and there is no answer. I try again, but the same thing happens. My mind goes to the worst possible places, thinking the worst thing imaginable has happened to her.

The panic slowly begins to settle into the marrow of my bones. I move down the hallway, my mind going at a million miles a minute. I knew I should have never left her on her own. She is barely two weeks out of the hospital, and now she is—

"Why does hell always break loose when Ginny's with Maria?" Dario growls, his voice tight with urgency. "First your son, now this?" He rakes a hand through his hair, already pulling his phone back up. "If your security's compromised, tell me. I'll triple it myself."

I grit my teeth but say nothing. He's not blaming me—he's scared. Same as I am.

"We move now," I snap. "You can yell at me after they're safe."

We burst through the front doors, adrenaline thundering in my veins. Dario is already dialing again, jaw clenched, his phone pressed so tight to his ear it might crack.

"Still going to voicemail," he mutters. "Fuck."

I don't wait. I throw open the driver's side door and slide in like the car itself might explode if I don't move fast enough. Dario jumps into the passenger seat, still trying Ginny, his knuckles white.

I slam the car into gear. Tires screech, metal groans, and we rocket out of the parking lot like demons are riding the bumper.

I dial Tony. One ring. He answers.

"Yes, boss?"

"Something's wrong. Get inside—now. Find Maria and Ginny. I don't care what you have to break down or who you have to go through." My voice is ice and steel. "And whoever's responsible? I want them breathing when I get there."

"Yes, sir."

The line cuts.

I push the car harder, redlining every corner, weaving through traffic like the city owes me its roads. Horns blare. Lights blur. My pulse pounds against my ribs like a war drum.

Dario turns to me. "If she's hurt—"

"She won't be," I snap. But the fear is clawing up my throat like smoke in a burning house.

The penthouse isn't just a home. It's supposed to be a fortress.

But now it feels like a trap.

You promised me, amore—stay alive.

I grip the wheel tighter. *Just hold on.*

I'm coming for you.

And may God have mercy on the one who dared touch you—because I won't.

27

MARIA

The woman in front of me is wearing Emily's face—but there's a stranger staring back.

Her eyes don't blink. Her smile doesn't reach her soul.

And I finally understand—I was never safe here.

There's no trace of the kind, composed woman I once trusted.

Murder—that's what I see in her eyes now. Deranged. Focused.

The woman I once knew is gone. In her place stands something brittle and rabid—eyes wide, jaw clenched, teetering on the edge of madness.

She clutches the knife tightly in her hand, her knuckles white from the force of her grip. Her lips curl into a bitter smile, her breathing uneven.

"You were meant to be dead," she spits out through gritted teeth. "I gave you double the poison. Why didn't you die!"

My breath catches. Ginny clutches onto my hand tightly, and I feel the rush of blood move past my ears. My heart hammers hard in my chest, the adrenaline triggering my emergency response.

I swallow hard, taking a slow step back and pulling Ginny with me. "Emily, please… you don't have to do this. Just talk to me."

"No, we're past talking! You should've stayed gone!" She waves the knife and then points it right at me. "You need to leave so that I can keep him. Things were better when you weren't here. You were never supposed to come here, that wasn't the plan! Why didn't you die like her!"

My stomach turns. So it's true—every lingering look, every carefully placed lie—it was all her. She wanted me gone from the start.

Ginny shifts subtly in front of me, placing herself in Emily's line of sight.

"Emily, listen to me. You don't want to do this. This isn't you."

Her voice is calm, firm. But I see the tension in her jaw—she's gauging every twitch of that knife.

"Just put it down. We can walk away. No one else has to get hurt."

But Emily keeps going, her voice rising with every word, her eyes locked on me like I'm the only thing she sees. "Matteo was never meant for you. I was there before you. I took care of him, I understood him. And then you showed up, and suddenly, you matter?" She shakes her head violently.

"He looks at you like you're the only thing that exists. He touches you like he's forgotten everyone who came before." Her voice quivers, steeped in resentment. "You stole him."

"Emily, stop," Ginny cuts in. "You don't need to do this. Matteo doesn't love her. You were right all along."

Her tone is sharp and practiced. A lie, but a smart one.

Emily falters—just for a second.

I try to steady my breathing and keep my voice calm. Something within her snapped. I can see it from the deranged look in her eyes. All the sanity has left her, and all that remains is this crazy woman who seems in love with Matteo.

It all makes sense now. The way her eyes would linger on me. His mother's necklace that she insisted I wear. All this time, she has been trying to sabotage us. The lingerie, the dinner, she knew all those things would only make him push me away further. It's what she wanted.

"Emily, listen to me. You know Matteo doesn't love me. He is just pretending with me like he did the last time. None of it is real." I try to reason with her as I take another step back. Ginny and I are trapped in the sunken living area, and the only way to get out is to move toward her direction. "He doesn't love me, and I can't love a man like him."

I will need to play along with whatever narrative she has built in her head.

Her eyes snap to mine, dark and manic. "Oh, but he does. And that's the problem." She steps closer, waving the knife in the air. "He never loved Beatrice, not like the way he loves you. I saw it in his eyes. I saw the way he moves and gravitates toward you."

Out of the corner of my eye, I see Ginny scanning the room. Her gaze flickers—to the fireplace, the candlestick, the hallway beyond.

She's reading the space like a battlefield.

She's not just scared—she's calculating.

I freeze, my heart hammering. The longer we stay here, the more likely we are to be stabbed. I can't have survived her poisoning only to be met by her knife.

Emily tilts her head, her smile widening. "All I had to do

was wait. If you just died—like Beatrice—then everything would go back to the way it was supposed to be. He would fall in love with me again. I just needed him for one night, that's all. One night and I would fuck you right out of him."

A chill runs down my spine. She is demented. This woman is a literal psycho who has been right under my nose this entire time.

"But it's fine. I will kill you so he will come back to me."

This can't be how it ends—not after everything. Not here, not by her hand.

With a shrill cry, she lunges in our direction.

I barely have time to react. I drop Ginny's hand as Emily makes it over the couch and swings the knife around, trying to nick one of us. Ginny and I scatter in opposite directions, forcing Emily to hesitate as she decides whom to go after. Her wild eyes settle on me.

Of course.

She grips the knife tightly and charges again. I grab the first thing I can reach—a small side table—and shove it toward her. The force isn't enough to stop her completely, but it throws her off balance for a second. Just enough time for me to scramble toward the other side of the room.

"I am going to kill you, bitch!" she roars.

The words send a wave of cold terror through me, but I push it aside. I need to focus. I need to survive. Emily swings again, and this time, I don't have anywhere to run. I duck, the blade missing me by inches. The movement sends me crashing to the ground, and before I can get up, she's on me.

I barely catch her wrist before the knife plunges toward my chest. Her arms shake as I hold her back. I don't have my full strength back, but it's enough to keep her at bay.

"You ruined everything!" she hisses, pressing down with

more force. The blade inches closer. My arms burn with the effort of holding her back, but I won't let her win. I can't.

With a burst of desperation, I shift my weight and roll us over, knocking the knife from her grasp. It clatters to the floor, and before she can reach for it, I throw a punch, my fist connecting with her cheek.

She lets out a blood-rippling scream that pierces my eardrums.

I scramble up, my breaths ragged, limbs trembling with exhaustion. I glance around frantically—where is Ginny? My chest tightens. Did she make it out? I don't know. I don't have time to find out. Emily is already coming at me again, eyes wild, hands clawing for skin.

Before she can reach me, there's a sharp crack.

Emily's body goes rigid. Her eyes widen in shock before rolling back, and she collapses onto the floor, motionless. Ginny stands behind her unconscious body, holding a heavy brass candlestick, her breathing just as ragged as mine.

She meets my eyes, her face pale. "Dumb psycho bitch. Are you okay, M?"

For a moment, neither of us moves. Then I blink, my instincts returning to me. I lift my gaze from Emily and grab Ginny's hand.

"We need to get out of here," I whisper. "Tony should be just outside."

Ginny nods, her hand tightens around mine, and we take off for the door. The only thing I can think about is the promise I made to my husband before he left.

Stay alive... If I have only one reason to survive, then it will be him.

Ginny and I race to the door, our footsteps pounding against the marble floors of the penthouse. We rip the door open and see Tony already there with his weapon drawn. I let out a scream and move to the side.

Tony has his eyes set behind me, and he moves into the penthouse. "Boss is on the way, get out of here, Maria."

I don't need to be told twice. I race with Ginny down the hallway and toward the elevator. When the doors open, I am met with a pair of familiar eyes. Without a second thought, I launch myself at him, not sure how he got to me so quickly.

"Amore." Matteo buries his nose into the crook of my neck. "Are you okay?"

I don't speak. I simply allow him to hold me. My body trembles as the last of the adrenaline seeps away.

"Gin, I got your message." Dario is beside my husband, and he gathers his wife into his arms. "What the hell happened?"

I pull away from my husband, now noticing that he's holding the elevator door open. I walk out into the hallway, now feeling safe with him here. Tears brim in my eyes.

He always somehow makes it just in time to save the day. "You're here."

"I am." He cups the side of my face. "What the hell happened, Maria?"

I shake my head, not even knowing where to begin. "Emily... she was behind it. The poisoning. From the start."

I swallow hard. "And she... she said I was meant to die... like her."

A beat of silence.

Matteo stiffens. His breath hitches.

Then his whole body tenses, like a loaded gun cocked and ready.

His grip at my waist tightens—not to hurt, but to anchor. To keep himself from shattering.

"What did you just say?" he asks, quietly. Too quiet.

His jaw is clenched, stone-hard. A storm flickers behind his eyes.

"She said I was meant to die like Beatrice," I whisper again.

He exhales—slow and sharp. Fury coils around every line of his body.

Tony comes back, panting for breath. "Boss—she's gone."

"Gone?" Ginny and I say at the same time.

No, no, there is no way that she can be gone. I saw her unconscious body lying on the floor only seconds before he arrived.

"What?" Matteo's tone is ice-cold, but I can hear the fury brewing underneath it.

Tony shakes his head, almost like he too is in disbelief. "I searched the house. She's not there. I think she may have taken the secret elevator in the kitchen. There are no other exit points but the front door."

A shudder runs through me. The last thing I saw was her body hitting the ground. She should still be there. A part of me thinks I should've killed her. I should've taken the chance—ended it then and there.

But I'm not a killer.

Matteo exhales sharply, his jaw clenching. His grip on my waist tightens as if grounding himself. "Don't just stand there. Gather the fucking men and find her. I want eyes on every street, every alley. Lock this fucking city down. You find that bitch and you bring her to me alive. And get Valerio on this and debrief him. I need all hands on deck for this one."

Tony nods. "Yes, boss."

All this time, the snake was in our backyard, and we had no clue. She was the one who taught me how to get close to

Matteo. The one I confided in when the pain got too heavy. I thought she was my friend, but I was wrong.

Trust is a dangerous game in this world—and if today proved anything, it's that putting it in the wrong hands can get you killed.

I shake my head in complete and utter disbelief. "She said I was meant to die... like the one before me." I swallow hard, tears burning. "She killed her, Matteo. She killed her."

I don't realize I am crying until I taste the saltiness of the tears on my lips. As one tear falls, another comes in its place, and soon I am sobbing softly.

My husband pulls me closer into his chest. He soothes my back, holding me tight to his chest—and I cling to him like he's the only thing holding the world together. Because right now, he is.

28

MATTEO

Maria is wrapped in the sheets beside me, her breathing soft, steady. One of her hands rests near my chest, fingers slightly curled, as if even in sleep, she's reaching for me. I kiss the top of her head, and she stirs a little and moves in to capture more of my warmth. She sighs and settles back into her sleep.

After the debrief, I took her to our room and lay beside her until sleep finally took over. I held her while she stared at the windows that looked out to the skyline. She didn't speak. She didn't cry. She just allowed me to hold her.

She is struggling. I know that much. She trusted this woman, and I believe, to some extent, she was friends with Emily. It hurts to feel so betrayed by someone, to have them come into your life and then try to tear it all apart.

My blood seethes again as I think of the lengths Giacomo has gone to. He's the one who sent her—Emily. The woman I've known for years—the one Beatrice trusted and hired—is the one who did this. Not only did she kill Beatrice, but she tried to kill Maria.

There will be hell to pay for what she did.

I am livid. How could I have been so blind?

The conversation from earlier replays in my mind, vivid and sharp as a blade. I had stormed into the study, and Dario and Valerio were already there, grim-faced, waiting.

I had barely stepped two feet into the room when Dario grabbed me by the collar.

I remove his hand and shove him away. "Watch it, Dario. You're here because I let you be."

Dario has always been a hothead. "How the fuck do you let this happen? The help? Really, Matteo? You used to be more vigilant than this."

"Do you think that I don't know? This caught me off guard, but make no mistake—I will have her head on a silver platter."

"Not before I feed her to my dogs. The bitch pulled a knife on my wife. Someone will have to answer for that." Dario is fuming, and for good reason. His wife was also caught in the crossfire. "First, you have your Giacomo mess, and now this? What the fuck is going on in your life, Davacalli? Were they working together?"

"It can be assumed so," Valerio speaks up for the first time. "We went to her apartment, and we found some wire transfers on her computer from Giacomo."

The rage scorched my muscles. I feel it take over every inch of my body. I feel like I am seconds away from exploding, so much so that I feel the steam coming out of my ears.

"Beatrice..." Her name leaves my lips, and I go still.

Valerio looks at me solemnly. "He planned her death, Matteo. Everything seems to point to that. It all makes sense. He said he was going to take everything from you that you took from him. Beatrice and—" He cuts himself off before he can say my son's name.

Dario clicks his tongue on the roof of his mouth. "I know that he's not your son. Talk."

"What? How?" Valerio looks at Dario suspiciously.

"After you warned me about Giacomo and what he is peddling in the streets, I decided to do my due diligence. I uncovered a lot of shit that you all tried to keep hidden—like the fact that Beatrice was sold to Gia and you saved her from the abusive bastard and married her to place her under your protection."

"Well shit, can no one keep a secret these days?" Valerio throws his arms up dramatically. "I don't need to remind you that what you just said is extremely private information that should not be divulged to anyone, including your wife."

"She already knows; in fact, she is the one who made the deduction when she saw Giacomo at the gala. She said that you look nothing like your only heir, while Daniele carries very similar features to Giacomo and your wife." Dario looks at me like it's the most obvious deduction. To be fair, he isn't wrong. "The only question that remains right now is what the fuck are we going to do about this?"

"We?" I cross my arms over my chest.

"You are out of your depths here. Giacomo is unhinged and on a rampage for revenge. Now, with my wife taking a liking to yours; that means I have a vested interest in this because if your wife dies, mine will be sad, and I hate when my wife is sad."

I blink. "Charming."

Dario steps toward me, the tension in the room as thick as tar. "Look, Giacomo came after my wife today. I don't take lightly to her life being in danger, and I will make sure that he pays for what he did."

The silence stretches on. Neither Dario nor I blink as we stare each other down. We've never needed friendship to understand each other—but he's one of the few men I respect in this world.

"To war?" I hold my hand out to him.

He takes mine into his with a smirk playing on his lips. "To war."

The memory slips away, and I'm back in our room—back beside her.

But before the anger pushes me too far, I take one last look at the woman sleeping beside me.

Beatrice, my son, and now my wife. It has gone on for too long. Giacomo has taken things too far, and he will answer for this.

I have always been a cool and collected man, but right now, my mind is moving on pure instinct.

That is the only thing on my mind. I don't know exactly what my plan is, but I do know that it involves causing pain to Giacomo in some way, shape, or form.

I finally remove myself from under my wife. I can't stay when my blood is bubbling the way that it is. I have a thirst for blood—his blood—and my gun has been itching to be shot.

Carefully, I shift away, peeling her fingers from my skin one by one. She stirs slightly, murmuring something incoherent under her breath. Her features contort into a frown before they smooth, and she is back to sleeping peacefully.

I push back the covers and rise from the bed, moving through the room until I am at the door. I glance back one last time. She looks so peaceful in that bed, and I would do anything to not see her in pain the way she was when those elevator doors opened.

I tighten my jaw and force myself to step into the hallway, shutting the door softly behind me.

Two of my men are already standing post outside the bedroom. Tony is running point with Valerio. I need both of my finest at the forefront of this job. Their backs straighten as I approach, their hands hovering near their weapons.

"At ease. No one gets in or out," I say quietly. "Not until I return. And if anyone tries to force their way in, shoot first."

They exchange a quick look but don't question me. They have one task and one task alone—keep my wife safe.

Satisfied, I pull out my phone as I make my way downstairs, dialing Valerio. If I am going to do what I'm about to do, I need to at least alert my second just in case I don't make it back alive.

He picks up immediately. "Matteo?"

"I'm going to Giacomo's club." There is no need for pleasantries at 1:00 a.m.

He is quiet for a moment. I think that maybe he hung up. Then I hear some rustling before he speaks again. "Are you out of your goddamn mind? Are you high right now?"

"I need to do this. Emily likely reported back what she did, which means he likely expects me to try something tonight. He has been goading me into making a move for weeks now—well, here it is."

"Matteo, we spoke about this with Dario. We need to wait for the most opportune time. You can't just decide that you want to go rogue all of a sudden. We stick to the plan." Valerio is in a bit of a panic. "Fucking hell, don't let your heart make you reckless."

He is trying to be the voice of reason, and maybe that's why I called him. Maybe I want someone with logic to talk me out of this. The only problem is that my anger is louder than my logic. I won't be satisfied until he is bleeding at my feet.

"I will be at his club downtown. He won't kill me, I know he won't. This isn't about killing me; if he wanted to do that, he would have pulled the trigger. This is about making me suffer the way he believes I made him suffer."

Valerio curses under his breath. "Boss, listen to me—"

I hang up before he can say anything else. I already know this is reckless. But that doesn't matter. He's been waiting for me to break, to blink first. Well, here I am, motherfucker. Staring you down.

I storm out my door and make sure my gun is loaded. If tonight is the night I end it, then so be it. My phone buzzes in my pocket, but I ignore it. Valerio knows where I will be, and he will come. I know he will.

I DRIVE FOR TWENTY MINUTES, moving through the streets of New York like a man possessed. I park my Range Rover right out front, and when the guards see me, they aren't moved by my presence.

Of course not. He is expecting me. Normally, they would have jumped me at first sight. This is enemy territory, after all, and their motto is shoot to kill.

I walk to the door, and the bouncers don't even bat an eye. They open the door for me and let me in. They're not stupid—they know who I am.

The gentleman's club is exactly what I expected—loud, dimly lit, and a knock-off version of The Vortex. Pitiful. The man has the originality of a brain-dead vegetable. The scent of sex and whiskey clings to the air, masking the stench of blood and sweat beneath it.

As soon as I step inside, every set of eyes in the room snaps to me, a ripple of tension spreading through the space. Some recognize me instantly. Others glance toward the VIP section at the back, where Giacomo sits pretty, surrounded by half-naked women moving their bodies sensually to the music.

Giacomo raises his whiskey glass in the air and beckons me over. That little shit. The metal of the gun digs into my skin. I have an itch to reach for it, but not yet.

I walk straight toward the man I came for.

Giacomo sits at the head of a long, private booth, a cigar burning between his fingers.

"Matteo," he drawls, exhaling a stream of smoke. "Right on time."

I don't speak. I don't even fully think. I simply swing.

My fist crashes into his jaw with enough force to send him sprawling across the booth. His cigar tumbles to the floor, landing in a pile of spilled whiskey.

The room erupts into chaos.

Half a dozen men reach for their weapons, but before they can aim, Giacomo lifts a hand, blood dripping from his lip.

"Put them down," he orders, his voice eerily calm. "Nothing but a greeting between old pals. Isn't that right?"

They hesitate but obey.

He wipes the blood from his mouth and grins up at me, eyes gleaming with something dark, something twisted. "There he is. I was wondering when you'd finally show me your real face. Ladies, please make yourself scarce. I have a conversation to have with my friend over here."

The half-naked women leave the booth, and Giacomo and I are the only two left. The room is still filled with a heavy tension that doesn't seem to let up even as the seconds tick by.

My hands flex at my sides, my pulse pounding in my ears.

"You made a mistake coming here," he continues, shifting back into his seat as if he isn't still tasting blood. "Now, let's talk about how you are going to pay for what you've done."

I exhale sharply, rolling my shoulders. "I don't owe you a damn thing."

He lets out a low chuckle. "No?" He leans forward, his voice dropping. "You stole from me. My wife. My son."

My jaw tightens. "Beatrice ran from you. She hated your guts, and she sought to seek shelter. I never stole anything."

"No, Matteo. This is personal—between you and me. That bitch belonged to me, and I paid a hefty price for her. Then you go and take her away from me and raise my blood—my heir—as some kind of half-bred mutt. Cunt."

A muscle ticks in my jaw. His insults roll off me like water but if he mentions my son again, I am going to lose my shit.

Giacomo exhales, his smile fading. "Tell me, did you like my little surprise? It's unfortunate that Emily went a little rogue and fell for you. What she sees in you, I don't know."

"I didn't take you for a man who would send some pussy due to his dirty work." I am goading him. I want him to lose all sense and composure. The more unhinged he is, the better for me.

"Nice try, Matteo. But your playground tactics won't work on me, I'm afraid. Using Emily was one of the smartest things I have ever done. She was the enemy from within—the Trojan horse."

I grind my teeth together. But I don't speak because the truth of the matter is that he is right. She did slip through the cracks.

"Enjoy the time you have left with your wife, Davacalli. Because the pain I'm going to inflict on you—on her—will be glorious." His eyes gleam with quiet, terrifying promise. "Tell me, do you think she will ride my dick as well as she rides yours?"

I watch his eyes flick to my waistband, and I know instantly what he wants me to do. I won't give him the satisfaction. He knows I am carrying, and he wants me to pull the trigger.

This is all about whoever shoots first and ignites the war.

"You are going to die, Giacomo, and when you do, it will be at the mercy of my bullet." I turn and walk out, my hands still clenched into fists. I feel the eyes follow me as I exit out of the club.

The cool night air does nothing to calm the fury thrumming through my veins. My knuckles ache, the skin split and raw from the punch I landed on Giacomo. Not an ounce of satisfaction fills me.

I exhale sharply, running a hand through my hair just as a familiar voice calls out from behind me.

"Matteo."

I turn to see Valerio standing against my car, arms crossed, his expression unreadable. His gaze flickers to my bruised knuckles before meeting mine. He's pissed, I can see it but his body remains cool and collected.

"Do you feel better?"

"No." I walk toward the car. I come to a halt beside him and lean against it too. "The asshole somehow always seems to be two steps ahead every fucking time. He used Emily, Rio. Emily, of all people. He was able to get that close, and I... I couldn't do anything to stop him. If Ginny hadn't caught the poison in time... Maria could've been gone."

I didn't even want to think of what could have happened today.

"I know," is all he manages to say. Truthfully, there are no words that he can tell me to make any of this better.

"I should have killed him," I mutter. "I should have pulled the trigger and killed him."

Valerio exhales, shaking his head. "No, you shouldn't have." His voice is steady and holds the control I wish I had. "Not yet. We have a plan in place, and we just need to stick to it. I know it sucks that we have to wait, but patience is a virtue. You taught me that."

I don't argue, even though the need to spill blood is still clawing at my insides. He is right, and I am thankful that things didn't escalate beyond what happened.

"Go home to your wife, Matteo. She's been calling, asking for you." He pats my shoulder. "After today of all days, she will need you."

"She's awake?"

He nods. "She woke up just after you left and started calling. She's worried about you. Don't keep her waiting."

Crap. I sigh heavily and lean against the car even more. Yet again, I dropped the ball. She isn't meant to be awake. I don't want her to see me like this. Knowing her, she will try to take on my burden as her own.

Valerio studies me for a long moment, then tilts his head toward the car. "Go home, Matteo."

I don't need to be told twice.

By the time I step inside the house, the world is quiet again. But that doesn't mean I am. I walk up the stairs, my body aching in ways that have nothing to do with the fight and everything to do with the rage simmering inside me.

I pass the guards, and they greet me and remain on their posts.

When I push open the bedroom door, I find Maria sitting up in bed, her hazel eyes filled with something I don't deserve—concern.

"You're back," she murmurs, her gaze flickering to my hands. "Valerio told me what you were up to. First off, are you out of your mind? And second, don't vanish without telling me where you're going. You hate it when I go rogue, so don't think you get a free pass to do the same. I'm your wife, you need to tell me these things."

I exhale slowly, shutting the door behind me. "I'm sorry."

The apology has a double meaning. I am apologizing for what I did and leaving her after the kind of day she endured. But I am also seeking forgiveness for other things I fear she may never look past.

I sit on the edge of the bed, flexing my fingers, wincing at the pain shooting through them. Maria reaches for my hand carefully, her touch hesitant but gentle.

"You're hurt," she whispers.

"It's nothing."

"If you're bleeding, then it's not nothing. Let me see."

I watch as she studies the bruises, her fingers lightly tracing over the broken skin. She is soft, and her touch seems to offer me comfort that leaves my heart feeling warm. She creates this safe bubble where I am free to take off the armor I wear for the rest of the world.

She makes me feel safe and vulnerable. She makes it okay for me to let her see the things that pain me.

"Daniele isn't mine." The words come out rough,

weighted with something I can't quite name. It's the first time I am uttering the secret that only a handful of people know. A secret I promised to take with me to the grave.

Maria stills, her eyes snapping to mine. "What?"

I inhale deeply, finally saying the truth out loud. "Daniele isn't my son—not biologically."

She stares at me, waiting, letting me take my time. So I do. I mull over my words in my head and try to think of the best way to explain it to her.

"Beatrice was engaged to Giacomo before me," I continue, my voice quieter now. "He hurt her. He raped and abused her in the year leading up to their union. Her father had a debt he couldn't pay, and Giacomo opted for her as payment. She was already pregnant with Daniele when she begged me to take her away from him."

Maria's grip on my hand tightens slightly. "So you did."

I nod. "I married her to keep her safe. Giacomo lost his mind when he found out. He swore he'd kill me, swore he'd take them both back. And when he couldn't—when he failed—he blamed me for everything. This entire thing is happening because he wants revenge—on me. That's why he came after you."

Maria doesn't speak right away. Then, softly, she asks, "Did you love her?"

I stare at our joined hands, at the way hers fits so easily against mine. Like she is my perfect match in every way, and yet we are so vastly different—night and day.

"I did love her, so much," I say quietly. "In the only way I knew how, back then. I thought she was it for me—my first real connection, someone I wanted to protect. And I did. I protected her with everything I had."

I pause, searching Maria's eyes.

"But then she died... and I met you. And suddenly, I

realized what I felt before—it wasn't the kind of love that scorches through your veins and leaves nothing untouched. It wasn't the kind that consumes you, ruins you, and rebuilds you in its image. Not like this. Not like you."

I exhale, my voice rough. "You broke me open, Maria. You showed me what it means to love so deeply it hurts. What it means to be terrified of losing someone because your soul wouldn't survive it. What I feel for you... it rewrote everything I thought I knew."

I swallow hard.

"I cared for Beatrice. I did. But I've never loved anyone the way I love you."

Maria nods slowly, absorbing my words. "And Daniele?"

I exhale, running a hand down my face. "He was never mine. But I raised him like he was. I held him through every scraped knee, every sleepless night, every heartbreak. I taught him to walk, to fight, to stand tall. He may not be my son by blood, but he is my son in every way that matters. He was raised through my hands, he carries my name, my values—he is mine."

My throat tightens slightly. "And it will be a cold day in hell before I let Giacomo have him."

Maria looks at me for a long time, something shifting in her expression. Then she moves closer, her fingers sliding up my arm, over my shoulder. She doesn't say anything at all. Then she pulls me into her for a firm hug.

She just holds me. And for once, I let her, I allow her to hold the cracked pieces of me. I close my eyes, resting my forehead against hers, permitting myself a rare moment of stillness.

"I'm sure it wasn't easy to share that with me." She pulls away to look into my eyes. She presses her lips to mine briefly for a short peck. But that small kiss alone is enough to soothe many of the jagged edges in my heart.

At that moment, I make a vow that when this is all over, I will tell her about Antonio. After feeling the weight lift off my chest, I know that the right thing to do is to tell her. I just hope that when I do, she doesn't walk away. Because if she does... I'm not sure I'll survive it.

29

MARIA

The morning light filters through the curtains, casting a golden glow over the bedroom. But the warmth of it does nothing to chase away the heaviness in my chest.

I feel the absence of his warmth before I even open my eyes. Normally, his arm would be draped over me, pulling me into him. Slowly, I blink my eyes open, and when I do, I find him sitting at the edge of the bed, his back to me, his posture tense.

His bare shoulders rise and fall with a slow, measured breath, but I can feel the storm beneath his calm exterior.

Last night's conversation lingers between us. I still can't believe it. There were a million and one things that I was expecting to come out of his mouth, but not once did I think it would be *that*. But the longer I sit with the information, the more I see the connections.

I have only seen this man, Giacomo, once, and from what I remember, he has the same eyes as Daniele. They carry the same features, and it is almost uncanny how similar they are.

"Matteo." I sit up and stare at his back. "Matteo, come back to bed."

He looks over his shoulder at me, and then he turns back to the window. He places his elbows on his knees and sighs. "Go back to sleep, amore. It's early."

"I will... with you back in this bed with me."

He doesn't say anything. I can tell that his shoulders are weighed down by the weight reality carries. I hate seeing him like this. So lost, so vulnerable... so human. This man moves like he is invincible, but for the first time, I see him falter.

The sheets pool around my waist as I reach out and press a hand against his back. His muscles tense for a split second before he exhales, relaxing just slightly beneath my touch.

"You didn't sleep," I murmur. It's not a question. I felt him stirring the entire night.

Matteo turns his head slightly, but not enough for me to see his face. "I got enough sleep to make it through the day."

I hesitate, then run my fingers lightly along his spine. "Talk to me."

A bitter laugh escapes his lips, but it lacks humor. "You want me to tell you that everything will be fine?" He finally turns to look at me, his dark eyes filled with something unreadable. "Because I won't lie to you, amore mio. This war? It's going to be brutal, and there is a chance that we won't make it out the other side."

A shiver runs down my spine.

I swallow, pushing past the unease curling in my stomach. "Whatever's coming—I want to face it with you. I want to help. I know that I can't do much, but I want to be able to ease this burden you have chosen to carry on your own."

Matteo's expression shifts, something dangerous flashing in his gaze. "All you need to do is stay alive."

I sit up straighter. "You don't get to shut me out of this war. Not when it's coming for both of us."

His jaw tightens. "Maria—"

"No," I cut him off. "I'm done being kept in the dark. I'm done being the woman who sits at home, waiting to see if her husband will come back in one piece." I meet his gaze, unwavering. "Giacomo is coming after me. He wants to end my life, and that makes me a part of this. And as a part of this, it means I get to play a role in how we both save my life."

Matteo watches me carefully, his silence heavy.

Then, finally, he exhales, dragging a hand through his hair. "You don't know what you're getting yourself into, Maria."

"I don't care."

His dark eyes burn into mine, filled with something raw, something lethal.

"If I let you get too close, you could die. And if that happens—everything I'm fighting for would mean nothing."

"And if you go into this alone, you will die. So if you're stepping into the line of fire—I'm stepping with you."

"I can't lose you, Maria."

"Then don't make me watch you walk into hell without me. Because losing you would destroy me just the same."

Matteo studies me for a long moment, his sharp eyes scanning my face as if searching for hesitation, for fear. But he won't find either. I have already made up my mind. I know what I want, and I know who I want.

Finally, he exhales, running a hand down his face before he leans back against the headboard. His movements are slow, deliberate, and controlled, except for his hands. His fingers twitch slightly, like they want to curl into fists, but he's forcing himself to stay composed.

"There are ways and laws of how war is fought in this world. Giacomo knows that he can't just outright come and start a war with me. There needs to be grounds for it, or else the rest of the families will see him as a radical and look to try and end him."

This is all news to me.

"What he has done is grounds for me to retaliate. He came after you, and he has been deep within my territory," he says, his voice quieter now but no less dangerous. "The other families are waiting to see how it all unfolds. Some will side with us—the ones who know that Giacomo is a psychotic bastard. Some won't—those who want to see my empire crumble to the ground."

"And what happens if they don't choose a side and allow Giacomo to keep running a rampage?" I ask.

Matteo's jaw tightens. "Then the city will burn, and it could all be reduced to nothing but ash."

A cold chill runs through me, but I refuse to let it show. "And Daniele?"

Matteo lets out a low breath, shaking his head. "I have no idea where my son's head is. I have tried to speak with him but he doesn't want to speak with me. Giacomo has corrupted him and made him feel like he can't trust me— like he doesn't know me."

Even with Daniele having sided with his enemy, Matteo still speaks of him as his own. I can see the pain swimming in his eyes. I can hear the anguish laced in his words.

There is blood on the Davacalli name—even Faravelli blood. Could this be what he meant when he saw me that day? Is this what he had been trying to hint at all this time?

I hesitate, watching the way his expression hardens when he says it. "He will come to his senses eventually."

His dark gaze snaps to mine. "I don't know, amore. I know my son pretty well, and I feel as though he has made up his mind when it comes to this. I am the bad guy in this story. I don't know how much Giacomo told him of what he did to his mother, but I'm sure it wasn't the full truth." His voice lowers, dark and unforgiving.

I swallow, gripping the sheets beneath my fingers. "So you should tell him. As much as I think he feels betrayed and hurt to learn that you aren't his true blood, he should learn the kind of man you are. The man who took in a woman who was scared out of her mind and chose to raise a child who did not share an ounce of his DNA."

I don't know if my words ease anything within him. He remains rigid and stiff as a board.

Matteo turns so that the majority of his body is facing me. He cups the side of my face, and the pad of his thumb strokes my cheek. His touch leaves little hot trails of tingles up and down my cheek. I lean into his touch, and when I turn, I kiss the inside of his palm tenderly.

A weighted silence stretches between us.

I place my hand on top of his and grip his large one tighter. "You won't lose me, Matteo. I know you are scared, and you feel a little out of your depth. But you won't lose me, okay? We have come way too far to let things like this break us apart."

Matteo watches me. The shine in his eyes penetrates right through me, and I feel warmth spread throughout my body.

"You won't lose me," I reassure him again, wanting him to know that I am not going anywhere. I am here with him. I will move through the storm with him. "We will get through this. If war is where we have to be, then war we shall have."

The air sits softly with my confession that lingers in the air. I mean every single word that I utter.

"You," he murmurs, his voice rough, "are the one thing Giacomo won't take from me. I won't just kill for you, Maria. I'd suffer, crawl through fire, lose everything—die a thousand deaths—if it meant keeping you breathing."

"I'm not willing to lose you. We get out of this together, or not at all. I want to hold your hand at the end of it all." I pull his hand from my cheek and thread our fingers together. I kiss each one of his knuckles, and then I tuck our joined hands under my chin.

A slow, steady beat of silence passes between us.

It's not a shock that I am falling in love with this man. He has captured my heart and pulled me into his web, and now I can't get free. Not that I want to be freed.

I lean forward and press my lips to his. I moan into his mouth, and my muscles relax. Our tongues move in perfect sync. The familiar dance that only our tongues could understand continues. It's this ebb and flow of emotion that passes through our bodies and settles deep into the marrow of our bones.

Every time we collide, it's like this cosmic out-of-this-world experience.

When we break apart, I am left breathless. My chest heaves up and down as I try to bring more air into my lungs. I look up at him through my eyelashes and catch his heated stare.

"Shower?"

Blood rushes down to my core, and I smile, already knowing where this is heading. "Shower."

He gets up from the bed and pulls me toward the shower so we can get ready for this new day.

The water pours over our bodies, hot and unrelenting, but it's nothing compared to the heat between us. Our mouths collide like we're starved—tongues tangling, teeth grazing, lips swollen from the force of it. It's messy and intense, but it's ours. This is how we come together: fierce, raw, no holding back.

Every time he kisses me like this, it feels like the first time—and the last. Urgent. Desperate. Fated. It's not just lust, it's gravity. Matteo isn't just touching my body—he's claiming every inch of it.

The steam swirls thick around us, fogging the mirrors, clinging to our skin. It feels like we're suspended in another world. A private one, where nothing exists outside this shower but his breath against mine and the need spiraling through me like wildfire.

When he pulls back, I'm panting. My lips are tingling. His eyes are locked on mine, sharp and dark, but there's something softer buried beneath the heat—something that makes my knees weak.

"I'm starving," he murmurs, voice low and teasing. "Think I'll start with breakfast."

My brows furrow, breath hitching, but then—he sinks to his knees.

The cool tile presses against my back as he guides me gently, reverently, and something tightens in my chest. I'm already trembling, and he hasn't even touched me yet. He looks up at me like he's about to worship, not devour.

My thighs part slowly, deliberately. A silent offering.

"Tell me what you want, Maria," he says, voice like velvet dragging over steel.

I swallow. His voice makes my legs shake, my heart's racing, but it's not fear—it's anticipation. "Your mouth."

"Where?"

He kisses the inside of my thigh, soft and slow, like he has all the time in the world. Each kiss sends a pulse of heat straight between my legs, the ache building with every breath.

He trails higher, closer—until his lips hover just above my clit, teasing, cruel, deliberate.

"On my pussy," I whisper, already trembling, my voice cracking under the weight of need. "Please, Matteo."

"Good girl," he breathes. His hands grip my hips, strong and grounding. "Leg up."

He lifts my leg over his shoulder with ease, his eyes never leaving mine. Then his mouth finally covers my clit—and I shatter.

A sharp cry escapes me as he sucks hard, his tongue drawing lazy, controlled circles. He's not rushing. He's savoring. Drawing it out like he knows how close I already am.

My back arches off the wall. My hands find his hair, fingers tightening, anchoring me.

He groans into me, the vibration sending a fresh wave of heat spiraling through my core.

"You taste like sin," he growls into me. "The sweetest fucking sin."

I whimper as his tongue slides down to lap at my folds, slow and methodical. He works me like he's crafting a masterpiece. His beard is rough against my inner thighs, every graze of stubble adding another jolt of pleasure.

"You're so wet already," he murmurs. "All this for me?"

"Yes," I gasp. "Only you."

A finger slides inside me, then another. He pumps slow

and deep, curling his fingers just enough to make my knees buckle.

"Matteo, I—I can't—"

He rips his mouth away, licking his lips like he's drunk on me. "Yes, you can," he growls.

"Don't run from it," he says, dragging his tongue back up to flick over my clit. "Take it, Maria. Let go."

His fingers keep moving, his mouth never stops, and I'm unraveling. My breath comes in sharp bursts. I want to cry and scream and beg, all at once.

"Matteo—fuck—don't stop. Please don't stop."

He groans again, tongue working faster now, fingers pressing deep. My orgasm builds slowly, torturously, a wave that keeps climbing.

Then—

He sucks hard, just once, and the world explodes.

My body convulses. My head thumps against the tile. I cry out his name like it's the only word I've ever known. My legs shake around his shoulders, but he holds me through it —steady, relentless, insatiable.

Even after I come, he doesn't stop right away. He licks softly now, like he's easing me back to earth, and I can't tell if I want to push him away or beg for more.

When he finally pulls back, I can barely breathe. My body feels boneless. My skin is flushed and tingling.

He rises slowly, watching me like he's proud of what he's just done—and maybe a little smug.

"You're fucking divine," he murmurs, voice rough with arousal. His cock presses hard against my thigh, thick and aching. "Turn around."

I do, limbs shaking, and press my hands against the fogged-up glass. My breath leaves soft marks on the surface as I wait for him.

Then his body molds to mine, chest against my back, cock sliding through my folds.

"You want me?" he asks, dragging the head of his dick along my slit.

"Yes," I whisper. "God, yes."

"Then beg."

"Matteo, please. I need you inside me—I need all of you."

A rough growl escapes his throat. Then he slams into me.

I cry out, the stretch shocking and delicious. He doesn't wait—his thrusts are slow but deep, grinding, like he wants to carve himself into me inch by inch.

"You were made for me," he grits out, voice thick with need. "No one else could ever fuck you like this. Tell me who this belongs to. Say it," he growls.

"You," I gasp. "It's yours—it's always been yours."

His hand slides around to rub my clit again—small, punishing circles that make me see stars.

My second orgasm creeps up slower this time, but it's deeper, heavier. I can feel it in my spine, in my toes, in the way my walls clench around him like I'll never let him go.

"Come on, baby," he groans. "Show me how much you need me. Fuck me back," he pants. "I want to feel you take me. I want to feel you break."

I thrust into him, meeting every stroke, every slap of skin. "Harder," I cry. "Matteo, give me all of it!"

The pressure builds again. I'm right there, clenching around him, needing the release like air.

"Come for me," he hisses. "Come all over my cock, baby."

I break.

This one doesn't hit—it erupts. It crashes through me

like a second wave, even harder than the first. I can't breathe —I don't want to. I want to scream his name—my legs trembling, my body falling over the edge again. But I don't scream this time. I gasp. I whimper. It's too deep for words. My body tenses, then melts into his, like I'm dissolving around him. I don't feel the ground. I don't feel the water. I only feel him. And it's everything.

My vision blurs. My walls clamp down around him, and he groans like I'm pulling his soul out of his body. He follows with a shout, spilling inside me—thick and hot—as he thrusts one last time.

He gathers me close, our bodies still shaking in the aftermath.

When it's over, he pulls out slowly and turns me in his arms. His hand cups my cheek. His breath fans across my lips.

"You ruin me," he murmurs, eyes softer now. "And I love it."

His autumn eyes gleam, turning molten—more caramel than gold, like hot chocolate on the coldest winter day.

"Breakfast was amazing," he laughs and kisses me with a softness that I am quickly getting accustomed to. "We should have that every morning."

I laugh into his chest and reach up to press my lips to his. I want to live in this bubble forever. But the storm's still out there, brewing beyond these walls. But I know that whatever is coming, we will face it together.

Giacomo will not win, even if I have to pull the trigger myself.

30

MATTEO

A week has passed. The events of last week still haunt me, the ghosts of that night still whisper in my ear. I can't believe that I had been so blind.

The weight of the past days still lingers, but the storm inside me has calmed—at least on the surface. I know Maria can see the fractures beneath, the unspoken thoughts that keep me awake at night, but she doesn't push.

I am not a man who makes mistakes. My judgment and intuition have served me well for years. They have gotten me to this point in my life. So how did they fail me when it came to my wife's safety? How did I not see the signs?

I do my cufflinks up and look at myself in the mirror. The suit is perfectly tailored to my body. My hair is gelled back, and I am freshly shaven for the gala. My dark brown eyes are darkened with worry of what is to come next. The war's brewing in the background; I can feel it. All the other families are on high alert, waiting to see what happens next.

Tonight, I need to be seen. The gala is more than just an event, it's a message. I need to remind everyone in the room who I am. Word traveled fast about what happened to

Maria, and I know they are looking at me as weak. The great Matteo Davacalli hassled by a man who is meant to be more of a cockroach than an adversary. But that all ends tonight. They need to see my wife and I as a strong and unified front.

I am so lost in my own world that I don't hear Maria come up behind me. Her sweet scent of vanilla wafts into my nostrils, drawing me back to the closet.

"Are you okay?" She comes to stand beside me, looking like perfection.

Christo santo. Jesus Christ.

She is a vision. Her beauty surpasses any woman I have ever laid eyes on in my life.

She is dressed in emerald silk that drapes over her body like a second skin; she is a walking temptation, a carefully crafted weapon. The slit in her dress teases glimpses of smooth, golden skin, and her lips—painted in a soft, sinful red—dare me to claim them.

Something in the center of my chest stirs, and I have to push back the need to pin her against this glass and have my way with her. We won't ever leave our home if I indulge my greed.

"Yeah," I say through the lump that has formed in my throat. I turn, taking a step closer, trailing my fingers along the exposed skin of her back. She shivers, her breath catching for half a second before she composes herself.

I love the way her body always reacts to me. It fills me with pride to know that I am the only man who has ever made her feel like this. And that I am the only man who ever will.

The heat that passes from my hand to her back intensifies the hunger within me. My eyes swoop over her lightly done face. Her lips part ever so slightly as my hand moves lower to sit on the top curve of her ass.

"Amore," I murmur, my voice low.

She meets my gaze, her hazel eyes holding a flicker of amusement. "Matteo," she returns, tilting her head to the side.

I smirk. I love how free and comfortable she is with me now. After the hospital, I was unsure of how this would all play out. I didn't want her to question my intentions—to question my feelings for her. But as the days have passed, I can feel us just going from strength to strength.

"You look handsome."

"And you look ravishing." I dip my head low with every intention of connecting my lips to hers, but she presses her fingers to my lips.

"I have lipstick on, and I don't want it to smudge." She laughs when I lick her fingers, and she immediately retracts her hand. "Ew, Matteo. That's gross."

"You didn't think it was gross when you were choking on my cock this morning."

She blushes. "Please stop."

"Never." I give her ass a little light tap and she shakes her head with a blinding smile on her lips.

I pull her in so she is flush against me. I feel her warmth against mine, and the blood rushes down to my groin. When it comes to her, I am insatiable—I will never get enough of her.

"You look divine, amore." I kiss her cheek instead to save her lipstick from being ruined. I watch the blush deepen in her cheeks before she dips her head low. "This color is made for you."

She rolls her eyes at my playfulness. She's one of the few who can bring out this side of me—the one that doesn't live inside his burdens.

I let my hand linger on her back a moment longer,

savoring her warmth before stepping away. "We need to leave before I start to do the things my mind keeps thinking up."

She nods. "Yeah, we don't want to be late."

I offer her my hand, and she interlaces our fingers together. We walk out hand in hand into the shark-infested waters that are the gala. If this wasn't necessary, I'd have kept her far away. But certain things cannot be avoided in this world.

We walk into the grand hall arm in arm after a long drive from our building. My wife squeezes my arm tightly as all eyes move to us. The soft violins serve as backdrop music as the crowd becomes nothing more than hushed murmurs.

I look over the sea of people, making sure to eye every single one of the men who dared think me weak. I didn't get all the way to the top by simply lying down. If they've forgotten who I am, tonight will be their brutal reminder. My roots run deep in this city; I cannot easily be taken down.

"It's going to be a long night," my wife mutters as I usher her into the battleground.

"Stay close to me, and we will be fine." I move my eyes over the area. I catch a few stares, but the majority of people avert their eyes and look elsewhere. "Two hours tops, and then we leave."

"Okay." She steels her back. "I can do this."

Gold chandeliers cast a warm glow over the ballroom, illuminating the faces of politicians, businessmen, and criminals. I see Governor Raynes by the bar—a man whom I helped to fund his campaign. They move through the room with carefully rehearsed smiles, masking their true intentions beneath expensive suits and designer gowns.

The crowd parts like the Red Sea as we make our way to the bar. I hear the murmurs, and I feel the stares, but I hold my head high, and so does Maria.

"Maria!" Ginny's voice rings out, and within seconds, she's beside us, dressed in a crimson gown that screams confidence. Dario follows closely behind his wife. His expression is blank, but his eyes tell me that his mind is ticking away.

Ginny launches herself at my wife and envelops her into a tight hug. They both laugh, and when they pull apart, they wear matching smiles. It's nice to see that she and Maria have found friendship. After what happened with Emily, I was scared she would close herself off.

Ginny grins. "Oh my God, this dress is stunning on you. Emerald is definitely the color for you. Matteo, your wife is a vision—careful, or the vultures might start circling."

I scoff. "I would love to see them try."

Ginny rolls her eyes. "How romantic. Have I ever told you what a walking cliché you are? You remind me of my husband. Brooding, silent, and rich."

I quirk my eyebrow at her. "Funny."

"It's a joke, Matteo." My wife laughs and presses her hand on my chest. The small gesture is enough to temper my hardness. I have been on edge since the moment we walked in here. "Smile, my love."

"No." I grab her waist and pull her in closer to my side. I press my lips on the side of her head and give her a slight squeeze. Having her near me helps to dull the sharpness in my chest. "Dario, I see you're well."

"Well enough." Dario then moves his eyes to my wife. Surprisingly, there is a softness when he addresses her.

"How are you, Maria? The last time we saw each other... things were pretty rough."

Maria leans into me, her hand coming to rest on my chest. "I'm doing well, thank you. A lot better, actually."

An awkward silence passes between us, but Ginny quickly fills it with a story about their vacation to Jamaica last week. After the incident, Dario thought it would be good for her to get out of the country for some time.

He was right. Ginny looks lighter now. The day of the Emily incident, Ginny had put on a brave face, but I knew better. She was hiding her true emotions for the sake of my wife. And for that I will be grateful.

"...the beaches were to die for. We need to visit together, Maria. You will love the..."

And then I hear it—a laugh I know too well. My head snaps to the left, and there he is.

Daniele.

He's leaning against the bar, a whiskey glass dangling from his fingertips, his tie undone, his body language radiating 'fuck off' energy. His usual sharpness is dulled, his gaze heavy with intoxication.

Great. He's drunk. My son has officially gone off the rails.

Maria senses my tenseness and she follows my eye line. Her muscles go rigid against my body as she sees my son. I know how she feels about the current situation, and she is wary.

The fibers in my arm twitch, and my jaw locks in place. I watch as he brings the glass to his lips and takes a long swig of the brown liquor. He slams the glass back onto the bar and points to the bartender to give him another.

"For fuck's sake." I need to get over there.

"Whatever you do, be calm, Matteo." Maria tries to ease

my irritation, but it doesn't work this time. "He is your son, but he is working with Giacomo."

"I know."

Dario and Ginny both turn to look where we're staring. I can feel the strain in the air, like it has teeth. I feel Dario's eyes but I don't dare look his way. I already know the judgment waiting there.

I release Maria with a murmured, "Excuse me."

I only make it three steps before my wife's hand grabs mine. I look back at her worried expression. Her eyes dart from Daniele to me and then back again.

"Matteo..." The plea in her voice is evident.

"It will be fine, amore. I just want to talk to him, like you said I should. I will be calm, I promise."

She seems unsure, but she still drops my hand and allows me to make my way to my son. I have not seen this boy in weeks. And within that time frame, he somehow managed to plant doubt in Maria's head.

I come up beside him and lean my elbows on the counter. At first, I want to come in guns blazing and drill into him for being so stupid, but my wife's voice rings in my mind like my conscience telling me to keep things in check.

The boy reeks of whiskey and cigars.

"Daniele."

He doesn't acknowledge me at first. Just tips his glass back, draining the last of his drink before setting it down and looking to get another. He drank two in the five minutes it took me to walk over here.

"I see you're doing well," I say, my tone carefully neutral. Daniele is like a bomb. One snip on the wrong wire and he'll blow. I need to proceed with caution.

Daniele lets out a sharp, humorless laugh. "I see they let

the trash in again—I had hoped that a bullet would find its way into your chest by now, Papá."

I hear a gasp from nearby, and several people turn their heads to us, but no one intervenes.

"You're drunk," I state, eyeing the way he sways slightly as he reaches for another glass. I grab it before he can get hold of it. "Give him another and I will have your hands sliced clean off."

The bartender's eyes widen, and he nods frantically before taking the glass from my hand and walking away.

Daniele clicks his tongue on the roof of his mouth. "You ruin all my fun, Matteo. Surely you have better things to be doing than bothering me. How about killing more of your in-laws?"

I step closer, looking around to see if anyone has heard his words. "I think you have gone a step too far, son."

Daniele rolls his eyes, his breath fanning my face as he straightens to look me dead in the eyes. "And what are you going to do about it, Davacalli?"

I keep my expression unreadable. "I'm still your father. And I always will be."

Daniele's smirk is slow, bitter. He lowers his voice just enough for only me to hear. "Are you, though? The last I checked, we don't share an ounce of DNA." He tilts his head to the side. He looks me up and down in disgust. "You are nothing to me, Matteo. Not anymore."

Everything inside me turns to ice. My heart clenches at his words, and I feel the guilt slowly creep out from beneath the surface. I don't move, don't react, but the toxic concoction of rage and pain fills my system. It sears through my veins and scorches every part of me.

I see the way he watches me—waiting to see if I'll snap. He's testing me. Pushing me. And it takes everything in me not to wrap my hand around his throat. But then there is another part of me that wants to pull him to my chest and remind him that he is my son—blood or not.

"Tell me, Papá, how well does your new bitch fuck? I should have taken her for a test drive before I left Italy; that body of hers is enough to make a man weak in his knees."

"Daniele." My blood rises in temperature. "Watch yourself."

"Or what?" Daniele shoves me back, but I only stumble a few steps. The little jab is enough to earn us more eyes.

Before I can do anything, Dario is suddenly between us, a firm hand pressing against my chest. He gives me an eye, telling me that I need to keep my emotions in check.

"Oh, goody, the class monitor is here to save the day," Daniele mocks. "Dario, I see you have decided to side with the scum of the earth."

"Enough," Dario says, his voice calm but edged with warning. "Daniele, I suggest you walk away before things turn ugly for you. Your father may not want to ram your head in due to his love for you, but I am not your father and will level you where you stand."

Daniele smirks like he's won something. He takes a slow step back before he does a dramatic bow. "Enjoy the gala, Don Davacalli. I would watch your step these days, though. People are feeling a little trigger-happy lately—me, to name one. It would be a shame if one of my bullets found its way into you or your wife."

I let out a low warning growl.

Daniele's smirk deepens. "I will be seeing you very soon, Davacalli."

I watch my son walk away from us. With each step he takes, I feel the heaviness in my chest cement itself further.

My fists clench at my sides, and then I move my gaze to Dario. "Thank you."

"I think it would be better that you don't get into a fist-fight with your son in the middle of this shitshow of an event." Dario pats my shoulder. "We do need to speak about something, though."

Immediately, I am on high alert again. "What?"

Dario watches me for a long moment before shaking his head. "Not here. Come."

I look back to try and find my wife.

"Maria will be fine. She has Ginny, and I have guards posted all over here," Dario reassured me. "This can't wait."

I take his word for it and follow him out of the ballroom. We make our way to a terrace, the chill of the New York air whipping against my skin. But the cold does give me some relief from the tension riddling my body.

Dario rubs a hand down his face. "Emily's been spotted."

"Where?"

"New Jersey," he says. "She was moving with someone called Blade, a glorified henchman. He has ties to the Russian Bratva and Giacomo."

"Fuck. Do we have an exact location of where she is? An address? She could be on the next plane out of the country for all we know."

"I've kept my eyes on her. If she so much as breathes, I will know about it," he tries to assure me. "We need to keep her alive for now; her time will come. The first one we need to go after is Giacomo."

We exchange a look, one that says more than words ever could. We both want to put the bastard down once and for all. He came for our women and threatened their lives. No one does that and lives to tell the tale.

"We're going after his trafficking ring," Dario says. "We

burn it down. Every contact, every operation. We make it impossible for him to do business and cripple him. Like we discussed earlier with Valerio. We now have an exact docking date."

I nod once.

"The only concern we will have is your son." Dario holds my gaze. "When it comes to it, Matteo, you will likely be on opposite sides with him. Meaning his gun will be pointed right at your head."

That is something I am unwilling to accept. I will bring sense back into my son, even if it is the last thing I do.

"I will handle my son, Dario."

His eyes tell me that he doesn't believe me, but he doesn't voice his opinions, thankfully. I am in no mood to get into it with anyone else tonight. War is on the horizon, and we need to all be ready.

We'll strike first. And this time, we finish it.

31

MARIA

"They are fine," Ginny gives my arm a reassuring squeeze. "You don't need to worry."

"What if something is wrong?" I hold onto my flute tightly. "Maybe I should check on him."

I start to take a step, but Ginny pulls me back. "Maria, I love you, but there's nothing you can do to stop them if they're in some kind of standoff."

She's right.

Matteo and Dario walked out of the ballroom almost twenty minutes ago, and they have not returned. Daniele had also done his own disappearing act, blending into the sea of people without a trace. I wanted to speak with him, hoping to reason some sanity back into him.

"Here," she takes my flute from my hand, "let me get you another one."

I don't need one, but I let her go to the bar. I stand at the edge of the ballroom, watching the people milling around and mingling. It's so strange to see criminals, politicians, and mafia bosses all moving within the same space. But I guess they all have one thing in common—the greed for power.

It's all a game to them. Seeing who can overpower who to get to the very top. They all want to sit at the high table, but very few manage to make it there.

I bite down on my lip and look at the door where Matteo walked out. Where is he?

I'm so lost in thoughts of my husband that I don't notice *him* until he's right beside me—and a chill runs down my spine.

"My, my. Don't you look ravishing, Mrs. Davacalli?" His chilling voice reaches my ears, and I whip to the side so fast I lose my footing.

His hand darts out, grabbing my elbow to steady me. "Careful now, wouldn't want you to break something."

"Giacomo," I say his name under my breath as if it is a name that should not be uttered. "Let go of me."

I rip my arm from his hold and step back. I glare at him, wishing my glare could melt him with the heat radiating from my pupils.

"So rude." He presses a hand over his chest, feigning offense. "No, thank you. A lady of status should know manners."

I don't speak. I simply stand there, toe to toe with the monster trying to take down my husband and have me killed.

"You look lovely tonight, cara mia."

"Fuck off, Giacomo." I apply as much venom to my words. "I'm sure you're aware that my husband is here. It's best you walk away before he comes back."

"Then he never should've left you unattended in the first place." He places his hands in his pockets. "Sharks lurk around every corner." His eyes dance over my body in a rather provocative way.

"Walk away," I murmur, keeping my voice steady.

Giacomo chuckles, the sound low and amused. "Now, now, is that any way to treat your elders? Remind me again, how old are you?"

I scoff. "Go to hell."

"Can I take you with me?" He's like a mosquito—persistent and poisonous.

I hold steady. Where the hell Ginny has gone? I know Giacomo won't try anything with me here, but still, being this close to him sends me over the edge.

The violinists change their tune to a waltz piece, and the dance floor fills with various couples moving to the soft melody.

His eyes gleam with something unreadable. "May I have this dance?"

I shake my head. "Not a chance."

Giacomo tuts under his breath. "I insist."

Before I can react, he reaches out, his fingers curling around my wrist—not tight enough to hurt, but firm enough that resistance is useless. He pulls me toward the dance floor, leading me effortlessly into a waltz before I can even protest.

He places my free hand on his shoulder, and I give in and accept the dance. I could easily scream bloody murder, but I am aware of what tonight is for. Matteo and I are meant to be putting up a front of an unshakeable partnership. I need to exude the role of the strong and capable wife.

The room spins slightly as I move with him, my heartbeat thrumming in my ears. Every so often, my eyes dart around the room in search of my husband.

Where are you, Matteo?

"You're tense," he observes, his voice smooth. "Relax, Maria. People are watching."

I grit my teeth. Bastard.

I force my body to move with his, keeping my expression neutral. I won't give him the satisfaction of rattling me.

The music swells, and Giacomo's grip tightens slightly as he leans in. "Tell me something," he muses. "Are you happy, cara?"

I stiffen. "Excuse me?"

"In your marriage," he clarifies, his lips curling into something dangerously close to mockery. "Is Matteo everything you dreamed he would be?"

I don't answer.

He tilts his head slightly, his voice dropping into something lower, more cryptic. "You know, it's quite pathetic—the way he plays the devoted husband now."

His thumb brushes the back of my hand. "Almost makes you forget what kind of man he really is."

I swallow hard, keeping my expression unreadable. "My marriage is none of your business."

"Oh, on the contrary, I think it is." He shoots me a wicked grin. "I was shocked to learn that he was in search of a new bride for his—oh, excuse me—my son. Only to be even more shocked when I learned that *he* married you instead."

"What point are you trying to get to, Giacomo?" My voice exudes the confidence I don't have.

Giacomo chuckles under his breath. "I see you are an impatient one. But do you ever wonder why Davacalli—arguably one of the most influential crime bosses in the state—would want to align himself with your family? No offense, of course. But you had nothing to offer him that he didn't already have. So why, oh why, would he arrange a marriage?"

I clench my jaw. I don't want to admit it out loud, but these questions did play in my head in the very beginning. "I know exactly why he married me."

"Do you?" His voice is a taunt now, curling around me like smoke. "Because from where I'm standing, it looks like a man trying to bury his guilt."

I keep moving, keep swaying to the music, but his words sink their claws into me.

He watches my expression carefully, reading every flicker of emotion I try to hide. "You're smart, Maria. Surely, you've asked yourself why Matteo was so adamant about making this marriage happen. The man needed nothing from you— fuck, with the kind of wealth he's sitting on, he could have any woman he wants. So why you? Why your family?"

I want to shove him away. I want to turn and walk off this dance floor and pretend none of this is happening. But I don't. Because he's not finished yet. His grip on me tightens, and he pushes me into his body.

Giacomo's smirk deepens as he reaches into the inner pocket of his suit jacket. "Consider this a wedding gift," he murmurs, bringing his lips right to my ear. He slips something cold and hard into my palm.

A flash drive.

My pulse spikes as my fingers curl around it.

"I think this will answer all the questions that you just can't seem to figure out."

A sharp breath leaves me. I stop moving. My body locks in place.

Giacomo pulls back slightly, his eyes filled with something sinister. "Be careful who you lie with, cara mia. You could be sleeping with the devil and not even know it."

His eyes flick over my shoulder before cutting back to me. "Looks like our dance is over. Until next time, Mrs. Davacalli."

And then he releases me, stepping away as if nothing happened. The music continues, the world moves around me, but I can't move. My feet feel rooted to the dance floor, my fingers gripping the small device as if it might disappear.

My heart pounds, my mind racing with the weight of what just happened. His words play in my head over and over again like a broken record.

I don't even register Matteo's approach until his voice cuts through the fog.

"Maria."

I blink, my head snapping up to meet his gaze. His expression shifts instantly—his sharp eyes scanning my face, reading the tension in my body.

He steps closer, lowering his voice. "Are you okay? What did he want?"

I swallow the lump in my throat, forcing myself to school my expression. "Nothing. He was just being weird and trying to get in my head."

His jaw tightens, but then, when his eyes take in my face, his gaze softens. "You look pale. Are you sure you're okay?"

"I'm fine," I lie smoothly, slipping the flash drive into the folds of my dress. "It's just been a long night. And Giacomo showing up just bubbled up some not-so-great memories."

Matteo doesn't look convinced. His fingers brush against my elbow, grounding me. "Come."

He leads me off the dance floor, toward a quieter corner of the ballroom. The moment we stop, he turns to me fully, his hands on my waist. "Tell me."

I shake my head. "There's nothing to tell."

Matteo exhales sharply, his grip tightening. "Maria, I need to know if—"

"I said I'm fine, Matteo." My voice is sharper than I intended, but I can't afford for him to see through me right now. Not when my thoughts are still tangled in Giacomo's words.

Matteo studies me for a long moment, his expression unreadable. Then, finally, he lets out a slow breath, running a hand through his hair. "I will not fail you."

I blink. "What?"

He steps closer, his voice lower, rougher. "I failed once. I won't fail again. With Emily... I should've seen it coming."

He meets my eyes, unwavering. "I know you said you're fine—that you're all right—but I'm your husband. My first duty is to protect you. And I won't let you walk into danger ever again."

I stare at him, my chest tightening. There's something raw in his expression—something that makes my heart ache.

I exhale, forcing a small smile. "You won't."

He watches me for a moment longer before nodding slightly. And just like that, the moment passes.

"Let's go home." He presses his lips against my forehead in the sweetest of gestures. "I think we proved our point being here. Dario and Ginny are leaving, too."

Matteo leads me out of the gala, his hand firm on my lower back as we move through the crowd. The weight of the evening settles over me as we step into the car, the city lights flickering past the tinted windows.

But my thoughts are somewhere else. Giacomo's words echo in my mind.

Be careful who you lie with.

I stare at the flash drive resting in my palm, my fingers curling tighter around it. I'm unsure if I'm more afraid of what's on it or what it might change. Caught between the urge to destroy it and the need to know what it's hiding.

The question is: Am I ready for what's inside—and will I ever be? And once I see it, could it change everything I've come to know and love about the man sitting beside me?

32

MATTEO

Something is off. I can feel it in my chest. My wife has been...different these past few days. After the gala, I noticed a shift in her behavior. She tells me she's fine, but I know her better than most—and I can feel that she's not. Something's on her mind—and every instinct points to Giacomo. The thorn that never stops digging deeper.

"I'm sure you're overthinking it." Valerio sits on the opposite side of my desk sipping a coffee. "Maybe she is just shaken up by what happened and then seeing Giacomo. Her head is probably all the way fucked."

I shake my head and lean further into my chair. "No, it's not that. She would tell me if it was. There is something else."

"Maybe—but until she does, there's no use worrying yourself over it. Just be there for her. Focus on what's in front of you." He sets his mug down and throws me the file he walked in with. "We know when the next shipment is for his trafficking ring. They are coming in from Western Africa, about fifty women—ten of them underage."

My lips curl up in disgust. "That ass has no moral code."

The men in this industry are far from saints, but we live by a code. We stand by the rules set out in order to keep all of us in check and from turning into absolute devils. The first and most important rule is that we don't touch women or children.

"He will be gone soon enough." Valerio adds, "We should have it intercepted by midnight before the ship officially docks. Dario lent us some of his men to make the bust."

I nod. "Never in my years did I think that I would ever align myself with Dario, of all people."

"Life has a crazy way of bringing the most unlikely people together. But we need to stay on high alert. I added three more guards to the penthouse, as you requested. We don't need another person slipping through the cracks."

I open my mouth to respond, but the shouting from outside stops me.

"You can't go in there, he's in a meeting!" I hear my receptionist call. "Please, just wait—"

Then the door swings open without warning. Valerio looks over his shoulder, and we both look to the only one who could make it into this building without issue.

Daniele.

"I am so sorry, sir," my secretary says. "I tried to stop him, but he—"

I raise my hand in the air to stop her. "It's all right. You can leave us."

She bites down on her lip, looking like a scared pup. She nods and closes the door as she steps out, leaving me with my son and Valerio. The tension in the air is thick and fills the gap that sits between us.

"Daniele," I say. "To what do I owe the pleasure?"

Daniele doesn't speak, he looks between Valerio and me. "Can't a son come and spend time with his own father?"

"Oh, I'm your father again?"

"No." His fists curl tightly at his sides, shoulders twitching like he's barely holding it together. His shirt is half-untucked, wrinkled like he slept in it, and there's a faint tremor in his hands—whether from anger or lack of sleep, I can't tell. Dark shadows bruise the skin beneath his bloodshot eyes, and a faint sheen of sweat clings to his brow despite the cool air of the room. "Leave, Valerio. This is a family affair."

"Nice to see you too, dear nephew. How have you been? Me? I have been fine." Valerio picks up his mug again and tips in the direction of my son. "Where are your manners, child?"

"I am not a boy. And I need you out, I have much to discuss with Mr. Davacalli." Daniele steps into the office. "I'm sure there is some errand you can go do. How about picking up my stepmom's dry cleaning?"

"Why, you—"

"Valerio, it's okay. Leave us. I need a word with my son."

Valerio looks like he wants to argue, but he nods and gets up from his chair. "I will handle our issue. Call if you need me, boss."

Valerio walks to the door but not before bumping shoulders with Daniele. The two make a show of sizing each other up before he walks out of the office.

Daniele stands in front of me, his jaw clenched so tightly it looks like it might snap. His suit hangs off him like an afterthought, tie undone and collar askew, as if getting dressed was a battle he barely won. His expression is a storm I can't name—rage, pain, maybe both—but whatever it is, it's brewing fast.

We haven't spoken to each other properly in weeks. It has been hatred-filled stares and almost-brawls every time we have come in contact. This time, I'm hoping we can be a little more productive.

"I fucking hate you," he says. "I really fucking hate you, Matteo Davacalli."

The words cut through me like a blade. I don't react. I don't let it show. Instead, I just hold my nerve, and I hold his stare.

Ticking bomb... ticking bomb...

I need to handle this with care. I need to choose my words carefully and try to bridge this gap between us.

Instead, I exhale slowly, placing my pen down with precision. "Son, I want you to know how deeply sorry I am that I had to lie to you. It was never my intention to hurt you."

Daniele lets out a sharp, bitter laugh. "Hurt me? You didn't hurt me, Matteo. You awakened me to who I truly am. You showed me my true birthright—my true bloodline."

My stomach turns.

I rise slowly, rounding the desk to stand in front of him. "Daniele, whatever Giacomo is feeding you, he is lying. He cannot be trusted. The man is a fraud and a psychopath."

His nostrils flare. "No, he's not. He told me everything. Everything!"

His neck flushes crimson, the veins in his temple bulging as rage blazes through his eyes.

"You killed my mother. That poison story? A lie. She wanted to go back to him—and you stopped her. Because you needed to control her."

The air leaves my lungs. The world tilts for a split second, like the floor's been yanked from beneath me.

My breath catches.

I take a step forward, my voice low, disbelieving. "What did you just say?"

Daniele stalks forward. "I know what you did. He showed me the true toxicology report. She died of an overdose—it was never poison."

Damn you, Giacomo.

He's been poisoning the boy's mind—feeding him lies like scripture.

No wonder he looks cracked at the seams—like he's barely holding himself together.

He truly believes I killed his mother.

The woman I once loved.

I grit my teeth. "I would never hurt Beatrice, and you know that. I loved your mother."

"Liar!" he roars.

"Daniele, calm yourself." I watch his movements carefully. I can't see a weapon on him, and that gives me some relief. "I am telling you the truth, I would never have hurt your mother. How could I? She gave me one of the greatest gifts in my life—you."

Daniele steps closer, his eyes burning into mine. "You took her away from him. You took her—and when she finally wanted out, she died. And you think I'm just supposed to believe that was a coincidence?"

His voice shakes now, fury laced with something more fragile. "She was trying to tell me something. I could see it in her eyes that night—like the truth was clawing at her throat. But she was scared. Of what, I don't know. Of you? Of him? Of both of you?"

He presses a trembling hand to his chest. "And then the next morning... she was gone. Just like that."

His jaw clenches, but his eyes are wild, haunted. "I've played that night over and over in my head, trying to figure out what I missed. What I didn't see. And now I know—she was silenced."

I stare at him, my pulse hammering beneath the surface. "That's not what happened."

"Then tell me, what happened?" His voice cracks slightly, the pain beneath his fury bleeding through. "Because I spent my whole life wondering why I never felt like I belonged. Why I always felt... out of step with you."

I clench my fists at my sides. "I raised you as my own. I watched you take your first breath, first steps. I am the one who taught you how to hold a gun. Yes, we may not be blood. But you are my son. My. Son."

"You lied to me—pretending I was your own." His chest rises and falls with ragged breaths. "All my life, I was the shadow of something you didn't want to claim. The son you tolerated because you had to."

My stomach twists violently. "That's not true. I love you, Daniele."

Daniele lets out another sharp laugh, but it's hollow. Empty. His voice lowers into something more venomous. "Isn't it? You never looked at me the way a father looks at his son. I saw it in your eyes—pity, obligation. And now I know why."

I take a step forward, holding my hands out to show him I'm not a threat. "That's not true, and you know that. He's been feeding you poison and trying to fully turn you. I am your dad, Daniele. I gave you your name. I love you, and I loved your mother with everything I had inside of me."

Something inside me fractures. The silence between us

stretches, heavy with words neither of us can take back. Then, Daniele exhales, his expression hardening into something distant. Something unreadable.

"For the rest of my life," he says, voice like stone, "I will hate you."

I inhale sharply, my chest tightening. "If you hate me so much as you claim to, Daniele, why are you here? Why are you standing in this office with no weapon on you, only your anger?" No gun. No backup. Just fury and grief. That tells me everything.

Silence. He stands there with tension riddled all over his body.

"Because you don't actually hate me, do you?" I move closer toward him, but only by a step. "You're angry. Your mind is confused, and your heart hurts, and you are trying to make sense of the truth.

"You want the truth? Fine. Here it is. Your mother was never supposed to be with Giacomo. She was sold to him—given away by her father like property to pay off a debt. He was cruel from the beginning, but over the years, he became something worse. A monster. He beat her, broke her spirit, and treated her like she was nothing. I saw the bruises, Daniele. I saw the terror in her eyes. I was the one who found her unconscious—bleeding on the cold tiles of a bathroom floor after he'd nearly killed her.

"That was the night everything changed. She was pregnant with you. And she knew… she knew if she didn't escape, he would destroy both of you. So she ran. To me. For safety. For salvation. And I took her in. I gave her my name. My home. I married her not because I had to, but because I loved her. And we raised you together, as our son. We were a family, Daniele. A real one. And we were happy—until now."

He takes a sharp step back, shaking his head. "Stop. Just stop. I've heard enough of your fucking lies, Matteo. You think you can rewrite the past to make yourself the hero? Save it. I'm done listening to your bullshit.

"They aren't lies. And you know they aren't." I step closer, but he takes two steps back again. "I am sorry if I ever made you feel like you were never good enough for me, Danny boy. You are my world, and you always will be."

The silence that stretches between us is loud. I want to reach for him and hold him to my chest the same way I did when he was just a boy. But I hold myself.

The ball is in his court now.

"Fuck you and fuck your stupid empire that meant more to you than me." He turns on his heels sharply and walks out, leaving nothing behind but the wreckage of everything I tried to hold onto.

For the first time in a long time, I feel something I cannot control.

Loss.

And worse than that—

Defeat.

The door slams shut behind him. The silence that follows is unbearable. I stand there, unmoving, staring at the space Daniele just occupied, his words still ringing in my ears like gunfire.

"For the rest of my life, I will hate you."

I press my fingertips against my temple. Control. Breathe. But it's useless. The tension in my chest is unbearable, pressing down like a vice, suffocating me in ways I refuse to name.

Daniele is my son. My son.

Not by blood. But by something far greater.

And yet, he looks at me as if I'm nothing to him. As if the

years I spent raising him, protecting him, guiding him, none of it ever mattered. I should be furious. I should get up, go after him, shake him by the shoulders until he sees the truth. Until he sees me.

Giacomo.

He's poisoned my son's mind, twisted his grief into something sharp enough to drive straight into my chest. And Daniele—angry, lost Daniele—has swallowed every lie whole.

You never looked at me the way a father looks at his son.

I am reminded of how Beatrice never wanted him to know the truth of his paternity. She wanted him to know only me as his father. I promised her that I would keep this secret, and now I've failed her, too.

How the fuck do I fix this?

Daniele isn't a child anymore. He's a grown man, one who has been made to believe that his entire life was built on a foundation of lies. And the worst part? He's not entirely wrong.

I should have told him the truth—I should have gone against Beatrice's wishes and jumped the gun. Maybe then Giacomo wouldn't have had the ammunition to turn him against me.

"Fuck." The curse is felt right down to the very depths of my soul.

A knock sounds at the door.

I already know who it is.

"Come in."

Valerio steps inside, his usual smirk absent. His sharp blue eyes scan me. He exhales, shutting the door behind him.

"Well, that went about as well as we knew it would." He sighs heavily. "I'm sorry, boss."

Valerio comes to stand beside me. "I think if we kidnap him and lock him up and starve him a little, he will come out right. We could add in a good spanking or two."

I let out a breath that's almost a laugh. Almost.

"This isn't a joke."

Valerio shrugs. "Didn't say it was. I'm entirely serious. What did he say?"

"He hates me."

Valerio exhales sharply, running a hand through his hair. "Matteo…"

I don't need his sympathy. I don't need anything. What I need is to fix this and get my son back.

"Giacomo fed him a story—one where I stole his mother away, ruined her life, and then had her killed." I shake my head, jaw clenched tight. "And he fucking believes it."

I pause, trying to breathe through the storm building in my chest. "She was everything to him, Valerio. His sun, his constant. He clung to her like a lifeline. When she died… he shattered. I watched it happen, piece by piece. And I didn't know how to fix it. I didn't know how to reach him."

My voice lowers, rough. "And now Giacomo's dug his claws into that grief—twisted it until it's poisoned him. Turned his love for her into hate for me, turning it into a weapon—and aiming it straight at me. And he's not just angry, Valerio… he's grieving all over again. Only this time, I'm the villain in his story."

Valerio's expression darkens. "That son of a bitch."

I glance at him. "Daniele or Giacomo?"

Valerio snorts. "Both."

I tilt my head to the ceiling, feeling the weight of everything come down on me. I run a hand down my face. What the fuck am I supposed to do?

Valerio watches me carefully. Then, in a quieter voice, he says, "Do you want my advice?"

I exhale through my nose. "Do I have a choice?"

"Nope." He nudges his shoulder against mine. "Don't fight him on this."

I narrow my eyes. "You want me to just let him believe Giacomo's lies?"

"No," Valerio says smoothly. "I want you to give him space. Right now, he's drowning in anger, confusion, and grief. His world just got turned upside down—and now he knows he's not your blood. It's a lot for any man to take. If you push back, it'll only make him fight harder. Let him burn himself out."

My stomach twists at the idea of doing nothing. But Valerio isn't done with his advice.

"And when the time comes," he continues, "when Giacomo finally shows his hand, when Daniele sees what kind of monster he really is—then you step in."

I roll my shoulders, considering his words. It's a risk. But maybe he's right. Daniele has to see the truth for himself.

And if he doesn't? If he stays loyal to the man who has orchestrated this entire war?

Then I will have to do what I've always done.

Win.

No matter the cost.

The weight of Daniele's words lingers, pressing against my chest like a slow, suffocating vice. I sit on the edge of the desk, letting the silence stretch between Valerio and me, knowing that no matter how much I try to shove this feeling away, it refuses to be ignored.

I hate you. Three words I never thought I would hear from him.

I glance at Valerio, who is watching me with an unusual

seriousness. He knows me too well—knows that I am at war with myself right now.

Finally, I exhale, forcing the tension in my shoulders to ease. "So what do I do in the meantime? Just let him run a rampage in the streets of Manhattan?"

Valerio smirks, but it doesn't quite reach his eyes. "You do what you do best."

I arch a brow. "Which is?"

His grin turns sharper. "You destroy the bastard who put you in this position in the first place."

A slow, dark chuckle escapes me. There it is, that familiar, ruthless focus settling back into place. The storm inside me shifts, redirecting itself toward the man who has orchestrated this entire disaster.

Giacomo.

"Then let's make him bleed."

Valerio nods approvingly. "Now that's the Matteo I know."

I look at the clock. I've been away from Maria for too long.

"Send word to Dario," I say, already moving toward the door. "I want every lead on Giacomo and Emily verified within the next twenty-four hours. I want this issue done and over with within the next two weeks. Enough is enough."

Valerio grins. "You got it, boss."

I step out of the office, my thoughts already shifting to the next battle. I lost the last two, but the war isn't over yet.

As I make my way down to my car, my mind begins to shift focus to something else—or rather someone else.

Maria.

She is my anchor in all of this. The one person whose

loyalty is unwavering. The one person who doesn't see me as a monster or a king of sorts—just as Matteo.

And yet, she's hiding something from me.

She thinks I don't notice but I do. The way she hesitated after the gala. The flicker of something in her eyes when I asked if she was okay.

She's keeping something from me.

And I intend to find out what it is.

Whatever she's hiding... I'll tear the truth from the shadows myself.

33

MARIA

I wake up in Matteo's arms. For a moment, I let all the doubt slip away and allow myself that one singular moment of reprieve.

His warmth surrounds me, the steady rise and fall of his chest against my back grounding me in the early morning stillness. His arm is draped over my waist, his hand resting just above my hip, holding me close even in his sleep.

For a brief moment, I allow myself to sink into it—to close my eyes and pretend that nothing is wrong. That there isn't a flash drive hidden in my nightstand, waiting to unravel everything. That I'm not holding a secret inside me, a possibility that could change my life forever.

But the moment doesn't last very long because I feel movement behind me.

Matteo shifts slightly, pressing a slow, lingering kiss to the back of my shoulder. "You're awake," he murmurs against my skin, his voice thick with sleep.

I force a small smile, even though my stomach twists uncomfortably. "I was just enjoying the quiet."

He hums in response, his hand skimming lightly across

my stomach before settling against my waist again. He doesn't say anything, but I can feel him studying me, his gaze heavy with unspoken thoughts.

"You're tense," he finally says, his voice still low, but sharper now.

Crap.

I stiffen slightly, but then I school my expression, turning in his arms to face him. "Just tired."

Matteo's eyes search mine, and for a second, I think he might push—might call me out on the lie. But then he brushes a strand of hair behind my ear and presses a kiss to my forehead. "I'll have someone bring you breakfast in bed."

I shake my head, sitting up. "No. I'll be fine once I'm up." I force another smile. "Besides, I don't like people preparing food for me anymore."

I wince as soon as the words leave my mouth. I shouldn't have said that. The last thing either of us needs is to be reminded of the Emily incident.

"I'm sorry," I mutter under my breath.

"I understand. The fridge has everything you could want. But I'll ask Valerio to make any runs you need—for anything. I don't want you wandering outside for too long."

He brushes the back of his hand over my cheek. I lean into his touch and revel in its warmth for a moment longer. I close my eyes and will myself to hush the internal voice that keeps roaring loudly in my head.

When my eyes open, I meet his raging pupils that stare into the deepest parts of my soul. "You should get to work."

His eyes flick over me once more before he finally nods.

I watch as he rises from bed, the muscles in his back flexing as he moves toward the closet. Matteo is not a man who misses anything, and I know that even though he's letting this go for now, it won't be for long.

So I do what I have to.

I fake another smile. I kiss him goodbye. I let him think that everything is fine. And then, as soon as the door closes behind him, I let out the breath I've been holding.

I fall back onto the bed, staring at the ceiling, wondering if it's even worth looking at the flash drive—or if it'll just bring new battles we'll have to face.

The house is quiet as I make my way to the kitchen. A few of Matteo's men nod in greeting, but I barely acknowledge them—my mind too tangled in itself. At first, the extra security bugged me, especially with the fact that they were now inside the house.

But as the days moved on, I got used to them. Now, I barely notice their presence unless they speak.

I brew a cup of tea, wrapping my hands around the warm ceramic, hoping it will steady me. It doesn't.

My stomach churns, and for a moment, I think it's just the stress—the weight of everything piling onto my shoulders. But then a sharp nausea rolls through me, and I barely make it to the bathroom before I'm on my knees, retching into the toilet.

I gasp for air, my forehead pressing against the cool porcelain as my body betrays me. My mind runs with wild ideas of what could have possibly upset me this bad. Is it that drive? Or is it the fact that I'm hiding something from my husband?

The flash of my ring against the light makes me pause. I flush the toilet and get myself back on my feet. My ribs scream in agony from the force they just underwent. I can't remember the last time I got sick like this. Maybe it was what I ate yesterday—barely anything at all.

"Stress, it has to be stress," I say to myself.

I squeeze my eyes shut, gripping the edge of the sink, my

hair curtains my face as I blink back the moisture. My reflection in the mirror is pale, my lips slightly parted as I take slow, measured breaths.

The wave of nausea passes, but my mind won't quiet. Could I be…?

I shake my head, the blaring of my phone breaking my internal freak-out. I grab it with unsteady hands and see Ginny's name flashing on the screen.

I hesitate for only a second. "Hey."

The moment she hears my voice, she knows something isn't right. "What is it?" This woman has begun to know me all too well now.

I close my eyes, pressing my fingers against my temple. "I just don't… I don't feel well."

Ginny is silent for a moment. "Are you sick?"

"A lot on my mind, I guess… and I just threw up, so maybe it was the tea? Or something I ate last night. I don't know."

Ginny remains silent on the other side of the line. I remove my ear from my phone to see if maybe she hung up. No, she's still there.

"Ginny?"

She clears her throat but says nothing at first. Then she finally speaks, "Maria… when was your last period?"

The question lands like a punch to the stomach.

I blink. My mouth suddenly feels dry. It was the same thought I'd had just before she called—but one I refused to believe.

"I… I don't remember." I try to think back. I count back the weeks, and then I pause. "Oh, shit. Almost eight weeks ago, I think."

"Oh my God," Ginny breathes. "You need to take a test."

A heavy, sinking weight settles in my chest. "No," I say quickly. "It's just stress. It's—"

"Maria," Ginny cuts me off, her voice firm but gentle. "Just take the test. I can bring one to your house right now if you want me to and—"

"No, don't. You don't have to do that. I can just have one delivered here." I rush out, run a frantic hand through my hair, and then look up at the mirror. My eyes are wide, and I can see the fear floating in them.

Pregnant.

I grip the edge of the counter. My heart pounds so loudly, I can hear it echoing in my ears. A single word—pregnant—and it terrifies me more than anything I've faced before.

"You're scared to find out you might be pregnant?"

I open my mouth to give her an answer, but the truth is I don't know. With the flash drive nonsense still swimming in my head, I don't know if I want to be pregnant right now. Giacomo is still a problem, and Emily is wandering the streets of New York, likely biding her time.

I swallow hard, my fingers tightening around the phone. "I don't know. Matteo and I only just started getting along, and with him still at odds with Daniele, I don't know if now is the best time to... have a baby."

"Aww, honey. Whatever the outcome of the test, I am sure that he will stand by your side. The man loves you with everything he has in him."

"I know." The words slip past my lips, but I don't even know if I believe them myself. "Look, I need to go, I will text you later, okay?"

I hang up before she can say anything else. Immediately, I order the test online and have it delivered to the penthouse.

"Ten minutes." I check the delivery app—that's how long it says it'll take. My eyes lift back to my reflection, meeting it once more.

For a moment, I just stand there, staring at myself, my pulse echoing in my ears. My hand finds its way to my flat stomach, and this sudden warmth overtakes me at the thought of a little life growing inside of me.

A baby. Our baby.

Being a mother has always been one of my greatest goals in life. I know that I was put on this earth to be one.

Then, without another thought, I step out of the bathroom and walk to the foyer to await my delivery. The guards watch me curiously, but they say nothing to me.

The doorman finally calls, and I allow the delivery man up. He hands me the box, and I make my way back to my room. I close the door behind me and head into the bathroom to pee on the damn stick. All the while, my mind goes round and round in circles trying to think out all the different scenarios.

I read the instructions—three minutes. That's all it takes to rewrite my life.

I cap the stick, set it aside, and lay on the bed, trying to breathe through the storm building inside me.

The seconds tick by like minutes. Then my gaze snaps to the side table.

The flash drive—still hidden where I left it after the gala.

For days, I've gone back and forth, debating whether to open it.

"I need to know what's in this thing." I open the drawer and pull out the flash drive with shaking hands. I look back down at the pregnancy test that is still processing. "Let's do this."

I walk over to the desk where my computer sits, and with anxiety gripping my chest, I plug the drive into my computer. It's now or never.

I stare at the screen, my breath caught somewhere between my ribs. My hand hovers over the trackpad, the small, blinking folder taunting me. With a deep breath, I double-click the folder.

A single video file sits inside. *Antonio.mp4*

My stomach churns violently. Why would Giacomo give me a video with my brother's name on it? I already know that whatever is on this is going to shatter my heart. I can feel it.

My hand hovers over the play button, my fingers shaking. Every part of me is screaming to stop. To shut the laptop. To walk away.

But I can't. I have to know.

I press play.

The screen flickers, grainy footage filling my laptop. The timestamp in the corner is from that night—the night he died. *Oh my God...*

The camera is shaky, like it was taken from a security feed or a hidden vantage point. The warehouse in the background is familiar, but what catches my attention first is him.

Antonio.

My breath stutters as I see my brother alive again, even if just on a screen. He looks worn—tense, on edge. He stands with a few men.

Suddenly, a canister clatters across the concrete floor, spinning before releasing a thick cloud of gas that quickly spreads through the warehouse. The men inside react instantly—hands going to masks, bandanas, anything to shield themselves. Antonio pulls his biker mask over his face, eyes narrowing as the haze swallows the room. The edges of the footage blur slightly from the fog, but the tension only sharpens. This wasn't just a meeting. It was an ambush.

Then the warehouse door bursts open with a loud metallic bang. Figures step through the thick haze—shadows at first, until the camera adjusts.

My world tilts.

"He was there..." I barely hear my own voice.

I watch in a trance as he strides forward, his presence commanding even in the grainy footage.

Matteo emerges from the smoke like it parts just for him, moving with the kind of confidence that makes everyone else seem like background noise. His son is right behind him with a few other men, hands resting on their weapons.

As soon as they cross the threshold, they pull masks over their faces in one smooth, practiced motion—like they've done this before. Like they knew exactly what they were walking into.

Behind Matteo, his men fan out in swift, deliberate strides—ghostlike through the swirling gas, their silhouettes distorted in the flickering light. Everything is chaos: smoke clings to the floor, the hum of static from the footage cuts in and out, and every figure is masked, indistinct. It's impossible to tell friend from foe.

Suddenly, a man lunges from behind a support beam, grabbing Daniele and pressing a gun to his head. Matteo reacts instantly—raising his weapon, aiming directly at the man.

"Put the gun down!" Matteo's voice is firm, commanding, even through the haze of static audio. His gun doesn't waver. He's trying to talk the man down, waiting for the moment.

Daniele's eyes are wide, locked on Matteo.

And then—before Matteo can shoot, another figure leaps into the frame from behind, moving fast, colliding with him.

Even through the grainy footage, I recognize the way he moves.

Antonio.

My breath stops.

He slams into Matteo with full force, knocking him off balance. The two of them crash to the ground, grappling as Daniele seizes the distraction. He slams his elbow into the attacker's ribs, twisting hard, and manages to knock the gun away.

The fight splinters in two directions.

Daniele wrestles with the armed man, fists flying, until he grabs a broken pipe from the ground and slams it into the man's skull. The body slumps.

But Matteo is still struggling.

He and Antonio are locked in a brutal, fast-paced fight. Blows land hard. Grunts, the scuff of boots, the static buzz of the footage. Neither is holding back.

Antonio throws a punch that nearly connects, but Matteo ducks, slamming him into a crate.

The camera shifts just enough to catch the flash of a blade in Antonio's hand.

Matteo knocks it aside and reaches for his gun—but Antonio grabs his wrist. They wrestle, limbs locked, struggling for control. Somewhere in the blur—a gun catches the light. It shifts between them, caught in both their hands.

The camera trembles too hard to follow, turning the moment into a fever dream of chaos.

A shot rings out. Loud. Sudden.

A single, deafening crack that cuts through the static and smoke.

"No..." My fingers brush the screen just as someone pulls the trigger.

For a heartbeat, no one moves. No one breathes. The smoke swirls like a curtain over a stage, obscuring the cost.

I can't tell who fired.

Can't even tell, at first, who was hit.

But then—one of them drops.

Antonio.

Blood pools beneath him like ink spreading across paper.

Matteo stumbles back, breath caught in his chest, gun still trembling in his grip.

Antonio drops to his knees, then collapses to the floor, the mask still covering his face.

A sharp, gasping sob rips from my throat. I slap my hand over my mouth, my entire body locking up as the video keeps playing. Antonio lies motionless, but his chest lifts in short, shallow bursts. Still breathing. Still here.

Matteo scrambles forward, falling to his knees. His hands shake as he reaches out slowly—like something inside him already knows. He pulls the biker mask from the man lying in a pool of spreading red and freezes.

My stomach twists, bile rising in my throat.

He sees the face. The face of my brother.

Matteo goes pale. He recoils—his expression cracks—and for a single second, I see something flicker in his gaze.

Horror. Realization. Guilt.

Then the video cuts off.

The screen turns black, and it's all over.

Silence.

Five minutes, thirty-four seconds.

That's how long it took for my world to fall apart.

I sit frozen, staring at the black screen, my pulse

hammering against my skull. For the first time, my mind is quiet, still reeling from shock of what I just witnessed.

No.

This can't be real.

I can't breathe. Can't think.

It has to be manipulated—edited—something. Matteo wouldn't. He couldn't. But I saw it. I saw him do it.

My stomach twists uncomfortably, and before I can stop myself, I shove the laptop aside and sprint toward the bathroom. I barely make it before I'm on my knees, emptying what little's left in me.

Everything inside me rebels, my body rejecting what I just saw, what I now know. When there's nothing left, I slump against the wall, gasping for air, my vision blurring with unshed tears. I grip my stomach, my fingers digging into the fabric of my dress.

The timer on my phone goes off in my room. The test. The test is done.

I quiver against the cold tiles, but I find the strength to get back onto my feet. With shaking legs, I make my way back to my bed. I barely have the strength to hold myself up at the moment. I look down at my duvet, and I pause.

"Shit." The curse leaves my lips softly, but the gravity of sorrow that it carries is immense. I look down at it again, making sure that I am seeing things correctly.

Pregnant: 8-9 weeks.

My world shatters. The word screams at me. There it is in big, bold letters. My body feels disconnected from my mind, as if I'm floating outside of myself, watching this moment from a distance.

A baby.

Matteo's baby.

The man I just watched kill my brother.

A broken sigh escapes me as I stumble back against the counter, my stomach twisting into knots. My mind is a tangled mess of thoughts, none of them making sense, none of them offering relief.

Five minutes and thirty-four seconds. That's how long the video was. That's how long it took for my husband to shoot down my brother.

What the hell am I going to do?

I shake my head, whispering to myself, "No. No, this isn't real."

My brother is dead, and the man I love—the man whose child I am carrying—pulled the trigger. For weeks, I have mourned the death of my brother—my father's sole heir. The entire reason I had to get married in the first place.

Now it all makes sense. Giacomo's words to me the gala ring loudly in my head like a resounding gong. They clang against my skull with no remorse.

A sob claws up my throat, but I swallow it down, pressing my hand over my mouth. I can't afford to break. Not yet. I don't know how long I stand there, staring at nothing, lost in my own storm. Eventually, a soft knock at the door startles me back to reality.

"Signora?" One of Matteo's men speaks from behind my door. "Are you all right?"

"I'm fine."

A pause. Then, "Do you need anything?"

I shake my head even though he can't see me. "No. I just need a moment."

Another hesitation. "Very well, Signora. I can send for a doctor if you need it."

"No, I'm fine."

"Okay, you can just call if you need anything." I hear the footsteps retreat from the door.

I release a slow, shaky breath, forcing my body to move. I can't stay here.

With trembling hands, I walk back into the bathroom, and I wrap the pregnancy test in tissue and tuck it deep into the trash bin, as if hiding it could make it less real. As if pretending it doesn't exist will stop the reality from closing in on me.

I move on autopilot, walking back to the bedroom. The laptop is still on the bed, the flash drive plugged in, the black screen like a gaping void, pulling me back into the nightmare. I force myself to shut it, tucking the drive away where Matteo won't find it. Not yet.

Not until I know what to do.

Because right now, I don't.

I have no answers. No plan. No idea how to move past the crushing weight of knowing that my child's father is also my brother's killer.

All I have is this secret growing inside me. And a truth that could destroy everything—that has destroyed everything.

What the hell am I supposed to do...

Carry his child while burying my brother?

Love a man I'm not sure I'll ever be able to forgive?

And the worst part?

I don't even know if I want to.

34

MATTEO

The moment I walk into the penthouse, I can already tell that something is off. There is a shift in the air that unsettles me. The lights are all off except for the one that leads to our room.

"Maria?" I call her name. My voice echoes through the walls of the penthouse. "Amore? Where are you?"

I walk toward the stairs. I relieved Marco—her guard—as soon as I walked in. There are three more posted outside the door and five more around the building. No one could have possibly gotten in.

She is safe. She is safe.

I repeat the words in my head, over and over, as I ascend the stairs. I make my way to our room and pause when I see her sitting on the bed in her silk nightdress. I let out a sigh of relief, but it's short-lived when her eyes flick up to meet mine.

They're red and swollen. She's been crying, her cheeks stained with old streaks of tears.

"Maria?" I rush to her and sit beside her on the bed. "What's wrong?"

I reach for her, aching to hold her—but she pulls away.

Her hazel eyes—so warm, so full of life—are now filled with something I never wanted to see: a shattering sadness that hits me like a punch to the gut. I have no idea what the hell is going on, but whatever it is, I want to fix it.

"Did you kill my brother?"

My entire world seizes.

She doesn't blink, doesn't waver. Tears line her lashes, but she doesn't let them fall. She sits there, waiting, demanding the truth. She knows. I don't know how... but she does. She just wants to hear it from me. She wants me to admit the crimes that I have committed.

My throat is dry, my pulse pounding like war drums in my ears. I could try to explain, try to soften the words—but there's no dressing up something like this.

So, I give her what she wants.

"Yes."

The moment the word leaves my lips, her entire body jolts—like I've struck her. Then, the silence shatters.

A broken sob rips from her throat, her entire frame trembling as the truth crashes over her. She pushes to her feet, but too quickly—stumbling backward. Her hands cover her mouth, her breaths coming in sharp, erratic gasps.

"Maria—"

"No." She shakes her head violently, stepping farther away, putting as much distance between us as possible. "No, no, no."

The pain in her voice is unbearable.

I get up from the bed and take a step forward, desperate to reach her, but the moment I do, she lifts a shaking hand. "Don't. Don't you dare come near me!"

My chest tightens. "Please. Let me explain—"

"You killed him," she whispers, her voice hoarse—barely

a breath. "You—" Her eyes squeeze shut as another sob wracks her body. "It was your gun, Matteo. I saw it. You—you killed my brother."

Her words slice into me, deeper than any bullet ever could.

She's right.

It was my gun—my bullet.

I move again, reaching for her, but she shoves against my chest with everything she has. "Don't touch me!"

I don't fight it. I let her push me away, let her rage crash into me because I deserve it. My worst fear has now come true, and I have no idea what I'm going to do. My heart is cracking with each breath I take.

"I didn't know," I say, my voice rough, pleading. "Maria, if I could take it back—"

"But you can't," she chokes out, shaking her head. "You can't take it back! My brother is dead, and you are the one to blame. Oh my God, all those times you held me and tried to comfort me. The day in my studio..."

Her breathing is uneven, her body trembling like she's about to collapse under the weight of it all.

I take a step toward her, gentler this time, not wanting to alarm her. "Maria—"

She turns on her heel and runs as if she can outrun the truth. She dives into the bathroom, a sanctuary where she can be free of my presence. A second later, the door slams shut. I could follow after her, but I know she needs the space. She needs time to process.

I hear the lock click into place, and I know she's not coming out of there any time soon. And I can't be the one to force her out. I stand there, staring at the door, my heart pounding, my hands clenched at my sides.

So I wait.

Hours pass. The sun dips below the horizon, casting the room in darkness, but she stays locked behind that door. And I, Matteo Davacalli, a man who has commanded armies, torn apart empires, and walked through fire, can do nothing but wait.

Every so often, I knock. Hoping—praying—she will let me in.

I sit down by the door, leaning my back against the hardwood, trying to listen to what's happening on the other side.

"Maria."

Silence.

I try again. "Please, let me in."

Nothing.

I exhale sharply, resting the back of my head against the wood. I don't deserve to be on the other side of this door with her. I don't deserve her forgiveness. But I can't fucking lose her. She can hate me, scream at me, or beat me if she wants to. But I refuse to lose her.

"I know you're not going to open the door, and you're right, you shouldn't. What I did—accident or not—was unforgivable. I shattered your family, and there's no undoing that. I destroyed everything."

The words feel heavy, strained. My throat is tight, my chest burning from the weight of the guilt that I have carried with me for months.

"I know you may not want to hear this, but I need you to know the truth. I'm not making excuses for what I did. It was my gun—and I was the one who pulled the trigger. We got bad intel about a shipment in Florence possibly being stolen. We were given the address of a warehouse and thought we were going to meet the smugglers, but it turns out we were wrong. There was a mistake that night. A fatal one."

I pause, drawing in a breath.

"Antonio wasn't supposed to be there."

Silence.

Still, I go on.

"We thought we were walking in to reclaim what was stolen from us—almost twenty million dollars' worth of firearms. We came in there with a lot of heat and every intention of putting these thieves down. And when I saw the men, I thought it was them—the ones who took our shipment. But it was your brother—Antonio and his men," I say, my voice tightens. "The place was filled with gas. Everyone had their faces covered. The visibility was shit. I didn't even know who we were fighting."

I exhale shakily, my hands curling into fists. "Daniele was grabbed—a gun to his head. I had no choice but to protect him. I aimed, but before I could fire, someone hit me from behind. We hit the ground—fighting. I didn't know who it was. I just reacted."

I pause, eyes burning. "Your brother attacked me, Maria. I fought back. I had no idea it was him."

My breath stutters. "The gun was between us. We were both holding it. And then—"

I close my eyes, swallowing past the ache in my throat. "The shot went off."

My throat burns as I force out the words. "By the time I saw his face... he was already on the floor, bleeding out from my bullet."

Silence stretches between us again, but this time, it feels different. I don't know if she believes me. I don't know if this changes anything. I can only hope she opens the door and allows me the chance to earn her forgiveness—even if it takes the rest of my life.

For months, I've carried this guilt alone. I have lived with the weight of that night, with the knowledge that I stole a brother from his sister. A son from his parents.

There it is—all of it. The truth, laid bare, unforgiving, impossible to take back.

"I never meant for any of this to happen." My voice is rough, raw. "I can't make it right, I can't bring him back to life. But what I do know is that I love you, Maria. You are my soul and heart intertwined. I can take your hatred. I can brave your anger. But I'm begging you—please don't leave me. I... I love you."

Seconds pass, and for a moment, I believe that she is going to remain quiet. But then I hear some shuffling and the subtle sound of the door clicking.

The click of the lock is the loudest sound I've heard in my life.

I scramble to my feet and wait for her to open the door. My heart rests on the floor, the anxiety choking me. She stands there with red-rimmed eyes and flushed cheeks.

"You love me?"

Her voice is barely a whisper.

I look at her.

"I... I love you, amore mio."

There it is. I finally said it. And God, it hurts more than I ever expected. The words hang in the silence—louder than any gunshot I've ever fired.

"I thought after Beatrice... that part of me had died. That love—real love—was buried six feet under with her, left to rot where no one could ever touch it again. That those words would never tear their way out of my mouth... out of my heart. That part of me is dead, gone. I swore I'd never feel this again—never let myself feel this again. Not because I couldn't. But because I didn't deserve you."

I take a breath that burns all the way down.

"But now it's here. Ugly. Honest. Unstoppable. Not polished or perfect—just real. Just mine. Dragged from the darkest part of me and laid at your feet— like a wound ripped wide open,

like a prayer...and a curse all at once. A confession. A plea. A surrender. And maybe... a mistake. Because if you walk away now, I don't know if there's any part of me left that will survive it."

The silence between us stretches, taut and trembling, from seconds into an eternity. But I don't move—I can't. I just watch her. Watch as her eyes scan my face like she's searching for the man she once believed in. A thousand emotions ripple through them—rage, grief, disbelief, something dangerously close to hope—and I take it all. I take every silent scream behind her stare because it's all I deserve.

I open my mouth to speak again—one more plea— but the words are quickly swallowed by her kiss.

And in that moment, I know: She's the only mercy I'll ever be granted.

35

MARIA

Matteo kisses me like he's trying to erase every moment of pain between us.

His hands cradle my face, his touch rough and desperate, like he's terrified that if he lets go, I'll slip through his fingers. His lips move over mine with a hunger that steals my breath, swallowing every doubt, every fractured thought.

And for a moment, I let him.

I let myself drown in him. In his warmth, his scent, the way his body presses against mine like it belongs there.

Because the truth is, I want him. I want to lose myself in this—just for tonight. I want to forget what I know, forget the war raging inside my heart.

So I kiss him back. Hard.

His grip tightens, a low growl vibrating in his chest as he presses me against the door. Heat pulses between us, fierce and demanding, and when his hands slide down to my waist, pulling me closer, I let out a soft gasp.

He breaks the kiss just long enough to rest his forehead against mine, his breath ragged. "Maria…"

I close my eyes. If he says he loves me again, I'll break.

So I kiss him before he can. I don't want to think right now, I don't want to feel. I just want his body against mine. But then he rips his lips from mine again and presses his forehead against mine.

"Maria," he breathes. "We need to—"

"No, we don't." I grab the back of his neck. "You can either fuck me right here, right now, or you can leave this room and never come back inside."

My words are enough to ignite a fire within his eyes. He crashes his lips down onto mine. The kiss is searing and unlike anything he has ever given me before. It claims every cell in my body and torches me with his mark.

I need this tonight. I need him. Because after tonight, it will all fall apart.

Our mouths crash together with ferocity, tongues battling for dominance. He lifts me into his arms, carrying me to the edge of the bed before lowering me with careful hands. I rip my lips from his, breathless, staring him dead in the eyes.

"Get on your knees," I demand.

Something wild and dangerous flashes in his eyes. A challenge. For a heartbeat, I think he'll resist—Matteo has never been one to yield control. But then, slowly, deliberately, he sinks to his knees before me, his gaze never leaving mine.

Power surges through me, intoxicating and raw. I reach out, threading my fingers through his dark hair, gripping just tight enough to make his breath catch. His hands slide up my thighs, leaving trails of fire in their wake.

"Is this what you want?" he asks, voice rough like gravel. His thumbs trace circles on my inner thighs, inching higher with agonizing slowness.

I don't answer. Instead, I tighten my grip on his hair and pull him closer. His hot breath fans against me through the thin fabric of my nightdress, making me shiver.

"Maria," he breathes my name. "Tell me what you want."

Instead of answering, I simply place my foot on the edge of the bed and lift my dress to reveal my throbbing core. There is a buzz that moves through the air.

His eyes darken with a deep lust and passion. "You want me to eat you out?"

"Yes." I thread my fingers deeper into his hair. "I want you to make me come with your mouth. Make it feel like the first time you ever touched me."

I don't give him a chance to respond. I shove his head to my pussy, forcing him into action.

He gives himself to me completely, his mouth claiming me with a reverence that betrays his hunger. My head falls back as his tongue sweeps against me, precise and knowing. He remembers everything—every spot that makes me tremble, every rhythm that drives me wild.

I roll my hips against his face, chasing the pleasure that builds like a storm inside me. His hands grip my thighs, holding me open for him as he devours me. When he slides a finger inside, curling it just so, I cry out, my body arching.

"Oh, yes!" I sigh into the dimly lit room. "Fuck me with your mouth."

Matteo knows my body better than I do. He knows exactly where to press, where to lick, where to suck until I'm trembling and incoherent. My thighs quiver around his head, and I can feel his smile against me, smug and satisfied even as he worships me.

"That's it," he murmurs against my flesh. "Let me hear you, Maria. Come undone for me."

Another finger joins the first, stretching me, filling me, while his tongue continues its relentless assault. My thighs begin to shake. I'm close—so close—but I don't want it to end. Not yet. I want to prolong this for as long as I can.

I pull his hair again, forcing a grunt from deep within his throat. The sound drives me crazy.

"Don't stop," I command, my voice breaking as he circles my clit with maddening slowness. "Don't you dare stop."

He hums against me, the vibration sending a jolt up my spine. His hands grip my hips, pulling me closer to his hungry mouth.

"Fuck," I breathe. I feel myself nearing the edge. This man works me in ways that I cannot fully comprehend. "Matteo, I'm going to…"

He bites down gently on my clit and that is my undoing. The orgasm rips through me, splitting me in two.

"Yes!" My scream fills the room. My voice echoes against the walls as I roll my center into his mouth as the orgasm rides out.

Matteo hums in appreciation before he pulls away and looks up at me with shining eyes. He laps up my wetness, holding eye contact from knees, the crescendo of my orgasm dripping from his lips.

I grab his chin and slam my lips against his. I taste the sweetness, and my heart hammers in my chest. He rises to his feet, his hands making quick work of removing my dress. And then I stand before him naked and bare.

Usually, this would be the time that I would reach for his length and get on my knees. But I don't. This isn't about him tonight. Tonight, I take what I want from him. It's about my pleasure. My wants and needs.

"Take off your clothes," I command, ignoring the ache rising in my chest. "All of them. Now."

His eyes spark with a gleam of mischief, and he smiles. "Your wish is my command." And so he takes his clothes off, layer by layer, until he stands bare in front of me.

"Lie down," I say, voice steady. "I'm going to ride your cock."

A flicker of surprise crosses his face, quickly replaced by raw desire. I am normally the one who lets him take charge.

He moves to the bed, lying back against the pillows, his arousal evident. I follow, my confidence growing with every step. Tonight, I'm going to get my fill of him.

I climb onto the bed, straddling him. His hands immediately reach for my hips, but I catch his wrists, pinning them above his head.

"No touching," I whisper against his ear. "Not until I say so."

His chest rises and falls with heavy breaths. "You're killing me, Maria."

"Good." I position myself over him, teasing us both by sliding against his length without taking him in. His hips buck involuntarily, seeking what I'm denying.

His eyes are dark with need, his lips parted, waiting. I place my hands on his chest and slowly take him in, inch by inch. We moan in unison, the sound filling the large room. The sweet scent of our joint arousal takes over, only driving me further over the edge.

I take him all the way in, until my hips press against his—then I pause, letting my body adjust to his massive size.

"You're so beautiful, it hurts," he murmurs, reaching for me.

His words are like a sword to the chest.

I slap his hand away. "No touching."

I lift myself up and then slam myself down. I repeat the

motion again, and we both nearly come undone from that stroke alone.

His groan tears through the room as I set a merciless pace, rising and falling on him with deliberate slowness, then quickening until we're both gasping. I grip my breasts, squeezing so tight that I feel the ache in them. His hands fist in the sheets, knuckles white with restraint.

"Maria," he pleads, his voice strained. "Let me touch you."

I shake my head, rolling my hips in a way that makes his eyes roll back. Power surges through me, watching him come undone beneath me. This man, who has always been so controlled, so commanding, is now at my mercy. It's invigorating.

Sweat glistens on his chest as I ride him harder. I lean forward, changing the angle, and gasp as he hits that perfect spot inside me. His eyes lock with mine, dark and desperate. I remove my hands from my breasts and place them firmly on his hard chest.

"That feels so good," I breathe, my nails digging into his chest. "So fucking good."

Something cracks open inside me with every thrust—a dam of emotions I've kept buried for far too long. Grief, rage, love, guilt—they all collide in a violent storm beneath my skin, threatening to swallow me whole. But I don't let them. Not now.

Right now, I need to stay inside my body. I need to feel every inch of him, every burn of friction, every heartbeat against mine.

The pain, the betrayal, the chaos of what comes next—

That can all wait.

Tonight, I choose this. I choose him. One last time.

"Touch me. Touch me, Matteo," I breathe, the words trembling on my lips.

Because this isn't just lust.

It's more.

It's a silent goodbye between lost souls, wrapped in pleasure and pain.

I want to memorize this—burn it into my skin. The way his hands fit around my waist. The heat of his chest against mine. The way his breath falters when he looks me in the eye.

His heartbeat. His gaze.

I felt it—the pain in his voice when he told me he loved me. Words torn from the ruins of his soul. Knowing this might be the end. Knowing that losing me would break him.

And I want to hold on to all of it.

Because after this… I don't know if I'll ever feel it again.

Matteo grabs my hips and lifts himself so he can take control of the pace. He rams into me with such force that my scream is a mixture of both pleasure and pain—the good kind. "Fuck, baby!"

"Oh, yes!" My breasts bounce up and down mercilessly. "I'm almost there."

Matteo lowers himself and then presses his hand against my back so that we come together—chest to chest. His arms circle around me, pulling me in tightly. His assaults on my core relentless and merciless until I finally feel the thread snap and my walls collapse around him.

"Matteo!" I bury my nose into the crook of his neck and allow the orgasm to overtake me. My walls carry him over the edge, too, and he finds his release at the very end.

We ride out our orgasms until our bodies melt into each other, and we are left satiated and spent. For a long moment, we stay like that, tangled in each other, our breaths mingling, hearts pounding in unison. His arms remain wrapped around me, holding me against his chest as if he can keep the world at bay just a little longer.

I should move. I should pull away. But I don't.

Instead, I let myself sink into the warmth of his embrace, memorizing the feeling of his skin against mine, the steady rhythm of his heartbeat beneath my ear.

Matteo's fingers trace lazy patterns along my spine, sending shivers across my sweat-dampened skin. He presses a gentle kiss to my temple, so different from the desperate ones we shared earlier.

"I love you, Maria," he whispers, his voice rough with emotion. "You're the gravity that holds me together. Without you, I'll fall apart."

He doesn't say the words, but I feel them—the plea buried in his silence: *Don't leave me.* It trembles beneath the surface of every breath. He doesn't dare ask, not out loud. Not with the weight of everything between us.

I want to answer him, to say something—anything—but the pain and betrayal tighten around my throat like a vice. The words die before they ever reach my lips.

So, instead, I shift from his chest and slide quietly to his side. "We should sleep," I whisper, barely audible. "We'll talk in the morning."

He doesn't fight me—thankfully. He simply pulls me in closer and presses his lips to my forehead one last time before we slip into silence.

I don't know how long I lie there, waiting—until the steady rise and fall of his chest tells me he's asleep.

For a moment, I allow myself to sink into his warmth, wishing this little bubble we've created could last forever. That maybe, just maybe, love could be enough.

But reality knocks—loud, insistent, unforgiving. I have

to follow through—because if I don't, everything I'm fighting for slips away.

Carefully, I slip out of his arms and move with practiced quiet. I retrieve the note I wrote before he came home and place it by the lamp, my fingers lingering on the paper for a beat too long.

Then I rush to the closet, pull on a pair of sweats, and grab the suitcase I'd stashed away.

I have minutes at most. I need to be quick.

I look at my phone and see that my mother has responded to the text I sent her a few hours ago.

I'm coming home, Mamá. I will explain when I get there.

Your room is ready, amore. Let me know when you're on the plane.

I walk back into the room and see that Matteo is still fast asleep. The sheets pool at his waist, and his chest rises and falls gently. My heart squeezes, aching with the weight of what I'm about to do—but I know it has to be done. I have to leave.

I make my way out of the room carefully and shut the door behind me. I race downstairs, making sure to keep quiet to not alarm the guards that stand outside the door. If they catch wind of this, then I am finished.

There are two ways of leaving this fortress—the main door and the secret elevator by the kitchen. I choose the secret elevator. It's the path of least resistance, and I need every advantage right now.

The kitchen is dark and silent as I slip through it, my footsteps barely a whisper against the marble floor. The service elevator is hidden behind a pantry door—the escape route Emily used. Ironic how I'm now using it to escape my husband.

The elevator descends slowly, each second stretching

into eternity. I clutch my suitcase tighter, wondering if I've forgotten anything important. It doesn't matter. I can't go back now.

When the doors slide open, I'm met with the cool night air of the underground garage. My car is waiting, the keys ready in my hand. The car had been a gift from Matteo that I never got around to using until now.

With adrenaline pushing me forward, I slip into the sleek Range Rover and peel out of my spot, and head for the airport without looking back once. I am only four blocks from the building when I feel the pain behind my eyes.

Tears prick my eyes as I drive. I try to push it all down, but now that I'm alone with my thoughts, I can't hold it back any longer. I allow them to trickle down my face so I can begin to grieve the man I love.

The night air bites at my skin as I step out of the car, dragging my suitcase behind me. The distant hum of airplanes fills the air, the glow of terminal lights stretching into the dark sky. I move forward, my breath slow and steady—my heart, anything but.

"Don't look back, don't look back," I repeat the same low chant to myself, trying to find the willpower to do this. "Do this for your baby."

The pain is too much. The love I have for him, deep, soul-consuming, clashes violently with the truth and the betrayal that sticks to the chambers of my heart.

I can't pretend I didn't see it. I can't pretend he didn't shoot my brother down like it meant nothing.

No matter how hard I try to justify it—no matter how many times he says it was a mistake—I can't erase the moment he raised that gun.

The image is seared into my memory.

Burned into me.

And it won't let go.

Tears prick at my eyes again, but I force them back. There will be time to cry—later. Right now, I need to get off American soil.

I weave through the parking bay, the small wheels of my suitcase dragging against the pavement. The terminal entrance is just ahead, glowing like a beacon—my ticket home.

Then, I feel a sudden movement in the air. The hairs on the back of my neck raise in awareness, and my head whips around, trying to see the threat that seems to be looming just around the corner.

My pulse quickens, my instincts screaming at me to move, but my feet feel like they're sinking into the ground. I inhale sharply, trying to convince myself that I am overthinking. I take another step forward—

"Gotcha, bitch." Strong arms come around me, and a cloth covers my mouth.

I have no sense of my bearings. My head is tilted upward, and the sharp scent of some chemical fills my nostrils as I try to struggle against the person who has me gripped.

I thrash, my suitcase slipping from my grip as strong arms yank me backward. A muffled scream claws its way up my throat, but the fabric they hold against my mouth blocks the sound, turning it into nothing more than a desperate whimper.

No, no, no!

I kick, twisting in my attacker's grip, but whoever they are, they're too strong. I feel myself being lifted, my feet barely brushing the ground as I'm hauled toward something —a car, maybe. The more I fight, the more strength I seem to lose, until my muscles eventually give way, and my vision blurs as it slowly dips into darkness.

The last thing I remember hearing is a familiar voice. One that only sends fear to my belly.

"Time for a joy ride, step-mommy."

And just like that, the darkness swallows me whole.

I thought leaving Matteo would hurt the most... until the real nightmare begins.

36

MATTEO

I notice how cool I feel before I even open my eyes.

At first, my sleep-clouded mind doesn't process it. My hand reaches instinctively, expecting to find the warm curve of Maria's body, the soft hush of her breathing pressed against me. But all I touch is the cold sheets.

My eyes snap open.

"Maria," I call out her name in the thick of the darkness. I look at my phone on the bedside table and see it is almost three in the morning. "Maria?"

She's not here.

A sharp pang of unease coils in my chest as I sit up, scanning the dimly lit room. Her nightgown lays on the floor where I stripped it off of her. The closet door is slightly ajar. The lamp on her nightstand is still on, casting a golden glow across the bed.

My gut twists. I try not to let my mind wander too far. Maybe she's just downstairs in her studio, sketching out the storm in her chest—waiting for me to come and talk to her.

Swinging my legs over the edge of the bed, I stand quickly, my heart slamming against my ribs. I scan the room again, looking for anything, any sign, of where she might have gone.

Then I see it.

A folded piece of paper, placed neatly by the lamp. I snatch it up, my fingers tightening around the edges as I unfold it.

Some things can't be undone, Matteo. And I don't know how to be whole in your world anymore. I need to remember who I was before you. Please... let me go. Before I forget how to breathe without you. Before I forget what you took from me. —M

The breath I take is sharp, my pulse roaring in my ears.

"No, no, no!" The desperation in my tone is evident. I grab my phone from the nightstand and immediately call her.

"Hi, you've reached Maria Davacalli. Please leave a message after the—"

Straight to voicemail.

My jaw clenches so tightly it aches. I try again. The same thing—voicemail. A cold rush of panic floods my veins. I pull at my hair, feeling like the world is closing in on me.

I dial a different number, one I haven't called since the wedding.

"Fuck." I sit on the edge of the bed and wait.

"Davacalli. Bit late for a call in your time zone." Maria's father's voice is sharp, clipped—no room for pleasantries. "You have three seconds to explain what you've done."

"Where is she?"

There's a pause. A measured silence that grates against my already fraying nerves.

"My daughter," he says slowly, as if the word itself is a correction. "She's coming home. And now I get to ask—what did you do? I told you not to hurt her. Are you incapable of even that small task?"

A muscle ticks in my jaw. "Italy? She's flying back to Italy?"

His voice is clipped, a warning beneath his tone. "My wife received a message from her earlier. I sent another, but she hasn't responded yet."

I inhale through my nose, forcing my rage back. "And when was that?"

"About three hours ago."

The pit in my stomach deepens. Three hours?

"Did she say anything else?" My grip tightens around the phone. "What flight is she going to take? Did she tell you when she was boarding?"

There's another pause, and that does nothing to ease the panic that riddles my bones.

"She never confirmed whether she boarded a flight," he finally says. "Or what flight she was taking. I was going to tell her to wait a few hours for our jet so she could travel more comfortably, but she never responded. I just assumed she was already in the air."

My breath comes out slow, controlled. But inside, a storm is raging. Something is very, very wrong here. I can feel it right down to the marrow of my bones. It's an unsettling feeling, one I felt when I first found Beatrice lying on the floor, unconscious.

I pull the phone away from my ear and switch screens. I tap into the tracker I had placed on Maria's car, watching as the signal pinpoints her last known location.

JFK. The car's at the airport—but if she's not answering her father, maybe she never boarded a flight at all.

The thought twists in my gut. Why wouldn't she? I don't even want to think about it. All I know is I need to find her.

I put the phone back to my ear. "She never got on a flight."

A sharp exhale from the other end. "What?"

"Her car is at the fucking airport," I say, my voice deadly calm. "If she got on a flight—any flight—she would've told someone. You or your wife."

I take a breath, my mind already racing.

"Wait. I need to make a call."

Before he can respond, I hang up the phone and dial Ginny's number. I hold it to my ear, praying that she answers the phone.

"Hello?" Ginny's sleep-laden voice croaks through the phone.

"Have you spoken to Maria?"

"Wait—what's going on?"

"Goddamn it, Ginny, focus." My voice is a growl of barely restrained panic. "Have you spoken to my wife in the last three hours?"

I hear some rustling and then a clearing of a throat. "No, I last spoke to her last night when she—what's wrong? Did something happen to her?"

"Maria is missing, and I don't know where the hell she is." I try to keep the panic out of my voice, but it slips through. "Her car's at the airport, and her number isn't going through. With Giacomo running loose, I... I need to find her."

I pause, swallowing the rising dread. "If you haven't heard from her, and neither have her parents, then something's wrong. Seriously wrong."

"Oh my God," she gasps. I hear her shift away from the phone, her voice low as she speaks to someone beside her. "Hold on—I'm handing you over to Dario."

"Matteo? What happened?"

"Maria's gone. I tracked her car to the airport, but her

phone isn't going through. No one's seen or heard from her in hours."

I move to the closet, pulling on clothes as I speak, my voice tight with fury.

"That bastard took my wife. I know he did."

"I thought you had men watching that place. Clearly, your security is a joke."

"Not the time, Dario," I hear his wife hiss in the background.

"Matteo, go to the airport. We'll start mobilizing things on our end. We'll find her."

I agree with her, stepping out of the closet and heading for the door. I hang up on Dario and immediately call my second.

He answers on the first ring. "Boss?"

"There's a situation," I grit out, slipping on my jacket as I stalk toward the door. "Meet me at the airport."

No questions. Just a sharp, "On it."

I hang up, shove my phone into my pocket, and step into the hallway. My mind is already racing through every possibility.

If Maria had left me, I could've taken it, giving her space, if that's what she needed.

Even if it tore me apart to watch her walk away.

But this?

This feels like something else. Something worse.

Her being taken—that's what truly unsettles me.

I get to JFK in record time. The moment I pull into the parking lot, I spot it—Maria's sleek Range Rover parked near the entrance. Everything looks normal on the outside, no signs of a struggle.

I step out of my car, my movements sharp, every nerve in

my body screaming at me. The closer I get, the colder my blood runs. I keep my gaze locked on the perimeter.

As I near the car, that's when I notice something on the windshield.

A note.

I yank it free, my fingers tightening around the edges as my eyes scan the words. A single sentence.

Looks like it's my turn to take your wife, Matteo. —From your old friend G.

The world narrows. Every sound fades. Every thought burns away, leaving only one thing—cold, murderous intent.

I turn sharply, heading back to my car, one thought blazing through me like fire: *Kill him.*

But before I can get in, tires screech against the pavement. A black SUV pulls up fast, and Valerio steps out before the engine even fully dies. His eyes land on the note in my hand, then flick to Maria's empty car.

"Fuck," he breathes. "Tell me this isn't what I think it is."

"I need to go."

Valerio's face darkens, his jaw tightening as he stalks toward me. "Boss." His voice is sharp with a clear warning. "Think before you fucking act."

I shove the note into his chest. "There's nothing to think about."

His gaze scans the words, then snaps back to mine. "This is a fucking trap."

"And you think I give a shit? He's got my wife, Valerio. My wife." The words taste like blood in my mouth because saying them makes it real. "He won't hesitate to kill her. You know exactly what kind of monster he is."

Valerio curses under his breath, dragging a hand

through his hair. "I know you don't give a damn when it comes to her," he says. "But if you charge in without a plan, Maria dies. You could die. Then what the hell will it all have been for?"

He locks eyes with me. "I need you to calm down—we need to come up with a plan that'll actually work."

The words slam into me, white-hot and suffocating. My hands shake, my breaths coming in sharp, uneven bursts. I know he's right. I fucking know. But every instinct in my body is screaming to move. To hunt. To kill.

Valerio steps closer, his voice low but firm. "Listen to me. We will get her back. But we have to be smart about this. Giacomo won't just kill her like that. This whole game he is playing is about making you suffer in the worst way possible. He won't kill her yet."

Logically, I know he's right. But logic doesn't register right now. All I can think about is that my wife is with him.

My pulse pounds, my mind at war with itself. The need to act is crushing, suffocating—but the truth in his words is undeniable.

I force out a breath. A slow, lethal inhale.

"We head back to the penthouse and track Maria's phone to see where it last pinged," I tell my second. "Then we meet with Dario and his men and come up with a solid plan of attack. I'd say we've got roughly two hours to get our shit together."

The timeline alone rips the hope straight out of my chest.

Two hours. That's two hours too long.

Giacomo could do so much to her in that time.

And the worst part? There's nothing I can do to stop it—not yet.

"Okay, I'll drive. Leave your car here," Valerio says, already moving toward his.

I follow close behind.

Valerio slides into the driver's seat, his hands tight on the wheel. I settle into the back, gripping my phone so hard I'm surprised it hasn't shattered.

The screen lights up—a photo of Maria on our wedding day, looking as beautiful as ever.

I exhale sharply through my nose, forcing my rage into focus. I can't afford to let it consume me. Not yet.

Then, the blasting of my phone pulls me from my innermost thoughts.

An unknown number stares at me, my lips peel away from my teeth in a sneer. I already fucking know who it is.

I answer without hesitation. "Where is she?"

A chuckle. Slow. Cruel. Mocking.

"Matteo, Matteo," Giacomo drawls, as if we're old friends sharing a drink. "You sound a little tense. It's so early in the morning, too. Shall we book you for a Swedish massage? It did wonders for my back."

My entire body goes rigid, my fingers curling into a fist. "Where is my wife, you sick, twisted bastard?"

"Tsk." He clicks his tongue. "So demanding. And here I was, hoping we could chat. After all, I am the one who called you. Not her."

I grit my teeth, my heart pounding. "Where is my wife, Giacomo? If you hurt her, then I will—"

He chuckles again—darker this time. "You'll kill me?"

A pause, heavy and deliberate.

"We both know that's how this ends. So, why not have a little fun before the curtain falls? Come on... where's your spirit?"

My jaw locks. "Giacomo—"

"My God, I don't remember you being so whiny," he sighs dramatically like I'm straining him. "Maria is still in one piece—for now. I can't just take her and kill her. Do you give me no credit for my craft?"

A sharp breath escapes my teeth. "What do you want?"

Giacomo laughs. "Isn't it obvious by now? I want you to suffer. I had Daniele... and now I've taken Maria. And the cherry on top?" His voice drips with venom. "She knows it was your cold-blooded hands that killed her brother."

He pauses, savoring the moment.

"Tell me—how did she look at you when she found out the truth? When she realized the kind of monster you really are? God, I wish I'd been there. I've been sitting on that little piece of information for a long time."

He was the one who told her.

A fire ignites in my chest, blinding. "If you touch her—"

"If?" He tsks again. "Matteo, Matteo. Let's be honest with each other. We both know you're running out of time. But seeing as it took you so long to figure out the warehouse, I'm going to throw you a bone. Call it my one act of kindness this year."

My knuckles turn white, gripping my phone for dear life.

Valerio grunts under his breath, his own hands tightening around the wheel. I feel the car push forward as he makes his foot heavier, increasing the speed.

Giacomo's voice drops into something colder. Darker.

"You have until noon," he murmurs. "Or I start delivering Maria to you—piece by piece."

My stomach twists. A growl rips from my throat. "You mother fu—"

"Ah, ah, ah. Careful now, you wouldn't want to upset me.

I get a little handsy when I'm angry." Giacomo's amusement only grows. "As for that bone I said I was going to throw you. Listen very carefully, my old friend. You will need to catch this one quickly if you wish to save the damsel."

I clench my teeth, my breath coming fast and hard. "Out with it."

"Return to the ghost of the past, of the one you cherished last. Some memories you shared once you cared. Out with the old and in with the new. She looks oddly familiar to her, too."

The line goes dead, and he hangs up. I hold the phone to my ear, the words playing off in my head over and over again.

What could it all possibly mean? I wrack my brain, playing the words over and over again. For a split second, my mind goes blank. But then—

He's talking about Beatrice. I know that much, but what could it be that she cherished last? She loved so many things: her family, a good glass of wine, the mountains in Aspen, and...

"I know where she is," I say under my breath.

I built her a cabin about five years ago. She loved to go there every fall to sit among the pine trees and breathe in the freshness of nature. The last time we went was only a few months before she passed.

My pulse slams against my ribs, and I'm already dialing Dario back.

He picks up instantly. "Talk."

"He has her at my family cabin. It's about an hour out of the city." My voice is razor-sharp. "I will send you the address, and you can meet us there."

"We need to move now if it's an hour out—we don't have long until daybreak," Dario says, his tone sharp. "I've got a team ready and assembled. We keep the squads small—he'll be expecting firepower. We outmaneuver them. Be smart, be fast. We get her out first. Then, we take the shot and put this fucker down."

And that honor will be all mine.

I hear some shuffling in the background before she comes back on the line. Her voice is thick with emotion—like she's been crying.

"Matteo," Ginny says, breathless. "There's something you need to know."

My grip tightens around the phone. "Know what?"

Something in her voice—sharp, trembling—makes the air shift.

"Maria might be pregnant."

The world tilts.

For one long, brutal second, I forget how to breathe.

Everything fades—the car, the road, the sky bleeding into dusk.

Maria. Pregnant.

A baby.

My blood. Our future.

I clutch the phone so hard it creaks in my hand. "What did you just say?"

Ginny exhales shakily. "She wasn't feeling well, Matteo. I told her to take a test, and she said she'd let me know once she found out... but she never got back to m—"

I can't hear the rest. My heart is pounding too loudly. My vision blurs. I don't even realize my hand is shaking until Valerio looks back and grabs my wrist. Steadying me.

"Boss," he says, voice tense, urgent. "You okay?"

I inhale sharply, locking my focus back into place.

"Yeah," I swallow hard. "I'm fine. Head to the cabin. I will call in the reinforcements and make sure they meet us three miles out. We are shooting to kill, but leave Giacomo for me. It will be my bullet that ends him."

Valerio presses on the gas and floors it down the road straight into battle.

You wanted war, Giacomo? Prepare to die in it.

37

MARIA

A dull throbbing pulses through my skull as I come to, the metallic taste of blood heavy on my tongue. My eyelids feel like lead, but I force them open, blinking against the dim, flickering light of a single bulb overhead. The air is damp, thick with the scent of pine—and something far more rancid.

Rotting wood… and death?

I scrunch up my nose and groan as I try to get my bearings.

What the hell happened? I blink again, trying to make sense of the confusion that litters my body.

I'm in a cabin.

Panic rises in my chest, cold and sharp. My wrists burn where they're bound, the rope digging deep into my skin. My legs are numb, tied just as tightly. I glance down at the chair beneath me, lit only by a single overhead bulb that barely cuts through the darkness.

I tug, testing my restraints, but they don't budge. The rope mars my skin and aches my joints.

"No, no, no…"

Every inch of me aches with rage—but it's not just anger. It's desperation. An overwhelming urge to break free.

I want to scream. I want to fight.

But all I can do is listen to the whispers of my own helplessness.

The betrayal, the grief—they claw at me from the inside out.

Should I surrender?

Part of me wants to. Part of me wants to give in, to fall into the enemy's hands and let it all go.

Because I can't ignore the truth: Matteo killed my brother.

But I can't give up.

Not now. Not when I carry life inside me. His child.

My heart feels like it's being torn in two, each half at war with the other.

I don't know who to trust anymore—not with everything that's happened.

But one thing is clear now: I won't give up.

Not when there's someone else who needs me to survive.

A soft, unhinged giggle draws my attention to the darkened corner of the room. I know that voice, and it is the last thing I expected to hear in the thick of the tension.

"Emily." Her name comes out as nothing more than a whisper, a curse that should never be uttered out loud.

"Oh, goody."

She steps out of the shadows like a slithering monster from the dark. "And here I thought you'd forgotten all about me."

She sways slightly, her pupils blown wide, fingers twitching like she's not fully in control of her own body.

Her lips are stretched into something that might be a grin—but her eyes... her eyes are wild.

Glitching. Unhinged.

"She's awake," she singsongs, taking a stumbling step toward me. "Finally. Daniele, look."

At the mention of his name, my eyes flick to the other end of the room. And there he stands, his back pressed against the wall and his eyes watching me with an incredible intensity. His voice is the last thing I remember before I was plunged into a sea of unconsciousness.

"Daniele." Emily smacks her lips together. "Come see."

I stare at the brooding man on the other end of the room. He doesn't speak, doesn't move. If not for the barely-there movement of his breathing, I wouldn't have known he was alive.

He looks exhausted—like a shadow of the man I once knew. But beneath that exhaustion... there's something else now. Hesitation.

The anger and hurt that burned in his eyes over the past few weeks have faded, dulled, giving way to something else —something I can't quite name.

Emily crouches in front of me, tilting her head like a bird of prey. "Do you know how much I hate you, Maria?" she whispers, the venom in her words coating her words. "Do you have any idea what it feels like to be invisible? To be nothing? For years, I've wanted him, watched him, only for you to come and take him from me."

I meet her gaze, keeping my voice steady despite the terror clawing up my throat. "You are a crazy woman, I hope you know that."

Her eye twitches. "Because I thought—" She stops herself, shaking her head like she's trying to silence her own thoughts.

She clearly chooses to ignore my words and keeps rambling. "I thought he would love me. I thought that once you were out of the picture—once you were gone—he'd finally see me."

I remain silent. There's nothing I can say or do to de-escalate the situation.

This woman has created an entire parasocial relationship with my husband.

If I'm going to get out of this, I'll need to keep a level head.

My life—and the baby's—depend on it.

Emily takes my chin into her icy hold, her nails digging into my skin. "What makes you so special? What do you have that I don't?"

A hand clamps down on her shoulder, yanking her back.

"Enough," Daniele growls. "This isn't about your sick obsession, Emily. Back off."

Emily glares at him, lips curling in disgust, but before she can speak, the door creaks open, silencing all of us. A cold shiver travels down my spine at the shift in the air that moves in the room.

It's him.

Giacomo strides in, bringing with him a gust of cold night air. His presence is suffocating, his energy a black void that sucks all warmth from the room—not that there was any to begin with.

He takes in the scene before him—Emily trembling, Daniele rigid, me bound and silent. His expression barely shifts as he pulls out a gun. The shot rings out before any of us even have a chance to react. It's swift, precise, and lethal.

The gunshot cracks like thunder. The bullet rips through Emily's chest, blood spattering as it slices through her like paper. She stumbles back, eyes wide, mouth opening in a silent scream as a wet, gurgling sound bubbles in her throat. Then her knees buckle. She crumples to the floor like a marionette with its strings cut—lifeless before she even hits the ground.

And just like that, she's gone. Erased from the world in a blink.

I flinch, my breath catching in my throat. Daniele stands there looking just as shocked, but he does a better job of recovering and schooling his features.

Giacomo exhales, lowering the gun like he's just swatted a fly. "I don't take kindly to disobedience. She had one job—make sure Matteo went down. Instead, she fell in love with the fucking target."

Daniele stares at Emily's lifeless body, his face blank, but his hands tremble at his sides. That's when I see it—the small shroud of humanity that still lives within him.

"Dispose of that," Giacomo orders, waving a hand toward the corpse like it's nothing more than trash.

Daniele hesitates for only a beat before moving to obey, already working to get rid of her.

As Giacomo's loose ends are tied up, he turns to me, offering a maniacal smile. "As for you, cara mia... I do hope you're comfortable. The finale is about to begin."

My stomach twists violently, but I refuse to give him the satisfaction of seeing my fear.

"Cat got your tongue, bella?" He clicks his tongue against the roof of his mouth. "No matter. I've waited years for this moment. Over two decades, and now... my revenge is finally at hand. And you, my dear, will have the best seat in the house."

He spreads his arms out wide and smiles. Never in my life have I ever seen a man so unhinged and tactful.

"You lied to Daniele," I spit. "About Beatrice—and God knows what else. You twisted everything he believed in.

Broke him from the inside out. And you will pay for what you've done, Giacomo."

He blinks, casting me an amused gaze. "From where I'm standing, amore, it seems that I have the upper hand right now."

He does—for now. But I know Matteo. By now, he's already looking for me, which means whatever grand finale Giacomo has planned... it's about to become reality.

I'm torn—caught between the desperate hope that Matteo finds me and the gut-wrenching fear that he'll walk straight into this psychopath's trap.

Giacomo chuckles, amused, striding toward the door. "I have business to attend to," he says, with a grin that curdles my blood. "But don't worry—I'll be back soon."

His gaze flicks to Daniele, who's just re-entered the room.

"Make sure she stays put," Giacomo orders. "I need to make a call to our guest of honor."

And then he's gone, leaving me in the cabin with Daniele.

The moment the door shuts behind him, the tension in the room thickens. Daniele remains frozen, his fists clenched, his chest rising and falling too fast. I can tell that he is barely holding on to whatever sliver of light that remains in him.

I swallow hard, my voice coming out softer than I intend. "Daniele."

He doesn't look at me.

I press on, my voice low but urgent.

"You know what he's doing to you, don't you? I know you do—otherwise, you wouldn't be standing there like you're about to tear yourself apart. This was never about love.

Never about family. He didn't bring you back to rebuild something—he brought you here to use you."

I lean closer, locking eyes with him.

"You're not a son to him, Daniele. You're a weapon. A tool he's been sharpening for years—just to aim at your father. This was always about Matteo. Always about revenge."

His jaw ticks. It's all the encouragement I need to keep going. I know I can reach him. I know the Daniele I knew is still in there.

"He lied to you, Daniele. Matteo didn't kill your mother, he's the one who saved her. He's the one who protected you and your mother all these years."

Daniele exhales sharply, finally turning to me. His eyes are glassy, conflicted. And in that moment, I see it—a flicker of hope, a fracture in the armor he's worn for so long.

"You are a Davacalli," I say, voice trembling with urgency. "Matteo never treated you like anything less than his son."

Daniele swallows, his Adam's apple bobbing. *Come on, Daniele. I know you are in there somewhere.*

"He killed my mother," he says hoarsely.

"No." I shake my head. "Giacomo is the one who destroyed your family. And Emily—" I pause, waiting for him to meet my gaze. "She killed Beatrice. She poisoned her the same way she was poisoning me. He manipulated both of you."

Daniele flinches. "Liar."

I don't break eye contact. "You know it's true."

A loud silence passes between us. Neither one of us daring to speak.

"Help me escape," I whisper, the plea breaking in my throat. "Please, Daniele. He's going to kill me—and when he's done, he'll come for you too. You know it."

I lean forward, forcing him to meet my eyes.

"He doesn't love you. He never did. You're not his son—you're just a shadow in his war. And the moment you stop being useful... he'll erase you like you were never here."

Silence.

His hesitation is a knife against my throat. For a long moment, he just stands there—silent, still—as if the war inside him might tear him apart.

For one agonizing second, I think he's going to walk away.

Then—

A sharp breath. A muttered curse.

Daniele steps forward and pulls out a knife, his jaw clenched tight.

I hold my breath as he cuts the ropes at my wrists, then my ankles, the strands falling like dead weight to the floor. My skin burns where they once held me captive.

I'm free.

"We have to go," he says, his voice low, urgent. "If we want to get out of here alive, we need to move. Now."

I nod, scrambling to my feet, fighting against the weakness in my legs. I use the thought of the small little life growing inside of me to push me forward and give me the strength to make it.

We move quickly, creeping toward the cabin door. Daniele peers through the cracks, body coiled like a spring. He looks over his shoulder at me and gives me one simple nod.

Stay close, his look states.

Then, in a blur, he bursts forward, kicking down the door.

The first guard doesn't even have time to react before Daniele slams his knife into his throat. The second one fumbles for his gun, but Daniele is faster, grabbing him by the wrist and twisting until there's a sickening snap. The guard drops, groaning in pain.

Daniele doesn't hesitate. One quick, brutal strike to the temple, and he's out cold.

"Move," he hisses, grabbing my wrist and dragging me toward a car parked near the tree line.

We're so close.

But then—

A gunshot splits the air.

Daniele shoves me behind him just as Giacomo's voice roars through the darkness.

"I should've fucking known! You're just like that treacherous bitch, Beatrice!" His snarl cuts through the night like a blade. "Going somewhere, son?"

Giacomo steps forward, raising his gun—but the wet earth betrays him.

His boot slips on the muddy ground, throwing him off balance. He stumbles with a curse, arms flailing, struggling to stay upright.

"Run!" Daniele growls, yanking me by the wrist. "Now!"

We tear into the woods, swallowed by the dark.

The cold air claws at my lungs as I force my legs to keep moving. Every footstep is heavier than the last, my breath coming in ragged gasps, my body screaming to stop. But I can't. Not when my child needs me to keep going. Not when every second could be the difference between life and death.

Gunshots explode behind us—deafening cracks that send my heart slamming against my ribs.

"Move faster!" Daniele shouts, gripping my wrist so tightly it feels like my bones might shatter.

My legs are about to give out, but the thought of my baby pushes me forward.

"Faster, Maria."

I'm trying. God, I'm trying.

My lungs burn, my legs scream, but the fear of what happens if we stop is stronger than the pain.

A bullet tears through the bark of a tree, just inches from my head. I yelp, ducking instinctively.

"Keep going!" Daniele growls, his grip tightening as he yanks me forward. "Don't stop!"

The trees blur together, shadows twisting and morphing in the dim moonlight. The deeper we go, the more the gunfire fades.

But I know Giacomo isn't far behind.

He won't stop until he has me—or until we're dead.

I steal a glance at Daniele, his jaw clenched, his body tense as he pushes forward. There's a wild look in his eyes, a battle raging within him. He saved me, yes, but I don't know if that means he's fully on my side.

I have to trust him. Because right now, he's all I have.

The terrain grows rougher, the ground uneven and riddled with roots and decaying forestry. My ankle twists, pain lancing through me, but I bite back a cry and force myself to keep going.

"Shit," Daniele mutters, pulling me behind the thick trunk of a tree. His chest heaves, breaths fast but forced into control. "We need a plan. Now."

"There's no plan," I pant, gripping the bark for support. "We keep running."

He shakes his head, peering around the tree. "We won't make it to the road before they catch up. There are guards littered all over this place."

He's right. We're exposed out here, too easy to track. The only thing working in our favor is the darkness.

My fingers curl into fists. "Then what do we do?"

Daniele presses his lips into a thin line, then, to my horror, he starts shrugging off his jacket.

"What are you doing?" I hiss.

"Giving them a trail."

He throws the jacket down and grabs a branch, dragging it through the dirt to erase our tracks.

"We need to split up. You head north—there's an old hunting cabin about half a mile up. If you make it there, you'll have a better shot at hiding. I'll come for you."

"No," I whisper harshly. "I am not splitting up."

His eyes flash in the darkness. "Maria, listen to me—"

"No! I'm not leaving you, Daniele. We need to get out of this together."

His expression tightens, and for a second, I think he's going to argue. But then his gaze flickers over my shoulder, his pupils dilating.

I don't need to ask why. The snap of a twig. The shuffle of boots on leaves. They're coming.

Daniele grabs my face, his fingers rough but steady. "You trust me?"

I swallow. "I—"

"Do you trust me?"

I hesitate, then nod. Something shifts in his expression, something I can't quite place. Then he's pushing me back, stepping into the open.

My heart stops.

"I messed up," Daniele breathes, every word cracked and raw. "I spent so long living in the shadow of the man I thought I was supposed to be—following orders, playing his game. I never wanted to be this person. I betrayed the only man who ever gave a shit about me." He swallows hard. "I don't know if he'll ever forgive me—and God knows I don't deserve it."

His voice cracks, but he forces the words out.

"But if I can do one thing right... it's this. It's getting you back to him. Alive."

I shake my head, but he grabs my shoulders, grounding me.

"Go to the cabin," he says, voice low and urgent. "I'll find you once I've handled this. But if I don't make it back—if something happens—tell him I'm sorry. Tell him I was trying to make it right."

His eyes glisten in the dark. Not with fear, but with something that guts me deeper—hope. Hope that he can be better than the man he became.

"What are you doing?" I whisper, my throat tight. "Why are you making it sound like goodbye?"

But he just stares at me for one long second, something silent passing between us—a promise, a regret.

Then he lifts his hands into the air and yells, "I got her!"

The blood in my veins turns to ice.

I lurch forward, but Daniele shoots me a warning glance so sharp and deadly, I freeze mid-step.

His voice carries through the trees. "She's hurt. She can't run anymore. We got her!"

My stomach churns violently as I watch him take slow, deliberate steps toward the sound of approaching footsteps, and they make their way in our direction.

Daniele.

I can't breathe. I can't move.

And then—just before he disappears into the shadows—he does something that nearly breaks me.

He winks and offers the smallest smile...

And then he's gone.

It might be the last time I'll see him alive. The last time

I'll see that small, fleeting glimpse of the man he could have been. I can't let his sacrifice be in vain. I won't.

I swallow back a sob, my hands trembling. He's giving me a chance. This is the opening.

I don't waste another second. I spin on my heel and bolt into the darkness, ignoring the guilt that claws at my chest. I have to make it to the cabin. I have to survive. Because if Daniele just risked his life for me, I refuse to let it be in vain.

The moment I take off into the darkness, the guilt slams into me like a bullet to the chest. Every instinct in my body screams at me to turn back, to stop Daniele from walking straight into the lion's den.

But I can't.

I have to trust him.

I have to run.

The forest swallows me whole, branches clawing at my skin, my breath coming in sharp gasps. Every footfall feels like an earthquake, every snapped twig a gunshot. The cold seeps into my bones, but I push forward, willing my body to move faster.

Daniele's sacrifice will mean nothing if I don't make it out.

38

MATTEO

The night feels endless—a cruel abyss stretching before me as Valerio floors the gas.

The speedometer climbs, tires screeching against the wet pavement. The rain has let up, and the moon now hangs above us, bright and unbothered.

I tighten my grip on my gun, my knuckles bone-white. Every muscle in my body is locked, my breaths short and ragged. Rage pulses through my veins, dark and consuming. I can barely hold it in.

Giacomo will pay for what he's done. And now that I know my wife is carrying our child, the fire in my veins burns even hotter.

Every inch of me aches with rage, but it's not just that. It's the thought of losing Maria—of not being there to raise our child. I can't let that happen. Not now. Not when everything I've fought for is finally within reach.

Even if she never forgives me for what I've done, I have to be there for our child. I've already lost too much—I can't lose this. I can't let Giacomo take them from me or let my past mistakes cost me the future I'm fighting for.

No. This time, I'll protect what's mine.

Valerio's voice cuts through the thick tension in the car. "Focus, Matteo. Breathe. This isn't the time for rage." His fingers tighten around the wheel. "I need you to keep your head, boss. If you lose control, she dies."

I suck in a sharp breath through my teeth, forcing my vision to clear. "I'm fine."

"You're not fine," Valerio growls, his own voice tight with frustration. "You're thinking about murder, not strategy. That's going to get us all killed."

I slam my fist against the dashboard, my control cracking. "What the fuck do you want me to do, Valerio? Sit here and be calm while Giacomo holds a gun to Maria's head?"

Valerio doesn't even flinch. He keeps his eyes on the road, jaw locked. "No. I want you to focus. I want you to use that sick fucking mind of yours and outthink him. That's how we win."

He's right. But knowing it doesn't make the fury go away.

I drag a hand down my face, exhaling slowly. "We take out every single one of his men—no loose ends, no mercy."

"Agreed," Valerio says. "But we secure Maria first. You get reckless, you put her life in danger."

I know. It's the only thing keeping me from losing my mind completely.

My ringtone blares in the car.

Dario.

I snatch it up, pressing it to my ear. "Talk."

"We're two minutes behind you," he says. "My men are in position—three miles out, just like you said. Once we get the signal, we move in."

"Good."

I hear muffled, frantic voices in the background. Then

Dario exhales sharply. "Matteo, listen to me—Giacomo is counting on you to be blinded by rage."

He's right.

"Don't let him win. He is going to try and bait you into reacting instead of thinking," Dario says, his tone serious. "He wants you to break. To make a mistake. To play into his game."

I close my eyes for half a second, grounding myself. "I won't."

The call ends, and we continue on our way. Valerio pushes the car harder, the trees whipping past in a blur.

The second Valerio slams the brakes, I'm already out of the car, my boots hitting the mud with force. The earth beneath my boots is slick, like it's fighting me with every step.

Cold air bites at my skin, and I taste the sharp sting of rainwater mixing with the sweat of my own rage. But I don't care. I barely register the rain soaking through my shirt.

All I hear is the distant echo of gunfire. The fight has already begun. We're walking into a live battleground—and we need to keep our heads.

Dario's SUV is already parked, his men positioned around it like sentinels in the dark.

Weapons drawn. Eyes sharp. They're primed for war.

I meet Dario's gaze. "Position?"

"Two of Giacomo's men posted near the perimeter," he replies, voice low and clipped. "A few more scattered deeper into the forest. I'd say eight to twelve total. He's expecting resistance—but he has no idea just how fucked he really is."

He nods to one of his men, who gestures toward the trees. "There's a clearing about half a mile in. We saw movement during the initial sweep—before the gunfire started. There's a small hunters' cabin we should check."

I already knew that. I spent years at that cabin. But hearing it spoken out loud? It makes my fucking blood boil.

Giacomo is in my house. With my wife. Playing a game he has no chance of winning.

I adjust my grip on my gun, jaw tightening. "We move fast. Quiet. We take out every last one of them."

Valerio smirks. "No survivors?"

I shake my head. "Not a fucking chance."

Dario's eyes gleam. "That's what I like to hear."

Then—

A gunshot cracks through the air. Too close. Too fucking close.

Maria.

My body moves before my mind can catch up, launching into a sprint toward the trees, each step echoing my need to save her.

Dario curses under his breath and follows, his men right behind him.

Valerio is at my side, his expression grim, eyes cutting through the dark in search of movement.

The forest is thick, the undergrowth heavy, but I push through it like an animal. Twigs snap beneath my boots.

We fan out, ghosts among the trees, covering ground with deadly precision.

I hear the shouts and screams of various voices, but none of them are hers.

Then, another round of gunfire erupts, and I hear a voice I know all too well.

"She's over here!"

Daniele.

I'd know his scream anywhere. My stomach twists at the thought of my son being on that man's side. I grip my gun tighter and push down every hesitation, every shred of doubt.

I catch a glimpse of him, and for a split second, I see the boy I once loved. My son. The memories flood me—how we used to be. But that fleeting image is swallowed by the darkness of the life he's chosen. If it comes down to it... If I have to pull the trigger on my own son—I will. But I can't shake the hollow ache in my chest.

Two of Giacomo's men stand guard near the tree line.

Idiots.

They're not expecting us. I exhale, steady. One shot. One kill. The first guard falls before he can blink. The second drops like a fly.

I don't stop.

My feet carry me toward the sound of my son's voice. I don't know what I'm about to walk into, but I know this: Whoever stands in my way will meet the same fate as those two.

Hold on, Maria. I'm coming.

39

MARIA

Fear claws at my chest, but there's no time to process it. I push my legs harder, not caring which direction I'm going—only that I keep moving. My pulse pounds in my ears, drowning out everything but the sound of my footsteps as I break through the trees

I have no real bearing of how much half a mile is, all I know is that I keep moving and winding through the thick tree, trying to make sure that I'm hard to shoot. I make it a few more feet before I catch sight of a familiar figure.

Matteo. It's him.

He's standing at the edge of a clearing, his gun raised, his sharp gaze sweeping the forest like a predator searching for his prey. A sob rips from my throat, my body lunging toward him before my mind even catches up.

"Matteo!" I scream, my voice raw with desperation.

His head snaps in my direction, his eyes locking onto mine. Relief flickers across his face for the briefest moment—

Then, a gunshot rings out. Pain explodes in my arm—white-hot, searing.

I cry out, my momentum cut short as I crash to the ground. The world tilts. Dirt and leaves grind against my cheek. My arm burns. Warm liquid trickles down my skin.

No. No, no, no.

I grit my teeth and force myself up, blinking through the haze of pain. I can hear Matteo's furious shout, the rapid fire of bullets.

Giacomo is here.

I have to move.

I push off the ground and stumble forward, my vision swimming. I don't stop. I don't look back. Somehow, through sheer will, I make it to the hunting cabin. I slam the door behind me, chest heaving, blood dripping from my arm. The cabin is dark and silent except for the storm raging outside.

I stumble toward the small closet, my body screaming in protest, and press myself against the cold wall, seeking refuge in the shadows. The pain in my arm is sharp—unrelenting. When I glance down, I see the wound is shallow; the bullet merely grazed me, but the sting is still unbearable.

I press the back of my head against the wall, squeezing my eyes shut, trying to steady my breath. I don't have time to think, but I trust that Matteo or Daniele will find me before Giacomo does. They have to.

I close my eyes, praying to whatever higher power might be listening, begging that we all make it out of this alive. I can't let this be the end.

Time stretches, each second an eternity. The silence of the cabin presses in on me, suffocating, broken only by the frantic thumping of my heart. Then, I hear it—the slow, deliberate creak of boots on the wooden porch. My breath catches in my throat as I press myself deeper into the shadows.

Who is it? My pulse spikes.

I don't dare move, don't dare make a sound. I can't. I hold my breath, listening intently. The cabin is too quiet—my heartbeat too loud, the rush of blood in my ears drowning out everything else. The door creaks open, the sound slicing through the stillness like a knife.

I stay hidden, every muscle in my body coiled tight. I need to remain unseen. I need to survive.

I slap a hand over my mouth to keep from gasping. Heavy footsteps echo against the wooden floor, slow and deliberate, each step sending ice through my veins.

The terror that overtakes me is enough to tell me that it's Giacomo. I know it's him—he is the only one who can bring out that kind of reaction from me.

I slip backward, careful not to make a sound, but my breath is too loud, my chest rising and falling in sharp, shallow heaves. My arm burns, the blood soaking my sleeve, but the panic gnawing at me is worse. Every instinct tells me to stay quiet, but fear is drowning me. I inch toward the corner of the closet, desperate to disappear deeper into the shadows.

A floorboard groans under my weight.

I freeze.

"I know you're in here, cara mia," Giacomo chuckles, low and menacing.

Terror lances through me, but I don't move. His boots scrape against the floor—slow, measured. He's taking his time, savoring the buildup of this hunt.

"I have to admit," he muses, "I didn't expect Daniele to betray me so easily. But his betrayal was inevitable. He never had the stomach for this life—just like his mother. I'll deal with him later."

Silence follows his threat.

Then, I hear the sound of tapping against the wood, like metal coming in contact with the surface.

He's close.

"I wonder," Giacomo drawls, his voice dripping with malice, "what Matteo would do if he walked in and found your lifeless body—bullet between your pretty little eyes. His precious wife, gone—just like the first."

He tilts his head, grinning.

"Or maybe we make it more entertaining. He walks in and finds you on your knees—used up, broken, just another one of my discarded toys. I bet he'll get a real kick out of that."

I bite my lip so hard I taste blood. My stomach churns at the brutality in his voice.

"Do you think he'd beg for your life?" He hums as if considering. "No... Matteo Davacalli doesn't beg. But he does bleed."

The closet door rips open, unexpectedly. A scream catches in my throat as Giacomo's cold hand clamps down on my wrist, yanking me from my hiding spot.

I thrash against his grip, but he's too strong. The fire in my arm flares, a burst of agony shooting through me, and I cry out as he shoves me into the center of the room. Tears blur my vision, my breath coming in short, panicked gasps.

He lifts his gun, pressing the cold barrel to my forehead.

"There you are, amore."

The front door slams open with a deafening crash.

"Let. Her. Go."

Matteo.

"Oh good, the guest of honor has finally arrived." Giacomo cackles. "Now the fun can truly begin."

Giacomo's fingers dig into my arm like a vice, his gun pressed so hard against my temple that I swear I can feel the cold metal seep into my skull. My breath is ragged, my vision blurred from pain, fear, and the blood trickling down my arm.

But none of it matters. Not now. Because Matteo is here. There's still a chance—maybe the only one I have—that I might make it out of this alive.

He stands in the doorway, his gun trained on Giacomo, his body rigid with fury. His chest rises and falls in jagged, controlled breaths, but his eyes—those dark, stormy eyes—are anything but controlled. They're wild, frantic, and filled with terror.

Not for himself. For me.

There's a slight hesitation in his stance, a flicker of doubt in his movements. And in that moment, I know—he's on the back foot.

"Let her go," Matteo growls, his voice low, deadly. His finger twitches over the trigger. "Now."

Giacomo chuckles, his grip tightening as he pulls me against his chest like a human shield. "Or what, Davacalli?" He cocks his head mockingly. "You'll kill me? Go on, then. But you'll have to shoot through your little wife first."

Matteo's jaw clenches, his nostrils flaring. I see the battle in his eyes—the hesitation that tugs at him, pulling him in two different directions. I know what he's thinking: If he moves too fast, if he takes the shot, I'm gone. I feel the weight of his choice pressing down on him. I see the fear—not for himself, but for me. He's stuck, caught between saving me and holding on to his humanity. And in that moment, I feel the pain of it all—the agony of loving me and knowing he might lose me forever, no matter what he does.

I swallow hard, the tears spilling over my cheeks as I struggle to hold myself together. I don't want to die. But the thought gnaws at me, the cold reality that if I do, my baby will die with me. The thought is unbearable, but it's a truth I can't escape.

Matteo takes a slow, measured step forward, his gun steady in his grip, but his eyes—his eyes are filled with a storm. "This isn't a game, Giacomo," he growls, his voice low but heavy with conviction. "All your men are down. I've cleared this whole forest. You're outnumbered. You're outgunned."

His words slice through the tension in the room like a blade. He means it. He's not just threatening anymore—he's in control. But I can feel the tightrope he's walking, the delicate balance between keeping me alive and ending Giacomo's reign.

Giacomo laughs—a low, guttural sound that sends a chill down my spine. "Do you think I fear death, Matteo?" He tilts his head, eyes gleaming with twisted satisfaction. "I didn't come here to survive. My only purpose is to make sure you lose everything—it's to ensure that you suffer. That you watch everything you hold dear crumble, piece by piece, until you have nothing left. Nothing but the ruin of your world."

He drags the barrel of his gun down my cheek, the cold metal sending a shiver through my body. My muscles lock up, bile rising in my throat.

"Take the shot if you must," Giacomo purrs, his voice oozing with malice. "But know this—you'll have to shoot through her first. And my finger?" He pauses, a cruel smile playing at the corner of his lips. "It'll be just as fast in ending her life as yours."

Matteo shifts ever so slightly—just an inch—but I see it: the war inside him. The agony, the hesitation. I know it as well as I know myself. He won't risk taking the shot. Not with me in the way.

And Giacomo knows it, too.

I close my eyes, taking a breath, trying to find the strength I've been holding onto for so long. The resolve hits me like a wave, and with a tremble in my chest, I open my eyes again, meeting Matteo's gaze.

"Take the shot," I whisper, my voice barely audible but heavy with finality.

The room falls into a heavy silence. Both men turn to me —Giacomo's smile full of disbelief, Matteo's face twisted in pain as he shakes his head.

"Take the shot, Matteo," I repeat, the tears slipping down my cheeks, hot against my skin. "Take it."

If this is how it ends, then so be it. I hope he knows that whatever happens, I don't blame him.

"Maria..." His voice cracks.

"Take the shot," I say again, my heart breaking with every word. I lock eyes with him, the man I've fallen in love with, the man I've given every part of me to. "I will be okay."

"You heard her, Davacalli. Take the shot. See what happens." Giacomo presses the gun tighter into my temple, his smile widening. "I dare you."

The tension in the room is unbearable, thick with impending tragedy, the air charged with the promise of a decision that will change everything.

40

MATTEO

The room is heavy with tension, the silence suffocating. The air feels thick, like it's holding its breath, waiting for the next move to shatter the stillness. The weight of the gun in my hand is a stark contrast to the weight of everything I've lost.

Then, the door behind me bursts open—and in walks my son with his gun raised, pointed directly at Giacomo, his face set with grim determination.

"Put the gun down, Giacomo," he says, voice cold and unwavering. "You lost."

The sight of him, standing tall and unwavering, is a shock to my system. I thought I'd lost him forever. I never expected him to turn on his own father. But here he is—standing side by side with me.

I don't have time to revel in this newfound victory. My eyes lock on my wife—her tear-stained face the one thing that grounds me.

"You're a fool, Giacomo," Daniele spits, his voice laced with bitterness. "You thought you could control everything, that I'd be your puppet. But you were wrong."

Giacomo's face twists in fury, his eyes blazing with rage. "You think I'm the fool? You, who couldn't even obey the laws of our world? You're a disappointment—a weak shadow of what I made you. You betrayed everything I taught you, everything I gave you. You were nothing but a weak boy, just like your mother."

The words hit Daniele like a slap, but he doesn't flinch. He's grown into a man, not just in stature but in resolve. His grip on the gun tightens as he steps forward, his eyes never leaving Giacomo.

"I did what was right," Daniele retorts, his voice low but steady. "You're the one who lost your way—so consumed by rage and pride, it led to your own downfall."

I can see the fury burning in Giacomo's eyes. "You want to die for this, boy? You think your little rebellion matters? You're nothing but the scum beneath my feet. "

Daniele's eyes flash with something cold, something sharp. "I'm not your little boy."

The room is on the edge of breaking, and just as the silence becomes unbearable, Giacomo's voice slices through the tension—dripping with venom.

"You want to kill me, huh? You want to end it here? Then lower your weapons, or I swear to God—I'll kill her."

My heart stops. My breath catches in my throat, but I refuse to lower my gun.

The tension between the three of us thickens—each of us waiting for the other to make a move.

"Do it," Giacomo sneers. "Take the shot, boys. Let's see who's faster."

The weight of his words hangs in the air. The room seems to tilt as if gravity no longer works in our favor.

My thoughts are a whirlwind. My gun is steady, but I can feel my control slipping.

One wrong move, and everything will shatter.

Then, without warning, Giacomo's eyes narrow. His gun swings away from Maria—aiming directly at Daniele.

"No!" I shout, but the sound is swallowed by the deafening crack of gunfire.

The shot rings out—sharp and fast.

Daniele stumbles back, a gurgled gasp escaping his lips as blood blooms across his abdomen.

My heart seizes in my chest.

"No!" I roar, my finger tightening on the trigger without thought.

The shot I take is swift. Decisive.

Giacomo's head explodes in a spray of blood and bone.

His body hits the ground hard, blood pooling beneath him, eyes staring blankly at nothing.

I rush to Daniele's side, my gun falling from my hand as I kneel beside him. He's bleeding heavily, his face pale, the life draining from him with every passing second.

"Daniele, stay with me!" I shout, my hands pressing against the wound, desperate to stop the blood from flowing.

He struggles to open his eyes, his voice barely a whisper. "Papá... forgive me... I... I didn't mean... to..."

"Danny, no," I choke, my voice cracking. "Shh... save your strength. I'm here, my boy. I'm here." Tears blur my vision, but I don't care.

"Just stay alive," I beg him, my hand trembling as I press it to his chest. "Please."

His eyes flutter open for the briefest moment, a faint smile curling at the edges of his lips. "I'm sorry..." His words fade, and with one last shaky breath, his eyes close.

"Daniele!" I scream, shaking him, but there's no response. The world around me tilts and sways, and for a moment, everything goes dark. I can't breathe, can't think, can't process it.

And then I hear it. A soft, sickening thud.

I turn, and my heart freezes.

Maria.

She's collapsed on the ground, her body unmoving, her face pale.

"Maria!" I shout, stumbling toward her, grief and fear crashing over me. My hand trembles as I reach out, fingers brushing her skin, feeling the chill.

And then, from somewhere far off, I hear the wail of sirens, ambulances drawing closer.

But in that moment, all I can think about is her.

My heart pounds in my chest, its rhythm erratic, jagged. Daniele's body lies next to me, the blood soaking into the floor, and Maria... Maria is still unconscious, her body cold to the touch.

I feel like I'm drowning, like the world is closing in around me. I can't breathe, can't think straight. I need to save her. I need to save them both.

I pull Maria's limp body into my arms, pressing her against me, desperate to feel the warmth of her skin. Her breath is shallow, but it's there. The faint rise and fall of her chest keeps me grounded, pulling me back from the edge of insanity.

"Maria," I whisper, my voice breaking as I shake her gently. "Please, come back to me. Please..."

Her eyelids flutter, and my heart skips a beat. A flicker of hope, the smallest spark in the darkness. But then her eyes remain closed, and I feel the weight of despair settle heavily over me.

The door bursts open, and a team of paramedics floods into the room—their presence like a breath of fresh air in a world suffocating with grief.

They move with practiced precision. One of them immediately kneels beside Daniele's body, assessing the damage, while another approaches Maria, who is still in my arms.

"Get them out of here," I demand, my voice hoarse, desperation threading through every word. "Now. Both of them. Don't waste time."

Valerio rushes in, his body splattered with blood—none of it his. His eyes sweep over the scene, and he curses under his breath when he sees Giacomo lying dead, a bullet hole in his skull.

I allow the paramedics to take her from me, to do their job—to get her to the hospital.

I rise to my feet, pressing down the emotions threatening to break loose.

There's no time. We need to take care of this mess. The last thing I need is the authorities on my ass.

"I need this handled," I say to my second. "We need everything cleaned up—quickly and quietly. Call the governor. And the congresswoman."

"Got it, boss." He places a hand on my shoulder. "They'll be okay."

I know words are meant to serve as encouragement, but they do nothing to ease the despair in my chest.

The paramedics move swiftly—loading Daniele's body onto a stretcher, then Maria.

The life in her is fading fast, but they're not going to let her go without a fight. I follow them, my steps unsteady, the weight of everything pressing down on me like a hammer.

I barely register the movement around me: the sound of the ambulance doors slamming shut, the rush of people speaking in low, urgent voices.

My mind is consumed by one thought, one singular focus: my family. My wife and son.

The journey between the cabin and the hospital is nothing but a blur. My mind is too lost in the events of what happened to fully comprehend much.

I sit beside her, my fingers wrapped around hers so tightly, my grip a silent plea to keep her here. I'm afraid I might crush her, but I need to feel her—need to make sure she's still here.

We reach the hospital, and the moment the ambulance comes to a stop, the doors are flung open. I don't wait. I don't even hesitate.

I follow Maria and Daniele as they're rushed into the emergency room, watching helplessly as the team works to keep them tethered to the land of the living.

Time becomes a blur after that, seconds dragging like hours. I've lost track—minutes, hours? I don't know how long I've been sitting in the sterile waiting room. All I know is I'm sitting there, a prisoner of my own thoughts.

I can't focus. My mind is a storm of fears. The waiting room is filled with the dull hum of fluorescent lights and the occasional shuffle of footsteps, but all I hear is the loud thudding of my own heart.

Valerio sits beside me, his face pale and drawn, his hands clasped so tightly I can almost see his knuckles turning white. Dario and Ginny sit across from us, her head resting on her husband's shoulder as we wait for news on either of them.

"They will make it out, Matteo. They are fighters." Valerio places his hand on my shoulder. "They will be fine."

I don't answer him because he doesn't know that. No one knows the outcome of what is happening in those operating rooms.

My entire world is on the other side of those doors, and I am helpless to do anything to fix their pain.

Finally, after what feels like an eternity, the door swings open. A doctor in a green surgical gown steps inside—his face impassive, his eyes tired. He walks straight toward me, and I can't read his expression well enough to know if he's carrying good news... or the kind that breaks you.

The four of us rise from our seats, waiting for him to speak.

"Mr. Davacalli," he says, his voice calm but firm. "Your wife is out of surgery. She had significant internal bleeding, but we were able to stop it. We also placed a shunt in her chest to drain excess fluid."

"And the baby?"

"The baby's fine. Strong heartbeat." He offers me a small smile. "Maria is still unconscious, but I can take you back to see her."

A rush of relief floods me, my chest tightening in a way that almost hurts. I stare at the doctor, trying to process what he's just said, but his words barely register.

But the relief is short-lived.

"What about Daniele?"

The doctor's face falls, and his next words make my stomach drop.

"Your son, however..." He pauses. "He must've hit the floor hard before you got to him. There was significant hemorrhaging in his brain, and it swelled during the chest surgery. We were able to relieve the pressure, but..."

He hesitates just for a moment. "He's on life support. As it stands, there's little to no brain function. We're not sure he'll regain it. You'll need to start considering your options."

The room spins around me. The air thickens. For a moment, I can't breathe.

My son.

I swallow hard, nausea rising like a tide. My throat tightens as the words sink in—slowly, painfully.

Daniele. My son.

I force myself to nod. "I... I understand."

I can feel Valerio, Dario, and Ginny looking at me, pity swimming in their eyes. But I don't dare look at any of them.

"Can I see my wife?"

The doctor nods. "You can, but only for a few minutes. She's still unconscious, and we will need to transfer her to the ICU after she is done in post-op. We need to monitor her closely. The next forty-eight hours will be critical for her and the baby."

I don't care. I don't care how long they'll let me stay or how long I've been waiting. I just need to be near her. I need to feel like I'm still connected to her in this storm of chaos and loss.

I leave the three of them and follow the doctor down the hall, the walls closing in around me, and enter the room where Maria lies. She's hooked up to machines, a quiet beeping sound filling the otherwise silent room. Her body is pale, almost translucent against the white sheets, but she's breathing.

She's still here.

I pull a chair to her side, my eyes never leaving her face. I reach for her hand, brushing my fingers over hers as I hold it gently. I let the silence stretch between us, the only sound the soft rhythm of the machines.

"Please," I whisper again, the words a prayer.

"You need to pull through this, amore. I can't lose you, Maria. Not when our child needs you to fight to be here. Not when I haven't told you how sorry I am. Not before I make up for what I did. Please... come back to me."

Never in all my years have I felt so helpless.

All the power and money in the world, and I still couldn't save my son—and now my wife's life hangs in the balance.

Fuck.

I don't care how long I have to wait—I'll be at her side, willing her to open her eyes again.

She needs to wake up because without her, there's no version of me that can exist.

41

MARIA

Pain lances through my chest like a thousand needles, and I gasp, trying to force air into my lungs. The sterile sting of antiseptic burns my nostrils, mixing with the metallic taste of fear. I wince, but the fog in my head doesn't lift, and my body feels like it's been broken and pieced together wrong.

It comes to me in flashes.

The cabin. Daniele. Gunshots.

My eyes snap open, and the harsh fluorescent lights above me feel like a cruel assault on my senses. I shut them again, overwhelmed by the brightness. After a few seconds, I force them open once more, the world blurring in and out of focus. My head spins, every movement heavier than the last.

I blink a few times, trying to clear the fog in my head. A dull ache builds between my eyebrows as I come to. I try to lift my hand, but it feels heavy. Sluggish. My body aches in places I don't remember.

"The baby..." I choke out, my hand moving to my flat stomach.

The steady beeping in the background spikes as panic surges through me.

"My baby."

"Maria."

A familiar voice breaks through the heavy silence. "You're okay. Calm down... you're okay."

His tone is soft, thick with something I can't quite place. The warmth in his voice is a lifeline, but it feels distant, like I'm hearing him from underwater.

As I turn toward him, I see him sitting by my bedside—his face pale, but his eyes warm, watching me with that familiar, intense gaze that always makes my heart ache in a way I can't explain.

"Maria," he whispers, leaning closer, his hand reaching for mine. "You're awake. Finally."

I want to speak, to say something—but my throat feels raw, and I struggle to swallow.

The panic that had gripped me slowly begins to fade... but only for a moment.

I look down at my stomach, waiting—hoping—to feel something inside me.

"The baby is fine," he says, a small smile pulling at the corners of his lips, though it doesn't reach his eyes.

"The doctor said the baby has a strong heartbeat," he breathes out, "and everything looks stable."

At his words, I ease a little. I sink back into the bed and let the fatigue pull me under—but only for a moment, as the thick silence lingers.

"How are you feeling?" he asks gently. His thumb strokes over my knuckles, comforting me.

I see the way his eyes roam over my body, searching for any sign of lasting damage—anything I might have woken up with.

"You gave me quite the scare there."

I nod, but I still feel uneasy... unsure.

He knows about the baby.

When I left, he didn't know a thing—and now he does. He knows I'm carrying his child.

He catches the look in my eyes, and his expression shifts—like he knows exactly what's going through my mind.

His voice is shakier now. "You're... you're about eight weeks along, at least from what the doctor said. I... I understand why you didn't tell me, amore," he adds, his voice breaking slightly, like he's afraid of pushing me too far.

I want to say something, but the weight of his words presses down on me harder than the pain in my chest.

I feel the sting of his words more than I should. It's not just about the baby, not anymore. It's about the lies, the silence, the secrets we've kept buried beneath the surface of everything.

The anger that had twisted in my chest for so long still lingers, hot and bitter. But now, under the weight of his remorse, I can't help but wonder... can love overcome all of this? Can I forgive him, not just for what he did to me, but for what he did to my brother?

I close my eyes, trying to shut out the turmoil inside me, but it's all still there—bubbling beneath the surface, threatening to spill over.

"I... I was scared, Matteo," I whisper, my voice trembling, betraying the rawness I'm desperately trying to contain.

My throat feels tight, like every word is a struggle to get past the lump that's lodged there. I push through it, but it feels like there's so much more I can't say, so much I'm still trying to understand.

"I didn't know how to tell you," I continue, my chest tightening. "After everything that happened with my brother... and then finding out it was you... It was too much to process, too much pain to carry. I couldn't think straight, couldn't breathe with the weight of it all."

I pause, swallowing hard, trying to steady myself, but the words feel like they're choking me.

"I need to get my head right, Matteo. I need space to figure out how to face you, to make sense of everything... because I still don't know how I feel about what I saw. About you."

The confession hangs heavy in the air between us. I feel the pull of everything that's left unsaid, the guilt of not being able to fully give him the truth, and the confusion of not knowing where I stand anymore. How can I reconcile the man I love with the man who killed my brother? How can I love him in spite of everything he's done?

Matteo's eyes flash with a mix of regret and guilt. "I'm sorry, Maria. I can't begin to make up for what I've done."

His voice cracks—raw with remorse and pain—but I can't tell if I'm ready to forgive him.

"I don't deserve your forgiveness. Or your mercy. Even if it was an accident—a horrible, terrible mistake—it doesn't change the fact that I killed your brother."

The words slice through me like a double-edged sword.

"I was hurt, Matteo," I continue, my voice trembling now as the weight of the words press down on me. "And I was angry. Oh, God, I was so angry. I wanted to hate you. I wanted to hate you so badly because the truth was too hard to face—I was in love with you."

I pause, the rawness of the confession hitting me like a wave. It's painful, but it's the truth. I can feel the walls around my heart start to crumble as the memory of him in the cabin floods my mind—the way he rushed to me, how his fear was written all over his face. How, even after everything, he still cared.

In the silence that stretches between us, it feels like I can hear my heart beating—steady, insistent, pulling me toward him. But the weight of what we've lost, of what he's done, threatens to tear that connection apart.

I've spent so long convincing myself that love could be enough—that if I just held on tight enough, we'd find a way through.

But love built on broken promises was never going to last.

And the illusion holding us together... it shattered the moment I watched my brother fall.

"But then, in the middle of all the rage and confusion, I saw you, Matteo. I saw you in the cabin, coming for me—fear etched across your face. I saw the man who would do anything to save me. And for a moment... I wanted to believe that was enough. That despite everything, despite the pain, I still loved you. That I could still believe in us. In that moment—so close to death—it wasn't dying that terrified me. It was the thought of letting go of you. Of waking up in a world without you in it."

I shake my head slightly, the ache in my chest tightening. "But love isn't supposed to feel like this—like a wound that never heals. And every time I look at you, I see what I lost. Loving you feels like betraying him... like turning my back on my brother. Like every beat of my heart for you erases a piece of him—and the memory I'm still trying to protect."

My voice falters, the rest of the words lodged painfully in my throat.

He doesn't speak. Doesn't reach for me. He just stands there—still, silent—like he knows that any wrong move might break me completely. And somehow, that silence gives me the space I didn't even know I needed.

"Over the past few months, I've come to know you—your character, the kind of man you are. And that man doesn't shoot innocent people in cold blood. You're not perfect. You live in the gray, and sometimes you make impossible choices... You protect what's yours. You act when you're cornered. And maybe that's why it hurts so much—because deep down, I still believe you're not the villain in this story."

His expression shifts—something flickers in his eyes, raw and unspoken—but it's quickly replaced by a deep sadness that makes my heart ache.

He doesn't say anything at first, just stares at me, as if trying to process what I've said.

"I shouldn't want to still be with you. In fact, I should run for the hills and never look back. That would be the safest option—the only logical answer for me. And yet... somewhere along the way, against every ounce of reason, I fell in love with you, Matteo," I whisper, my fingers curling around his. "But love isn't always enough. Not when it's built on pain. Not when it costs me pieces of myself."

I gently pull my hand from his, the ache rising in my throat.

"I love you... but I can't stay—not right now. Maybe not ever. Because if I stay, I'm choosing you over the part of me that's still grieving him. And I don't know how to live with that."

His eyes shine, the emotion in them breaking something inside me. He leans forward, presses a kiss to my forehead—soft, reverent, like goodbye.

"I never wanted to hurt you," he murmurs, his voice thick with regret.

We hold each other's gaze, a thousand words spoken in silence.

And for one final, fleeting moment—I wish things had been different.

But love alone won't carry us through this storm.

Not this time.

But just as the silence settles between us, my thoughts shift—and a sudden panic grips me. "Daniele," I whisper, breaking the fragile stillness. "How is he?"

The weight of Daniele's fate crushes me in a way I can't fully grasp. His apology, his regret—it feels like a final breath he'll never get to exhale.

And the man who should be at his side... is here, with me.

I want to push him away, to make him feel the guilt I carry for still loving him despite everything.

But I don't. Not yet.

Because my heart aches for the son he's about to lose—and some part of me still needs to hold on, if only long enough to survive this moment.

Matteo's face tightens, and I see the anguish in his eyes before he speaks.

"He's on life support, Maria. There's little to no brain function. The doctors... they don't think he's going to make it."

The room goes still.

The words hit me like a freight train, and for a moment, I forget how to breathe.

For all he did, in the end, he found his redemption. He tried to correct the mistakes he had made.

I squeeze Matteo's hand, my chest tightening with grief —grief for Daniele, yes, but also for the man I love, who is shattering before me.

"I'm sorry, Matteo. I'm so sorry."

I open my arms to him, and he lets me pull him into a warm embrace.

Nothing will ever soothe this kind of heaviness—but I will do whatever it takes to make sure he never feels alone.

"In the end, he was sorry—for how everything played out. He loved you with everything he had, and he wanted to get me to safety... to make up for the wrong he'd allowed."

Matteo stares at me, his face caught between deep sorrow and acceptance—like he's already mourning the loss of the son he tried so hard to protect. His eyes hold a pain so raw, so real, that it twists in my chest. He's not just losing Daniele—he's losing the future they both fought for.

I can see the heaviness in his gaze—the quiet desperation to be there for Daniele in his final moments.

And I know what he needs to do.

"Go to him," I say quietly, urging him. "Go be with your son. I'll be okay here for now."

He looks at me, uncertainty flickering in his gaze. But I know he has to be with Daniele. He has to say goodbye—and we don't know how much time he has left to do that.

"Here. Take my phone," Matteo says, his voice shaking as he hands it to me. "Call your parents. They've been worried about you, and I promised them you'd call as soon as you woke up. They were set to land in two days."

I nod, trying to keep myself composed. I don't want to fall apart in front of him and make him hesitate.

He needs to go. He needs to be with his son.

After Matteo leaves, I stare down at the screen—my mother's number already open, waiting for me to dial.

I let my fingers hover above the phone, frozen.

My hands tremble as I lift the phone to my ear. The room is quiet, sterile. A faint beeping from the monitors is the only sound as I sit curled on the hospital bed, wrapped in a blanket that doesn't quite chase away the cold.

The phone rings three times before my mother answers. "Maria? Dios mío—are you all right?"

"I'm okay, Mamá," I whisper. The lie tastes like ash on my tongue. I wish I could believe it.

"I just wanted to tell you… I'm coming home."

There's a long pause. I can almost hear her heart pounding through the silence.

"We've been so worried, Maria. We've missed you so much."

"I know, Mamá."

"When will you be here?"

"Soon," I say softly. "There are just a few things I need to do first."

I don't explain. I can't. There's too much she wouldn't understand—too much even I don't.

Matteo is losing his son. And for everything that's happened between us, I can't walk away. Not yet. So I'll stay beside him through this. I'll help him say goodbye. I'll be his strength—until he no longer needs mine.

And then… I'll leave.

Not because I stopped loving him—

But because sometimes love isn't enough to survive what's been lost.

42

MATTEO

It's crazy to think that I've watched this boy go from diapers to grade school to being a full-grown man. I've been with him every single step of the way. I was there for every milestone, every smile, every tear. Not once did I leave his side.

And now, here I stand, watching him lie on this damn hospital bed, and I can do nothing to bring him back.

The beeping of the machines is the only sound filling the room, and it's the harshest noise I've ever heard in my life. I've taken on live gunfire and had explosives detonate in my face, and still, the chilling, steady beat of the monitor is the most terrifying sound to me.

His heart still beats. His chest rises and falls in a mechanical rhythm, as if he's still here—but I know the truth. His body is hanging on by threads, and his soul is somewhere I can't reach.

"Your son is brain dead."

The words echo loudly in the deepest chambers of my heart.

I place my hand gently on his, feeling the coldness in his skin. He has numerous tubes and wires attached to him, trying to keep him anchored to the land of the living.

"Daniele," I whisper, my voice cracking, "I'm so sorry, my boy. I failed you."

I've never been one for prayer. Never needed to ask for guidance or strength. But right now, standing at the edge of my son's life, I don't know what else to do. So I close my eyes, the weight of everything pressing down on me, and I pray. For the first time in my life, I beg the heavens to give me just one more moment with him.

"Please," I murmur. "Just one more conversation. Let me tell him I love him. Let me make things right. He needs to know that I love him—that I forgive him."

I take my seat beside him and hold onto his hand for dear life. The tears prick at my eyes but never fall. I simply sit in the silence, the only background noise the steady beating of the monitor behind him.

"Come back to me, my boy. Even if it's just for a moment. Come back to me."

Never in my life have I felt so broken. The woman I love hates me. My son is between life and death. And all I can do is stand and watch the wreckage that follows.

I don't know if my words will reach anyone. Heaven, fate —whatever it is that might hear me. But I say them anyway, desperate for any kind of intervention.

The minutes tick into hours, and the sun dips just below the concrete horizon. The streams of light that filter in are from the last remnants of the day.

Will I have to make the choice to take him off this machine? Would it be cruel to hold out hope for a miracle?

I have scorned heaven enough times for it to ignore my cries.

But still, I plead with them anyway—
Hoping.
Praying.
For a miracle for a sinner like me.

I blink my eyes open and look down at his face again, expecting to see his sleeping form—but I'm stunned. I see his lids twitch, the tube in his mouth shifting ever so slightly.

"Daniele..." I whisper his name. "Can you hear me?"

And then, it happens. The soft flutter of his eyelids.

I watch, breathless, as his eyes blink open. There's a flicker of disorientation, but then they find me. His gaze is uncertain, slightly confused—but it's there. He's looking at me.

And for the first time, I see the apology in his eyes. He can't speak, not with the tubes in his throat, but I hear him anyway. I feel the weight of what he's trying to say—the regret, the understanding.

I feel it too.

Maria's words hit me again, this time with far greater force now that I'm standing at his bedside.

"Daniele," I say softly, my voice barely a whisper as I lean closer, still holding his hand. "I forgive you, my boy. Okay? I know you were just angry, confused, and lost. But I forgive you. I forgive you, and I am so, so sorry. I never wanted you to feel like you were unworthy of being my son, because that was the furthest thing from the truth. You may not be my blood, but you are my son. You've always belonged with me—DNA was never what made us family. You didn't need my blood to be mine... You always were."

The words hang in the air. A promise. A release. It's all I can give him now. I am powerless to offer anything else.

A single tear slips from the corner of his eye, the light in his blue gaze locked on mine.

And then, just as quickly as the spark of life returned, it fades.

The monitors flatline.

The beeping morphs into a deafening silence.

His chest stills—and I know.

He's gone.

"Daniele..." I whisper his name into the sterile room, the scream of the flatline echoing in the background—but I can't even hear it anymore. "Go well, my boy."

I swallow the lump in my throat, forcing back the grief that threatens to consume me.

My son—my precious son—is no longer here.

The words I should have said years ago.

The things I should have done.

They're all left behind.

But at least I had that one moment.

The one confession I needed him to hear.

I stand there for a long while, staring down at him, willing my heart to accept what's happened.

But it doesn't. It never will.

A parent is never meant to bury their child.

It's the kind of heaviness that refuses to leave you—even as the years drift on.

And I will carry this hurt for as long as I live.

And that's okay.

Because the pain I carry will always be proof of the love I still hold for my boy.

Until the day we meet again—

Wherever that may be.

∼

A WEEK LATER...

The rain pelts down as I stand at the gravesite, the umbrella above me doing little to shield me from the weight of it all. I watch as my son's coffin is lowered into the earth, the finality of it hitting me harder than I ever could've imagined. My chest aches—a raw, bleeding wound that won't heal. I thought I could bear this. I thought I was prepared. But I wasn't. No one ever is.

Maria stands beside me, her presence the only thing keeping me anchored. Her hand rests in mine, and she hasn't let it go since we left the church service. True to her word, she has stayed by my side while I face the worst pain of my life. I've never needed to lean on a woman before her. But now, for the first time in my life, I allow myself to break. I allow myself to be weak—if only for a moment.

I glance to the side, my gaze landing on Beatrice's tombstone—the grave next to Daniele's. The two of them are together now, buried side by side. It seems fitting, in a way. They were always so intertwined in life, even if we never really acknowledged it.

"As his soul has left this earth, we lower his body to the ground, and I ask that..." The reverend begins his speech, but I'm too far gone to process his words.

The ceremony passes in a blur—the somber rituals, the weight in the air. I can hardly feel anything except the cold numbness creeping into my bones.

And then, when it's finally over, we return to the manor for the wake. A place I haven't set foot in since Beatrice's passing.

It took Beatrice dying for me to leave this estate I had built for our family. And now, it's taken my son's death to bring me back.

The family home he grew up in and loved so dearly.

The house feels just as hollow as I do. Filled with mourners, yes—but also filled with ghosts. Still, there's a strange comfort in being surrounded by these familiar walls.

43

MARIA

I thought the halls would feel haunted.
I thought they would scream at me, curse me—because these were the walls she walked.

These were the walls where she created a family with him.

But there's a strange comfort that comes with being here. It feels... like a home. Not like the penthouse we've been living in these past few months. There's a warmth that carries across the marble floors.

A life that once was still lingers in this palace of a house.

I press my hand over my belly and watch the garden outside the large floor-to-ceiling window. I needed some time for myself. The funeral was suffocating, and watching Matteo in so much pain tore at the deepest parts of my heart.

I said I'd be there for him, but this weight... if it feels this heavy on me, I can only imagine how much heavier it must be for him.

I hate seeing him like this. But he needs to grieve. He

needs to mourn his son fully, and then—maybe—make space to heal.

I don't know if I'll still be there when that time comes. I made a promise, but being this close to him after everything that's happened… It's hard.

"Amore."

My father comes to stand beside me. His familiar scent brings a flicker of comfort to my chest. "I was looking for you."

I turn my head to the side. "Papá, I just needed some time away from everything."

His lips tilt upward in a small smile, though it doesn't quite reach his eyes. "How are you, cara?"

I sigh, the weight of the past few days pressing down on my chest. "As well as I can be. We eradicated the man responsible for all this strife. But in the process, we lost Daniele. And it feels… bittersweet. Like we won—but we also lost."

"Come, cara."

My father pulls me into his arms and holds me.

I've always been independent. I never needed to be coddled. I stood well on my own.

But in this moment, I curl into him like the little girl who always found safety in her father's arms.

"You are far too strong for your own good," my father mutters into my hair.

"I need to be, Papá. He needs me. I can't leave him right now."

When I pull away, I see something flash in my father's eyes—a mixture of regret and sorrow swirling in the deep waters of his gaze.

"What is it, Papá?"

He doesn't respond at first. The tension between us thickens with every second that passes.

"Papá?" My stomach churns as I search his face.

He sighs. "Maria, I need to tell you something."

I frown. "Tell me what?"

He pauses, gathering the courage to continue. "Maria... I can't carry this any longer. You need to know what really happened the night Matteo shot Antonio."

"We already know what happened, Papá."

He shakes his head. "There's more to the story, cara mia. Far more that I need you to prepare yourself for."

Dread seeps into my bones, oozing from the marrow into my bloodstream. "What do you mean there's more?"

A heavy silence falls between us before Papá finally fills it.

"Your brother, cara... he was working with Giacomo." His mouth moves, but the words don't register at first. "I know it's hard to accept, but it's the truth. He wanted to be part of this world—this blood and war."

The disappointment in his voice cuts deep. My father tried for years to distance us from this life. He ran to Italy to give us a chance at something different—something normal. A life untouched by violence and legacy.

"He chose to live by the code." The words escape my lips in a whisper of disbelief. "But... I don't understand."

"Antonio was sent to kill Matteo. That was his mission. The day he died... Matteo was ambushed. Giacomo orchestrated it—and Antonio led the charge."

I stare at my father, stunned. The words reach my ears, but my mind struggles to make sense of them.

"Papá... are you saying..."

He nods slowly, grief shadowing his expression. "Yes, Maria. He chose the traitor's side. Manipulated by Giacomo's lies—just like Daniele. Antonio organized the ambush at the warehouse. He wanted to be fully immersed in this life. He wanted to make a name for himself."

He pauses, voice shaking.

"I didn't tell you because I was ashamed. We're the ones who need forgiveness. He tried to kill the man who's done more for this family than most ever will—a man we owe far more than we admit." His voice dropped lower.

"Antonio fed Matteo false information about a stolen shipment worth millions—it was a trap. Matteo was the real target. And Antonio... he didn't hesitate to follow Giacomo's orders."

I stand frozen, my mind racing.

"After Antonio's death, I requested an autopsy. The report said he died from suffocation. The gunshot wound was superficial. He would've survived with just a scar if he hadn't been suffocated. I started digging. One of Antonio's men came to me—he found footage from that day. It showed what really happened."

His voice breaks slightly.

"Antonio attacked Matteo from behind. In the struggle, Matteo didn't even know it was him. The shot went off by accident—they were fighting over the gun. When Matteo saw Antonio's face, he panicked. He and Daniele rushed out to get help to take him to the hospital. He was alive."

"But someone else was there. A shadow approached. Antonio was weak from the wound... and he was suffocated. By the time Matteo returned, Antonio was dead. He thought he'd died from the bullet."

"They got him to the hospital within ten minutes."

He looks away.

"I was furious. I wanted to destroy the man who killed my son. But then I saw the footage. I saw the truth. I spoke to Matteo. Told him everything. I needed his conscience to be clean—because he wasn't the one who should feel guilty. We should. My son... was the traitor."

His eyes shimmer. "Matteo begged me not to tell you. He didn't want you to remember your brother that way. He chose to protect your memory of Antonio—even if it meant losing you forever. But I can't stand by and watch him break. Losing his son, and now the woman he would give his life for..."

He places a hand gently on mine.

"Maria, you have to forgive him. It wasn't his fault. Matteo's shot was meant to save his son, while Antonio's was meant to kill him. In the end, Matteo won the war. But he lost so much more. He lost his family twice."

My breath catches and I have to use the wall to steady myself. I feel like the world tilts on its axis. I feel the air evaporate from my lungs.

"He... he didn't kill my brother," I utter the words. "He... he is innocent."

My father places his hand on the small of my back and pulls me into him. I allow him to hold me while I crumble. All this time I have been moving between love and hate, trying to make sense of the violence that tore my family apart.

I pull away from him, tears streaking down my face. "I need to find him, Papá. I need to..."

My father grabs my hands and kisses the back of my knuckles affectionately. "He's on the balcony on the second floor. I left him there before I came to see you."

I don't respond to him. I simply pull my hand from his grasp. My feet are already moving by the time he is done speaking. My pace is quick—frantic and desperate to get to him. My heart roars in my chest at this newfound revelation that has leveled my entire psyche.

Antonio.

My brother.

A traitor?

No. No, not him.

But then—yes. Maybe.

I didn't know anymore.

And Matteo...

The man I'd hated.

The man I'd loved anyway.

The man I'd cursed for taking my brother away.

He didn't do it.

He didn't even know.

My brother—my sweet Antonio—had been the one to start all of this. For months, I mourned him as a victim, believing he'd been gunned down in cold blood. But the truth? He chose the side of the true devil in this story—the cold, unscrupulous murderer who's left nothing but blood and ruin in his wake. The man who hunted Matteo, who terrorized this family without mercy.

My heart still aches for him. I still grieve the boy I grew up with, the brother I once believed incapable of betrayal. But now, I see him in a new light—not a monster, not a martyr. Just... human. Flawed. And heartbreakingly lost.

I don't love him any less. But the truth has cracked something open in me. It changes everything.

"One day," I whisper into the silence of the hallway, the marble echoing beneath my feet. "One day, I will forgive you."

My heels echo against the marble floors of the mansion as I move through the halls in search of my husband. The pain and despair that have consumed me for weeks now begin to lift, dissolving into something quieter—something purer. All that remains is love and grief. Love for him. Grief for everything we've lost. Matteo.

I pick up my pace, searching the hallway. By the time I make it to the end, to the door that leads to the balcony, I am panting.

Then I see him through the glass. He stands stoic, hands pressed against the concrete ledge, looking out at the rolling hills of the Davacalli estate. My heart clenches in my chest —seeing him look so... devastated pains me.

His pain is mine.

I push the door to the side and step out into the cool chill of the autumn air. The wind blows through my hair, cooling the heat at the back of my neck. "Mat..."

I try to call his name, but a lump lodges in my throat and steals the rest of my words. So I say nothing. Just stand there, watching him from a distance.

He turns slowly, and when he sees me—when our eyes meet—I see it all. The weight of it. The months he'd carried it. The guilt. The silence. The grief he thought he had no right to feel.

"You know," he says quietly when I reached him.

I nod. "Yes."

"I told him not to tell you."

"He told me that, too."

A silence stretches between us—long and tight, the kind that sits between heartbreak and hope and doesn't lean either way.

I finally ask, my voice barely more than a breath, "Why? Why would you carry that alone?"

He glances at me, then down at the ground like the truth still weighed too much.

"Because your brother didn't deserve to be remembered

as a traitor. Not by you. He was just a lost soul... like Daniele. A good heart who lost his way before he even knew how to come back."

My chest aches, sharp and slow. "And what about you?"

"I'm not the one you loved."

The words shouldn't have hurt—not after everything—but they did. Because he still didn't get it. He still thought he wasn't enough. Still believed that losing me was just the cost of his silence.

"You ran out to save him," I say, my voice steadier now. "You could've walked away, but you didn't."

"I was too late," he mutters.

"But you tried."

He looks away then, his jaw locking like he's holding back everything that has been building inside him for months.

"I hated you," I whisper. "I woke up with it. Slept with it. Carried it like a second skin."

He didn't flinch.

"I know," he said.

"And still..." I swallow. "I kept loving you."

His eyes flick to mine, the faintest shimmer in them.

"I know that, too."

I take a step closer. Then another. The space between us wasn't cold anymore. It was full. Full of things we hadn't said, and things we still couldn't.

"You should've told me."

"I didn't want to take your brother from you twice."

And that... that is what finally breaks me.

The tears come then—not for Antonio, and not for the war that stole everything from all of us.

But for him. For the man who carried every burden alone except the one that mattered most—his heart.

I step into his arms without thinking, and he pulls me in like I am something precious. Like he doesn't quite believe I am real. Like letting go would cost him everything.

"You didn't kill him, Matteo," I whisper against his chest.

"Doesn't change what happened."

"No," I say softly, pulling back just enough to look at him. "But it changes everything else."

He doesn't answer. He just looks at me like he wants to believe it—like maybe hearing it out loud will make it true.

I reach up, my fingers brushing along his jaw, rough with days of exhaustion and silence.

"You've punished yourself long enough," I whisper. "Let me carry some of it now."

His eyes flutter shut, just for a second. And when he opens them again, something in him has shifted.

Not all the weight was gone—it wouldn't be, not yet—but something inside him had cracked open.

He leans in, not all at once, but slowly, like he was waiting for me to stop him.

I don't.

Our lips meet—soft at first, uncertain. Then deeper. Like we were are trying to memorize the way this feels after everything we've lost, everything we've nearly destroyed.

It doesn't erase the past.

But it feels like a beginning.

When we pull apart, his forehead rests against mine, breath warm and uneven.

"I love you," I say, because I can't hold it back any longer. "Even when I tried not to. Even when it hurt."

His hand cradles the side of my face, gentle, reverent.

"I never stopped," he murmurs. "Not for a second."

We stand there for a while, just holding on. Just breathing.

Grief doesn't disappear. Love doesn't fix everything.
But sometimes, it is enough to know the truth.
Sometimes, it is enough to come back to each other.
Even if it is through fire.
Even if it is after everything.

Three months later...

Three months have passed since the funeral, but the weight of our loss still clings to the penthouse like an unshakable fog. I watch Matteo struggle in silence—burying himself in work, speaking less, retreating into his own world. He is a strong man, a powerful man, but even the strongest have their breaking points. And I fear he's nearing his—or he's already found it and is simply existing now.

The scent of warm bread and sugar fills the small bakery as I stand beside Ginny, watching as the baker carefully packs the gender reveal cake into a pristine white box. It's a delicate thing, hiding within it a secret that will soon change our lives forever.

I can't contain my excitement. The thought of a little human with equal parts Matteo and me growing in my belly... This baby is a beacon of hope in the midst of the deep grief we're moving through—our small light at the end of the tunnel.

Ginny glances over, smiling softly. "How are you holding up?" she asks, running a hand over her small bump.

Yes, only a few days after I found out I was pregnant, Ginny found out she was expecting again. Nico and Sofia, her wild little twins, are currently running circles around us, their laughter echoing through the bakery like little bursts of joy.

There's something so comforting, so grounding, about going through this experience alongside her. Watching her with her two little ones, knowing she's done this before—it gives me a strange sense of peace.

I feel a gentle kick and instinctively rub my bump, letting this little one know I'm right here.

I sigh. "I'm okay. I think Matteo is the one I worry about the most." I meet Ginny's gaze. "I don't know how to help him. He won't talk about it. He just... works. I get that he doesn't want to drown in his sorrow, but I worry that avoiding it will only cripple him down the line."

Ginny nods knowingly. "It's hard. These men—they carry everything on their shoulders, thinking they have to be strong for everyone else. Sometimes they forget that we're strong, too. We made vows to them just like they did to us."

I chuckle. "Exactly. I just want to be there for him, but I don't know how to break through."

"You just have to keep trying," Ginny says. "He'll let you in when he's ready. And in the meantime, you just love him. Hold him that extra bit longer, kiss him softer and more often, and remind him you're there. That's what we do."

I exhale and nod, accepting the advice. "You're right. He needs time."

The baker hands us the box, and I smile in gratitude before we walk out to our cars. I see my bodyguards posted up by the back door waiting. Neither Dario nor Matteo lets us touch the wheel while pregnant, and though I wanted to fight him at first, I know he does it for his own peace of mind.

"Dinner at our place next week?" Ginny offers. "He won't

admit it, but I know Dario is dying to get another round of chess in with Matteo."

I laugh. "Those two are secretly besties."

"Yup." She laughs with me. "How does Thursday sound? Maybe tacos—I've been craving Mexican food like crazy."

I nod. "That sounds perfect."

We hug briefly before parting ways. I place the cake gently on the passenger seat before settling in and letting Tony drive me home. My fingers tap anxiously against the leather of the seat as I think of my husband—of how distant he's been. Maybe tonight will be the night I reach him.

When I arrive home, the penthouse is quiet. Matteo's study door is slightly ajar, and I peek inside to see him hunched over his desk, paperwork spread across the surface, his brows furrowed in deep concentration.

I step inside, my voice soft. "You've been at this all day."

He looks up, the dark circles beneath his eyes evidence of too many sleepless nights. But when he sees me, something in his face softens.

"I have to make sure everything is in order," he says, leaning back in his chair. "I don't have the luxury of slowing down."

I approach, resting a hand on his shoulder. "You do," I whisper. "You just don't let yourself."

Matteo reaches up, taking my hand in his and pressing a kiss to my palm. "I can't lose you, too."

I swallow the lump in my throat, then slowly guide his hand to my small but growing bump. "You won't," I promise. "The threats are gone, and there's peace—well, as much as this world will allow, anyway. We're okay, amore mio. We're fine."

His eyes soften as he runs his fingers gently over my

stomach. The baby instantly recognizes their father's touch and starts jumping.

"I'll protect you. Both of you. Always. How was our little mango today?"

Matteo has a pregnancy app on his phone that shows the baby's size each week. He takes such pride and joy every time we reach a new fruit or vegetable. This week, we're a mango.

"They were fine." I smile, brushing a kiss against his forehead. "But I think it's time we finally figure out exactly what we're having. I got the cake—it's in the kitchen."

He looks at me, confused for a moment, before realization dawns. I grin and nod toward the kitchen.

"Come on," I say, tugging at his hand. He threads his fingers through mine and lets me lead the way.

Matteo follows me into the kitchen, his fingers laced tightly with mine, the warmth of his touch grounding me. The cake sits on the counter, an innocent thing hiding a life-changing secret. I grab two glasses of sparkling juice, handing one to him as excitement flutters in my chest.

"Close your eyes," I say, my voice filled with a mix of nerves and anticipation.

He raises an eyebrow. "Really?"

"Yes, really," I laugh. "Just trust me."

He exhales, shaking his head but complying. We both close our eyes, and I count down. "Three... two... one."

We dig into the cake, pulling out a slice, the sound of glass against porcelain the only noise in the room.

"Okay, are you in?" My voice shakes with anticipation.

"Yeah." I can hear the rapid rise and fall of his chest.

"Okay." My heart pounds as I peek open one eye, and the sight steals my breath.

Blue.

I gasp, and Matteo's eyes snap open. He looks down at the glass of cake in his hand, at the unmistakable blue filling, and for the first time in months, his face truly lights up.

"A boy," he whispers, as if he can't quite believe it.

Tears prick my eyes as I nod. "A son."

He sets the glass down and pulls me into his arms, his embrace firm and unwavering.

"Maria," he murmurs into my hair, his voice thick with emotion. "A son."

I wrap my arms around him, feeling the weight of his grief lift—if only for a moment. This is exactly what we needed.

"We're going to be okay," I whisper, pressing my lips to his jaw. "All of us."

Matteo pulls back just enough to look at me, his eyes shining. "I swear to you, I will do everything to protect this family."

His arms tighten around me, and I feel the tremor in his breath.

"Daniele would have been so happy," he murmurs, voice breaking slightly.

I nod against his chest, blinking back tears. "He would have been the best big brother. I wish—" My voice catches, and I take a steadying breath. "I wish he could be here. But I know he's looking on with joy in his heart over this moment."

Matteo exhales sharply, pressing a lingering kiss to my temple. "I miss him every second."

I lift my head, cupping his face in my hands. "Me too. But he lives on with us, amore. And he would want us to live—for you to live."

His gaze softens, and for the first time in months, I see something beyond the sorrow—a quiet acceptance, a flicker of hope. He places his palm against my stomach once more, his fingers spread protectively over our growing child.

"A son," he whispers again, as if grounding himself in the truth of it. "Our son."

I lean into him, letting my forehead rest against his. "And he's going to have the best father."

Matteo kisses me deeply, pouring every unspoken word into the press of his lips. When we part, he holds my gaze, his voice unwavering.

"Forever and beyond, Maria?"

"Forever and beyond."

There is no man I would rather face life with than him.

44

MATTEO

I step through the door, the familiar scent of tomato, garlic, and rosemary filling the air as I take in the sight of Maria—barefoot and glowing—standing in front of the stove. She's humming softly to herself, clearly lost in the rhythm of preparing dinner.

I've loved watching her body shift and change to grow our son over the past few months. Pregnancy looks stunning on her. She rubs her belly affectionately as she stirs whatever's on the stove, a smile on her face.

Her head lifts and she shoots me a wide smile that's almost blinding. "You're home."

My heart skips a beat seeing her like this—pregnant and radiant, a beautiful contrast to the chaos of the world outside. Coming home to this—to the estate—is always something I look forward to.

"Hey," I greet her softly, my voice full of warmth, as I walk over and wrap my arms around her waist. She leans back into me, the curve of her belly pressing against my chest.

"Hey," she replies, turning her head to look up at me. "How was your day?"

I chuckle, brushing my lips across her forehead. "Busy, but nothing I can't handle. And you? How was your day?"

She gives a little shrug, her fingers dancing on the spoon as she stirs the pot. "Just the usual. A lot of quiet time, but I've been trying to get things ready for our little guy." She lets out a soft, contented sigh.

There's something sacred about this moment—just the two of us, suspended in quiet before the storm. In a world built on blood and strategy, this kitchen, this woman, this child—they are the only things that feel real.

"Crazy to think eight months has flown by like... nothing."

I can feel her energy, the excitement in her words, and it lifts my own spirits. The anticipation of meeting our son, of finally holding him in my arms, is enough to make me feel like I'm walking on air. But I can't escape the slight tinge of sadness I always feel when I realize that Daniele won't be here to see his little brother.

I walk over to the stove to look at the pot she's preparing. Never in a million years did I think I'd move back to the Davacalli estate—or be so... domesticated. She's really slowed my life down in the best way possible.

"Do you need any help, amore?" I taste the sauce she has in the pot with a spoon, but when she doesn't respond, I look up at her—and I pause. "Maria?"

Her body tenses, and her hand grips the edge of the counter. Her breath catches, a sharp gasp escaping her lips.

"Maria?" I ask, stepping closer, my voice full of concern. "What's happening?"

Before I can even process it, she doubles over in pain, a

scream tearing from her throat. Her eyes widen, and she looks up at me, panic flickering in her gaze.

"My water just broke," she says, breathless.

It's like the world shifts beneath my feet. I don't move for a second—I just stand there, trying to process her words.

Water breaking. Baby coming. She's in labor.

"You're in labor," I say, almost too casually. But then it all clicks, and I'm panicking. "Oh—fuck. Okay. You're in labor. Right. We've trained for this," I mutter, half to myself. "Where's the damn hospital bag...?"

"Matteo," she breathes, her eyes shining with a mix of fear and excitement. "I need you to be calm. Because if you freak out, I'll freak out—and I need to be zen when I push a human out of my vagina."

"Okay, okay," I stammer, my mind rushing as I scramble to grab her hospital bag from the corner by the door—thank the heavens my wife is a micromanager and prepares for things in advance.

Maria stands by the counter, breathing in and out through her mouth as she sways from side to side like her doula showed her. All those birthing classes, and I'm blanking on every single lesson.

I feel like I'm moving in slow motion, my thoughts tumbling over each other as I try to stay calm. "We need to go. We need to get to the hospital. Now."

Maria winces again, her hand gripping the counter, but she nods. "I know. Let's go. He's coming—I can feel him."

I'm frantic as we rush to the car, my heart hammering in my chest. The roads blur as we speed toward the hospital, the sound of her labored breathing beside me grounding me. Her hand grips mine, squeezing with every contraction, and I squeeze back—my nerves tangled with pure, raw excitement.

When we pull up to the hospital, I don't wait for the valet—I just rush inside, Maria at my side, the weight of her pregnancy anchoring me to the present.

We're here. It's happening.

Our son is coming.

OUR SON IS COMING.

They take her straight to a room, and I'm by her side every step of the way. The nurses move quickly, getting her set up on the bed, hooking her up to the monitors. My eyes stay fixed on her face. I've watched this woman stare down the barrel of a gun and hold strong—and now I'll watch her bring new life into the world.

The last time I was in a situation like this, I was watching Daniele come into the world. And now, here I am again—with the one who brought meaning back into my life.

She's scared—I can see it—but there's something else in her eyes too: hope. Anticipation. She's been waiting for this moment her whole life. She was born for this role.

"I'm here," I whisper, brushing her hair back from her face, trying to comfort her, though I'm equally shaken. "You're doing great."

"I'm scared, Matteo," she admits, her voice trembling slightly, but she forces a smile. Small beads of sweat dot her forehead as she tries to breathe in and out. "What if I can't do this?"

I lean down, pressing my forehead against hers. "You can. You're stronger than you think. You're incredible."

The hours seem to fly by—or maybe they slow down, I can't tell. All I know is that before long, the doctor is telling us that it's time.

I stand at her side, gripping her hand, feeling her squeeze it in return with every push. I'm watching her—

watching the strength in her face, in her body—as she brings our son into the world.

And I fall in love with her all over again.

I can hardly believe it's happening.

This is real.

And then, after four hours of labor and six strong pushes, we hear it. A sound I will never forget for the rest of my life.

Our son's cry—raw, pure, and full of life—pierces the air, and it takes everything in me to hold it together.

The nurse places him on Maria's chest, and his cries instantly calm. I'm overwhelmed. I look down at his tiny face, the soft strands of black hair on his head, the little fingers that curl instinctively.

He's perfect—just like his mother.

Maria's tired eyes meet mine, and she smiles, her face flushed but radiant. "He's here," she whispers.

I glance down at our son again, overwhelmed by a love so deep it threatens to spill over. And then, we both know. We've been talking about names for months, trying to figure out which one fits best. But in this moment, there's no hesitation.

"Antonio Daniele Davacalli," Maria says softly, her voice full of emotion as she gazes down at him. "He should carry his brother's name—and his uncle's, too."

I nod, my throat tight as I try to hold back the tears. "I love it," I tell her, my voice thick with emotion. "It's perfect. Antonio. Our perfect little boy."

He blinks slowly, his tiny chest rising and falling.

And for a moment, the world outside this hospital room ceases to exist.

This—this is everything.

The quiet of the hospital room settles around us as we

sit in the soft glow of the bedside lamp—the three of us, finally complete. Antonio is wrapped snugly in a blanket, his tiny fingers grasping at the air as if trying to touch everything at once. His little face, though scrunched from the world's first tastes of reality, is a vision of pure innocence.

I will do whatever it takes to make sure this baby is safe and protected. Nothing will ever harm him in this world as long as I live.

Maria leans back into the pillows, exhaustion etched into her features, but there's a soft smile playing on her lips. Her eyes are on Antonio, the love she feels for him overwhelming—and I can see the bond between mother and child forming in an instant.

"He looks so much like his Uncle Antonio—it's almost uncanny," I mutter, eyes fixed on his tiny face.

"I see it too," Maria whispers, her voice full of wonder. "The name is fitting for him, I think. I've been thinking about it for weeks now."

I walk over to her and lean down to give her a gentle kiss on the lips. The exhaustion in her eyes softens.

"It's perfect. You gave me a new life, Maria. Saying 'I love you' doesn't even come close."

She lets out a tired laugh, her hand coming to gently cup my cheek. "I love you, Matteo. I love you both."

Just as the quiet begins to settle, my phone buzzes. Of course it does. Only one person would dare interrupt this moment.

"You can't avoid him forever. He's probably camped outside right now, waiting to come and meet him," Maria laughs.

"Fine," I sigh, swiping the screen and pointing the phone at a sleeping Antonio.

"He's so freaking cute!" Valerio's voice rings through the

speaker. "Oh my God, he's got hair—a freaking gorgeous baby."

"Valerio," my wife and I say at the same time.

"Oh, sorry. Dammit—I'm going to have to start being PG," he laughs softly. "You did good, Maria. You did so good."

I turn the phone to Maria, and she smiles through her exhaustion. "Thank you, Valerio. I presume you're already in the waiting room?"

"Been here for almost three hours," he says, beaming. "I'll come up just now—need to grab my gift from the car first."

Before we can say anything else, he hangs up. Maria and I exchange a smile. Aside from us, Valerio has been the most excited for Antonio to arrive.

"You hear that, son? Your crazy uncle is on his way up," I coo at Antonio, who is now fast asleep in my arms.

"And we love him all the same," Maria chuckles. "Antonio is already so loved."

He is.

The future we never thought we'd have—right here in our arms.

The proof that love—real love—can rise from ashes.

Our son.

Antonio Daniele Davacalli.

EPILOGUE
MARIA

I stare at the ceiling, my heart sitting completely in my stomach. I've been feeling off the last few days. My mood has been horrendous, and I've been overly emotional about everything. Antonio fell over last week, and you would've thought the world was ending with the way I cried, convinced he was in the worst pain imaginable.

I glance at my husband, sleeping soundly beside me. The tension in his features has completely melted away, and he's finally found rest. The sound of the waves is a beautiful backdrop to our sleep.

"Could I be..." I whisper to myself. "No. We just started trying again."

But there's only one way to know for sure.

I peel myself out of bed, the soft sheets cool against my skin as I slip into the quiet of the morning. The sun hasn't even risen yet, but I can't sleep any longer. My heart is pounding in my chest as I tiptoe to the bathroom, careful not to wake Matteo. I don't want him to know I'm taking the test—no point in giving him false hope.

I close the door gently behind me and head to the

drawers beneath the mirror. I take the box out and stare at it for a moment. The last time I took one of these, our lives looked a whole lot different than they do now.

"Okay, let's see." I walk over to the toilet, slip my shorts down, and get on with it. I tell myself not to overthink it—just take it one step at a time.

Everything I've been feeling lately—the dizziness, the nausea, the strange cravings—has been leading me to this moment. But still, I'm nervous. What if it's negative? How will I handle that disappointment? I love having Antonio, but I would really love to give him a sibling—like I had.

As the minutes tick by, I stare at the test in my hand, my heart pounding in my ears. The wait feels like an eternity.

I close my eyes and wait for the beep to alert me that it's done. I brace myself for whatever I'm about to see on that tiny screen. I peel one eye open, slowly, cautiously, and...

Pregnant.

It's positive. I blink, unsure if I'm seeing it right. My hands tremble as I stare at the word in bold, clear writing. I can't believe it...

"Oh my God..." My hand flies to my mouth in pure and utter shock. I had a feeling—and now I know I was right.

Tears well up in my eyes before I can even process them. We're going to have another baby. Our family of three is about to grow to four, and I...

I laugh through my tears, clutching the test to my chest. My silent prayer to the heavens has been answered, and I can feel the joy radiating through my entire body.

I stare down at the test again, wanting to make sure I read it correctly.

"I need to tell him," I whisper to myself, the excitement bubbling up inside me. "But how..."

I want to do it in a special way, but I also know I won't be able to hold this in for more than an hour—it has to be this morning. The last time he found out I was pregnant, I was lying in a hospital bed, barely clinging to life. He deserves a joyful experience now—one we can look back on with warmth in our hearts.

I take a few deep breaths to steady myself and quietly leave the bathroom, walking down the hall to our son's room.

He's still asleep, his little body curled up in the 'big boy bed' we assembled when we arrived at the vacation house.

I smile softly as I watch him. My baby boy. He doesn't know it yet, but soon he'll be a big brother—and he'll form one of the most sacred bonds between two people: the love of a sibling.

I go to his dresser and grab one of his white tees. Carefully, I pull a marker from one of the drawers and write the words "Big Brother" across it. I hold it up, admiring my work.

This will do nicely, I'm sure.

"Mamá?" His tiny little voice cuts through the thick fog of emotion. "Mamá?"

I turn to face my little one and smile. His eyes are so bright and vibrant—just like my brother Antonio's. It's uncanny how much of him I see in this little face.

"Buongiorno, tesoro." Good morning, my treasure. I walk over to his bed and kiss his little head. "Come on, we have a surprise for Papá. Do you want to help me?"

Immediately, the sleep vanishes from his face and he beams up at me, nodding with enthusiastic little jerks of his head.

"Good," I say, kissing his chubby cheek. "Let Mommy help you put this on."

I carefully dress Antonio in the shirt, my hands shaking

slightly with excitement. Once he's ready, I scoop him up and tiptoe back to our room. He rests his head on my shoulder, his small hand laying over my chest in the sweetest gesture.

I never knew the capacity of my heart until I brought my own into the world in human form. There is no love quite as potent and intense as the love a mother has for her child.

I bring Antonio onto the bed and gesture for him to wake his father. He smiles and toddles over to where Matteo's head rests, placing his little hand on his face.

"Papá," he says softly. "Wakey ups."

Matteo stirs, groaning as he blinks his eyes open, still groggy. I quickly scoop Antonio off the bed, making sure to cover the shirt from Matteo's view. I don't want him to see it just yet. We need to go down to the beach first.

His voice is thick with sleep. "Amore?"

I smile down at him, my heart racing as I hold Antonio up for him to see. The moment Matteo's eyes land on his son, his expression softens.

"Let's go watch the sunrise."

He blinks up at me, looking like I've lost my mind. "You? Want to watch the sunrise? Since when do you like mornings?"

I shrug. "Well, just not today. Come on, let's go."

He sighs and rubs his eyes. "Do we really have to?"

"Yes. Come on or we'll miss it." I give him a no-nonsense look, and he lifts his hands in mock surrender before peeling the sheets off and pulling on a shirt.

"The things I do for you." As we head toward the sliding door, his palm gently smacks my bum. "It can only be love."

We step outside onto the private beach, the sun's rays just starting to kiss the edge of the night sky, slowly giving way to dawn. I breathe in the sea air and press a kiss to my little boy's head as he babbles to his father, excited as ever, while we make our way down to the shore.

Once we're far enough from the house, I feel my heart pick up pace. The jitters settle into my limbs, and Matteo pulls me into his side, kissing the top of my head. He breathes in my scent and lets out a soft, satisfied sigh.

"I didn't take you to be a morning person," he says, breaking the silence between us. "You've been sleeping a lot, actually."

I lick my lips, nerves consuming me. "I think there might be a reason for that."

Now or never…

"Here," I say softly, placing Antonio in his arms—careful to turn him just enough so the words on his shirt are clear.

He chuckles, eyes still on our son. "What's this little guy wearing today?"

His gaze drops to the shirt.

"Big brother…" he reads aloud, the words trailing off into silence.

There's a pause. His brow furrows, lips part slightly as the realization begins to sink in.

He looks up at me, eyes wide. "Wait… Maria—are you…?"

I nod, tears stinging the corners of my eyes, my voice thick with joy. "We're having another baby."

His expression softens, tears gathering in his eyes. "Are you serious?" His voice is filled with awe, and I nod again, tears now spilling freely down my cheeks.

"I'm sure," I whisper, my voice thick with emotion. "We're going to have another little one."

Matteo pulls me into his arms, and for a moment, everything feels perfect. His warmth, the scent of his skin, the steady rhythm of his heartbeat beneath my ear—it makes everything else fade away. I let myself sink into him, closing my eyes as the reality of the news settles in. We're going to have another baby. A sense of peace washes over me—one I haven't felt in a long time.

He pulls back slightly, his hands framing my face as he looks at me, his smile wide and full of joy. "I can't believe it," he whispers. "I thought we were going to have to keep trying... This is everything. You're incredible, Maria."

I let out a shaky laugh, brushing away the tears that continue to fall. "I guess we didn't need to try for long. I'm so happy... Are you?"

He blinks away his own tears and kisses our son, who remains blissfully unaware of what's happening—but happy just to be in his father's arms. Matteo's gaze softens as he looks at Antonio, still nestled against his chest.

"He's going to be the best big brother," Matteo says, glancing back at me with that familiar twinkle in his eyes.

I nod, my chest swelling with love for the little boy who's already captured so much of our hearts. I can already imagine the bond they'll share—the way Antonio will hold his little sibling, teach them everything he's learning. A bond like the one I shared with my brother.

I turn my gaze to the rising sun, the sky painted in shades of gold, pink, and soft orange. I know they're both watching with smiles on their faces.

"We're so blessed," I whisper, reaching for Matteo's hand. "I love you, amore."

Matteo presses a kiss to my forehead, his thumb gently stroking my cheek. "I love you more than you'll ever know, Maria. You've given me a life I never imagined I could have."

"And it's only just the beginning," I reply, my heart full of hope and excitement for what's to come.

We still live in a world laced with danger—one that will

always linger at our doorstep because of the life my husband leads. But I am prepared to stand beside him through every battlefield, every fire, every storm. Because no matter what we face, I believe in us. And I know we will emerge on the other side not just surviving, but stronger than we ever were before.

"Papá, pretty." Our son points to the sunrise, his little chubby cheeks rosy from the whipping wind that kisses them. "Mamá, look!"

"I know, baby. So beautiful," I say, looking toward the horizon. "I know they would be so happy."

I don't need to explain—I know Matteo understands I'm talking about Daniele and Antonio. They are huge missing pieces in our lives, but they live on, and every time I look at the sky, I find them in every ray of sunshine and every painted horizon.

I lean into my Matteo and savor this precious little moment on the beach. "I think it's a girl."

Matteo hums in agreement. "I had a dream you were playing with a little girl last night."

I turn my head to look up at him. "Really?"

"Yup. And she was the spitting image of you. Perfect in every way." He leans down and kisses me, which makes Antonio squeal and bounce in his father's arms.

"All right, all right—enough from you, little one."

Matteo pulls away and starts tossing our son into the air, making him laugh. They run around on the beach, and I sit on the sand, watching my tiny, perfect family.

I glance down at my still-flat belly and place my palm over my womb. "You are so loved already, baby girl. I can't wait to meet you."

Who would have imagined that marrying a mafia boss would lead me to the very life my soul had always craved?

Life has a curious way of coming full circle—guiding us to where we were always meant to be. And just when you least expect it, it gives you exactly what you never knew you were searching for.

As the sun continues to rise, casting its warm glow across the shore, I wrap my arms around myself, still holding onto the bliss of this morning. A new life growing inside me, laughter ringing out from my boys on the sand, peace woven into every breath I take. For the first time in a long while, I feel like maybe—just maybe—we've outrun the shadows.

But peace, in our world, is always fleeting.

A sound breaks the quiet—the hurried crunch of footsteps on the gravel path leading from the house.

I turn around just as Valerio appears, breathless, his face pale with something that doesn't belong here—urgency.

His eyes land on Matteo.

"Val?" Matteo says, suddenly alert. He sets Antonio down gently in the sand and strides over to meet him. My heart drops.

Valerio grabs Matteo's arm and pulls him aside. His voice is low, but the wind carries enough of it to reach me.

"Someone's found a woman—alive—locked inside a room in one of Giacomo's old properties."

He pauses, eyes flicking toward me for the briefest moment.

"She claims her name is Beatrice Davacalli."

The world stills.

Matteo turns, slowly, his eyes locking with mine.

And just like that, the past—one we thought buried—begins to stir again.

Hope is no longer the only thing rising with the sun.

Something else is coming. Something we never expected.

Something that could change everything.

Forever.

THE END

If you enjoyed *Mafia King of Lies,* then you'll also like *Dark Mafia Heir*.

(CLICK HERE to get Dark Mafia Heir)

STOLEN from the altar by her father's sworn enemy, Vivienne becomes the obsession he'll never let go in this ruthless arranged marriage, secret baby mafia romance. **Read Chapter One on the next page!**

45

SNEAK PEEK

Dark Mafia Heir SNEAK PEEK

ANTONIO

THE MOMENT I TASTED HER, I knew one thing—she was mine.

I stole her from her wedding and put a ring on her hand.

But there's an ache I can't ignore—I might never have her heart.

VIVIENNE COLE IS my enemy's daughter. My perfect revenge.

And now... my wife.

. . .

I PLANNED to use her as my weapon to rip her father's world apart.

But marrying Vivienne wasn't supposed to feel this good.

HER FIRE TEMPTS ME.

Her defiance dares me.

Her laugh makes me forget I'm a monster.

I SHOULD BREAK HER. Instead, I crave her.

She calls me a beast. She's right.

She hates me. She should.

BUT EVERY TIME SHE RUNS, I hunt her down.

She doesn't know that there's no way out.

THEN I SEE one of my men standing speechless at the door—and I know.

They took her.

AND SHE'S KEEPING a secret from me—one I'll kill for.

I'm going to be a father.

And I'll spill oceans of blood to protect what's mine.

VIVIENNE

. . .

The moment I kissed him, I knew—I was his obsession.

He stole me from my wedding, and now I carry his child.

Now I don't know if I want to run... or stay.

One stolen moment with a dark stranger, and my life was no longer my own.

Antonio Mancini is a ruthless monster made of secrets and sins.

He doesn't ask. He takes.

And on the night of my wedding—to another man—he does exactly that.

Ripped me from my world and chained me to his.

I swore he could have my body, my name, my vow...but he'd never have me.

But the more I fight him, the more I crave him.

And every battle ends the same. *He owns me. And I let him.*

I should hate him. And I do... until I don't.

I let him steal something even more dangerous than my freedom—my heart.

But how can I trust a man who was born to destroy?

. . .

I thought I could escape him.
Then I saw the test—two pink lines.

Antonio is about to become a father.
He'll never let me go.

(Click Here to get Dark Mafia Heir)

CHAPTER ONE
Vivienne

The man sitting across the club has his dark eyes pinned on me. He's swirling a glass of whiskey in one hand, while giving me a predatory smile that sends a shiver down my spine.

I'm celebrating my twenty-first birthday with my sister at De Angelo, one of the biggest Italian clubs in New York. My papa said today is the day I transition into full adulthood, which could mean a lot of things.

For girls outside the mafia, it might mean they've finally grown up to earn their freedom. But it's different for girls in my world. For us, becoming twenty-one only means we're way past the age to be traded off like breeding mares.

The man's smile turns into a smirk as he signals for me to come closer.

I cringe, almost rolling my eyes. Does he think I am a stripper or something? Whatever, I don't care. He gives me the ick.

I turn around to face my sister, who's vibrating with the music and flipping her hair. Honestly, I can't tell if she's very excited or if she's just drunk from all the drinks she's had—which is only a few shots, by the way.

Harper is nothing like me. I'm a party animal, and my sister is the ladylike one—the one with good grades who makes our father proud. And she's pretty, just like our mother used to be.

The only thing we have in common is our father's emerald eyes. I look more like our mother with my straight red hair.

I poke my sister's ribs to get her attention, and she shudders. "Are you okay?"

She stops flipping her hair and raises her head to look at me. Her emerald eyes crinkle under flickering neon lights, and she has the wildest smile plastered on her face. "I am. This is just so fun."

I chuckle as I hold her hand and join in her dance. The bass thumps through my veins, syncing with the pounding in my ears as I let the music take over. I'm not thinking about anything except the rhythm, how it moves through my body, the way it makes me feel alive.

But more than the music, I am glad Harper is having some fun at last. "Come on, Harp! Don't hold back!" I shout over the music, grabbing her hand and pulling her closer to the center of the dance floor.

We're both so lost in the noise around us that I don't notice the man from earlier striding towards me until he wraps his arm around my waist.

I jerk, repulsed by his touch, as I turn around to face him with a frown.

The asshole has the nerve to smile. "I see you girls are having fun," he says. "I want in, and maybe we can go somewhere else from here."

I tuck Harper behind me and square my shoulders. We'd

sneaked out tonight and there's no bodyguard here with us. A stupid decision I made in the heat of the moment—a decision I'm now regretting. Papa will be so mad if he finds out I put Harper in danger.

"The only place you'll be going from here is your grave if you lay your hands on me again." I tilt my chin, looking at him straight in the eyes, and ignoring the way my heart is pounding against my ribcage with fear.

"Feisty." He pulls on his lower lip, eyes glinting with irritating lust under the flashing strobe lights. "I like it. I like you."

I give him a once-over, at least making a feeble effort to assess him. His short, dark hair is in an unattractive mess, his nails have dirt in them, like he works on engines at a car shop, and, worse, he smells bad.

Imitating Papa's intimidating glare, I stand my ground and square my chin, hoping this loser gets the hint. "But I don't like you. Scram, Jerkface. I'm sure you'll find someone else to have fun with."

The wry smile melts off his face like heated wax rolling down a candle, and the real ugliness inside him is unmasked. Jerkface grabs my wrist, his fingers curling around my skin so tight, I know it'll leave a mark as bright as a ruby bracelet. Snarling, he yanks me forward, momentarily cutting the breath from my lungs. I stagger. I didn't see that one coming.

"Vi!"

"Stay back, Harper." I wave her away, not wanting her even an inch close to this madman. I am scared, terrified, in fact. My heart is running a marathon inside my chest, and my head is pounding.

But I'd rather fight until I draw my last breath than allow this man to even touch a hair on my sister's head. She's staring at me, lips quivering, fingers fidgeting helplessly, and eyes tearing up quickly. And I know, if I don't do something soon, Harper is going to call Papa. And then all hell would truly break loose.

"I'm warning you for the last time: let me go, or else—"

"Else, what?"

When his dirty finger touches my lips, my skin crawls, and a wave of nausea hits me at once. I want to puke and scrub off every trace of this man's hand on my skin.

The world around us is still in crazy motion. It's ridiculously loud. Neon and stage lights blink in rhythm to the ongoing beat while they jump, dance, and sing in unison to "Be My Lover."

The DJ cranks up the vocals, and the energy spikes to the roof. Jerkface pulls me closer, snaking his lean arm around my waist, while he peers into my eyes like he wants to steal my soul.

"Thinking of different ways you could scream, baby doll?" I hold my breath while his finger goes down my neck. His breath smells like citrus and rum, and it stirs the queasiness in my belly. "No one's going to hear you."

He is right, except I manage to release a supersonic scream; the party animals in this hall are most likely deaf. In a flash, an idea hits me; a sneaky strategy I'd seen Papa's men use during sparring sessions. All I have to do is distract him and make a run for it with Harper.

"Fine." His brow twitches, saying he doesn't understand. "Let me go, and I'll go with you wherever you want without making a fuss."

A frown crosses his lips. "That easily? All of a sudden, after you asked me to leave?"

I try to keep my expression neutral and my tone, resigned to make him believe I sincerely agree with him.

"Yes, because I am not stupid. I can see you are right; struggling is going to do no good in this noisy environment. So, let me go, and I'll go with you."

Doubtfully, he looks at me, and I hold my breath, praying this tactic works—that he actually falls for it and releases his hand from my waist, giving me the opportunity I need.

Five seconds pass—*because my brain can't stop counting how long it'll take until freedom finally comes*—and, after watching me closely like a hungry predator, he finally shrugs and drops his arm.

Perfect.

Elation and adrenaline had to be the best combination of emotion and energy that a human could experience, because that powerful combo flows through my veins, fueling my burning desire to put a fist in the man's face, like dried sticks feeding a fire.

I don't hesitate. I don't pause. I curl my fist as tightly as I learned from Dabi, one of Papa's men, and swing my arm, aiming directly at Jerkface's jaw.

Screaming, Jerkface falls to the floor on his side, cursing, whimpering, and holding the side of his face.

But I am startled because my fist still hangs in the air. I didn't touch him.

"That was a friendly warning."

The rich, smooth, resonant baritone from beside me ignites a fire in my core, its vibrations coursing through me, spreading molten heat that tingles all the way down to my toes, and I turn around, only to be blown away by a sight too surreal to be true—like a perfect stranger from one of Alisha Rai's novels.

To top it off, he checks off all the other boxes; tall, dark-haired, and stunningly handsome. The type of handsome that makes you forget to look out for other characteristics of their personality. The type of handsome that makes a woman *feel* like a woman. She just wants to be in his arms, touch the hard lines of his muscles, and sleep on his chest. That type of handsome is this stranger standing beside me, glaring at Jerkface with cold, dark eyes that hold promises of death.

He slides his hand—the same one that sent the mad man crumpling to the ground—into one of his black dress pants pockets and raises a brow.

"What are you waiting for? Get out."

Jerkface doesn't waste another second. Without another word, he hops to his feet, clutching his bleeding mouth as he scurries away without looking back.

My hand drops to my side as Harper and I stare at this *hero* in awe. Even though I am the only one between us who appears grateful to the stranger for literally swooping in to save the day. Harper looks terrified, probably still deciding whether to call Papa or not.

Slowly, I muster a small smile at the stranger, who still has his eyes trained on the shadow of my harasser.

"Thank you..." my words hang in the air while I sweep my gaze over this man's striking features. Firm, bow-shaped mouth, chiseled jawline, eyes that don't just look but see, and a classic fifties pompadour haircut. The stranger appears young, but his aura, the way his shoulders stand stiff, the swiftness of his punch, the hard lines at the corner of his eyes... everything about him oozes years of experience navigating through this crazy world.

Regardless, I am not deterred. Older man or not, he rescued me from the snares of that idiot. So, he deserves my gratitude. I try again.

"Thank you, sir."

That startles him. A deep, *sexy* chuckle rumbles at the back of his throat, and with a smoothness that makes me fall even harder, he turns and faces me with a dazzling smile. Dark eyes, the color of molten chocolate, lock on mine, assessing every inch of my body, from my bare shoulders, down the length of my mini pink slip dress, sending a tingle across my skin. I am feeling light-headed, and I'm not sure if it's because of the few drinks I had, or the effect of this man not-so-subtly checking me out.

My knees wobble, and I clear my throat. *Damn.*

"Sir?"

I didn't take note of it before, but now, as I listen keenly, I hear an accent. And the best way I can describe it is as a tempting roll of the tongue—reminiscent of olive oil drizzled over fresh bread, with his words stretching long and smooth, like melted mozzarella. My ears itch to hear more of it. I beam back, easily forgetting what brought him here in the first place.

"Is it strange to be called that?"

A playful glint crosses his eyes, like it's fun to indulge me.

"No." He shakes his head, still giving me that dark, delicious, intense look that swallows up the noise around us and makes me feel like I'm the only one in the room. "I'd prefer if you called me by my name."

I suddenly remember that I'm not the only one in the room—Harper is here too. My eyes find hers, and I try to snap out of whatever spell this man has me in.

"I'm sorry, but we have to go."

He looks over his shoulder and smiles at my sister. "Don't you think I should buy your sister a drink? That man tried to ruin your night, but I can make up for it."

Harper does not look too convinced. Her eyes tell me

she is uncomfortable and wants to leave, but his charm seems to have worked on her, too, because she rubs her arm and nods. "Sure. You did help us, so I guess one drink is not too much to ask for."

"Grazie." Thank you.

And my stomach drops with a warm sensation, as if everything suddenly clicked into place. It makes so much sense, that poise, the insane level of unearthly beauty, and the accent.

He's Italian.

By the time I snap back to the present moment, he's telling Harper something about taking me to the bar across the street because the drinks there taste better. He extends the invite, but Harper doesn't want to join in. He directs her to stay in his VIP section because it's safer there and advises her to keep her phone close.

He's a stranger, and we should not trust strangers, but I can't help the tug in my chest as I watch their interaction and his gentleness with my sister.

Harper gives me a cautionary glance, one with a message: *don't hesitate to scream or call if you have to.*

I nod. Message received and sent back.

Satisfied, she clutches her purse and walks away with a bodyguard we hadn't even noticed before, leaving me and the perfect stranger alone.

"She's safe, don't worry." He turns back to me and extends his arm. "Shall we?"

The music pounds through my chest, a deep bass that makes the floor vibrate beneath my feet, although I think my heart is beating for some other reason.

Shyly, I blush and hook my arm through his, allowing him to lead us through the sea of gyrating bodies and smooching partners. His tall frame, standing out like a six-foot-three athlete, cuts through the masses like a knife, and I follow close behind, my fingers slipping into his without thinking.

We move towards the back of the club, away from the pulsing lights and sweat-slick air, to the back door with the neon exit sign gleaming atop. The heavy door creaks as he shoves it open, and a rush of cool night air hits me, sharp and refreshing against my flushed skin.

I laugh quietly when he closes the door, blocking the thrum of the club, and ushers us into the narrow alley, dimly lit by flickering streetlamps at the far end. It's quieter out here, but my heart's still racing, the adrenaline from the night pumping through my veins.

I brush my hair behind my ears. "This is crazy." I smile up at him. "I don't even know your name, and we're in an alley."

Mirth flashes through his eyes, but he just stands there in all his intimidating glory, with his hands tucked into his pockets. He looks sharper than a knife with a black button-down tailored for his broad chest.

"Antonio." His shoulders nudge towards the bar at the other end of the street. "And I really did bring you out to get a drink across the street."

Something crackles in the air between us, thick and suffocating, like static before a storm, and it pulses between us with every glance, every breath. It's a heat that crawls across my skin, shrinking the space between us, until it's just the two of us, locked in this silent, unspoken thing.

I swallow to find my voice. "But?"

There's a dark, sharp flicker behind his eyes, somehow daring me to look away, but drawing me in at the same time. When he takes steps towards me, I take a step back.

He moves again, and I move back, slamming into a wall

behind me. My pulse quickens, a steady thrum in my chest that echoes this tension cracking between us.

The corner of his lips curves upwards and I can tell he's enjoying this. I square my chin, narrowing my eyes with a feigned defiance. "The bar is across the street. Why aren't we moving?"

He's too close, not close enough, and every nerve in my body screams for more, for less, for something to break.

"Because, what's crazy is that I don't even know your name, and I feel a crazy urge to kiss you senseless, until one of us gasps for air."

Damn. That didn't just leave his mouth. Did it?

My breathing falters as the heat flares higher, the tension pulling tighter like a thin rope about to snap, and I know he feels it, too. It's in the way he's standing, just barely holding himself back, as if one wrong word, one wrong move, and we'd be crossing a line we can't come back from.

Nervously and on impulse, I blurt, "Vivienne. And it's my birthday today."

Hearing that seems to snap something inside him because his hands leave his pockets and find solace on my cheek, like he needed the slightest excuse to touch me. They are big and warm; I can't help but lean in.

"I should give you a gift then."

Gently, his fingers trace the curve of my mouth and the loud thrashing of my heart in my ears makes it hard to think or breathe. I should say no. I should turn on my heels and head back inside, grab my sister, and leave without looking back at this handsome Italian stranger.

This is escalating very fast, but I can't bring myself to move from this spot. My body calls to his own; a wild, irrational yearning to feel the weight of the man on me, to know what it feels like to be suffocated by his strength. I want—

no, crave—every inch of him. Every muscle, every taste of him.

He lowers his lips to mine, and my heart flutters when the dim streetlight casts a warm glow on his olive skin.

"*Buon Compleanno*, Vivienne." *Happy Birthday*.

When his mouth closes on mine, fireworks explode in my head. I grip his shirt, my fingers curling into the crisp fabric to steady myself. He cradles my face and moves against me like he fears I'll break. I moan into his hot mouth, tugging on his shirt. I don't want the restraint. I want him to unleash. For a moment, it's just us, lost in a bubble of wild passion with no cares or worries.

Then, a crack splits the air.

I recognize the sound too well.

Gunshot.

I freeze, breaking our kiss as I pull away from him, the sound ringing in my ears. Panic replaces passion, fast and hot, and my mind snaps back to reality.

My sister is inside.

"Harper!"

(CLICK HERE TO get Dark Mafia Heir)

Printed in Dunstable, United Kingdom